IN THE KENTUCKY NIGHT, MISTAKEN FOR THIEVES, THEY FLED FOR THEIR LIVES . . . AND DISCOVERED THEIR LOVE!

When they'd caught their breath, they looked at each other.

"You weren't hurt, were you?" Leah asked.

"A bloody side, but not bad," Wesley replied.

She moved closer to him, grabbing the buttons of his shirt.

"You sure are eager to get my clothes off, woman." He grinned down at her. "You are a very pretty young woman, Leah," he whispered.

The air was filled with the charges between them, dancing lights drawing them together.

Leah's fingers moved from the cuts on Wes's side to his dark, warm skin, upward to the dark mass of curling hair on his chest. She couldn't move away when his lips came near hers.

"We are still married, you know," he murmured . . .

Books by Jude Deveraux

The Velvet Promise
Highland Velvet
Velvet Song
Velvet Angel
Sweetbriar
Counterfeit Lady
Lost Lady
River Lady
Twin of Ice
Twin of Fire
The Temptress
The Raider
The Princess
The Awakening
The Maiden
The Taming
A Knight in Shining Armor
Wishes
Mountain Laurel

Published by POCKET BOOKS

JUDE DEVERAUX

RIVER LADY

POCKET BOOKS

New York   London   Toronto   Sydney   Tokyo   Singapore

This book is a work of fiction. Names, characters, places and incidents are either the product of the author's imagination or are used fictitiously. Any resemblance to actual events or locales or persons, living or dead, is entirely coincidental.

An *Original* Publication of POCKET BOOKS

POCKET BOOKS, a division of Simon & Schuster Inc.
1230 Avenue of the Americas, New York, NY 10020

Copyright © 1985 by Deveraux Inc.
Cover art copyright © 1985 Harry Bennett

ISBN: 0-671-70676-4

First Pocket Books printing December 1985

10 9 8 7 6

POCKET and colophon are registered trademarks of
Simon & Schuster Inc.

Printed in the U.S.A.

Chapter 1

Virginia Riverfront
September, 1803

The rain enclosed the little tavern, darkening it so that the lantern's golden light made eerie shadows on the wall. The late fall sunshine that had warmed the morning was gone now and the tavern was almost cold. Behind the tall oak counter washing pewter mugs was a woman, pretty, plump, clean, her soft brown hair caught in a white muslin cap. She hummed as she worked, smiling now and then and showing a dimple in one cheek.

The side door, not the door for patrons, opened and in a gust of cold, wet wind a girl slipped into the room, pausing for a moment until her eyes adjusted to the light. The barmaid looked up and, with a frown and a little click of disgust, hurried forward.

"Leah, you look worse every time I see you. Sit down here while I heat a toddy for you," the plump woman said as she pushed the shivering girl into a chair and went to set the poker in the fire, all the while surreptitiously studying her younger sister. If possible,

Leah had lost weight. Her unfleshed bones seemed to poke through her dirty, mended dress; her eyes were sunken, the skin under them blue, her nose sunburned and peeling. There were three bloody scratches running the length of one side of her face, and a long bluish-green bruise on the other side.

"He give you that?" the barmaid asked in disgust as she jabbed the hot poker into the mug of flip.

Leah merely shrugged and eagerly put her hands out toward the hot beer and molasses drink.

"He give any reason for hittin' you?"

"No more 'n usual," Leah said after drinking half the contents of the mug and leaning back in the chair.

"Leah, why don't you—?"

Leah opened her eyes and gave her sister a hard look. "Don't start on me again, Bess," she warned. "We've been through this before. You do what you must and I'll take care of me and the kids."

Bess stiffened for just a moment before turning away. "Layin' on my back for a few clean gentlemen is a lot easier 'n what you have to do."

Leah didn't even wince at Bess's crudity. They'd had this argument too many times before for her to be shocked. Two years ago, Bess had had her fill of their crazy father who beat them constantly because "women were born in sin." The older girl had left their poor backwater farm to find herself a job, and, on the side, she was "friendly" to a few men. Leah, of course, had been beaten for Bess's sins. Now, Bess was always trying to get Leah to leave their father's shack of a house. But Leah remained to care for her six younger brothers and sisters. She plowed, planted, harvested, cooked, repaired the house, and, most of all, she protected the little ones from their father's wrath.

"Look at you!" Bess said. "You look forty-five years old and you're what? Twenty-two now?"

"I think so," Leah said tiredly. It was the first time she'd sat down all day and the warm drink was relaxing her. "Do you have any clothes for me?" she whispered lazily.

Bess started to complain again, but instead she went behind the counter and reached for cold ham, bread, and mustard. As she set a plate on the table beside Leah, she took a seat across from her. Out of the corner of her eye she saw Leah hesitate before touching the food. "You even consider not eatin' that and takin' it back to them kids and I'll cram it down your throat myself."

Leah gave a little quirk of a smile and tore into the food with both hands. Her mouth full, her eyes downcast, she said, as if the answer meant nothing to her, "Have you seen him lately?"

Bess gave the top of her sister's dirty head a sharp look. "You're not still thinkin' . . . ," she began but stopped and looked back at the fire. A flash of lightning lit the tavern.

Poor Leah, Bess thought. In many ways Leah was like their father, as stubborn and hardheaded as a piece of stone. Bess could walk away and leave the little ones, but to Leah family was everything, even if a lunatic, rampaging old man was part of her family. After their mother died, Leah had decided that she was going to take care of the kids until the last one was old enough to leave. No matter what happened, or what was done to her, she refused to leave.

And just as Leah remained with her father, she stubbornly clung to a dream. The dream wasn't the one Bess had always wanted: food, shelter, and warmth. Leah's dream was one she could never attain.

3

Leah fantasized about one Mr. Wesley Stanford.

When Leah was a girl, Mr. Stanford had come to their hovel, asked her a few questions, and, in gratitude for her answers, he'd kissed her cheek and given her a twenty-dollar gold piece. When Leah had told Bess of the incident, there'd been stars in the young girl's eyes. Bess had immediately wanted to spend the gold on new dresses, but Leah had gone into a rage, screaming that the coin was from *her* Wesley and that she loved him and he loved her and when she grew up she was going to marry him.

At the time, Bess's only thought had been of that shiny gold coin hidden somewhere, unspent, all its glory wasted. She began to wish this Wesley had given Leah a bunch of flowers. She tried to forget about that coin, but sometimes she'd see Leah, plow harness about her shoulders, stop and stare into space. "What you thinkin' about?" Bess would ask, and Leah would say, "Him." Bess would groan and turn away. There was no need for Leah to say who *him* was.

Years later, Bess decided she could take no more of her father's hideous temper and the constant work, so she left the farm and took a job across the river as a barmaid. Elijah Simmons had disowned his eldest daughter and had forbidden her to visit the farm or see her siblings. But during the last two years, Leah had managed to slip away a few times to visit her sister and get the clothes Bess collected for her. The townspeople wanted to help the desperately poor Simmons family, but Elijah refused to allow his family to accept charity.

On her first visit to the tavern, Leah had asked after Wesley Stanford. At the time, Bess had been enthralled with having met all the rich plantation owners, and Wesley and his brother Travis were the wealthiest. Bess had talked for thirty minutes about how handsome Wes was, what a considerate man he was, how often he visited the tavern—and how happy Leah would be when they were married. To Bess, it'd been like the creating of a fairy tale, something to pass the cold winter evenings, and she thought Leah had seen it that way too. But a few months ago, with a laugh, Bess had told Leah that Wes had become engaged to a beautiful young lady named Kimberly Shaw. "Now who are you going to love?" Bess laughed before she saw Leah's white face. Under the bruises and dirt Leah looked as if her blood were draining away.

"Leah! You can't be serious about a man like Wesley. He's rich, *very* rich and he wouldn't let a couple of . . . of, well a 'lady' like me and a scrawny, filthy thing like you in his second-best parlor. This Miss Shaw is from his own class."

Quietly, Leah slipped out of her chair and headed for the door.

Bess grabbed her arm. "It was just a dream, didn't you realize that?" She paused. "But Wesley has a third gardener that just might be interested in a woman from . . . from our side of the river."

Leah didn't answer, but, still pale, she left the tavern, and the next time she visited, she acted as if she'd never heard that Wesley Stanford was engaged. She asked Bess for more stories about Wesley. This time Bess was reluctant, so she again tried to tell her of the engagement. Leah gave her sister such a chilling look that Bess turned away. For all Leah's look of frailty, there were times when she could be imposing.

Since then Bess hadn't tried to argue with her, and every visit she lifelessly recounted Wes's last time in the tavern. She didn't mention that he was in there more often now because the tavern was on the road between his house and the Shaws'.

5

Now Leah leaned back in the chair, slipped her hand into her much-mended pocket, and clutched the gold piece Wesley had given her years ago. Over the years she'd rubbed it so often it was completely smooth. There'd been many nights when the pain from one of her father's beatings had kept her awake and she'd sat on the straw tick rubbing the coin and remembering every second of the time she'd spent with Wesley Stanford. He'd kissed her cheek, and to her knowledge that was the one and only kiss she'd ever received. Sometimes Bess talked about him as if he thought of himself as a god, better than everyone else, but Leah knew how kind he could be, how he could kiss a skinny, dirty little girl he'd never seen before and reward her lavishly. Vain, arrogant men didn't do such things. Bess didn't know him as Leah did. Someday, she thought, she'd see Wesley again and he'd see the love in her eyes and—.

"Leah!" Bess half shouted. "Don't fall asleep. The old man will miss you before long. You have to get back."

"I know. It's just so nice and warm here."

"You could stay all the time if—."

Leah stood, cutting off Bess's words. "Thanks for everything, Bess, and I'll see you again next month. We wouldn't be able to make it if it wasn't for you and your—."

The heavy front door flew open and a man entered, his body filling the opening, pushing the door shut behind him.

"Oh Lord," Bess gasped, paralyzed for a moment before grinning and moving toward the man. "Awful wet for anybody to be out, Mr. Stanford. Here, let me help you with that," she said, taking his coat from his shoulders and glancing toward Leah, who stood stock-still, gaping.

He hasn't changed much, Leah thought. He was taller, even more muscular than she remembered, and more handsome. His thick dark hair curled damply about his neck and there were drops of water on his lashes, making his eyes look even darker, even more intense. Bess was standing on her toes and using her hand to brush water from his dark green wool jacket. Buckskin pants hugged his big, hard thighs while tall boots encased his feet and calves.

"I wasn't sure you'd be open. Doesn't Ben ever give you the night off?" he asked Bess, referring to her boss.

"Only when he's sure I'll put the night to good use. Ain't nobody around to spend this evenin' with so I might as well tend bar," she teased. "Now you sit down and let me get you somethin' hot to drink."

Bess began ushering Wesley Stanford toward a tall, sided booth, trying to keep his back to Leah, who still stood in the middle of the room, her eyes wide.

With a chuckle, Wes disengaged himself from her pushing hands. "What are you trying to do to me, Bess?" It was then he saw Leah, and Bess saw the brief flicker in his eyes. He was judging her as a man looks at a woman and as to where she belonged on the social ladder. He obviously found her wanting in both aspects. "Who's your . . . pretty friend, Bess?"

Manners, Bess thought. Those people must be taught manners from the cradle. "This is my sister, Leah," Bess said tightly. "Leah, you best be gettin' home."

"It's early yet," Leah said, stepping forward into the light; Bess looked at her sister as a stranger would and saw poverty and hardship hanging over Leah like a black cloud. But Leah seemed oblivious to her appearance. Her eyes were fixed glassily on Wesley, who was beginning to look at her in speculation.

"Perhaps you two ladies will join me in a glass of ale."

Bess put herself between Leah and Wes. Leah, in her innocence, was giving Wes looks that usually only a seasoned prostitute could produce. "I got work to do and Leah here has to go home." She said the last while glaring at her sister.

"Ain't nothin' waitin' for me at home," Leah said, deftly sidestepping her sister. "I'd love to drink with you, Wesley." She said the name as if she said it hundreds of times a day—which she did—and didn't notice the movement of Wes's eyebrows as she slid into a seat in the booth, looking up at him expectantly.

"The flip is good," she said.

Wes looked down at her dirty, scratched, bruised face for a second before taking the bench across from her. "A couple of flips," he said quietly to Bess.

Angrily, Bess flounced away toward the bar.

"You work for Ben now?" Wes asked Leah.

"I still live with my family." Her eyes were eating him, remembering every angle of his face, memorizing every curve. "Did you ever find your friend's wife?" she asked, referring to the first time she'd seen Wes.

For a moment he didn't understand. "Clay's wife?" he asked, then smiled, astonished. "You couldn't be that little girl who helped us?"

Silently, reverently, Leah pulled the worn gold coin from her skirt pocket and laid it on the table.

Wonderingly, Wes picked it up and held it toward the light to look at the rough hole drilled in the top of the coin. "How—?" he asked.

"A nail," she said, smiling. "It took me a while to

8

make that hole but I was afraid I'd lose it if I didn't tie it to me."

Frowning, Wes put the coin back on the table. It was odd that the girl would keep the gold when she obviously needed so many things. Her hair, greasy beyond belief, was pulled back from her head and, idly, he wondered what color it would be if it were clean.

As Leah reached for the coin, she touched his fingertips and, her breath held, she touched them with her two fingers, marveling at the cleanliness of his nails, the shape of his big square-tipped fingers.

Bess set two mugs of flip on the table with a splash, while glaring at Leah. "Mr. Stanford, why don't you tell my sister here about that beautiful young lady you're about to marry? Leah'd just love to hear all about her. Tell her how pretty she is, how she can dance, what pretty clothes she has."

Wes moved his hand away from Leah's and chuckled. "Perhaps you should tell her, Bess, since you seem to know so much about my wife-to-be."

"I think I'll do that," Bess said, grabbing a chair from a nearby table and moving it to the end of their booth. But a look from Leah stopped her from sitting down.

"I'd rather hear what Wesley has to say," Leah said quietly, but her eyes bored into Bess's.

Bess's eyes held her sister's for a moment. Why was she trying to protect her sister? Isn't this what she'd wanted her to do? If only Leah weren't so *serious* about the man. With a sigh, Bess left them alone.

Wes drank deeply of his steaming drink while he looked at the emaciated girl across from him, and wondered how long she'd been a prostitute. She certainly was good at getting a man's attention in spite of her unappetizing appearance. The way she looked at him made him feel as if she'd been waiting all her life just for him. It was flattering, but at the same time it was disconcerting. It was almost as if she felt he owed her something.

"You were saying, Wesley . . . ?" Leah prompted, leaning forward so that he got a whiff of her body odor.

"Kimberly," he said, only half-aloud. It might be better to think of Kim or, heaven help him, he might be tempted by this fragrant witch. "You're sure you want to hear? I mean, usually one woman doesn't want to hear about another woman."

"I wanta know all there is to know about you," she said with heartfelt sincerity.

"There's really not much to tell. We met about two years ago when she came to visit her brother, Steven Shaw. Their parents died when they were young and Kimberly was sent East to live with an aunt and uncle, while Steve stayed here with relatives."

Wesley's "not much to tell" turned into an hour of extended rapture. Wes had fallen for the beautiful Kimberly instantly, but so had twenty or so other young men, and he'd had a two-year courtship battle to win her. He talked about how pretty Kim was, how gentle, delicate, how sweet-tempered, how she loved beauty, books, and music.

Leah's hands gripped the pewter mug so hard her knuckles turned white. "And you're soon to be married?" she whispered.

"Early spring. April. Then the three of us, Steven included, are traveling to the new state of Kentucky. I've bought land there."

"You'll leave Virginia?" She gasped. "What about your plantation here?"

"I don't think Virginia is big enough for my brother

and me. For all my thirty-four years, I've been called Travis's little brother. It's made me want a place of my own. Besides, starting all over in a new land with a beautiful woman appeals to me."

"You won't return?" she whispered.

"Probably not," he answered, frowning at her intensity. In spite of her looks and her smell, he found himself drawn to her. "The rain's stopped and I better get home." He stood. "It was a pleasure meeting you." He tossed coins on the table for the drinks. "See you next week, Bess," he called as he started out the door.

Leah was after him in a second, but Bess caught her arm. "Are you sure you know what you're doing?"

Leah jerked away from her sister. "I always thought you wanted me to enjoy men."

"Enjoy them yes, but I'm afraid you're obsessed with Wesley Stanford. You're going to get hurt and hurt worse than from Pa's blows. You know nothing about men! All you know is how to plow and scrounge wild plants for food. You don't know——."

"Maybe I can learn!" Leah hissed. "I love him and he's leaving soon and I have this one chance and I'm going to take it."

"Please, Leah, please don't go after him. Something awful will happen, I know it will."

"Nothing *awful* will happen," Leah said softly and was out the door.

Wesley was just mounting his horse.

"Will you give me a ride?" Leah called, stumbling along the path in the dark.

Wes stood still, watching her in the moonlight and wishing with all his might that the girl would go away. There was something about her that was almost frightening, as if it were fate that had brought them together, as if what was going to happen were inevitable. And damn! He'd been so good, faithful to Kimberly since they'd become engaged, and he'd planned to remain celibate until they were married. But it wasn't worry of tumbling the girl that bothered him but her intensity, her seriousness. Why in the world had she kept that coin all these years?

"Let's walk," he said, holding the horse's reins, not wanting Leah's thin little body near his on the horse.

Leah had never felt so alive in her life. She was with the man she loved. Here and now was what she'd dreamed of since she was a child. With one hand on the coin in her pocket, she slid her other arm through Wesley's.

He looked down at her and, whether it was a trick of the moonlight or the concealing darkness, she looked downright pretty. The bruise and scratches, now hidden, had kept him from noticing her full lips and that her eyes were large, seductive. He gave the groan of a man lost and started walking with her.

Leah's heart was pounding rapidly by the time they left sight of the tavern. Her conscience, dulled by three mugs of beer, was telling her that Bess was right and she had no business here. Yet a part of her was saying that here was her one and only chance for love and she was going to take it. Later, when Wesley was in a faraway place and she was still toiling for her family, she could remember tonight. Perhaps he'd kiss her again.

With her thoughts in her eyes she looked up at him, and Wesley, with no thoughts at all, bent his head and kissed her.

She melted against him, her body feeling delicate and breakable in his work-hardened arms, but she kept her lips closed in a childish way. He drew back, his eyes twinkling. The girl was a mixture of accomplished whore and virginal innocence. With her eyes still closed, she moved her lips against his, put her mouth on his again, and Wesley nudged her lips open. He had a thought that she was a quick learner but soon no more thoughts crossed his mind.

The girl gave herself to him as if she'd been hungering for him, and Wesley responded with months of pent-up desire, his head pushing hers back, his hand burying in the gummy mass of her hair and turning her to better reach her lips. He withdrew, his eyes glazed, his breath coming hard. Her hair had come untied and hung to her waist; her lips were reddened.

"You're beautiful," he whispered and went for her mouth again as his hands tore at her dress top.

"No!" Leah said, suddenly frightened. A kiss was what she'd dreamed of, a kiss and no more, but as his hands sought her bare flesh, and even as she told him no, she knew she'd never actually deny him. "Wesley," she whispered as her hands ceased to fight him. "My own Wesley."

"Yes, love," he said distractedly, his mouth traveling down her throat.

The fabric of the coarse dress was old and tore away easily. Within seconds Leah was standing nude in the moonlight. Her thin body showed every bone, every muscle. The only sign of her womanliness was her full breasts, proud and perfect.

With great care Wesley lifted her in his arms, then lay her on his cloak, which had fallen from his shoulders.

Leah, not knowing what to do, how to return the pleasure she was feeling, lay still as he ran his hands over her and unfastened his clothes at the same time.

When he entered her, she screamed in pain. Wesley lay still a moment, touched her hair, kissed her cheek.

Leah opened tear-filled eyes to look up at him, and a

13

wave of great love came over her. This was her Wesley, the man she had always loved, would die loving. "Yes," she whispered, "yes."

Wesley continued quickly and only at the end did Leah feel even a tinge of pleasure. And when he finished with a hard thrust, he grabbed her shoulders and whispered "Kimberly" in her ear.

It was several moments before Leah understood exactly what had happened to her. *Kimberly,* he'd said.

He rolled off her, tired for the moment, his eyes half-closed, while Leah stood and pulled on the shreds of her old dress.

"Good girl," Wes said drowsily as he reached into the pocket of the pants he hadn't fully removed. "For your trouble." He flipped a gold coin toward her and it landed at her feet. "We keep meeting, you'll have a trunk full of those things."

Stunned, Leah watched him stand, fasten his pants, and pick up his cloak and hat. Reaching out, he touched her chin. "You, little girl, are going to get me in trouble." He drew back. "I hope *some* of you was clean." With that, he mounted his horse and rode away.

It was some time before Leah could move. What an absolute, total fool she'd made of herself, she thought more in amazement than anything else. She felt as if she were a child who'd just learned there were no fairy godmothers. All these years she'd been able to resist the horror of her life because at the end of the rainbow was the great god Wesley. But in the end he was just a man who'd taken what was freely offered to him.

"Free!" she exclaimed, stooping to grab the coin at her feet. Holding it for a moment, feeling how cold it was, she thought of all the food and clothes she could buy with the money and what it had cost her to obtain the coin. With a laugh at her years of childish dreams, she did what may have been the first totally impractical act of her life: she drew her arm back and threw the coin as far as she could, down toward the blackness that was the river, and when she heard a splash, she smiled.

"Not all the Simmons are whores!" she shouted at the top of her lungs.

Feeling better, willing herself not to cry, since she'd learned long ago that tears were useless, she started toward the place she called home. Her body ached and she moved slowly, knowing she'd never make it back before daylight and that there'd be a beating waiting for her. The loss of her dream made her feet heavy and she dreaded more than ever the life ahead of her.

Chapter 2

March, 1804

The tall, steepled building of Whitefield Church was beautiful inside, with whitewashed plaster walls and sun streaming in through round-topped windows. The pastor's box was high above the people's heads, a carved walnut staircase leading to it. Below, on hard benches inside short paneled walls, sat the congregation.

Wesley Stanford sat next to his bride-to-be, holding her fingertips under the concealing folds of her pink silk dress. Kimberly Shaw reverently kept her head up and her eyes on the pastor. She was a very pretty woman with plump cheeks, big blue eyes, and a soft, desirable mouth. Now and then she'd glance at Wesley and smile, her cheek dimpling.

Next to her was her brother, Steven Shaw, a tall, big male version of Kimberly, blond, handsome, with a cleft chin.

Beside Steven were two couples, Clay and Nicole Armstrong next to Travis and Regan Stanford. Travis was moving his big form about in the seat, obviously impatient to get home, and his pretty wife was just as obviously giving him deathly looks—looks that Travis was ignoring. Clay, on the other hand, was sitting quite still, only occasionally glancing at his dark little wife, as if he weren't sure she was really there.

Wesley, his grip tightening on Kim's hand, thought of all the things he had to do before he and she left for Kentucky in two weeks. They'd be married on Sunday, spend the night—oh lovely night—at Stanford Plantation, then set out early Monday morning. Awaiting them in the new state was Wes's land with a new house and barn on it, livestock tended now by a neighbor. For the first time in his life he'd be in a place where he wouldn't be judged by what his brother did or said.

It was while Wesley was contemplating this idyllic scene that the side door of the church flew open with a bang. Reverend Smyth paused in his monotonous intonation to glance toward the disturbance, but what he saw made him cease speaking.

Crazy old Elijah Simmons, his face red with fury, was pulling behind him, her hands bound with rope, what must have been one of his daughters, but the swollen, distorted face made identification impossible.

"Sinners!" old Elijah bellowed. "You sit here in the Lord's house yet all of you are fornicating sinners!"

He pushed the girl forward so hard that she stumbled to her knees. And when Elijah pulled her up by her hair, it was clear that she was pregnant. Her hard, round belly protruded from her gaunt frame.

"Travis!" Regan said with a plea, but Travis was already on his feet ready to stop the old man.

Elijah pulled a pistol from the pocket of his coat and held it to the girl's head. "The fornicating whore doesn't deserve to live."

"In God's house!" the reverend said with a gasp.

Elijah held the girl and backed up the stairs leading to the preacher's box. "Look at her!" he yelled, forcing the girl's body back to make her stomach more prominent. "What sinner did this?"

The preacher started down the stairs, but Elijah pressed the pistol deeper into the girl's temple. She appeared to be only half-alive, one eye swollen shut, the other drooping tiredly.

Travis slowly began walking around the walled bench. "Now, Elijah," he said soothingly, "we'll find out who did this and he'll marry her."

"The devil did it!" Elijah screamed, his head bent back, and the congregation, eyes on him, gasped in unison.

"No," Travis said calmly, inching forward. "A man did it and the man will be made to marry her. Now, let me have the pistol."

"There are no men!" Elijah said. "I kept her under my eye; I watched her day and night; I tried to beat some goodness into her, yet the slut—." He broke off as he bent the girl's arm backward. "The twelfth of September she stayed out all night. On the thirteenth of September I tried to beat some shame into her but she was born in sin and she will die in sin."

Wesley, his face turning whiter with each moment, saw his world collapsing about him. He knew the girl was Leah, the one with whom he'd spent an hour and whose virgin's blood he'd seen on his cloak the next morning. He knew, without a doubt, that the child she carried was his. If he went forward now, perhaps he wouldn't have to marry her, but he wondered if Kimberly would be able to forgive him his one lapse. But if he didn't step forward, the girl Leah might lose her life.

He stood.

"Stay out of this, Wes," Travis said from the corner of his mouth.

Wesley looked at old Elijah. "I'm the father of the girl's child," he said clearly.

For a moment all sound in the church ceased. The first sound was a half-gasp, half-sob from Kimberly.

"Take the sinner!" Elijah screeched, and he pushed Leah down the stairs.

Wesley and Travis worked together, Wes grabbing Leah and sweeping her into his arms before she hit the floor, Travis wrestling the pistol from Elijah's hand.

Everyone began to move at once, the congregation excitedly leaving the church, Steven holding Kim, who kept her head high and her eyes dry while Clay, Nicole, Reverend Smyth, Travis, and Elijah followed Wesley into the vestry.

Regan lifted her skirts and ran out the side door to the parsonage, where she demanded that hot water and clean cloths be brought immediately to the vestry. When she returned, everything was chaos. The girl lay lifelessly on a sofa, her bonds cut away, Nicole kneeling beside her. Clay stood beside Elijah, who was sitting, reluctantly, in a chair. Reverend Smyth cowered in a corner. And in the middle of the room were Travis and Wesley, bellowing at each other like two enraged bulls.

"You'd think you'd have enough sense to stay away from virginal young girls. What with all the—," Travis shouted.

"The bitch flung herself on me," Wesley answered. "How was I to know it wasn't her profession? I even paid her."

"You fool! Why did you have to pretend to be a saint and say in front of everyone that it was your kid? I could have handled it."

"Like you handle everything else in my life, Travis?" Wesley yelled, fists clenched.

The water came, the housekeeper left, her eyes wide with terror, and Regan knelt beside Nicole. Ignoring the two men in the center of the room, they began tenderly to wash the girl.

"You think Kimberly will still take Wes after this?" Regan asked Nicole, hope in her voice.

"Probably," Nicole answered, and Regan's shoulders fell.

"I wonder why she went to bed with Wesley if she was a virgin. And why she went back to that old man afterward. You know, don't you, about her sister?"

"I've heard," Nicole answered. Then, with eyebrows raised, she looked at Regan. "You're up to something."

Regan gave Nicole a look of pure innocence. "Look!" She nodded toward the frightened preacher. "They're scaring the reverend. Tell Clay to take Wes outside, and I'll get Travis out of here. I'd like to talk to this girl."

Regan had to put her small body between her husband and his brother and beat on Travis's chest with her fists to get his attention. "I want quiet in here!" she yelled up at him. "Go somewhere else and scream at each other."

"If you're telling me what to do—," Travis began, but Clay caught his arm. "Let's go outside. The girl is sick." He nodded toward Leah on the couch.

"Sinners! All women are sinners!" Elijah screeched, and Clay grabbed the old man's arm and hauled him out the door behind Travis and Wesley, who'd already resumed their argument in full gale. The reverend tiptoed out behind them.

"That's better," Nicole sighed when the room was quiet. "How do you stand both of them under the same roof?"

"It's a big roof," Regan answered, "but they're getting worse as they get older. No!" she said quickly to Leah, who was trying to sit up. "Just lie still."

"Please," Leah whispered through swollen, cracked lips. "I must leave now while he's gone."

"You can't leave. I doubt if you can walk. Now lie still," Nicole said.

"I think we ought to take her home and feed her," Regan said, and the unsaid words *and wash her* hung on the air.

"No," Leah said. "Don't want to cause Wesley problems. Marry his Kimberly. So sorry about baby."

Nicole and Regan exchanged looks. "How long have you known Wesley?" Regan asked.

"Always," Leah whispered, leaning back on the cushions. Through her one unclosed eye she saw two women who looked like angels, exquisitely pretty, with soft clouds of dark hair, dresses of fabric woven by gods. "I must go."

Regan gently pushed her down again and applied a cloth to her swollen face. "You've known Wesley always yet you only climbed into bed with him once?"

Leah's mouth gave what could have been a smile. "Only saw him twice." With that she fell asleep or into a state of half-sleep, half-consciousness.

Regan sat back on her heels. "I'd like to hear the rest of this story. What was Wesley doing with a girl such as this when he was supposed to be faithful to her royal highness Kimberly?"

"Her royal—," Nicole said with a smile. "Oh Regan, you haven't called her that to Wesley, have you?"

"No, but I did once to Travis. Stupid men! Both of them think she's the epitome of womanhood. You know, I'd almost rather see Wes married to . . . to that—," she pointed at the bruised mess that was Leah—, "than to the dear, delectable Miss Shaw."

Before Nicole could answer, the door burst open and in ran Bess Simmons, Leah's sister.

"I'll kill him!" she cried, falling to her knees and taking Leah's lifeless hand. "Is she alive? I'll kill him!"

"She's alive and which one do you plan to kill? Her father or Wesley?" Regan asked, standing over Bess.

Bess wiped away a tear. "The old man. Leah asked for what she got from Mr. Stanford."

"Oh?" Regan asked with interest, extending her arm to Bess to help her stand. "Then Leah did throw herself at Wesley."

"Oh yes. Stupid girl." She glanced fondly at the sleeping Leah. "She'd have done anything for Mr. Stanford."

Together Nicole and Regan ushered Bess to a chair. "Tell us," they chorused.

Within a few minutes Bess had told the whole story.

"It was through Leah that Clay found me on that island," Nicole said thoughtfully.

"And she's loved Wesley all these years?" Regan said.

"It ain't been *real* love," Bess said, "since she ain't seen him in all these years, but Leah's always had the notion that she was in love with him."

"Better than Kimberly," Regan said under her breath.

"Regan . . ." Nicole warned. "I don't think I like your thoughts."

"Bess," Regan said brightly, taking Bess's arm, "it

was so good of you to come by and I swear to you that Leah will be well taken care of." Expertly, Regan escorted the woman out the door.

Leaning on the closed door, Regan's eyes were bright. "The girl saved your life and she's been in love with Wesley for years."

"Regan, are you going to interfere in this? This is between Wesley and Kimberly. We should take the girl home, nurse her back to health, deliver the child, and perhaps find them a place of employment."

"And what about Wesley's child?" Regan said righteously. "Are we going to let it be raised by strangers?"

"Perhaps Wes and Kim could adopt—?" Nicole began but stopped. "Perhaps that is a bit farfetched."

"With dear, sweet Kimberly it is. I doubt if she'll be able to put up with the nuisance of her own children much less someone else's." Regan sat down. "Look at her, Nicole, and tell me how you think she'll look when she's healed and clean."

Nicole hesitated, but she did as Regan bid. Nicole had an idea what Regan was hinting at and she was sure she should stop her, but at the same time she agreed with Regan. For months now she'd been hoping something would happen to prevent Wesley from marrying Kim.

As dispassionately as she could, Nicole studied Leah's battered face. "She has good features, good bones. I can't tell about the eyes in this condition. She may never be pretty, exactly, but neither do I think she'll be ugly."

"Oh well, we couldn't hope to beat Kimberly's loveliness. Nicole!" she said, rising. "I think we should insist that Wes marry the mother of his child, that he do the honorable thing by her."

23

"Regan . . ." Nicole gave a sigh of exasperation. "It just won't work. You know Travis could fix it so the girl would never want for anything and Wes does *not* have to marry her."

"He'd more likely be happy with this stranger than he would with Kimberly. This girl *loves* Wes and I know Kim cannot love anyone except herself."

"But Wesley loves Kim," Nicole said stubbornly, trying to reason with her friend. "He does *not* love this girl. And besides, what do we know of her? Maybe she's worse than Kim ever thought of being."

Regan gave a snort of disbelief. "You heard the sister. This girl could have had an easy life in the tavern but instead, she chose to stay and support her brothers and sisters even though she had to bear beatings from that crazy old father. How many people do you know who would do that? Miss Shaw?"

"Maybe not Kimberly but—."

"We have a choice between Kimberly or this battered, unloved, unappreciated girl."

That made Nicole laugh. "Oh Regan, really, you do exaggerate so. None of what you're saying means anything. Wesley will make up his own mind."

Regan looked thoughtful for a moment. "If you and Clay agreed with me and we got Travis on Kim's side—Wesley *always* does the opposite of what Travis wants—we might be able to get what we want."

"Clay can't stand Kimberly," Nicole said, half under her breath.

"And what about you, Nicole, what do you think of Kimberly?"

Nicole looked down at Leah for a long moment. "I hate to see anyone I love unhappy. Wesley has borne Travis's criticism for so long."

"And wouldn't it be nice for him to have a chance

with a new wife in a new land—a *real* chance for happiness, not one doomed to failure?" Regan whispered.

"Clay *thought* he wanted to marry Bianca but fate stepped in and we were married instead," Nicole said under her breath.

"We're going to help fate a little, aren't we, Nicole?" Regan urged.

Nicole looked up, eyes laughing. "I'm afraid so—and *afraid* is exactly the right word."

In spite of Nicole's original reticence, she was the one most enthusiastic in bringing about Wesley and Leah's marriage. Clay looked into his wife's eyes and remembered too well how he'd wanted to marry one woman and had ended with another. Besides, he'd had too many run-ins with Kimberly to ever take her side.

Rubbing his jaw in some private memory, Clay said, "I owe Wes one. He helped me get away from Bianca. I just hope this Leah proves to be a better woman."

"That's my worry too," Nicole answered.

But when Clay, Regan, and Nicole reached the strangely quiet Wesley and Travis, there was no need to persuade anyone.

"You talk to him!" Travis seethed at Regan. "He thinks he has to marry the little two-bit whore. He's willing to give up his whole future because the cunning slut arranged it so he was her first customer. If he'd had any sense and waited a few minutes in the church, probably twenty men would have admitted to tumbling her. I wonder if she faked virgin's blood on *their* cloaks?"

Regan, her hand on her husband's arm, seemed reluctant to speak.

Nicole went to stand near Wesley, to look up into his bleak eyes. "You don't believe that, do you?"

Wes shook his head. "I don't want to marry her but it's my duty. She carries my child."

"And what about Kimberly?" Nicole asked softly.

"She—," Wes turned away for a moment. "That was killed when I stepped forward in the church."

"Wesley," Nicole said, her hand on his arm, "I don't know the girl, but I think she has qualities that could make her a good wife."

Wesley snorted. "She's fertile. Now, shall we get this over?"

"For God's sake, think about it for a few days at least," Travis exploded. "Maybe you'll come to your senses. We can find the girl a husband. The cobbler's boy is looking for a wife. He could—."

"Travis, you can take your cobbler and—."

"Wesley!" Regan interrupted. "Are you going to hate Leah when she's your wife?"

"I shall give her and the child the best of everything. Now, shall we go inside to my—," he smiled in an ugly way—"bride?"

Leah became Mrs. Wesley Stanford before the sun went down on that fateful Sunday. Through some inner strength, she held herself upright and answered the nervous preacher's questions firmly. She didn't quite understand how it had all come about, but it was so much like one of her dreams, standing in a marriage ceremony with the man she'd always loved, that the pain in her body seemed to slip away.

The solemn group didn't say a word when the service was complete. Leah was helped to make her mark beside Wesley's signature in the church registry, then

26

Clay's strong arms carried her to a waiting wagon. She was too ill to notice where she was or that her new husband and his brother refused to look at her.

She was placed in a boat, rowed upstream, and put into another wagon. At long last she was gently laid on a soft, clean bed.

"My room," Wesley snorted at Regan as Clay put the girl on the bed. "It's fitting then that I should leave."

"Leave!" Regan gasped. "With a new wife and—."

Wesley's look stopped her. "If you think I can look at that every day and stay sane you don't know me very well. I have to go away for awhile and get used to the idea." He pulled a carpetbag from a wardrobe bottom and shoved clothes into it.

"Where are you going?" Regan whispered. "You won't leave her and the baby?"

"No, I know my duty. I'll take care of both of them but I need some time to resign myself to . . . *that!*" He sneered at the sleeping Leah on his bed. "I'll go to my farm in Kentucky, do some work, and should be back in the spring. The kid'll be old enough to travel then."

"You can't stick us with your leavings," Travis said from the doorway. "You were the noble one who felt he had to make an honest woman of her. *Woman!* I can't even tell if she's human. Take her with you. I don't want to be reminded of your stupidity."

"Take the expense of her keep from my half of this place," Wesley shouted.

"Don't part like this," Regan pleaded, but Wesley was already gone. "Go after him," she told Travis.

"Nicole and I will take care of the girl. Don't part with your brother like this."

After hesitating, Travis touched his little wife's cheek, then tore down the stairs. From the bedroom window Regan watched the brothers embrace before Wesley started toward the dock and the boat that would take him west.

Chapter 3

Two days after Wesley left, Leah was delivered of a stillborn child. She cried over the tiny coffin then was ushered back to bed where she slept for days, waking only briefly to eat lightly.

When Leah finally woke and looked about her, she was sure she was in heaven. She lay in the middle of a big four-poster bed hung with cream-colored cloth. The walls were painted white and hung with pictures of sailing ships and men hunting, and there were chairs, tables, and cabinets such as she'd never seen before.

She allowed herself only a moment to enjoy the view before she swung her legs out of bed. She was wearing a cap on her head and a brilliantly white gown; wonderingly, she touched the garment while her head stopped spinning.

"What do you think you're doing?" asked a woman from the doorway. "Miss Regan!" she shouted over her shoulder.

When Regan arrived, Leah was struggling with the

woman to be allowed out of bed. "Sally, that will be all."

"You don't know what her kind's like," the maid said, sniffing, pushing at Leah's shoulders.

Regan drew herself up. "Sally!" she commanded. "Out of this room and I'll speak to you later." When she was gone, Regan turned to Leah, who was again trying to sit up. "You must rest."

"I have to see about the little ones. The old man'll let them starve."

Gently, but with force, Regan pushed Leah back into bed. "That's all been taken care of. Travis and Clay went to your farm and got all your brothers and sisters and they're being placed in people's homes. As for your father, no one's seen him in weeks, not since he . . . came to church. Right now all you have to do is rest, eat, and get well. When you're better, you can see your family. Ah, here's the food."

Leah was bewildered when a prettily painted wooden tray laden with food was placed over her legs.

"I didn't know what you'd like so I ordered a variety," Regan said, lifting domed silver lids to show fragrant, hot food.

"I . . ." Leah stammered.

Regan patted her hand. "Eat as much as you can and enjoy it, then I want you to sleep. We're going to fatten you up before we set to work. The chamber pot's under the bed." With that Regan left the room.

Leah tore into the food with both hands, eating as she always did—as fast as she could. She was unaware of the flecks of food she splashed on the bed hangings. When she finished, she used the chamber pot and emptied it out the window, just as she had at home. Scratching, she went back to bed and slept, missing

Travis's furor when he heard what Leah had done with the contents of the chamber pot.

For ten days Leah did nothing but rest and eat and, as her scratches and bruises finished healing, Regan looked at her in speculation. Regan had told Leah about Wesley's leaving for Kentucky, pretending that it was something he'd intended to do all along.

Leah learned to leave the chamber pot for a maid, but she never had the courage to leave the bedroom. She sat at the window and looked out at the acres of buildings that went with Travis's plantation, saw the hundreds of people moving about their jobs, and she began to feel restless.

"When am I gonna start that work you mentioned?" she asked Regan.

Regan took Leah's chin in her hand and studied her face in the sunlight. The bruises were almost completely healed. "How about tomorrow morning?"

"Good." Leah smiled. "You got anything I can wear? Somethin' old," she said, nodding toward Regan's blue silk dress.

"I don't think we'll worry about your wardrobe yet," she said thoughtfully. "Yes, I think we'll start tomorrow if Nicole is available." She gave Leah no time to ask questions. "I must go. There are so, so many preparations to make," she said distractedly as she left the room.

When Leah woke the next morning, both Nicole and Regan were standing over her wearing worn, coarse dresses of muslin, their hair covered, and stern expressions on their faces.

"It's not going to be easy," Regan murmured. "Where do we start?"

"Body first, hair tomorrow."

Before Leah could say a word, each woman grabbed an arm, pulled her from the bed, and led her out of the bedroom. Leah, while being half dragged, gazed about her in wonder at carpets, pictures, furniture of magnificence. They led her downstairs to a relatively plain room that was still beautiful compared to where she'd lived. "Is this gonna be my room? Wait a minute!" she gasped as Regan and Nicole practically tore the nightgown from her. She bent, struggling to cover her nude body. "You can't—."

"Get used to it, Leah," Regan ordered, "because you won't be wearing any clothes for a couple of days."

"You have no right—," she began, grabbing her gown from the floor.

"Get in!" Regan commanded, pointing to an enormous tub standing in the middle of the room.

Leah stood perfectly still where she was, holding her discarded gown before her.

Nicole took over. "Leah," she said firmly. "You're a Stanford now and with the name and the beautiful house go certain responsibilities. For one thing, you cannot sit at a dining table smelling worse than a mule, which you do right now. Therefore, Regan and I are going to devote the next few weeks—or months if need be—to making you into a Stanford. We're going to clean you, cream you, mask you, and when that's finished we're going to tackle your grammar, your walk, your manners, and anything else that needs work."

Leah looked from one woman to the other. "When you get through with me will I smell like you do? When Wesley comes back will he see me wearin' a pretty dress?"

Regan and Nicole exchanged smiles. "A beautiful dress. Wesley will be proud to have you as his wife."

Days later she wondered whether she would have gotten into that first tub of water if she'd had any idea what those two fiendish women had planned. She'd assumed they'd be happy with her clean skin, but Nicole clucked over her.

"This won't do at all. Too many years of neglect."

Leah, wrapped in a cotton robe, was led to another room and in this one sat a tub of . . . "What *is* that?" she said with a gasp.

"Mud," Regan answered, laughing.

So Leah was immersed in mud, made to stand in her birthday suit until it dried, and given three more baths. Then she lay on a table while Nicole and Regan tried to scrub her skin off with coarse leather gloves. She was put into another tub of water, this one greasy with vegetable oil, and when she was removed they rubbed her with cucumber cream.

"Not bad," Regan said at the end of the day, hair straggling in her eyes, her dress filthy. "I think we accomplished a lot." She smacked Leah on her bare bottom, handed her a robe, and escorted her upstairs.

Exhausted, but her skin feeling tingly and alive, Leah fell into the bed.

The next morning Nicole and Regan were there again. Leah groaned and pulled the covers over her head.

"Oh no, Leah," Regan said, laughing, "greet the day with a smile." She pulled the covers off, but Leah did her own walking downstairs to the torture chambers.

"I've been itching to do this," Nicole said, pulling the cap from Leah's dirty hair. "I wonder what color it is?"

Leah sat in a hard chair while Nicole took a stiff-bristled brush to her scalp, scrubbing so hard it brought tears to her eyes.

"Dandruff," Nicole murmured, but Leah didn't even know what that was.

While Nicole scrubbed, Regan applied a cornmeal mixture to Leah's face. When the mask was dry, they began washing her entire head. It took four shampooings to remove years of grease and dirt.

"I won't swear to it but I think there're touches of red in here," Nicole said.

Even wet, Leah's head felt lighter than it ever had, but before she could speak, Nicole began dumping handfuls of mayonnaise on her newly clean hair. Her head was wrapped in a very hot towel and she was left alone in the darkened room, her head leaning backwards, grated raw potato under her eyes.

Wesley, she kept thinking. I'm really, truly his wife, and he's worth all of this.

In the evening her hair was washed again and rinsed with rainwater mixed with lemon juice, vinegar, and rosemary. Nicole had covered all the mirrors on their path from Wesley's bedroom to the storage areas where they were working, so Leah had no idea how she looked, but as she sank into the bed she knew she smelled better.

Leah was appalled to learn that Nicole and Regan expected her to change her underclothes and bathe every single day. She felt that if it'd been done once it was done forever, but on the third day they pushed her into a tub again. They were determined to soften Leah's skin since it bore calluses from years of work. Her elbows and knees were scrubbed raw, then bleached with lemon juice and massaged with strawberry cream.

And always there were lectures. Nicole taught her how to care for her skin and hair even if she spent all day in a field behind a team of horses. Since Leah couldn't read, they made her memorize recipes for creams, facial masks, hair conditioners, and shampoos; on and on they went, making Leah recite them until she could repeat them even asleep.

After two weeks of treatments, Nicole, her hands in Leah's clean, soft, shining hair, stood back. "Do you think we can show her now?" she asked with a smile.

"Wait." Regan laughed. "Put this on, Leah." She held out a deep green silk taffeta dressing gown, embroidered with tiny, colorful birds.

"I couldn't." Leah hesitated, but Nicole's look stopped her. Leah dropped the plain muslin gown she wore and slid her arms into the silk, her eyes rolling slightly at the feel of it. "It's lovely."

"All right, now stand right here," Regan ordered, posing Leah before a full-length mirror that was draped with a bed sheet.

When Regan, with a flourish, pulled the sheet away, Leah made no reaction—because she had no idea who the person in the mirror was. She turned to see who was behind her, but when the reflection moved also, she stood still.

The woman in the mirror was not just pretty; she was beautiful. Long, thick auburn hair cascaded about her shoulders, down her back, and big green, intense eyes looked out of a square-jawed face marked with a full, sensuous mouth. Tentatively, Leah lifted her hand to touch her own cheek—and the next minute she collapsed in a heap on the bed while Regan and Nicole laughed.

"I think we've succeeded," Regan said in triumph, then her head came up. "I want to show her off. Just a bit, right now."

"It's early," Nicole warned.

"Come along, Leah," Regan said, taking Leah's hand.

Regan led Leah through a part of the house she'd never seen before, through long hallways, past a vast dining room. "Does this place have an end?"

"You'll learn your way around. Now we're going to Travis's office."

"Wesley's brother?"

Regan gave a short laugh. "Wesley is usually thought of as Travis's little brother."

"Not to me," Leah said with confidence.

Travis was sitting behind an enormous desk, ledgers open before him, one of his clerks beside him. Regan stood Leah before the desk and when the clerk looked up, his mouth dropped open in amazement. Travis glanced up, saw the man's expression, and turned to look at Leah.

"Good God!" he said, sucking air through his teeth. "She's not—."

"She is," Regan said proudly.

"Fetch us some tea," Travis commanded his clerk. "And stop gawking! Here, sit down. Leah, is it?"

As if she'd always been treated as a lady, Leah demurely sat on the upholstered chair Travis held for her. The robe had parted somewhat and was exposing a great deal of cleavage, which Travis was enjoying. He looked up to see Regan glaring at him.

"Filled out some, hasn't she?" he said with a grin.

The tea arrived almost instantly with two maids and a butler carrying a big silver tray, all three of them and Travis's clerk gaping at Leah.

"Out! All of you!" Travis commanded.

Leah sat still, returning all their looks with curiosity, wondering who they were and what their jobs were.

When the room was clear, Travis poured tea for Leah into a fragile porcelain cup and held it out to her with great politeness.

"I *am* hungry," Leah said and noisily moved her chair closer to the desk where the tray of cakes and sandwiches had been set. She blew loudly on the tea, slurped it so it bubbled through her teeth, set the wet cup down on the wooden desktop, then picked up three small pastries, mashed them in her saucer, poured cream from the silver pitcher over them, and began eating the concoction with her teaspoon. Halfway through she looked up to see Travis, Regan, and Nicole gaping at her.

Nicole was the first to recover. "We have a bit more work to do yet," she said softly before sipping delicately from her teacup.

"That you do," Travis said with a grunt.

Leah resumed eating.

Three days later Leah swore she hated those little cups and saucers that looked so pretty but seemed to always be falling apart in her hands. Regan threatened Leah's life if she broke one more piece of expensive imported porcelain, so Leah again tried to learn how to handle them.

"What does it matter *how* you eat as long as you get it inside?" Leah half cried as Nicole again corrected her use of a fork.

"Think of Wesley," Nicole said, using the phrase as a slogan to urge Leah on—and it always worked. The women used Wesley to entice Leah, to force her to be patient and learn the manners she needed to know. And they got the whole story from Leah about how she'd met Wes, how she'd loved him forever.

After Leah had been at the Stanford Plantation for

two months, her father, Elijah, was found dead in the river. Travis paid for a funeral that was beautiful. For the first time since she'd married Wesley, Leah saw her brothers and sisters. Each of them had gained weight, were unbruised and clinging to the hands of the people who'd taken them in. They looked at Leah with wide eyes, not even sure who she was, and left with their new families; Leah shed tears of joy because they seemed so happy now.

Once, Leah looked across her father's coffin and into the gaze of a beautiful young woman. But before Leah could even look her fill at this vision, Regan nudged her and Leah turned away. When she looked back, the woman was gone.

"Who was she?" Leah asked later.

"Kimberly Shaw," Regan answered tightly.

The woman who was supposed to marry Wesley, Leah thought, feeling very smug. She may have wanted him but I got him.

Seeing the woman, Leah resolved to work harder so she'd please Wesley when he returned in the spring.

Leah set her cup down easily, quietly, as if she'd always known how to eat and drink properly, leaned toward Travis, and smiled prettily. "And do you think this new cotton gin will help speed production? You don't think the cotton market will collapse like the tobacco market did?"

Regan and Nicole leaned back in their chairs and watched their protégé with pleasure. It had taken months of work, but Leah was passing the test. They'd never attempted to instruct Leah in *what* to talk about, merely how to say the words, so they were surprised when her main interest was farming. But of course she'd never been able to read—and they'd not yet tried to teach her how—so Leah talked of what she knew: farming.

And Travis was eating it up, Regan thought with disgust. Sometimes, when Regan was talking about household problems, she'd see Travis's eyes glaze over, but with Leah asking about his beloved fields, horses, and blacksmith shop, Travis was practically on the edge of his seat.

"In the morning," Travis was saying, "you can ride out with me and have a look at the tobacco."

"No," Nicole said softly. "Tomorrow Leah goes home with me. I have been away too long and it's time we dressed her."

"She looks dressed to me," Travis said appreciatively, looking at the low-cut muslin gown Leah wore.

"Travis," Regan warned, ready to tell him what she thought of his ogling of Leah.

Nicole laughed and prevented the impending quarrel. "No, Leah must go with me. The fabrics I ordered have come at last and my seamstress is there. Also, I'll start teaching her how to manage a plantation. She can start on someplace small before tackling this monster of yours, Travis."

After a frown, Travis smiled, then took Leah's hand and kissed it. "I'm going to miss your pretty face around here but Clay'll take care of you."

Later Regan walked with Leah to Wes's bedroom. "Nicole has an army of French craftsmen at her place. She and Clay went back to France last summer and returned with people Nicole had known when she lived there. Her dressmaker used to work for the queen. Now sleep well because you'll leave early in the morning. Good night."

Leah removed her dress, an altered one of Nicole's, put on a clean nightgown, and slipped into bed. It was

July now, she thought. There was all the winter to go and then spring before Wesley would return to her. Touching her clean, soft hair, she knew she looked very different, and she prayed that she'd please him when he returned. More than anything, she wanted to please him. "I will be the best wife in the world to you," she whispered and fell asleep smiling.

In the morning before it was even light, Nicole and Leah were escorted by Travis to the dock. In the five months that she'd been there, Leah had barely seen the plantation except from her window, because she'd always been inside with Regan and Nicole, practicing her walk, her grammar, her table manners, how to sit, how to stand, whatever ordeal could be imagined for her.

At the dock, Travis bent and kissed her cheek, and touching the place, Leah looked up at him in wonder. "We'll miss you," he called as a man helped Leah into the waiting sloop.

Smiling, she waved to them until they sailed out of sight. How heavenly, she thought, how warm and kind and loving everything was. For moments she could almost forget what it was like to be angry twenty-four hours a day.

She turned to Nicole, who was watching her. "If Wesley were here it'd be perfect," Leah said laughing, hugging herself.

"I hope you're right," Nicole murmured, mostly to herself, before looking away.

Chapter 4

At the dock of Arundel Plantation waiting to greet Nicole were identical twin boys, six years old, and two beautiful seventeen-year-old twins who were introduced as Alex and Amanda. Clay waited impatiently while everyone else hugged his wife, then he swept her into his arms for an embarrassingly passionate kiss, after which they walked away, each holding one of the boys' hands and looking into each other's eyes.

"They're always like that," Alex said half in disgust.

"They're in love, you idiot," Amanda snapped before turning to Leah. "Would you like to see the cloth that came in? Uncle Clay says it's for you."

"I have better things to do, so if you ladies will excuse me," Alex said as he mounted a beautiful roan horse and rode away.

"We don't need him anyway," Amanda said. "Come on, we have to hurry. Madame Gisele is awful when she's kept waiting. If she bullies you too much, just threaten to send her back to France. It makes her keep quiet for a few minutes at least," Amanda confided.

As Leah and Amanda walked together, Amanda chattering away, Leah was watching the early morning bustle going on about her as people went in and out of what seemed to be hundreds of buildings. Leah asked questions.

"The overseer's cottage, workers' quarters, ice house, the stables through there, the kitchen," were Amanda's answers. "She's upstairs waiting for us." Amanda led Leah through an octagonal porch at the back of a big brick house, up some beautiful stairs, past tables covered with freshly cut flowers. "Mom—I mean Nicole—likes lots of flowers. Here we are, Madame," Amanda said politely to a tiny little woman with a big nose and fierce black eyes.

"You have taken your time," Madame Gisele said in such an odd way that Leah didn't quite understand her.

"It's her accent," Amanda whispered. "Took me awhile too."

"Out!" Madame commanded. "We have work to do and you are in the way."

"Yes, of course," Amanda said, laughing as she curtsied before leaving the room.

"Insolent girl!" Madame snapped, but there was affection in her voice. Then her eyes were on Leah, walking around her, examining her.

"Yes, yes, a good figure, a bit large in the bosom but your husband likes that, no?"

Leah smiled, turned red, and began to study the wallpaper of the attic room.

"Come, come, don't stand there. There's work to be done. Show me what you like so we can begin." She motioned toward shelves along one wall that were loaded with bolts and rolls of fabric.

Leah stuck out her finger to touch a piece of deep blue velvet. "I . . . I don't know," Leah said. "I like everything. Nicole and Regan usually—."

"Ah!" Madame Gisele cut her off. "Madame Regan is not here and Nicole is no doubt in the throes of passion with that magnificent man of hers and she will be of no use for days. So! Now you must learn to rely on yourself. Stand up straight! No dress will ever hang properly if your shoulders droop so. Have some pride in yourself. You are a beautiful woman, you have a rich, handsome husband who will return to you soon and now we will dress you splendidly. You have much to be proud of so *show* it!"

Yes, Leah thought, she is perfectly correct. I *do* have a lot to be proud of. She turned toward the fabric. "I like this," she said, touching a rust-colored velvet.

"Good! And what else?"

"This and this and . . . this one."

Madame Gisele stood back for a moment, looked up at Leah, then gave a short laugh. "You may look frightened but you're afraid of no one. True, no?"

Leah considered the question seriously. "Nicole and Regan are so sure of themselves. Everything they do is perfect."

"They were born to wealth but people like you and me . . . we have to learn. I will help you, that is, if you aren't afraid of hard work."

Leah smiled at that, remembering the feel of the plow harness about her shoulders. "People who live in houses like this don't even know what work is."

"You will do," Madame Gisele said, laughing. "You will do."

What followed for Leah were days of measurements, pinnings, and being bullied by Madame.

"Lingerie!" the little woman said repeatedly. "You

may have to forego silk for everyday wear on that nasty farm you're going to, but underneath you'll be a lady."

At first Leah was shocked by the semitransparent garments of Indian cotton, but she soon grew to like them. Madame and her workers created a stunning wardrobe for Leah with many plain, everyday dresses of printed muslin and several silk and velvet creations for whatever society existed in the new state of Kentucky.

And always, Madame helped build Leah's confidence. "You are a Stanford now and entitled to the privileges that go with the name."

Unconsciously, Leah began to stand straighter, and within another month, she acted as if she'd always eaten her meals at a table and worn satin dresses.

When the fall harvest was in and Clay could relax, he began to spend time with Leah. Each morning they went out together and he taught her to ride.

"I like her," Clay told Nicole one night. "She's very serious, always wanting to please, trying to learn everything at once."

"It's for Wesley," Nicole said softly, looking up from the needlework in her lap. "Even after the way he's treated her, leaving her after their one night together and again leaving her after their marriage, she still believes the sun rises and sets on that man. I just hope . . ."

"You hope what?" Clay asked.

"Wesley is so much like Travis and when either one of them gets something in his head it's not easy to change."

"And what do you want to change?"

"Kimberly," Nicole answered.

Clay gave a snort of disgust. "Wes was saved when he didn't marry that bitch. Kimberly believes the world

44

should be laid at her feet, and, unfortunately, it generally is."

"And most often it's put there by Wesley. I don't think he's going to easily forget Kimberly."

"He will," Clay said with a chuckle. "Wes isn't stupid, and after he spends a few weeks alone with a beauty like Leah, he'll never even remember that Kimberly exists."

Nicole had her own ideas of the stupidity of men when it came to pretty women, but she said nothing as she turned back to her sewing.

It was that winter, as work on the plantation began to slow down, that Leah discovered weaving. When Nicole showed Leah the loom house, Leah was reluctant to leave. The beautiful cloth, the coverlets taking shape under the women's hands, shuttles flying, treadles working smoothly, fascinated Leah.

"Would you like to try your hand on a loom?" asked a big blonde woman who Nicole introduced as Janie Langston.

"I'm not sure I could do that," Leah said hesitantly. There seemed to be thousands of threads on the loom going in and out of looped strings, with a metal comb tied to a wooden bar.

"Would you like to try?" Janie urged as Leah reverently touched a piece of woven cloth.

"Very much," Leah said positively.

Nicole led Leah around more of the plantation, but Leah didn't see much of it because her mind was still on the fabrics she'd seen. "Do you *really* think I could make something like that?" Leah asked while she was supposed to be looking at the dairy cows. She'd milked cows since she could walk and they didn't interest her, but the idea of being able to create such beauty did.

"Yes, Leah, I believe you could. Would you like it if we went back to the loom house now?"

Leah's eyes sparkled in answer.

Leah spent the next months seldom more than a few feet away from Janie, who taught her everything from caring for sheep, shearing, and dyeing to spinning, dressing a loom, and weaving. And Leah took to it all as if she'd been born with a shuttle in her hand.

In the evenings she sat behind a spinning wheel and the threads she produced were even and very fine. During the days she put her stool near the loom heddles and pulled threads through according to Janie's intricate pattern without a single error and without losing her patience. When she wove she threw the shuttle straight through and brought the beater back with a great deal of strength.

In January, Janie said it was time to learn to draft her own patterns.

"But I can't read," Leah said.

"Neither can my other weavers. Now, first you learn to draw your pattern."

In the next few weeks Nicole twice found Leah asleep over a table covered with pattern drafts, intricate graphs of blocks of numbers and treadling charts, as well as tie-ups. She'd extended the numbers to draw the six harness patterns on paper to check herself for errors. There were names such as double chariot wheel, double bow knot, velvet rose, snail trail, and wheel and star.

Nicole helped Leah to bed, and in the morning Clay asked that she come to his office.

"I thought you might like to have this," he said, handing her a large book bound in blue leather.

"But I can't—," she began.

"Open it."

She saw that the pages were blank and she looked at him, puzzled.

Clay stood beside her. "On the cover it says, Arundel Hall, and every year I have several of the books bound to use for permanent records. Nicole told me of your loom patterns so I thought you might like to record them in this. You could take it to Kentucky with you."

To Clay's complete bewilderment, Leah collapsed in a chair, the book held close to her, and she began to cry. "Did I do something wrong?" he asked. "Don't you like the book?"

"Everyone is so kind," Leah cried. "I know it's because of Wesley but still—."

Clay knelt before her, put his fingers under her chin, and lifted her face. "I want you to listen to me and believe what I'm saying. At first we *did* take you in because you'd married Wes, but we forgot about him months ago. Nicole and I and our children have come to love you. Remember how the boys came down with the measles at Christmas and you stayed up with them? Your kindness, the love you've given us, have more than repaid us for what little we've done for you."

"But all of you are so easy to love," she answered through tears, "and you've given me the world. I've done so little for you."

Standing, Clay laughed. "All right, we're equal then. I just don't want to hear any more about what we've done for you. Now I need to go back to work."

Leah stood and on impulse threw her arms around Clay. "Thank you so much for everything."

He hugged her back. "If I'd known I'd get this kind of reward I would have deeded you the plantation. Now go on back to your looms."

Smiling, she left the office.

In February, Regan and Travis came to fetch her.

"You've had her long enough," Travis said to Clay while grinning at Leah. Regan had said, with some disgust, that Travis had quickly *forgiven* Leah for trapping his little brother after Travis saw how pretty Leah'd turned out to be.

With tears in her eyes, Leah hugged all the Armstrong family good-bye.

"Oh yes," Clay said, eyes dancing, "I thought you might like to have this." He nodded toward a wooden crate standing with several others on the wharf.

Puzzled, Leah walked toward the box. Behind it was a loom, a beautiful piece of work in cherry with brass fittings.

As Leah gaped soundlessly, Clay put his arm around her. "It breaks down for packing and you can take it to Kentucky with you. If you start crying again I'll keep it," he warned.

Again Leah hugged him as Travis said he'd send someone to get the loom. Leah, hating to part with the loom for even a few days, grabbed the long comblike reed and clutched it. As Travis lifted her into the little sloop, she held the reed and waved as long as she could see the Armstrongs on the dock.

On the sail back to Stanford Plantation, Regan asked Leah hundreds of questions and at the same time noticed the many changes in Leah. She held herself erectly, looked people in the eye, and her movements were unconsciously graceful.

As they walked from the dock to the house, Regan was thinking that Leah was ready for anything—until she looked up at the house. Standing on the porch, one hand delicately poised on the iron railing, was Kimberly Shaw, her blonde hair drawn back from her lovely face, rings of curls down her neck. Her fragile prettiness was set off by a silk gown and matching cloak of deep pink.

"Is she Wesley's Kimberly?" Leah asked in a whisper.

"*You* are Wesley's wife, remember that, Leah," Regan said under her breath as Kimberly walked down the stairs and toward them.

"Kimberly!" Travis said, pleased. "It's been so long since we've seen you." He caught her shoulders and kissed her cheek. "Have you met Leah, my sister-in-law?"

"Only briefly," Kimberly said in a pretty, soft voice as she held out her hand. "I am Kimberly Shaw."

To Regan's disgust, she could see Leah weakening before Kim. Kim had a way about her of apparent sweetness that made people want to do her bidding.

"I am very happy to meet you," Leah said softly.

"If you ladies will excuse me," Travis said, "I have to get back to work."

When he was gone, Regan invited Kim in for tea.

"If it's not too much trouble," Kim said. "I do have some news I want to tell."

"About Wesley?" Leah asked eagerly, following Kim up the stairs.

"You haven't heard from him?" Kim asked, eyebrows raised in speculation.

"Have you?" Regan interrupted, leading the way into the small parlor as she ordered tea from a servant.

"Not often," Kim said modestly. When they were seated, she spoke again. "I want to be honest about everything and I was, to say the least, very upset at what happened last year. I couldn't bring myself to even hear Wesley's name for months afterward."

Leah toyed with her fingers in her lap. She had given so little thought to how this woman must have felt at losing the man she loved.

"As you know," Kim continued, "it was planned that Wesley and I, with my brother Steven, would travel to Kentucky together and I'd looked forward to going to a new state with . . . with . . ." She stopped as the tea was brought in.

When the servant was gone, Regan spoke. "You didn't come here to tell us about last year's plans, so why are you here?"

Big fat tears clouded Kim's pretty eyes. "Since that day in church my life has been awful, just dreadful. Regan, you really can't imagine what it's been like. I'm laughed at constantly. Every time I go to church someone makes a remark about how I was . . . jilted." She glanced at Leah, who was still looking at her hands. "Even the children are making up rhymes about what happened."

She buried her face in her hands. "It's too awful. I can't bear it any longer."

In spite of herself, Regan felt her heart go out to the woman. "Kim, what can we do? Maybe Travis could talk to the people or—."

"No," Kim said. "The only way is to leave. Leah," she said, pleadingly, and Leah met her eyes. "You don't know me, but I want to ask you to do something for me, something that will save my life."

"What can I do?" Leah asked seriously.

"In Wes's last letter to me, he said he was returning at the end of March, then the two of you and my brother would start the journey to Kentucky."

A month! Leah thought. In just a month Wesley would be home and she would really be his wife.

"Let me go with you," Kimberly was saying. "I could

travel with Steven and the four of us could go somewhere where no one knows what's been done to me.
Please, Leah, I have no right to ask anything of you, I
know, but it was because of you that—."

Regan stood and cut off Kim's words. "I think you're
asking too much of Leah and I don't think she
should—."

"Please, Leah," Kim asked. "Maybe I can find a
husband in Kentucky. Here everyone laughs at me. It's
miserable, really miserable and you already have Wesley, the one man I've ever loved and—."

"Yes," Leah said firmly. "Of course you may go with
us."

"Leah," Regan said, "I think we should discuss
this."

"No," Leah said, looking at Kim. "It's my fault that
this has happened to you and I'll do what I can to give
you back some of what you've lost."

"That's not your responsibility," Regan began, but
Leah gave her a look she'd never seen before.

"Would you pour?" Leah said to Regan, and Regan
sat down and obeyed her.

Chapter 5

Leah put the last stitches in the border of the coverlet, a blue and white Irish chain pattern, and smoothed it in her lap. She looked up at Janie's laugh.

"Is it my imagination or are your hands shaking?"

Leah returned her smile. "I think they are a bit." She paused. "Was that the bell?"

Janie laughed harder. "I'm afraid not."

"You don't think they'd forget to ring it, do you? I mean, they wouldn't let Wesley arrive and not tell me."

"Leah," Janie said, her hand on her shoulder, "Travis and Regan are waiting to see him too. The minute he's sighted, they'll ring the bell."

At that moment came the loud, excited clang of the bell by the wharf.

Leah didn't move but her face drained of color.

"Don't look so scared," Janie said with a laugh. "Come on, let's greet him."

Slowly, Leah rose, looking down in doubt at her dress. She wore a deep rust-colored silk twill that brought out the auburn in her hair, and the high waist was trimmed with black silk ribbons, with more ribbons entwined in her hair, which was piled on her head in a mass of glossy curls.

"You look beautiful," Janie was saying as Regan rushed into the room.

"Are you going to stay here all day?" Regan demanded. "Don't you want to see him?"

"Yes!" Leah gasped. "Oh yes!" And together the three of them left the loom house at a run.

Two weeks before, Travis had received news from Wesley saying that he and Steven were returning around the second of April; today was the third. Travis had sent someone upriver to watch for the men, and the moment they were seen the big wharf bell was to be rung so everyone could come to greet the returning men.

Now, as Leah was running, she touched the gold coin pinned to the inside of her pocket, the coin Wesley had given her so long ago. Would he be pleased with the way she'd changed? As they drew near the wharf and she could see Travis talking to someone, she stopped running. I will make you the best wife in all the world, my Wesley, she vowed. You'll never regret having lost your Kimberly.

Leah was behind the gathering crowd as everyone pushed to greet the returning men, but as people moved about, Leah had her first glimpse of him. He'd put on some size while he'd been gone and now stood as big as Travis; covering his broad shoulders was an outrageous costume of pale leather, fringed about the shoulders and down the sides of his pants legs. Crisscrossing his shoulders were straps to a couple of pouches, one decorated with an intricate design of tiny beads. On his head was a broad-brimmed hat that looked as if it'd made the journey back and forth to Kentucky tied to the bottom of a wagon wheel.

Leah looked at him and felt her heart begin to beat faster, her throat closing in anticipation. She'd waited for this moment for years and years.

"Here she is," Travis was saying, slapping his brother's shoulder.

As he said the words, Leah saw Wesley's face turn from the joy of greeting to one of coldness, and she hesitated.

Regan came forward and took Leah's arm. "Come on. He doesn't even recognize you."

Hesitantly, shyly, Leah stepped toward her husband.

"She's changed some, hasn't she?" Travis was saying with pride. "Could have knocked me over with a feather when she cleaned up so pretty."

Blushing, but very pleased, Leah looked up through her lashes at Wesley. He was looking toward the fields over her head.

"You have to tell me how last year's crops were," Wes was saying. "And I'll need some seed to take back with me. Ah!" He smiled. "Is that Jennifer?" he called to Travis and Regan's five-year-old daughter who was running toward her uncle. "Excuse me," Wesley said and made his way through the crowd to greet the child.

For a moment everyone was too embarrassed to speak, but as they cast looks of sympathy toward Leah, the crowd began to break apart.

Leah, stunned at Wes's lack of greeting, watched as he and Jennifer walked toward the house.

"That bastard—!" Travis began, but Regan put her hand on his shoulder and shook her head. "I think I'll talk to him," Travis said and left Leah and Regan alone on the wharf.

"Leah—," Regan began.

"Leave me alone," Leah snapped. "I don't need sympathy from anyone. I was stupid to think there could ever be anything between us. I'm just a poor girl from the swamp of the river with a whore for a sister, so why should he even bother to look at me?"

"Stop it!" Regan commanded. "Wesley isn't like that. Maybe he was shocked when you were so pretty. After all, he's never seen you looking as you do now."

Leah gave her a look of contempt. "I am not quite that stupid."

"Let's go to the house," Regan urged. "Travis will talk to him and find out what's wrong." She took Leah's arm. "Please," she pleaded.

Leah allowed herself to be pulled along by Regan, but she held her head high as everyone they passed gave her a look of pity.

They were barely inside the house when the sound of shouting came to them, and both women stood paralyzed at what they heard.

"You expect me to stop hating her merely because she cleaned up pretty?" Wesley was shouting. "I've hated her from the moment I married her, ever since she made it impossible for me to have the woman I loved. All winter I worked long, long days trying to sweat out my hatred of her, but I couldn't. I wouldn't even sleep in the house knowing that the slut was going to be living in it. She's ruined my life and now you expect me to fall all over myself merely because she's washed her face?"

Regan didn't allow Leah to hear any more, except for a few crashes as a fight between the brothers seemed to break out, before she shoved Leah up the stairs to the room Leah was to have shared with her husband. Regan leaned against the door, so shocked and hurt that she couldn't move.

Not so Leah, who went to the wardrobe where her new dresses mixed with Wesley's suits. "I won't take much," Leah was saying. "But I'll need a few clothes. Perhaps you can sell what's left and the money will help repay what you've given me."

Regan took a moment to react to Leah's words. "What are you talking about?"

Leah folded two dresses, her hands and body shaking. "I'll go back to the farm. I worked it before and I can certainly work it enough to support myself. Maybe I can still have the loom Clay gave me and sell some weaving."

"You're running away?" Regan gasped.

The face Leah turned to her was filled with fury. "All of you may think I'm nothing, that because I grew up without the finer things of life that I'm not worth much, but I have my pride and I'll not stay here where I'm hated."

"How dare you!" Regan seethed, her teeth clenched. "No one before today has treated you with anything but respect and how dare you insinuate that we have!"

The women were practically nose to nose before Leah turned away. "I'm sorry," she whispered. "Please forgive me."

"Leah," Regan said softly. "Don't do anything you'll regret. I wish you hadn't heard what Wes said, but I'm sure something can be worked out."

"Such as?" Leah whirled. "Should I go to live in that house with him? My father always hated me, but he hated everyone else too. There was nothing personal in it. But now my . . . my husband hates *me* and only me. I never wanted to impose myself on him. I wish my father'd shot me rather than come to this." She went back to the wardrobe to take out a straw bonnet.

"Leah, you can't go back to that farm. That place is nothing but a breeding ground for mosquitoes and Travis said the roof fell in on the house this winter. You can't—."

"What are the alternatives? And don't say that I should stay here with you. I've never been an object of charity before and I won't be now."

"Damn that Wesley!" Regan said. "I thought that in a year he'd come to his senses. If he'd just open his eyes he'd see that Kimberly is—." She broke off, her eyes wide as she stared at Leah. "Leah," she said quietly. "If you go back to the farm and Wes returns to Kentucky with Steven and Kimberly, what are people going to say?"

Leah gave an exasperated sigh. "People from my class have never had the luxury of wondering what people will say. When your own father drags you, pregnant, into a church with a gun held to your head, there isn't much worse that can happen to you in your lifetime. People will just say I'm another Simmons whore and that they knew so all along."

"Is that what you want? Do you like the idea of walking into a store or the church and having people whisper about you?"

"As a Simmons, I've never had any choice in the matter."

"You *aren't* a Simmons. You're a Stanford. Did you forget that?"

"No one need worry. I'll give Wesley a divorce or an annulment or whatever he wants. There's no child, so he has no further obligation to me."

"Leah," Regan said and took her hands. "Sit down here and talk to me. You can't go running away from every adversity. Once I tried to run away from my problems rather than staying and trying to work them out. I put myself through a great deal of needless pain. You have to think of yourself and not sacrifice yourself because of one stupid man."

For the first time Leah realized Regan was angry at Wesley.

"Oh yes, I'm angry at him," Regan answered the unasked question. "Wesley has no idea what he's been saved from. I knew for a long time what his precious Kimberly was like and I took a chance that you weren't like her. You've lived with us for nearly a year and we've all, Clay and Nicole included, come to love you, and damn Wesley! I'm so angry at him I think he almost deserves Kimberly."

Suddenly Regan stopped. "That's it!" She gasped. "That's it!" She stood and walked a few feet away. "I know how to solve everything. We—," she broke off to laugh. "We are going to give Wes just what he *thinks* he wants—Kimberly."

"Good," Leah said tiredly, gathering her clothes in her arms. "I'm sure they'll be very happy together. Now, if you don't mind, I think I'll go."

"Leah, no," Regan said, halting her. "Listen to me."

Leah dressed carefully for dinner that night, wearing a low-cut gown of deep forest green that matched her eyes. In spite of her efforts, no one seemed to notice anything throughout the stilted dinner. Wesley was sporting a bruise on his jaw and Travis kept moving his left arm gingerly, as if it hurt him. Regan, after a few choice words about some of her furniture being broken, said nothing. The men ate in silence while the women remained quiet, picking at their food.

When Leah could stand no more, she rose. "I would like to talk to you in the library," she said to the top of

Wesley's head, and when he looked up at her with cold eyes, she returned his look with matching ice.

He gave her no answer, but when she turned, she heard him move to follow her.

When they were alone in the library, she offered a silent prayer that she'd be able to say what she wanted to. Regan's plan was a good one and would ultimately save Leah's pride, but for the moment the idea repulsed her. She wanted no part of this man who so obviously hated her.

"I have a proposition to make you, Mr. Stanford," she began.

"Oh come now, you can call me Wesley. You've certainly worked for that right," he said with a hint of a sneer in his voice.

Leah, her back to him, made her fingers into claws as she took several deep breaths to calm herself. She faced him. "I want to get this over as quickly as possible because I don't want to be near you any more than you want to be near me."

"That's probably true," he said with a snort. "No doubt you wanted this house and that pretty dress more than you wanted a man cluttering up your life."

"Why I did spend that one night with you is beyond my reasoning now, but the fact is that we are married and I'd like to do something about that."

"Ah, blackmail," he said in a self-satisfied way.

"Perhaps," she said as calmly as she could. "I have a plan." She went on before he could interrupt her again. "I believe I know how to get what we both want. You want your Kimberly and I want a decent place to live."

"Stanford Plantation isn't enough for you?"

She ignored him. "I apologize for our marriage, for my father having forced it. I even apologize for having . . . given myself to you that night, but I can't change

59

that now. If I gave you an annulment now I would still have to live here in Virginia and face down all the gossip over what has happened. But I have an alternate plan."

She drew a deep breath. "A few weeks ago your Kimberly came here and asked to accompany us to Kentucky in the hopes that she could escape the talk about how she was jilted and, perhaps, in a new state, she could find herself a husband."

It gave Leah no pleasure to see Wesley wince at the idea of someone else marrying the woman he loved.

"It seems that now," Leah continued, "our roles are reversed. I have heard how you hate me, that you cannot bear sleeping in a house I may some day live in and, whether you believe it or not, I have enough pride that I don't want to force myself on someone who detests me. Now! What I propose is this: that the four of us leave Virginia as planned, but once we're out of sight of people you know, I will cease pretending to be your wife—our marriage is no more than pretense— and will become your . . . cousin, I guess is good enough. Or perhaps I should be Miss Shaw's cousin if you can't bear any relationship with me. Kimberly can travel as your fiancée and when we arrive in Kentucky our marriage can be annulled or whatever, making both of us free."

"And how much am I to pay you for this generous offer?"

She sneered at him. "I will work on the journey to Kentucky in exchange for my bed and board, but once in Kentucky I'll set up my own weaving business and support myself. Regan has provided for me and we have an arrangement whereby I can repay her. You'll have no further obligations to me once we reach the new state."

He looked at her in disbelief. "You're willing to let me out of this marriage you worked so hard to get?"

Red rage filled her. "I never even suggested marriage! I did *not* come to you when I knew I was carrying your child. I tried to conceal the fact, but when my father found out he beat me senseless. Half the time in the church I wasn't sure what was going on. If you hadn't been so 'noble' and had waited, I would have asked you *not* to marry me. Now I'm attempting to get us both out of this situation. If you can't stand the idea of my going to Kentucky with you, let me know and I'll return to my father's land. In fact, on second thought, I think I should do that anyway, because I'm not sure I can bear your company on the journey. Excuse me and I'll go now and talk to Travis about the legalities of ending this marriage."

She shut the door behind her and for a moment leaned against it. Never had she been so angry before. Nothing her father had ever done had affected her as this did. Perhaps it was because it was the end of a dream. Regan's plan had seemed good when she first heard it and she would have liked to earn her living as a weaver and to get away from people who'd always call her "one of those Simmonses," but it had been an unattainable dream. With a caressing hand, she touched the velvet of her dress. On the farm there'd be no need of velvet dresses. With her shoulders straight, she went in search of Travis.

For a moment Wesley sat in stunned silence, then, with force, he threw his hat against the closed door. He didn't know which made him angrier, that the girl had overheard him or that she was taking everything so calmly. She was so cool, maybe a little angry, but certainly she didn't act as a *woman* should.

"Damnation!" he cursed under his breath as he went

to retrieve his hat. The last thing in the world he wanted was a woman who told him what to do and how to do it. All his life he'd lived under Travis's rule. Even when their parents were alive, Travis had been in control of his younger brother. When Wes was a toddler Travis had always been there, shouting orders, giving directions. It seemed to Wes that Travis had always been an adult, had never been a child, had never had a child's doubts as mortals did.

And Travis had never needed anyone. He was running most of the plantation by the time he was fourteen. Travis never read a book, never did anything that was just for pleasure. He was born knowing Stanford Plantation was his, and he had no qualms about treating everyone, including his parents, as employees.

When Travis met his wife he'd treated her as though she were someone who worked for him, and, because of this, she'd run away. Away from Travis, she'd managed to become someone in her own right, but she couldn't have done so while standing in Travis's overpowering shadow.

Wesley had always worked for Travis, but to escape he'd taken long trips all over the world. He'd drunk champagne from a beautiful woman's slipper in Paris. He'd made love to a duchess in England, and in Italy he'd nearly fallen in love with a black-haired singer.

In the end he'd known he was deluding himself. He was a farmer and he'd never be happy away from the land. But, as soon as he had returned home, Travis had begun giving Wesley orders about five minutes after his arrival. And it was then Wes decided he had to get away permanently. The new state of Kentucky was said to have rich, fertile land and he went to see it. He loved the state and the people, people who had a feeling that things were moving and changing. He bought several hundred acres of land near a little town called Sweetbriar, repaired the house that someone had built years before, and returned to Virginia one last time.

But he'd no more than returned when his life was forever changed: he met Miss Kimberly Shaw. For the first time, Wes had felt he was looking at a *real* woman, a woman who was proud of being a lady. Kimberly couldn't read a ledger of accounts, couldn't even really ride a horse. What Kim knew about were sewing, pressing flowers, what colors to paint a house—and most of all, how to look up at a man and make him feel like a *man*.

Wesley began to imagine returning home from the fields to the pretty little house Kimberly would decorate for them, putting his head in her lap and letting her soothe away all the tensions of the day. No doubt she'd have a dozen domestic crises a day, all of which Wesley would have to solve. Kimberly *needed* him. For the first time in his life Wesley felt wanted, felt as if he weren't just another strong back that would do as well as any other. When Kim looked up at him Wes felt twenty feet tall.

Everyone kept warning him that Kim was helpless, but no one understood that that was just what he wanted. He didn't want some woman who was as perfect as Travis, some woman who could run a plantation with one hand and raise children with the other. Kimberly was soft, sweet, clinging, and needed protection from all of life's hardships.

And now he'd lost her! This winter when he'd worked so hard on his new farm he'd had time to regret his rashness in marrying the Simmons girl. He knew the story of how she'd remained on her father's farm when

63

she could have run away. But instead she'd stayed with her younger siblings and done the work of a couple of men.

Wes was sure she was a paragon of all the virtues; if he died tomorrow and willed her the Kentucky farm, she could no doubt run it single-handedly; in fact she could probably run it better than he could. But what no one seemed to realize when they were telling him "for his own good" that Kim was a helpless butterfly was that she was exactly what he'd always wanted.

Crumpling his hat, he put his hand on the doorknob. Whatever the girl Leah was, she was his wife and he had an obligation to her. Maybe she had planted herself in his arms, maybe she had planned to get some money from him, but since he had been dumb enough to fall for her tricks he deserved what he got.

"Lord, protect me from competent women," he prayed as he went in search of Leah.

Chapter 6

Two minutes after she left Wesley in the library, Leah began shaking. At first she thought it was from anger, but she soon recognized it as fear. For the past year she'd tried not to think about what would happen when Wesley returned. She'd tried her best to hope that he'd hold out his arms to her and love her, but instead, he'd rejected her publicly.

Leah was accustomed to anger. Anger was what had fed her while she worked her father's farm. Anger had kept her from giving in and being beaten down. Her father had taken away everything except her anger and her pride—and both of these had come to the forefront with Wesley.

But now that she'd vented her anger she was frightened. She didn't want to go back, alone, to her father's farm. For a year she'd lived within the heart of two loving families and she'd had hopes of having her own family. If she returned to the swamp she'd no doubt remain there the rest of her life. Perhaps with her weaving . . .

"Leah."

Wesley's voice interrupted her thoughts. Immediately she straightened her shoulders. She was standing in the hallway and had no idea how long she'd been there feeling sorry for herself. "Yes," she said coolly, and braced herself against another of his attacks. This was the man she'd dreamed of so long and she'd thought that when she got him all her problems would be solved, but actually they were just beginning.

"I came to apologize," he began, watching her. She was pretty, he thought, in a haughty sort of way. Her eyebrows peaked in the middle, making her look arrogant, willful. "I haven't really had time to think over your plan but it sounds as if it could work. I don't imagine you want to stay here in Virginia any more than I do and I do have a duty toward you."

"No," she said quietly, her eyes smoky dark. "You have no obligation toward me. I have always taken care of myself and I will continue to do so. Our marriage will be dissolved and you'll be free of me."

The corner of Wesley's mouth quirked, but not in amusement. "I'm sure you're able to take care of any number of people, but would you rather farm that bit of filthy swampland you own or come to Kentucky and—what is it you want to do—weave?"

It flashed through Leah's mind to wonder what she'd ever seen in this autocratic man to ever think she cared about him. He offered her this choice as if he were amused because he knew how it wasn't really any choice at all. How she'd like to toss his offer back into his face! But for all her pride, she wasn't going to do something stupid.

"I would rather go to Kentucky," she snapped

angrily. "But I want it known that for all I am a Simmons and not of your class, I pay my own way. I will never be a burden to you."

"There was never a question of whether you would be a burden to me. I'm sure you can handle anything," he said with a hint of disgust.

He would have said more but a whisper of "Wesley" behind him made him turn. Kimberly stood there, her soft body encased in swirls of light pink silk, her big eyes already filling with tears.

Before Wes could move, Kim pressed the back of her hand to her parted lips and in the next second she started a slow sink toward the floor, her lashes fluttering prettily.

Wesley caught her in his arms long before she hit the floor. Sweeping her up, the pink silk floating about him, he looked down at her with concern. "Water!" he commanded to Leah, who was standing motionless. "And brandy!" Wes added as Leah turned away.

"My darling," Wes whispered as he sat down with her on a long bench against the wall.

Leah had never seen anyone faint before and she was sure Kimberly was dying. Lifting her skirts, she took off for the kitchens at a run.

"Leah!" Regan called, starting to run after her. "What's wrong? Did Wesley—?"

"Brandy and water," Leah demanded from the head cook. "And quick." She turned to Regan even as she grabbed the tray handed her. "Miss Shaw just fell to the floor. I think she's dying." With that she started running again.

"Kimberly faints regularly," Regan called. "And don't let her have too much of that brandy. She likes it too much."

"Regularly?" Leah gasped in disbelief. "The woman

must be ill." When she reached the hall, Kim was lying on the bench, Wesley kneeling beside her, holding and kissing her fingers.

"I'm such a burden to you, my darling Wesley," she said softly. "You are so good to put up with me, and especially since we'll never . . . I can never be . . ."

"Hush, love," Wesley whispered. "It's all going to work, you'll see." He turned, saw Leah, and his voice changed. "You took long enough. Here, love," he said, lifting Kim and holding a snifter of brandy to her lips.

Kimberly drained it all in a gulp.

"Not so fast! You'll choke!" Wes cautioned.

"Oh my. I'm just so upset I don't know what I'm doing. What did you mean when you said we'd work things out?" She glanced up at Leah, who was silently watching the scene.

Gently, Wes smoothed back a curl from Kim's temple. "The four of us, you, me, Steven and . . . Leah will leave for Kentucky and once we're there my marriage, such that it is, will be dissolved, then we can be married."

For a moment, Kim didn't say a word. "How will we travel?"

"Leah will be my cousin and you my intended."

Kim gave another glance to Leah. "Couldn't the marriage be dissolved just as well here in Virginia?"

A very slight frown crossed Wesley's brow. "I'm sure it could, but legally Leah is my wife and I have a responsibility toward her. If I left her here the gossips would kill her."

"Of course, Wesley dear," Kim said tiredly, fluttering her lashes. "Can you ever forgive me for being so insensitive? Oh dear! I seem to be suddenly quite chilled. Would you please get me a shawl? I do hate to be a bother."

"You could never be a bother," Wes said before leaving them.

When they heard his footsteps on the stairs, Kim opened her eyes, sat up, and gave Leah a wide-eyed look. "Are you really, truly going to give up Wesley?"

"Are you all right?" Leah asked, still shocked at Kim's fainting.

"Oh yes, perfectly. I would love some more brandy though. Brandy makes me feel so good. I always feel brandy is my reward for pleasing Wesley. He so loves for me to faint. Leah, I just knew you were going to be a kind person. I knew it when you agreed to let me travel with you to Kentucky. I've heard how you used to run that dreadful farm of yours and I know you'll be so handy on this trip. I can't cook or lift heavy things and horses terrify me. I just know you'll be wonderful to have around and we'll become great friends. Uh-oh, here comes Wes." She hurriedly put the empty glass on the tray, slid down on the bench, and resumed her helpless look.

"Here you are, dear," Wes said tenderly, wrapping the shawl about Kim.

Bewildered, Leah stepped back and watched as Kim allowed Wes to treat her as a helpless invalid. No one noticed when Leah left to return the tray to the kitchen. Leah wasn't sure whether to laugh or cry at the situation. Kim's "Wesley so loves for me to faint" made her want to laugh, but the idea of any woman playacting to attract a man disgusted her, and Leah vowed she'd never allow herself to faint, no matter how much it pleased a man.

Leah managed to avoid Wesley for the next few days, although she caught glimpses of him now and then through a window or from around a building. She dressed carefully each morning until she realized that she wanted him to notice her. The night of his arrival she put on her prettiest nightgown—just in case—but her husband stayed away from her. He was distantly polite when he saw her but nothing more. And as Leah went about her work of preparing for the journey ahead, her pride began to take over. She refused to allow Wesley's rejection to hurt her.

The day they were to leave dawned clear. The wagon was loaded high and Travis had tied a piece of canvas across the top. Wesley already sat on the seat, reins in hand. A cage of chickens was fastened to the back; a milk cow on a lead rope trailed behind.

"We'll miss you," Regan said, hugging Leah. "Tell Wesley what you want to say and he'll write it for you, but don't lose contact with us." She leaned forward to whisper. "I'm going to have a baby in the fall."

"Congratulations!" Leah laughed, hugging her again. "I hope it's a little boy just like Travis. Goodbye, Jennifer," she called, hugged Travis once again, and then was lifted onto the seat beside Wesley.

As Leah turned and waved, Wesley clucked to the horses and they started the journey.

As soon as she was alone with Wesley, Leah felt uncomfortable. She began studying her fingernails, but quit, tucked her hands under her, and sat on them. "We're to meet the Shaws at their place?" she asked, but when Wesley merely nodded she said no more.

They drove past the tavern where Bess worked and Leah wished she could stop and say good-bye to her sister, but one glance at the tautness in Wesley's profile and she knew she wouldn't ask him for a thing. She straightened her back and looked ahead.

The sun was barely up when they reached the plantation where Steven and Kimberly were staying. It was a tiny place compared to Clay's, and some of the outbuildings looked as if they needed repair. But what caught and held Leah's attention was the utter chaos surrounding a half-packed wagon. From out of the jumble of voices, boxes and animals, Kim came running toward Wes.

"Oh, Wesley, dearest," she called, "you have to help us. Steven is refusing to take all of my clothes and all of the beautiful things I have for our house. Please, you must talk to him."

Wesley jumped from the wagon, gave Kim a quick, reassuring caress with the back of his hand, then went toward the wagon. Leah was left to help herself down. When she reached the wagon it was easy to see what was wrong, yet even as she circled the mess she couldn't believe her eyes. None of the goods loaded on the wagon had been packed with any sense of order. A small, fragile hatbox was crushed under two fifty-pound bags of seed. A steel-bound trunk teetered atop the arms of a gilded chair.

"You can see there's no more room," came a man's voice from the opposite side.

Leah bent her knees and peeked through the arms of the chair to get her first glimpse of Steven Shaw. He was as lovely as Kimberly—blond, blue-eyed, cleft chin—perfect.

"Wesley, dear," Kim was saying, "you must find a way. I can't possibly leave anything behind. You wouldn't want me to be unhappy, would you?"

Heaven forbid that catastrophe, Leah thought as she began untying the ropes across the goods in the wagon. If it was repacked from the floor up, they'd probably be able to get everything on.

When Wesley walked to the side where Leah was untying the ropes he gave her a look of surprise; then

71

there was just a hint of disgust. He looked away. "Can you climb to the top of this mess and hand me that trunk?"

"Of course," Leah said, smiling to herself. Maybe he *did* realize his precious Kimberly was little more than an ornament.

"Somehow I was sure you could," Wesley said under his breath in a way that puzzled Leah.

Leah and Wesley worked well together, unloading then repacking the wagon, while Steven and Kim squabbled. Kim cried over her crushed hat while Steven complained about Kim's lack of help.

A couple of times Leah felt Steven watching her, but he looked away just as she turned.

When they finished Leah looked to Wesley, in truth expecting some sort of thanks, but all he did was grunt. "You can ride with Steven," he said as he tied the last rope.

Stunned, Leah watched him walk away. "With pleasure," she called after him and fought down the urge to throw a rock at the back of his head. Maybe she should set fire to the fringe on his buckskins.

A hand touched her arm and she looked up into Steven Shaw's dancing blue eyes. "May I?" he asked, nodding toward the wagon seat.

Instantly, Leah didn't trust him. When she was a girl her two older brothers used to bring men home and sometimes they had looks in their eyes such as the one Steven now had. Of course, she told herself, she was wrong.

Wesley and Kim pulled out onto the road first. No one came from the house to say good-bye and suddenly Leah felt very alone—among strangers, traveling to more strangers.

"Will you miss your friends?" she asked Steven, but

all she got was a sidelong look from him that made her stop talking.

They traveled west for hours, and Leah didn't try again to talk to Steven. They stopped for an hour to eat sandwiches Regan had sent, and Wesley hovered over Kim, who cooled herself with a sequined fan and unbuttoned the top buttons of her pale blue silk dress. Wesley was appreciative and Kim rolled her eyes in modesty.

"That Wesley's a lover," Steven said to Leah. "Only he can't have both of you." He gave Leah a look from head to toe.

Frowning, she moved away from him.

In the afternoon as they neared a cluster of houses four men rode toward them. Wesley shouted and Steven halted the wagon.

"Send Leah up here!" Wesley bellowed back.

Leah froze in place. She had no intention of obeying this man who ignored her all day yet ordered her about when it was convenient for him.

Steven gave one look at her face and chuckled. "She wants none of you, Stanford," Steven shouted. "Better leave her here with me."

With a curse Wesley bounded from the wagon. "They're coming to greet the newlyweds," he said tightly, looking up at her. "Unless you want all of Virginia to find out about us, you'd better come to the wagon with me."

"What do *I* care about Virginia? It's your name that needs saving."

"Damn you!" Wesley gasped as he grabbed her arm and pulled.

Leah wasn't expecting violence and so was unprepared for his strength. With a gasp she went flying into Wesley's arms just as the four riders reached them.

"Can't keep your hands off of her, can you, Wes?" said one man, laughing.

"Just lookin' at you, ma'am, I can see why Wes grabbed you off the church steps."

"Put me down!" Leah hissed at Wes, who was holding her as if she weighed nothing at all.

"We planned a little goin' away party and you're the guest of honor. We'd be pleased if you'd honor us with some of your time."

The fourth man was gawking at Leah. "Who'd think that one of those Simmonses would clean up to look like that?"

One of the men glared at him. "Excuse him, ma'am. Vern never did have no manners. We got everythin' waitin' at the inn. Bess Simmons is there."

"Sure, of course we'll be there," Wesley said.

"See you then!" they called as they turned to ride away.

"*Now* will you put me down?" Leah demanded.

Wesley turned back to his wife in his arms and for the first time he seemed to look at her—but the glance was broken after only seconds.

"Oh Wesley," Kim began to cry. "That was so humiliating to me. *I* should have been in your arms. They should be giving *us* this party."

Wes nearly dropped Leah as he ran to comfort Kim. As Leah steadied herself against the wagon Steven, above her on the seat, laughed nastily. "Haven't you learned how to fight with tears? My sister's an expert at it."

Leah ignored him as she walked to the back of the wagon to check on the animals. It was there that Wes found her.

"I think you better ride with me," he said tightly.

She glared at him. "If you're trying to save my

reputation, you needn't bother. I'm sure your friends will be prepared for anything when a Simmons is involved."

She turned away toward the cow, but Wesley grabbed her arm and pulled her to face him. "I don't give a damn if you don't care for your own reputation but I'll not have it said that Kimberly has broken us up. She's innocent in all this and I'll not have her name dirtied further."

She jerked away from his grasp. "I should have known that you were concerned only for your dearest Kimberly. So for your Kimberly I'm to play your wife for the night? The idea repulses me!"

He gave her a hard look as his voice lowered. "I will tell you this only once: Don't you ever again say anything against Kimberly. She has suffered a great deal because of you and if our spending one evening together will help keep her name clean you'll do it if I have to break some of your little bones. Tonight we'll be a loving couple, do you understand that?"

"Perfectly," she said through clenched teeth.

Wesley turned on his heel and left her, and as Leah looked up, in the distance stood Kimberly, smiling prettily and confidently before she swept away in a swirl of silk, Wesley trotting along after her.

"Damn, damn, damn!" Leah cursed under her breath as she angrily adjusted the cow's harness.

"My little sister does have a way of getting men," Steven said from behind her.

Leah ignored his ingratiating tone and blinked back tears. She would not cry!

"But then you have your own way of interesting a man," Steven said as he touched her arm. "Those friends of Wesley's were surprised to see a Simmons looking like you. Ol' Wes was lucky that night when you climbed in bed with him. Of course he wasn't so lucky when he had to marry you. Men marry women like my sister but women like you were made for only one thing—love. Now I could give you—."

He didn't finish his sentence because Leah grabbed the cow's feed bag and slammed it into the side of Steven Shaw's smirking face.

"Bitch!" he yelled, rubbing his face, but Leah was already running to the front wagon where Wesley sat waiting for her. Without a word, she climbed into the seat.

Damn them, she thought. Damn each and every one of them. Steven thought she was a whore, Wesley threatened her with violence if she didn't obey him, and Kimberly smiled and drank brandy like a sailor. I'll do what Wesley wants, she seethed to herself. Tonight I'll be the most loving wife this side of the mountains. We'll leave Virginia with everyone thinking we're so in love that Kimberly *couldn't* come between us. I'll save Miss Shaw's reputation, but I wonder if she's going to like the process.

Chapter 7

Leah didn't speak to Wesley for the rest of the ride to the inn. Even though she knew what she wanted to do, she wondered how in the world she was going to stand him long enough to pretend to be his wife. And, too, Leah began to wonder just how Wesley's friends were going to treat her. Already one of them had made a comment about her being a Simmons. Would they treat her as Steven Shaw did?

As they neared the inn, Leah steeled herself because ten men were waiting for them. The wagon hadn't rolled to a stop when all ten of them rushed forward, each pushing the other for the privilege of helping Leah from the wagon.

"Welcome, Mrs. Stanford."

"Wesley doesn't deserve someone as pretty as you."

"Clay says you like to weave. My sister sent some drafts for me to give you."

"And my mother sent you some flower seeds."

Bewildered, Leah looked from one smiling face to

another. "Th . . . thank you," she stammered. "I had no idea . . ."

One of the men gave a hard look to Wesley. "The women were pretty upset that Stanford Plantation didn't give a party to celebrate your marriage. We wanted them to come today, but they thought since they hadn't been invited maybe they weren't wanted."

It was Wesley's turn to stammer. "No, it was just that we . . . I mean no one . . ."

One man laughed. "Take a look at her, men. If you had a wife that looked like her, would you want to share her?"

Leah was so pleased by their compliments that she blushed.

"Come on inside. You all must be tired. May I?" The man held out his arm to Leah.

"Since when have you earned such a privilege?" another man asked, extending his arm.

"I believe I saw her first," said a third man.

"Here!" Wesley interrupted. "Before any of you start a fight, I'll escort my own wife."

Trying to hide her surprise, Leah took Wesley's arm and walked with him into the tavern.

Bess waited inside for her. "I'd never have known you," was all Bess could gasp, standing apart from her sister.

Leah left her husband's side and opened her arms to Bess. Hugging her sister, Bess laughed. "It *is* you, isn't it?"

"Every dirty inch," Leah returned.

"They're fillin' a tub for you now. Miss Regan said you'd be wantin' a bath, just like all the other ladies do." She looked up at Wes. "Now you behave yourself while she's gone and I'll return her to you soon enough."

Bess quickly ushered Leah upstairs where two men were filling a large tub. As soon as they were alone, Bess began undressing Leah.

"Bess, I can do that myself. There's no need for you to act as if you were my maid."

"Someone should!" Bess snapped. "Someone needs to be good to you after that story Miss Regan told me. Are you really going to give up your own husband willingly, without even a fight?"

"I have no intention of fighting to keep a man who doesn't want me," Leah said stiffly.

"Listen to you. You sound just like our old man. When you get somethin' in your craw there's no stoppin' you. Just for once, Leah, don't be so stubborn. Don't just *give* Wesley away."

"Bess, you're being silly. Wesley was never mine. He wants Miss Shaw and he shall have her. After tonight I'll not even be his wife in name. I'm going to be his cousin."

"Cousin, schmusin. You are his *wife!* Nothing will change that."

"It will when we get to Kentucky." Leah, nude, put one foot into the water. "It's amazing how easily one can get used to being clean. I think I'll stay in this water all night. If I did I wouldn't have to pretend to be my husband's dear devoted wife."

"That's a good idea," Bess said quickly. "You stay there and I'll get you some clean clothes."

Leah sat back in the tub, closed her eyes, but in minutes Bess returned, a huge grin on her face.

"There's trouble in paradise," Bess said gleefully. "Wesley and that Miss Shaw were having an argument."

"She'll forgive him," Leah said tiredly.

"Miss Shaw didn't like the idea of Wesley taking your

arm and Wesley said he had to pretend to be your husband. Miss Shaw wanted to know just how far he planned to carry the pretense. Wesley tried to calm her but Miss Shaw said that two could play the game and if he so much as touched you he'd be sorry."

"And?" Leah asked, trying to conceal her interest.

"Wesley said he didn't like being threatened and he was doing all this for her and he'd do his duty and do what he had to do."

"Duty!" Leah gasped, sitting up.

Bess smiled. "I guess he means his duty is to touch you."

Leah sat back in the tub. "Bess, there's a black trunk in the back of the wagon, on the left. Inside is a dress of gold velvet. Would you bring it to me?"

"A special dress, is it?" Bess asked.

"What little there is of it is special," Leah said, closing her eyes as Bess left the room.

Leah thought of the dress and knew that if Wesley didn't care for her, at least some of the men would notice her. Perhaps she wouldn't get as much attention as Kimberly, but it would be better than she got while riding on the wagons.

The door opened.

"That didn't take long," Leah said, opening her eyes to see Wesley standing there.

He didn't move as he looked at her, her beautiful body clearly visible in the water, her breasts just breaking the surface, her legs stretched out, parted.

"If you've seen enough, you can leave now."

Reluctantly, Wes looked back at her face. Steamy little curls touched her neck. "Bess said—." He didn't finish but turned and left the room.

With shaking hands Leah began washing herself, and she wasn't sure if she was shaking with anger or because she had suddenly and inexplicably remembered every detail of the time Wesley had held her in his arms.

When Bess returned with the dress, she had such a smug, knowing look on her face that Leah refused to say a word about Wesley's return to the room. Even when Bess gave broad hints, Leah still didn't comment.

The gold velvet of the gown made Leah's skin look even creamier, and the neckline was cut so low that only imagination was left.

"I can't do it," Leah said, looking at herself in the mirror. "There's too much of me and too little cloth. I told Regan I'd never wear this dress."

Bess adjusted the last curl on top of Leah's head. Her long, perfect neck eased down into the beautiful sculpture of her collarbone and breasts. "You will too wear it! I've seen ladies with even less on."

Leah gave her a look of disbelief.

"They just had a lot less to show than you so less looked like more."

"Oh Bess." Leah laughed. "I'm going to miss you."

"Not if I have my way and you get your husband back," Bess said with a sniff.

"I never had him to begin with."

Bess didn't answer but shoved her young sister out the door.

Standing at the top of the stairs Leah had a chance to survey the scene below. Kimberly sat in a chair wearing a sedate turquoise silk dress; she looked absolutely lovely and six men surrounded her. Wesley leaned against the cold fireplace, talking in a tight-jawed way to two men, his eyes constantly shifting to Kim, and there were sparks of anger in the looks. Leah wasn't sure whether she should laugh or be disgusted, but somewhere in her was a bit of jealousy.

As she began to descend the staircase, she was

pleased to see first one pair of male eyes, then another, travel upward toward her. At Stanford Plantation she'd always been treated with respect, but she often wondered if it was only because she was married to Wesley.

"May I?" asked one man at the foot of the stairs, his arm extended. The other nine men stood still, gaping in such a way that Leah felt her confidence return.

"Thank you," she said graciously, taking his arm.

Kim stood suddenly and said in an expert half-plea, half-command, "Am I to be left all alone? Do only *married* women get any attention?"

Quickly two men ran to her side—but eight stayed by Leah.

"Supper is waiting. Shall we go in?" a man asked.

Leah looked up to see Wesley, still near the fireplace, his eyes fastened to Kim's retreating back. He didn't seem aware that anyone else was in the room.

Leah, feeling a quick surge of anger, excused herself from the men near her. "Perhaps you should go ahead. My husband and I will follow you."

Leah planted herself in front of Wesley. "You're making a fool of yourself!" she hissed up at him.

He didn't hear her at first.

With disgust Leah used her thumb to poke him sharply in the ribs.

"What are you doing?" he asked angrily, then as his eyes focused on Leah, they turned smoky for just a second. He recovered himself. "Trying to show the men what they missed?" he asked, one eyebrow raised as he looked at the low, low cut of her gown.

She willed herself not to blush. "You're looking after Kimberly as if she were a bitch in heat. If you plan to save her name I think you should exercise a little control."

He looked at her in speculation. "Are you always sensible?"

"I try to be," she answered, puzzled.

"I thought so. Come on, let's be the loving couple." He took her upper arm in his hand and led her into the dining room.

They were greeted with uplifted tankards and one toast after another.

"To Wesley, who had the sense to look for a jewel where no one knew there was even a mine."

"To Leah, who agreed to put up with a cantankerous, stubborn mule who is only a little better than Travis."

The word *Travis* made them groan as Wesley pulled the chair of honor out for his wife.

Kimberly sat directly opposite Leah and gave her a hurt look that said Leah had betrayed her. Leah felt a pang of guilt as Kim turned away to talk to the man next to her.

For all the warning he'd been given, Wesley still watched Kim with hot eyes.

Telling herself she was doing this to save Wesley and his beloved Kim, Leah leaned across Wesley's arm to reach the pepper and pressed her breasts against him. Wes reacted instantly, turning surprised—and interested—eyes toward his wife. Leah smiled up at him sweetly.

"If you would pass me the pepper I wouldn't have to reach," she said softly.

His eyes flickered downward. "Reach, by all means. Reach for whatever you want."

"Wesley!" Kimberly said sharply, and he looked away from Leah. "I was just trying to remember when we last saw the Ellingtons. Wasn't it at the harvest ball?"

It was obvious to Leah that Kim was reminding Wes of some private, probably risqué, meeting.

Didn't Kim realize it was her reputation being saved? Leah clutched Wesley's arm, leaned into it, and looked up at him through her lashes. "The harvest ball and moonlit nights," she murmured. "Sometimes the moon causes people to do memorable things."

Wesley narrowed his eyes at Leah, then bent to put his lips near her ear. "You'd better stop this little game or you'll get more than you bargained for."

Quickly Leah moved away from him. What did she care if Wes made a fool of himself in front of his friends? Except that she had some pride, too. She didn't want to leave Virginia with people saying that maybe a Simmons could get a man but couldn't hold one. They'd probably never hear of her divorce unless Regan or Travis told, so there was some advantage in leaving the people with an impression that she was good enough to remain with one of the high and mighty Stanfords.

Chastised and no longer so sure of herself, Leah gave her attention to the food, pushing it around on her plate, her head down, speaking only when she was asked a direct question. She no longer felt like competing with Kimberly. Disinterestedly, Leah watched Kim flirt with one man after another.

As the meal progressed things began to change. The man next to Leah started talking about the new cotton gin and within minutes Leah forgot about Kimberly. From cotton the conversation went to sheep and the prevention of diseases in one's livestock. More men joined the talk.

Within twenty minutes, as Bess and two other women cleared the table, Leah, the ten friends of Wesley, and Wes himself were deep into a discussion of crops and animals. Steven ate, not interested in anything else, and Kimberly looked ready to cry, but Leah was oblivious to the looks directed toward her.

"My father lost nearly everything when the tobacco market collapsed and I'll not put everything into cotton now," one man said.

"I agree," Leah answered. "We're going to raise some sheep and I believe that someday American wool will be in demand."

"You'll not compete with the English markets."

"I'll hire spinners who can do as well as any Englishwoman!" Leah said vehemently.

"Can she spin, Wes?" a man asked, laughing.

Leah suddenly became aware of who she was and where she was and she looked down at the uneaten apple tart on her plate. "I'm afraid I've overstepped myself," she said softly.

To her surprise, Wesley put his arm around her. "To tell you the truth, I haven't been married long enough to know whether she can spin or not."

Astonished, Leah looked up at her husband. His eyes were bright and he seemed almost proud of her.

"Go ahead and kiss her, Mr. Wesley," Bess said from across the table. "You look like you're dyin' to, and we'd all like a little proof that you love her. Isn't that right, men?"

To Leah's anger, Wesley gave a glance to Kim.

He was *not* going to humiliate her. "I don't need much encouragement to kiss my own husband," she said seductively as she slid her arms around Wes's neck.

The moment her lips touched his, she began to regret her actions. She wanted to prove something to the strangers around her, show them she really was good enough to be loved by a man of Wesley's stature, but she forgot any sensible reasons for kissing him. For a year she'd lived with couples who loved each other passionately, and until she began to kiss Wesley she was unaware how this had affected her. She very much wanted to be touched, wanted a release for her passion.

At first Wesley was cool, but he felt Leah's excitement, felt the commitment in her kiss, and he responded. He forgot the people around them as he kissed her deeply, hotly, searingly. His hand covered her head, his fingers demolishing the ordered curls there.

"Wesley," someone said with some embarrassment, "maybe you should wait until later."

Leah was helpless in Wesley's arms, as helpless as she'd been on the one other occasion when he'd touched her.

A hand touched Wesley's shoulder just as he was beginning to seek the soft curve of Leah's breast. The man's hand tightened. "Wes!"

Gradually Wes began to surface, and when he broke away from Leah his eyes took a moment to focus.

For seconds, Leah lay back on Wesley's arm, her eyes closed, her dark hair streaming over his buckskins. When she opened her eyes and became aware of where she was, she sat up abruptly and her face turned several shades of red. Her one glance at Wes showed him to be looking at her with puzzlement, and a vein in his throat pulsed rapidly.

"I . . ." she began, pulling away from him. A hand on her head showed her hair to have fallen. "Excuse me, I must . . ." she didn't finish as she turned and fled through the room and up the stairs to her bedchamber.

She was barely inside when Bess burst in. "I have *never* seen a kiss like that. Not in all my born days have I seen somebody get kissed like that. That Wesley is some man! Not only is he the best-lookin' thing this side of the mountains, he's also the best lover."

"Will you *please* stop talking?" Leah half cried. "How can I face any of them again? They'll never believe I'm a lady now. I wanted to leave Virginia with the people saying I'd become a lady, but what do I do but act like a Simmons whore." She paused, then gasped. "Oh Bess, I am sorry."

"You haven't hurt my feelings, and those men down there are going to dream about you tonight."

"Just what I wanted," Leah said as she sat down heavily on the bed. "Do you think I could slip out the back door and never see anyone again?"

Bess chuckled. "Let me fix your hair and then you will go downstairs again. You should have seen that Kimberly's face. She was spittin' nails."

"I was under the impression you thought Miss Shaw was the perfect example of a lady."

"Hold still!" Bess commanded, her hands in Leah's hair. "I thought that before my own sister was transformed into the most beautiful, elegant lady that Virginia has ever seen."

"Bess," Leah said, turning, "go with us. I need a friend. I'll teach you how to weave and you can go into business with me."

"And leave my nice warm tavern and my nice warm men for a clackety ol' loom? Those Stanfords didn't teach you any sense, did they? You take your Wesley and live on your farm and milk hundreds of cows every day, but not me. I want a life of ease. There, you're all prim and proper again. Now go down and smile. You've got Kimberly on the run."

Leah laughed. "I will miss you so much. Kim will run straight into Wesley's arms as soon as this night is over and he'll kiss her so well it'll make our kiss—." She paused, remembering. "Our kiss will mean nothing," she finished quietly. "All right, I'm as ready as I can be. If my husband can playact a kiss I can at least recognize it as such."

"That was no playacting," Bess called behind her sister, but Leah either didn't hear or ignored her.

Chapter 8

It took all Leah's courage to face the people downstairs once again. She was so sure they'd treat her as if she were a whore that she wasn't prepared for the warm welcome. Three men had arrived while she was upstairs, two with fiddles, one with a banjo, and they were already beginning to play.

Before Leah had a thought she was shoved into Wesley's arms and he led her in the first minuet.

"You seem to have regained your composure," Wes said before Leah was taken away from him to dance with another.

For hours Leah was whirled from one man to another. Once, she saw Kim dancing with Wesley, and he was looking at the blonde woman with concern. Leah pretended she didn't see them.

Twice during the night she heard the name Justin Stark mentioned, but she never had enough breath to ask who he was.

At midnight Wesley announced that the party was

over, that they needed an early start the next morning. He took Leah's arm and half pushed, half pulled her toward the stairs.

Leah felt wonderful. She'd had much too much of the delicious punch Bess had given her and she was humming as she entered their room. On the bed was her most beautiful nightgown, a translucent concoction of silk and ruffles. Leah picked it up, held it close to her, and began dancing about the room.

"Are you drunk?" Wesley asked calmly as he slipped his buckskin shirt over his head.

"How lovely!" Leah said under her breath as she looked at Wesley, bare from the waist up.

There was a spark of interest in Wes's eyes—perhaps more than a spark.

Leah stopped dancing, although her head didn't stop. "Are you going to make love to me?" she whispered.

Wesley's face changed as he looked at her in the golden light of the single lamp in the room. He took a step toward her. "Maybe I could be persuaded."

Leah dropped the gown from the front of her and stood waiting for him, her breath held, her heart pounding. She wanted more than anything for him to hold her, to kiss her again. When he was close to her she touched his bare chest, her fingertips wrapping in the abundant hair on his chest. "Wesley," she whispered as his head moved down toward hers.

A loud, quick knock on the door wasn't even heard until the door opened and Steven Shaw entered. "It looks like my little sister was right."

"What the hell are you doing in here?" Wesley asked angrily.

"Unlike you, Stanford, I don't have two women in two rooms. My little sister is bawling her eyes out

because she believes you're doing just what you are."
He gave Leah a hooded look. "I told her what a man of
honor you were and that you could be trusted. Somehow, after seein' this little filly after you all night, I
knew I was lyin'."

"Get out of here," Wesley said tiredly, moving away
from Leah. "Tell Kimberly I'll be there in a few
minutes."

"As soon as you finish here?" Steven chuckled but
left the room before Wes could say a word.

"Leah, I'm sorry," Wes began.

Leah glared at him. Her mood, loosened by the
liquor, easily changed from love to hate. "Sorry you
didn't get to finish what you started? Sorry you didn't
get to take advantage of the weakness of one of the
Simmons whores?"

"I don't know what you're talking about," he said,
reaching for his shirt. "You're my wife and—."

"*I* am your wife? Do you mean me who has begged
you all evening to stop drooling over the divine Miss
Shaw?"

"I'd advise you to watch your tongue," he warned.

"My tongue!" She gasped. "Don't you know that we
Simmonses have better uses for our tongues than to
talk with them? Isn't it in our bloodstream?"

Calmly, Wesley pulled his shirt on over his head.
"Look, I really don't know what you're so upset about.
You were the one who wanted to travel as my cousin
and you've always known how I've felt about Kim. I've
always tried to be honest and fair."

"Fair! You nearly attack me in this room and you call
that fair?"

Wesley almost smiled. "You've done everything possible to entice me this evening, and that dress isn't
exactly made to calm a man down."

"I didn't wear it for you," she said softly as she turned away to hide her humiliation.

Wesley smiled at the back of her. "Leah, really, I *am* flattered that you'd go to so much trouble to get me into your bed. It made me feel good to have you flirting with me even while you were dancing with other men, and I'm sure you could have seduced me if Steven hadn't interrupted, but the truth is, I really should keep to our bargain. For Kim's sake I'm going to try to resist your considerable charms."

"You what?" she said breathlessly, turning to face him.

"I owe something to the woman I love and she needs me, all of me, to stand by her, and in the future I'm going to try to resist you."

"Is that what happened before?" she whispered. "That in spite of all you could do, you gave in to my enticement of you?"

"I really need to go, so maybe we could discuss this another time. But, yes, you did throw yourself at me once before."

"Throw myself at you? As I did tonight?"

"Leah," he began, taking a step toward her, "I think I've hurt your feelings."

"Feelings!" She gasped. "Women like me don't have feelings. Didn't you know that? Women from my class of people, women who didn't grow up wearing silk, are capable only of seductions and enticements. When we get to Kentucky, I won't open a weaving shop, I'll . . . I'll merely open my legs."

Wesley's face hardened. "You've misunderstood everything I've said. All I wanted was to thank you for the compliment of offering me your body."

"I won't do it again," she said coldly. "Next time I offer it, it will be to someone else."

"Not while you're my wife!" he snapped.

She gave him a nasty little smile. "Shouldn't you go to your Kimberly? If you make her cry too long her pretty eyes will be red. How does *she* seduce you? Do her tears pull you into her bed?"

"Kimberly is a virgin," Wes said tightly, his eyes narrowed.

Leah threw up her hands. "A whore and a virgin fighting over you. Poor Wesley, you must spend some sleepless nights. Go to her."

"Leah, I never said you were a whore," he began.

"Get out of here!" she screamed.

"If you need me . . ."

"Need you!" she yelled at him. "You're the last person I'd ever need. I wish I could go to Kentucky by myself and I'd never have to even see you again. Now go to your dear Kimberly. She *needs* you."

Wesley seemed to want to speak, but instead he turned and left the room.

Immediately Leah fell to her knees, the sobs tearing through her. Need him, he'd said. No, she didn't need him, but she *wanted* him, or wanted someone, a man who cared enough to jump when a tear ran down her cheek. A man who had never known her family, who didn't believe she was a whore before he even saw her.

Sometime during the night Leah removed her dress and slipped on her nightgown. She'd cried all she could cry and all that was left was an empty hollowness, a feeling that life was never going to change. She'd been born in a swamp and she'd always be a part of the swamp. Pretty clothes would never cover the vileness with which she'd been born.

In the morning as Leah lay awake, Wesley slipped into the room; Leah knew he didn't want anyone thinking he hadn't spent the night with his wife.

"You're awake," he said as the early light illuminated the room. "Leah, about last night—."

She rolled to the side of the bed, got out, and walked across the room to the small trunk that held her clothes. She felt as if her spirit were dead and she didn't care about anything. Without a thought she slipped the gown off, careless of her nude form presented to Wesley as she began dressing.

"You never give up, do you?" he exploded angrily.

But Leah didn't even bother to turn around. When she was dressed, she turned to face him. "I'm ready whenever you are. Your friends won't know where you slept."

Frowning, he put his hand on her arm. "Leah, I've never meant to hurt you."

She looked from his hand to his face. "Never touch me again. Do you understand me? Never, ever again do I want you to touch me." With that she opened the door, waited outside the room for him, and together they walked down the stairs, looking for all the world like a couple who'd just spent the night together.

Leah parted from her sister quietly, and just as quietly she mounted the wagon beside Wes. He reached out his hand to help her, but one look from Leah made him withdraw.

At noon she gathered wood, built a fire, and cooked a hasty meal while Kimberly bathed some of the dirt from her face. Steven conveniently disappeared and Wes was busy with the animals. During the meal Kimberly chatted about the last party they'd attended in Virginia and repeatedly told Leah she should have been there. Leah silenced Kim by saying she had been too pregnant at the time to attend a party.

While Leah cleaned up from the meal, Kim announced that it was time for Leah to ride with Steven and from now on she'd be Wesley's fiancée and Leah his cousin. She seemed to think there'd be some protest, but there was none.

Leah climbed onto the wagon beside Steven. He made one comment about how he'd be glad to replace Wes if she felt any urges, but when he got no response from Leah, he took the reins and shut up.

At night, while Leah prepared supper, Wes rode to the nearest inn, and when he returned he reported that the place was too filthy to inhabit and they'd camp with the wagons. Kim sniffed about how she needed a bath, so Wes hauled buckets of water, heated them, hung a blanket screen, and prepared a bath for Kim. She conveniently lit a lamp behind the blanket so everyone around was treated to a silhouette of Kim's languorous bath.

"No screams of jealousy?" Steven said to Leah under his breath as Wes watched Kim in obvious rapture.

Leah didn't bother to answer as she cleared the supper dishes.

The next morning dawned hot, and Leah unbuttoned the top of her dress.

"Is that for me or him?" Steven asked. "If it's for Stanford you may as well close it. All he's interested in is my sister and she's an expert at keeping a man tailing after her. You ought to learn something from her. Never be too honest, at least not with gentlemen like Stanford. He'd rather look at a woman from behind a blanket. But you and me," he said with a chuckle, "we like skin."

He clucked to the horses and they were off.

Leah tried to still her trembling. She prayed she was not like Steven Shaw.

Toward noon they had to ford a river. The water, heavy with spring melts, was over the hub of the wheels.

"If we take it slowly we'll be able to make it," Wes informed Steven as they all stood on the bank.

"I'm frightened, Wesley," Kim said, clutching his arm.

"Don't be." He smiled. "We'll come through this. What about you, Leah, scared?"

"No," she said flatly. "I think we'll make it. Others have before us."

"I knew you'd feel that way," Wes said before turning away.

"Hallo!" came a man's voice from across the water. A tall, slim man in buckskins similar to Wesley's waved at them.

"It's Justin Stark," Wes said, smiling. "He'll be traveling with us."

Leah paid no attention to the man waiting on the far side but turned back to the wagons.

Wesley eased his wagon and horses into the water with utmost care. The horses shied, but Wes controlled them.

"He's afraid!" Steven said contemptuously. "He's scared to risk his hide. Hiyah!" he called to the horses, cracking his whip over their heads.

"No!" Leah said. "Wait until they're across."

"I'm not spendin' all day here and I'll not let that Stark fellow think I'm a coward."

Steven whipped the horses forward into the deep water.

"What the hell are you doing?" Wesley bellowed back at them.

"Not eatin' your mud," Steven called as he pulled alongside Wes's wagon.

"Keep to the right! Keep to the right!" the man on the land shouted at them.

Leah, hanging onto the seat with both hands, repeated the man's instructions to Steven, but Steven ignored her as he cracked the whip again.

The right front horse stepped into an underwater nothingness, screamed, and pulled the other horses after him. The heavy wagon tipped to one side and Steven went flying into the water. Leah released her hold on the seat and grabbed two flying reins as Steven released them. The others fell to the side.

"Keep a tight rein!" the man on land shouted. "Control that horse!"

Leah tried to obey him, wrapping the reins around her arm while trying to ease down far enough in the seat to get the dangling reins.

"Help her, Wes!" the man shouted. "Let that woman drive and help the redhead!"

Leah barely heard the man's shouts as her fingers inched toward the reins. She screamed once, when the frightened horses pulled until her arm nearly came off.

"Leah!" she heard Wesley shout but couldn't understand what he was saying because Kimberly had started to scream hysterically.

Quick tears of relief blinded Leah for just a second when her fingers tightened over the loose reins. Using every ounce of her strength she managed to control the frightened horses, pull the wagon to the right past the deepest part of the hole, and inch them toward the far bank.

The stranger from the shore swam toward her. "Good girl. Now hold them steady."

"Steven!" Leah yelled down at him as the horses touched land. Even while the back of the wagon was still in the water, Leah was pulling off her shoes. She'd always been a strong swimmer and now she wondered if the others realized Steven had fallen into the river.

"Here!" Leah gasped, tossing the man the reins just before she jumped down from the wagon and into the water.

"What the hell—!" the man began and then gave his attention to the horses.

"Where's Leah going?" Wesley demanded of the man.

"She yelled something about Steven."

"He's not here?" Wes said, but was in the water after Leah in seconds.

Leah dived for what seemed to her like hours, but there was no sign of Steven. Wesley and the stranger joined her after a few minutes, and when she surfaced she told them where she'd already looked.

Near dusk they found him, lying at the bottom at the edge of the river, the side of his head dented from his fall. Wesley pulled him onto land.

Leah stood over him, panting, exhausted from the afternoon's search. After the first hour she'd discarded her dress, since the long skirt hampered her. Now, in her dripping underwear, she was too cold, too tired to care about proprieties.

Wesley, seeing Justin looking at Leah, removed his shirt and slipped it over her, concealing her almost to her knees.

"No! No! No!" screamed Kimberly as she came toward them, her eyes on her brother's body.

Wesley moved away from Leah to comfort Kim in her grief and, if possible, Leah's shoulders drooped even more. Kim and Wes walked away into the growing darkness, Kim's sobs breaking the nighttime stillness.

For a moment neither the stranger nor Leah spoke.

"You ought to get into some dry clothes," the man said softly, watching her.

Leah merely nodded once and stood there, shivering.

The man moved closer to her. "I'm Justin Stark and you're—?"

Leah couldn't even answer him as she stared down at Steven's cold, lifeless body. Tears began to roll down her cheeks.

Without another word, Justin swept Leah into his arms.

She tried to pull away, but she was too weak, or perhaps she needed comfort, even from a stranger.

"Go ahead and cry, little girl," Justin whispered. "Anybody as brave as you deserves to cry."

Leah wasn't sure where all the tears came from—or why they came—but she began to cry as she'd never cried before. It was so good to be close to someone, to be held in a man's strong arms.

When the man unbuckled a blanket from his horse, Leah was hardly aware of it. Even when he gently removed her wet clothing she didn't protest. He wrapped her nude, wet body in the blanket, snuggled her against him, and sat with her on a fallen log. At some time he began to rock her and Leah gradually stopped crying, but she clung to him. Even when she fell into a deep sleep, she still clung to him.

"Is she asleep?" Wesley whispered to Justin.

Justin nodded. "You have a bed made up for her?"

Wes glanced at his boot toe. "I only made one for Kim. Leah usually makes her own bed." Justin didn't say another word and Wes disappeared for several minutes. "It's ready," he said when he returned.

Very carefully Justin stood while holding the sleeping Leah, and as if she were a fragile piece of glass, he laid her on the pallet of blankets Wesley had prepared.

For a moment Justin knelt over her. Then he stood and motioned Wes away into the silence of the forest. "Who is she?" Justin demanded.

"My . . . cousin," Wes answered. "What difference does it make who she is?"

Justin looked at Wes as if he were crazy. "Difference? I guess it matters to me because she's the most magnificent woman I've ever seen. Did you see the way she handled that team? And the way she risked her own life looking for that guy that drowned? I could see you had your hands full with that screaming bit of uselessness. Lord deliver me from women like that! Who is she anyway?"

"The woman I'm going to marry," Wesley said rigidly.

"Oh well . . . ah . . . I didn't mean anything," Justin stammered. "It's just that when you see the two women together, it makes that blonde *seem* worthless. No, I didn't mean that exactly."

"I think you've said more than enough."

"Right," Justin said sheepishly, but quickly raised his head. "Who is she?"

"Kimberly Shaw. The man who drowned was her brother."

"Oh I see. That's why she worked so hard to save him. I wonder if any of my sisters would risk their lives for my dead body. He was a lucky man to have a sister like her."

"No," Wes said softly. "Kimberly is the blonde. Leah is the woman who did the diving."

"And what is her relationship to the dead man?"

"None," Wes answered.

Justin turned away toward the trees. "Your cousin, is she? You were born under a lucky star. She attached to somebody? No, don't tell me. I don't care if she's plannin' to marry somebody. I think I'd go after her no matter how many men stood in my way. How'd you like me for a cousin by marriage?"

"Wait a minute, Justin. You're going too fast. You know nothing about Leah. She's pretty, I grant you, but she's the kind of woman that makes a man feel useless. You spend an hour around her and you'll begin to wonder if men are needed on this earth. There isn't *anything* she can't do all by herself and she always lets you know she needs nobody else. You marry her and in a year she'll be running your farm and your life and you won't be worth your weight in horse manure to her."

After an astonished moment, Justin began to laugh. He slapped Wesley's shoulder. "You can have all your pretty little blondes who sit on a wagon and scream while their brothers drown, but for me, I want a *woman*."

"You don't know what you're asking for," Wes warned. "Two weeks with Leah and you'll be looking for someone to make you feel like a man."

Justin smiled. "All she has to do is be a woman and that makes me feel like a man. Now I think I'll bed down. Tomorrow I'm going to start courting."

"Courting? But—," Wes began.

"Do you have any reason to object?" Justin asked coolly.

Wesley could only shake his head.

"All right then. Let's go to bed. In the morning we'll have a funeral."

Wesley watched Justin lay out a pallet where he could watch Leah in her sleep, then Wes went to where his own bed was. "Poor man," he muttered. He wished there was some way to save Justin from himself.

Chapter 9

Leah woke early to the sounds of Kimberly's sobbing. Wesley was holding her and trying to comfort her, but Kim seemed inconsolable. With a groan for her aching head, Leah threw back the blanket covering her, then gasped because she was stark naked. With a blush that covered her entire body, she remembered what had happened the night before. A quick glance around the campsite showed that the stranger was not there.

"Wesley," Leah said through a hoarse throat.

Wesley, intent on Kim's problems, didn't hear her.

Leah cleared her throat. "Wesley!" she said urgently.

He looked around, obviously annoyed. "Yes?"

"Could you get me some clothes?" She hated to ask him, but she wasn't going to parade before him wrapped in a skimpy blanket.

With one eyebrow raised, Wes left Kim to go to the wagon and extract a brown cotton dress for Leah, not bothering with her underwear. "You certainly do make an impression on a man when he first meets you," he said, eyeing her bare shoulders.

Leah snatched the dress from him. "Go back to your Kimberly," she said angrily, just as Kim let out a loud wail.

With resignation Leah dressed under the covers, rose, and gathered the water buckets. On her way to the river she saw Justin, the man who had recently joined them, stripped to the waist, digging a grave.

"Good morning," he called to her, his eyes alight.

Leah could barely murmur a reply because she ducked her head in embarrassment at the memory of being undressed by this man.

Immediately Justin was beside her, taking the buckets away from her. "Sleep well?" He laughed when she merely nodded, still not looking at him. "You're not going to let a little thing like a lack of clothes come between friends, are you? Why I've undressed hundreds of women."

She looked up at him, eyes wide.

"Maybe not hundreds." He smiled, his eyes almost eating her. "And certainly none as pretty as you. Don't turn away. Are you always so shy?"

She lifted her chin and looked at him. "I don't think I'm ever shy, but now I am . . ." She wanted to change the subject. "You'll be traveling with us?"

"All the way into Kaintuck." They were at the river and he took the buckets from her to fill them. "I grew up in the town where Wes bought his farm. All winter he worked like a demon on that place. I guess he was trying to get it ready for Miss Shaw."

"I guess so. Do you also farm?"

"Sure, and a little huntin' on the side. No, I'll carry them," he said when Leah reached for the full buckets.

"I can take care of my own jobs, thank you," she said stiffly.

Justin smiled at her, and his already handsome face looked even better. "I have no doubt you could carry a hundred buckets, but would you be so cruel as to deny me the pleasure of carrying them for you?"

For a moment, Leah didn't answer, but then she smiled. "I would hate to be called cruel. By all means, Mr. Stark, carry the water."

"Justin," he said with a laugh. "All my ladies call me Justin."

"*All* of them?" She laughed in return and felt better than she had in weeks.

"You two certainly seem to have forgotten what happened yesterday," Wesley said, glowering down at them. "I'd think you'd at least have a little respect for Kimberly's grief."

Justin's face lost its smile. He was a smaller man than Wes, but he didn't back down. "I think Leah showed a great deal of respect when she nearly drowned searching for a man who isn't even related to her. Just because that woman of yours cries loud doesn't mean she's willing to risk anything except tears."

Leah glanced up at the two furious men and excused herself because she was afraid of letting them see her smile. Justin's words made her want to smile all over. With a lightened heart she set about her chores of tending the animals, cooking breakfast, and readying the wagon for the day's journey. She didn't know if Wes and Justin continued to argue, but when they all gathered at the grave site, the two men seemed to have come to terms. Kim leaned heavily on Wesley's arm while he talked about what a good man Steven Shaw had been.

After the service, such as it was, Kim allowed Wes to help her inside the wagon where she lay down.

Justin tossed his pack and saddle in the second wagon, tied his horse behind, and climbed on the seat beside Leah, taking the reins from her. "I don't know if that woman and I are going to get along at all."

In spite of Leah's denial that she was shy, she really didn't know what to say to Justin. But she needn't have worried. Justin told her about his hometown of Sweetbriar, about his three sisters and four brothers, about his nieces and nephews. He told stories about who was in love with whom in the town and about how pretty Miranda Macalister was driving all the single men crazy.

"You included?" she asked timidly.

"I've looked at her a few times, but I've always had an idea of what the woman I wanted was like."

"And?" Leah encouraged.

"She's like you, Leah," he said softly, looking away only when the lead horse stepped into a rut.

Leah felt a wave of fear go through her. This man knew nothing about her, that she was a Simmons from the Virginia swamps, that she had a whore for a sister and her father had been crazy. It was a while before she talked, and then it was only in monosyllables about her weaving.

They stopped briefly to eat cold meat and potatoes, and Kim didn't leave the wagon. At night Leah made dinner over a fire she'd built. She watered and fed the animals. Justin cut firewood while Wes tended to Kim, who was distraught and incapacitated by her grief over her brother.

For days they traveled west with Justin beside Leah, talking to her, asking her questions, and each day

Leah's sense of guilt grew. Regan and Nicole had been kind to her in spite of the fact that she came from the swamps. But they'd always known about her. She felt she was leading Justin on, lying to this man who was so nice to her. If he knew what she was really like, where she was from, he would probably treat her as Wesley did.

A week passed and Kimberly's grief did not subside. Leah began taking Kim's meals to her in the wagon, where Kim clung to Leah and cried.

"Don't," Justin said one evening, putting his hand on Leah's arm as she filled a plate for Kim. He turned to Wes. "Isn't it about time she stopped being a princess? Leah isn't her waiting woman."

"Kim's still grieving for her brother," Wes said stubbornly.

"Then you wait on her. Not Leah!" He grabbed the plate from Leah and thrust it at Wes.

They ate in silence and Kim came out of the wagon to sit, leaning against a tree while Wes hovered over her.

With seeming disgust, Justin threw the last of his coffee into the fire. "We all need a rest. There's a waterfall a few miles from here and I thought maybe tomorrow Leah and I could ride over there." He smiled at her across the fire. "Maybe do some washing."

Leah looked down at her cup. "I do need to do some washing," she murmured.

Before the morning was fully awake, Justin was standing over Leah, wanting her to hurry up so they could go.

"But what about breakfast?" she asked, gathering dirty clothes into a bundle.

"Let the duchess fend for herself for a day."

Leah suppressed a giggle. "I'm ready."

"Leah!" Kim called and came running to them. She

was very pretty in the early light. She held out a couple of dresses and some underwear to Leah, "Would you mind? It looks like I have all the camp work to do today since you're going off to have fun, so could you do this little thing for me?"

"Of course," Leah answered, but Justin grabbed the clothes.

"You can do your own laundry," he began.

Leah put her hand on his arm and took Kim's clothes. "Of course I'll wash them."

"Come on," Justin said in disgust, half-pulling Leah to his saddled horse. "Why do you let her take so much from you? You're worth fifty of her." He mounted the horse then pulled her up behind him.

"No I'm not," Leah whispered, but she didn't think Justin heard her.

They traveled north for over an hour, away from the houses that dotted the countryside, away from sight of other wagons that traveled westward. After another hour, Justin dismounted and lifted his arms up for Leah. When he held her aloft, hands on her waist, he lowered her slowly and kissed her gently.

Leah felt no sparks, but it was a pleasant kiss. She looked away when he set her on the ground.

He looked at her, a puzzled frown on his brow. "Who's hurt you, Leah?" he asked softly. "I've never met a woman as pretty as you who hung her head all the time and thought she was another woman's slave."

"There are things about me you don't know," she said, pulling away from him, but she kept her chin up. "And I'm no one's slave."

"Then why are you so frightened of Wes?"

"Frightened?" She gasped. "I'm not afraid of him—or any man!" She lowered her voice. "But there are things between Wes and me, things you know nothing about." She could feel the anger in her growing. "I'd better get started with the washing."

"Forget the washing!" Justin said fiercely, grabbing the bundle from her. "What's between you and Stanford?"

"Not what you mean," she flashed at him, eyes bright with anger. "Wesley Stanford hates me, just as I hate him and all his kind who let my family starve while they spent money on fine clothes and horses. Wesley's horse cost more than what all nine of us lived on for over a year."

She moved away from him, knowing she'd disgusted him. He wouldn't care about her now that he knew who she was—and she wasn't going to let him see how his change hurt her. "You and your fine manners," she said, seething. "All of you men are alike. You think because we're poor you can get what you want from us. But let me tell you that only *one* of us Simmonses is a whore."

"Is that what you think of me?" Justin gasped. "That I think you're a . . . a . . ."

"Go on and say it!" she shouted at him. "I've certainly heard the word enough times from men and women like you. Pretty clothes on the outside and filth inside."

Justin stood still for a moment, looking as if he were in shock. "Is that what you think I am? Some rich dandy that grew up in a big house with servants to wait on me?" Quickly he turned around, and when he looked back he was grinning. "I wish the people of Sweetbriar could hear this. One of the Stark boys accused of having manners and riches. Oh Leah," he said, beginning to laugh. "I don't know how poor you grew up but you'll have to go some to beat me. Sit down here and let me tell you the *true* story of my family."

Bewildered, Leah sat beside him on the ground and listened to the true version of Justin's life. It wasn't that he'd lied when he'd told her of his family earlier, but he'd left out all the bad—because he thought Leah was a lady born and raised, and he didn't want to shock her with the tales of his life.

Justin told about his father, Doll Stark, who, it was rumored, was the laziest man east of the Mississippi. It might have been a joke to others, but to the rest of the family it was a constant battle to survive. Doll would spend his days in the Macalister trading post, laughing, enjoying himself, while his wife and children tried to feed themselves from a few acres of overworked land. Justin, the oldest boy, grew up hating his father. Doll would eat a massive breakfast, for which the family had worked, disappear until nightfall, come home, eat more, then spend hours trying to impregnate his wife. Justin would lie awake and hear the quiet sounds and hate his father even more. As for Doll, he never asked how his family fared or how Justin worked long, long hours to keep meat on the table.

And the town merely joked about Doll's laziness. The only time they interfered was when Justin's oldest sister, Corinne, told some lies and caused some trouble with the town's precious Macalisters.

"Is this the Macalister with the pretty daughter?" Leah was beginning to understand that Justin was one of her kind, not Wesley's. Maybe Justin wouldn't hate her, as Wes did, because of where she came from.

"The same one," Justin said. "Now tell me of your family."

Leah hesitated. At least Justin's lazy father was liked

by the townspeople. What good could she say about her own family? A glance at Justin showed her that he was prepared to wait until doomsday for her to speak.

She began slowly, watching for signs of revulsion from him, but when she saw only interest and concern on his face, she launched into her story rapidly. She told of her eldest brother kidnapping a woman, of her sister's prostitution, of her father's insanity, the way he beat his wife and children. And last of all, she told of the constant, backbreaking work she'd always had to do.

The forest seemed especially quiet when she finished and she held her breath for Justin's reaction, afraid to look at him.

"And even though you were Stanford's cousin, he let you suffer through that? He's never said, but isn't he rich?"

"Massively," Leah murmured, still not looking at him.

"What made him finally rescue you? Or did he hire you to wait on his princess Kimberly?"

Leah took a deep breath. "My father died and the children were adopted by other planters. I . . . wanted to come west, to go where no one knew me, so Wesley's sister-in-law gave me money to start a weaving shop and Wesley allowed me to travel with him."

Justin was silent for a while and Leah wondered if he believed the last part of her story. "Where did you learn your pretty manners?" she asked tentatively.

"Macalister's wife. An English lady. And you?"

Leah began to smile as she briefly told of Regan and Nicole's transformation of her. It was beginning to sink in that this man didn't mind that she was a Simmons. Perhaps not all men were like Wesley. Perhaps in this new state she wouldn't be judged by who her father had been.

"They sure did a good job." Justin laughed as he stood. "Now that's enough seriousness for today. Come on and see the waterfall." He grabbed her hand and led her up the steep, rocky hillside. There at the top was a pool and a short, hidden waterfall.

"Not the biggest I've ever seen but one of the most private. How about a bath?"

Instantly Leah's eyes narrowed at him.

He ignored her obvious suspicion. "You go first while I wait down the hill for you and when you're finished, give me a call." With that, he turned and left her alone.

Leah hesitated only seconds before removing her clothes and climbing into the pool. Using soap she'd brought for the laundry, she shampooed her hair and used the waterfall for rinsing. The pressure of the water nearly pushed her under. When she emerged, a long time later, she felt better than she had in months. She was no longer burdened by a secret past; a handsome man waited for her; she was on her way to a new land, new people; she had her weaving—and now she had clean hair. What more could a woman want in life?

She was laughing when she reached the bottom of the hill and Justin.

"I won't be but a minute," he said, racing up the hill to the pool for his own bath.

With energy Leah knelt on a rock and began the laundry, and a very short time later Justin joined her. With a grimace he started to help her rinse the clothes.

"And does this little frilly nothing belong to princess Kimberly?" Justin asked, holding up a nearly sheer chemise trimmed with tiny silk ruffles.

Her face red, Leah snatched it from him. "That one happens to be mine."

"Oh?" he asked, one eyebrow raised. "Then this is her ladyship's." He lifted a pair of drawers that were faded yellow and torn at the waistband. "She may be a lady on the outside but not where it counts. We ought to do her a favor and lose these."

Before Leah could blink, Justin tossed the worn-out drawers into the river.

"No!" Leah gasped, laughing as she hitched her skirt to her knees and walked into the river, following the underwear, which was rapidly heading downstream.

Justin came wading in behind her, grabbed the drawers, and caught Leah's arm at the same time, purposefully nearly causing her to fall. "Watch yourself." He smiled as Leah clung to him. In an instant his arms were around her and he was kissing her, and Leah liked this so much better than the first time he'd kissed her.

Neither of them heard Wesley plowing through the brook until he'd grabbed Justin's shoulder and shoved him into the water. "Is this how you're to be trusted?" Wesley bellowed. "Do you always attack the women you're supposed to be caring for?"

Justin came out of the water in a rage and Leah knew this was the beginning of a brawl. She put herself between the two men. "You have no right to interfere in my life," she yelled up at Wesley.

"Interfere?" he spat back at her. "You're my . . . You're in my care," he finished. "Damn you, Justin, what if you caught a man behaving like this with your sister?"

"I'd demand he marry her," Justin said calmly. "I'm leaving, Wes, because I don't want this to become a fight. I don't want there to be hatred between a woman's husband and her relatives." With that he walked out of the water toward his waiting horse.

Wesley didn't speak until he heard Justin's horse moving away. "Who does he mean by 'husband'?" he asked accusingly.

Leah snatched Kim's underwear from the driftwood where it had caught and started out of the river. There was no need to lift her skirt since it was soaked.

"I asked you a question," Wes demanded once they were on the bank.

"I didn't tell him about us if that's what you mean," she snapped. "You can relax. Your pure Stanford name wasn't sullied by me. Now if you'll excuse me I need to rewash a garment of your fiancée's."

Wesley's mouth hardened. "Is that what you two were talking about so long? Kim?"

She threw Kim's wet drawers on his boots. "It may surprise you to know that we lower class people have things to talk about other than our betters."

"It didn't look to me like you were doing much talking when I arrived. Both of you were wet. Did you go swimming together? Did you let him take your clothes off *again?*" He took her shoulders and pulled her to him. "When he kissed you," he whispered, "did he make you feel like you do when I kiss you?"

Leah would have given a great deal not to react when Wesley touched her, but she was utterly powerless. It wasn't the same as kissing Justin; this was surrender. His body crushed next to hers, his lips touched hers, and she felt or saw nothing else. She remembered no hate, had no thoughts at all.

When he released her, she was dazed, barely able to stand upright.

"It didn't look as if you were feeling like that in Justin's arms," Wes said so smugly that Leah's eyes flew open.

She knew with every fiber of her body that she *had* to

113

wipe that look off his face. Without thought, she used a trick her brother had taught her. She brought her knee up between Wesley's legs.

Immediately he crumpled, and Leah ran to his horse, mounted quickly, and started back to camp. As she rode, knowing he'd have to walk back, she laughed with pleasure, but after a few minutes she halted the horse. Maybe she'd injured Wesley. She had a right to be angry, but she didn't feel right in hurting him.

She was still hesitating when Wesley dropped from a tree above her, catching the horse's reins.

"How—?" she began.

He didn't answer her but began to lead the horse back to the waterfall. She didn't like the look of blind anger in his eyes and she dared not speak to him. Would he beat her?

At the river he stopped. "Get down and get the clothes," he said in a steely voice.

Leah obeyed him.

He mounted his horse, took the wet laundry from her, and offered his hand to help her behind him. She was afraid of the look on his face, scared to refuse him, and when seated she tried to keep from touching him, not wanting him to remember she was there.

Once, the horse stepped sideways and Leah nearly fell off.

"If you can't bear to touch me at least hold onto the damn saddle," he said with a growl, and again Leah obeyed.

They were silent the rest of the way to the camp and Leah might have thought Wes hated her before, but now his anger was like a hot red cape encircling him—a cape that would burn one's fingers if one dared touch it. She was careful to avoid him.

Chapter 10

Two days later they met the Greenwoods: Hank and Sadie and their three little boys. Leah was the one who suggested they travel together. For the last two days it had been very unpleasant traveling with Kim, Wes, and Justin. Wesley kept watching, staring at her with dark eyes, while Justin treated her as if she might break at any moment, and Leah was beginning to find his hovering an annoyance. Kim seemed oblivious to the tension and just kept demanding more and more from Wes.

The Greenwoods and their noisy, active children were exactly what was needed to take away some of the tension within the group. There were many travelers on the road heading for Kentucky and even farther west. They were drawn by the enticement of riches beyond belief, of fertile, virgin land that was theirs for the asking. There was no longer an Indian problem and Kentucky was a state, so they felt safe, protected from hardship. Some of the travelers were well prepared, their wagons loaded with goods. They'd sold their farms and had money to buy new land in the west. But too many others had merely walked away from where they'd lived, their families trailing behind them with no more than the clothes on their backs and a sackful of food.

All along the way were inns, and although the majority of them were too filthy to consider, they charged much for their services and received whatever they asked.

Leah was reminded of her own childhood when she'd see a family of children dressed in rags, looking gaunt and worn-out but trudging westward, dutifully following their parents. At first secretly, she began to feed some of these children, not letting Wesley see her because it was, after all, his food. The evening of the day they met the Greenwoods, while everyone was sitting around the campfire she'd tentatively suggested that they offer food to some people with several children who were camped not too far away.

It was one of the few times Kim expressed a strong opinion. "Aren't you being awfully free with someone else's goods?" Kim asked. "People should learn to take care of themselves. If we start giving them things they'll never learn to depend on themselves. They'll always expect us to take care of them."

For a while no one said a word and when someone did speak, it was about something else.

That night Leah stayed awake for a long time, and when she thought everyone else was asleep she threw back her blankets, crept silently to the wagon to get the bag of food she'd secretly prepared earlier, and made her way through the darkness toward the people camped nearby. They had four young children and nothing but a handcart of goods. Silently she set the bundle of food near the cart and started back toward her own wagon.

She'd gone only a few yards when a voice made her jump in surprise.

"Quiet or you'll wake them," Wes whispered, motioning for her to follow him further into the trees.

Leah swallowed hard, knowing he'd caught her stealing from his supplies. She prayed he wouldn't return her to Virginia. She stopped when he did, but she couldn't meet his eyes.

"What did you give them?" he asked.

"Bacon, flour, p . . . potatoes," she stammered, then looked up at him beseechingly. "I'll pay you back. I didn't mean to steal the food. It's just that the people looked so hungry and—."

"Ssh," he said, and she could see in the moonlight that he was smiling. "Look there." He pointed.

Through the trees she could see the people's banked fire. By the cart was her bundle and near it was another bundle just like hers. She looked up at him quickly. "Yours?" she asked, astonished.

He grinned. "Mine. I couldn't stand to see them hungry either."

They were silent a moment, sharing their secret. "How long have you been . . . ?" Wes began.

Leah looked at her bare feet. "Since we started. That's why I haven't minded being in charge of the food. No one else looks at it but me so I know how much I can afford to give away and not be discovered. I didn't mean to steal," she began again, looking up at him.

"I can afford a few potatoes," Wes said. "I'll bet we're pretty low on supplies."

Leah looked guilty. "Very low. I was planning to tell you soon but . . ."

He chuckled. "As soon as you absolutely had to, no doubt. In the morning make me a list and I'll get everything. Maybe you ought to double whatever you think we'll need. Now let's get back before we're missed."

Leah hesitated. "Wesley," she whispered. "I don't know how to write. How can I make a list?"

He turned and looked at her, and his look made her blush. Once she would have run into his arms. She wished she could forget how she'd once loved him.

"I guess you'll have to go with me," he said, so softly she barely heard him.

Together they went back to their own camp. Wesley walked Leah to where her bedroll lay and when they stopped, he smiled at her in conspiracy, gave her a wink, then turned toward his own bed on the far side of the camp.

Leah fell asleep with a smile on her face.

In the morning Leah didn't want to look at Wesley because she was afraid she'd see hatred in his eyes and that the night before would turn out to be a dream.

"You're sure you don't mind us traveling with you?" Mrs. Greenwood asked for the hundredth time.

Turning, Leah smiled at her. "Of course not. I'm looking forward to spending time with your children. Until this trip, I've always been surrounded by children, and I miss them."

Sadie Greenwood laughed. "You may get more of them than you want. My three are a handful."

At that moment the baby began to cry. "Let me," Leah said, running toward the toddler, Asa, who'd just fallen. The boy was used to strangers; he clung to Leah, and as she held him hot tears came to her eyes.

"Are you all right?" Wesley asked from behind her;

it was as if he'd been watching her and came when she needed him.

"My child would have been nearly his age," Leah choked out, hugging the boy who was no longer crying. She turned back to the wagons.

"*Our* child," Wes murmured, but she didn't hear him.

The next few days were very pleasant. Leah rode with Mrs. Greenwood and they swapped recipes, Sadie's of food, Leah's of how to concoct beauty creams, and talked endlessly about children.

"And which one of those men are you going to choose?" Sadie asked.

Leah kept her eyes on the horses. "I don't know what you mean."

Sadie chuckled. "At first I thought it was Justin, since he's always hovering over you, but then that good-looking Wesley could never take his eyes off you, so I asked him how closely you were related."

"You *asked* him?" Leah said with a gasp.

"Years ago I quit trying to cure myself of nosiness—and so did Hank. Or maybe he just gave up on me. It's an absolute curse on me. I always want to know everybody's business."

"What did Wesley say about our relationship?" Leah asked softly.

Sadie gave her a quick look from the corner of her eye. "He said you were cousins by marriage and not blood relatives at all."

Leah laughed at that. "That's certainly true," she said, and to change the subject she asked Sadie something about the children.

That night Sadie had her first run-in with Kimberly. It had started quite innocently. Sadie was used to taking charge, used to organizing people to get things done. Leah, Wes, Justin, and Hank were seeing to the livestock while Sadie was starting supper and managing the children, who were restless after riding all day. She began giving Kimberly things to do. At first cooperative, Kim obeyed Sadie, but after being given five tasks in a row Kim set the pan down, murmured, "I have to go into the woods," and didn't return until everyone was sitting down to eat.

Sadie was silent all through the meal, but twice, when Kim asked Wes to fetch something for her, Sadie gave Kim hard looks. After dinner, Leah began clearing the dishes when Sadie stood.

"I think Miss Kimberly should clean up since she didn't bother to help make camp or cook the meal," Sadie said loudly.

Her husband looked as if he wanted to crawl under a rock. "Now Sadie," he began, "I'll help clear."

Kimberly was already on the outskirts of the camp, obviously preparing to escape.

Leah looked at Wes, but he was studying his empty plate. Justin was watching Sadie with interest.

Sadie stood firm. "She didn't help this morning or at noon. She didn't help with the animals or tonight's meal. She won't drive a team nor does she help load or unload. I'll not be anybody's servant, Hank Greenwood. I'm a free American."

Kimberly was obviously too astonished to speak, but now she looked pleadingly at Wes.

Slowly, Wes stood. "Come on, Kim," he said softly. "I'll help you clear the dishes."

The group broke apart immediately. Hank grabbed Sadie's arm. "Are you happy now that you've made a scene? It's their business who does what around the camp." He led her away into the shadows.

Kim started crying. "How could you let her say those things about me?" she wailed, falling into Wesley's arms. "You know I'm not strong like the rest of you. I wish I could be like Leah but I just can't. And no one seems to care about how much Steven's death upset me. It's so difficult for me to adjust to his being gone. Oh Wesley, please don't leave me. I need you so much. I just couldn't live without you."

Leah stood rooted to where she was, watching Wes comfort Kimberly.

"Walk with me?" Justin said, pulling Leah by the arm, leading her into the darkness. "Sadie said what I've wanted to for a long time. What amazes me is how Wes can put up with her."

Leah jerked away from him. "I'm getting tired of hearing about how bad everyone thinks Kim is. Maybe she senses how much you dislike her and that's why she refuses to help." She stopped. "I'm sorry. Maybe I'm just tired in general. I think I'll go back." Quickly she turned and ran back to the camp.

Wesley was just pouring hot water into a pan to wash dishes while Kim, looking sulky, was prepared to dry them.

"Go away," Leah told Wes gently. "Kim and I'll do the dishes." She barely glanced at him but he left the women alone.

"I didn't mean—," Kim began. "That woman is so awful. Does she know my brother just died?"

Leah started washing dishes. "I think she believes that even grief is no excuse to get out of work. Tomorrow morning why don't you stay by me and I'll help you stay busy?"

"But, Leah, I do stay busy. I always have so much to do. I have to look nice for Wesley and my hair takes so much time. Sometimes I wish I were like you and didn't

121

worry when I get grease stains on my clothes or soot smudges on my nose. Justin likes you as you are, but Wesley wants me to be beautiful and I have to be. Doesn't anyone understand that?"

Leah rubbed her cheek on her shoulder and glanced down at her dress. It was indeed stained.

Kim moved closer to Leah and began to whisper. "I'm beginning to worry about Wesley. He doesn't kiss me as often anymore. He used to always be clutching at me, but now he just looks at me."

"Kim," Leah said in exasperation. "Why are you telling me this? How can I help you?"

"I just thought you might know some enticements because you're a . . . well, because you're not a virgin and I thought maybe your sister might have given you some hints." She stopped at Leah's look. "I didn't mean to offend you," she said as if wounded. "I just thought you might know some things."

"Kimberly," Leah said evenly. *"You* wash the dishes." With that she turned away.

That night Leah was awakened by a touch on her shoulder and looked up to see Wesley leaning over her.

He put his finger to his lips and motioned her to follow him. She slipped her dress over her head and went into the woods behind him. When they were far enough away, he turned to her.

"About a mile down the road is a family that needs help. I made up a package of goods and thought maybe you'd like to go with me to deliver it. Unless you're too tired."

He sounded like a little boy, afraid she'd turn him down. "I'd love to," she answered.

They walked for a while, not speaking.

"Pretty night, isn't it?" Wes asked.

"Very."

"You and Justin have a fight?" he asked bluntly.

She shot him a look of challenge. "You and Kimberly have a fight?"

He grinned at her, and she grinned back.

"You like him, don't you?" Wes persisted.

"He's one of my kind. We both grew up poor."

"Oh," Wes said. "I always had money but I also always had Travis. I'm not sure if I wouldn't give up the money if I could have grown up without Travis."

"Only a rich man would say such a thing. *No* brother is worse than poverty."

"At least you were free to think your own thoughts. Travis always told me what to think and how to think it. That's why Kim—." He stopped.

"Why Kim what?" Leah asked quietly.

"Kim needs me," he said, stubbornness in his voice.

"Kim needs something," Leah answered. "But I wonder if anyone knows what it is. Is that the camp?"

"No, it's farther away. For some reason they camped in a little canyon. If a rain came they'd never get out fast enough. You don't mind a bit of a climb in the dark, do you?"

Leah shook her head, but later she wished she'd questioned his idea of a "bit of a climb." They seemed almost to scale a rock wall in order to reach the bottom of the canyon. Wesley went first, then as Leah came down above, he took her ankles, moved his hands— quite unnecessarily, Leah thought—up her legs to her hips, then plucked her off the wall and set her on the ground. She meant to speak to him about his conduct, but he was grinning so winningly she laughed with him. He grabbed her hand and started down the canyon.

"There it is." He pointed. "You stay here while I deliver the package, then we're off again."

Leah crouched down behind a rock and watched as

Wes made his way toward the sleeping travelers. She almost felt like a thief, as if they were doing something wrong, skulking about in the middle of the night, intruding on sleeping people.

Wesley was just entering the camp when Leah saw a man coming from the opposite direction, a long-barreled fowling gun slung across his arm, a big dog at his feet. Instantly she knew there was going to be trouble.

She stood just as Wes saw the man and dog. Wes raised his hand to give greeting, but the dog set up a howl and ran toward Wes in attack and the man raised his gun. Wesley sensibly dropped his bundle, turned, and started running back toward Leah.

"Go!" he shouted over the growing din of voices and barking dogs.

"Come back here, you thievin' varmint!" someone shouted, close behind Wes.

Leah grabbed her skirts and took off at a dead run, inches in front of Wesley.

The gun went off and the air exploded with bits of shot. Behind her Wes grunted, but when Leah looked back he shoved her shoulder. "Up the damned wall!" he said with a growl, and the next thing Leah knew she was grabbed by a big hand on her seat and shoved upwards, her cheek grazing rock.

She scrambled up the side of that rock like a fly, heaving herself over the top and crawling on her hands and knees before running with all her might.

Wesley tackled her, slamming her into the ground just as more of the fiery shot whizzed over them.

"What *is* that?" She gasped from under him.

"Quiet!" he hissed, covering her head with his hands, protecting her slight body with his own.

124

Leah couldn't breathe, but she was much too frightened to need to breathe.

"They got away!" came a voice from below them. "Leastways I ain't goin' up that rock to look for 'em. I reckon they'll think twice before they try stealin' again."

For a long while they lay quietly.

"Wesley," Leah managed to say. "I can't breathe."

He rolled off her, stood, and grabbed her hand. "Let's get out of here."

He pulled her along behind him at a galloping pace until he stopped and leaned against a tree, his chest heaving. Leah did the same.

When they'd caught their breath, they looked at each other.

Wesley was the first to grin. "So much for our Good Samaritan acts."

Leah gave a little laugh. "We could have been killed."

Wes grinned wider. "Wonder what he'll think when he finds the bag of food?"

Leah couldn't refrain from laughing any longer. "I hope his dog doesn't get it sooner. Oh Wesley, I never went up a rock faster in my whole life! I thought you were going to throw me over the top."

"I tried to. That dog was so close I could smell its breath." He laughed. "You weren't hurt, were you?"

"A few scrapes and bruises, that's all. I'll be sore tomorrow. What about you?"

He was still laughing. "A bloody side, but not bad."

That sobered her. "Where?" she demanded, moving in front of him and grabbing the buttons of his shirt.

"You sure are eager to get my clothes off, woman." He grinned down at her.

"Shut up, Wesley," she said conversationally, unbuttoning his shirt. In the moonlight she could see two long, deep scratches. "They don't look bad, but they ought to be washed. Let's get to the water."

"Yes ma'am," he said happily, following her as she walked through the woods to the nearby stream.

Wesley removed his shirt while Leah tore part of her petticoat away to wash the cuts. "What would men do without women's petticoats?" Wes murmured. "You are a very pretty young woman, Leah," he whispered, then touched her chin so she looked at him.

The air was filled with the charges between them, dancing lights of the moon on the water drawing them together.

Leah's fingers moved from the cuts on Wes's side to his dark, warm skin, upward to the dark mass of curling hair on his chest. She couldn't move away when his lips came near hers.

"We are still married, you know," he murmured.

Leah awoke from her trance. "If you're trying to seduce me, Wesley Stanford, you have just failed. Here! Clean your own wounds." She jumped up and started back to the camp.

Wes grabbed his shirt and ran after her. "I didn't mean anything, Leah, honest," he pleaded. "I just thought—."

She whirled on him. "You thought that I was an easy woman and available so you'd take what you could get, didn't you? Why didn't you ask your virginal Kimberly out tonight and try to seduce her? Because she's good and I'm bad, right? It's all right to try what you can with a Simmons but not with a lady like Miss Shaw. Well, you were wrong! I gave myself once to you because I *wanted* to, and the next time I'll choose the man and he won't be one who tricks me."

126

"You mean Justin," Wes said angrily, then changed his tone. "Leah, I didn't mean to trick you. Everything just sort of happened. I wasn't trying to seduce you because you're experienced, but you're a pretty girl and—."

"And any pretty, experienced girl will do, is that it?"

His face changed, his pride took over. "I'm not Justin and you're not Kimberly, so we're even." He brushed past her to return to the camp.

Instantly Leah's anger drained away and she knew she'd been wrong. Wesley was right. What had happened had not been planned and she'd been wrong to ruin the moment.

She started to call out to him but stopped herself. It was better this way. Lately they'd been becoming too friendly. When it came time for their separation and his marriage to Kimberly, she didn't want to be in love with him. Yes, it was better to stay away from Wesley and concentrate on Justin. Perhaps Justin could make her forget all the feelings she'd ever had for Wes.

Chapter 11

Leah found it quite easy to concentrate on Justin. He always seemed to be just a few feet away from her, always ready to help with any chore. He smiled at her a great deal and gave her flowers.

One evening as Leah was standing by the wagon holding a handful of wildflowers Justin had given her, Sadie approached. "So you're thinkin' of choosin' the little one," Sadie said.

"I'd hardly call Justin small," Leah answered, not pretending to misunderstand. "Besides, there's never been any choice in the matter. Wesley Stanford is engaged to Kimberly and he's very much in love with her."

Sadie snorted. "He may have been at one time, but that was before he had to spend twenty-four hours a day in her company."

"What do you mean?"

"Don't act innocent with me, young lady," Sadie chided. "I know very well that you can sense what's going on between them."

"I haven't seen anything," Leah said. "And besides, it doesn't matter to me what Wesley does. I think I may be falling in love with Justin."

Sadie only grunted as she went into the woods to empty a pan of dirty water.

Two nights later they camped near three families, one of which played fiddles, and they invited everyone to an impromptu dance.

Leah spent a long time choosing her dress and in washing and brushing her hair until it shone and sparkled like melted rubies. Her low-cut dress was deep rose-colored silk that caught the light when she moved. Darker rose ribbons were entangled in her hair and tied under her breasts.

"You look like a princess," Sadie's oldest son said with a gasp when he saw her.

At the dance were five women and fifteen men. Four of the men were the big, good-looking, energetic sons of one of the women, and they caught the hands of Leah and Kimberly instantly, leading them into romping dances near the cooking fire.

"I don't like this," Kimberly said as she tried to catch her breath between dances.

Leah didn't have time to reply as another man pulled her away to dance with him.

"You seem to be enjoying yourself," Wesley said later as he pulled her into his arms.

"I don't want to fight you," she said, enjoying the music and the moonlight.

"You look beautiful, Leah," Wesley whispered. "You've changed since—."

He stopped at the sound of Kimberly's insistent voice from across the camp. "Wesley!" she demanded.

"You'd better go," Leah said, starting to pull away from him.

Wesley wouldn't relinquish her hands. "Not yet," he said, his jaw set. "I'll go when *I'm* ready."

She gave him a cold look. "You'll leave when Miss Shaw pulls your chain," she said hotly. "Now if you'll excuse me I'd rather dance with someone else."

She was shaking as she walked away, and when she saw Justin she clung to his arm. "I need to get away from this crowd," she murmured, and Justin led her into the dark forest.

Once out of sight of the people, Leah nearly flung herself into Justin's arms and planted her lips on his. She needed to feel she was a woman. She was sick of rejection, sick of feeling as if she'd been discarded. She'd thrown her body and her love at Wesley and he'd used what he wanted and told her he wanted no more. Kimberly sat on her throne and Wesley knelt before her, offering gifts.

"Marry me," Justin whispered, kissing her face and neck. "Marry me tonight."

She drew away from him. "You don't have to marry me," she said. "Just because I tend to . . . throw myself at men doesn't mean one of them has to marry me. Or marry me forever," she added.

"Leah," Justin said, grabbing her shoulders. "I don't know what you're talking about. I love you. I've loved you from the beginning and I want to marry you. I want you to be my wife and live with me."

"For how long?" she snapped. "Don't you have a girl back home?" She pulled away from him. "I can't marry anyone." Turning, she ran back to their own wagons, only to nearly run into Wesley and Kim.

"I can't go back there," Kim was saying, tears in her voice. "I'm so tired and all those men kept touching me. I don't like it."

"You don't seem to like for any man to touch you," Wesley said. "Even me."

"That's not true. I don't mind when you touch me except when you hurt me. Please, Wesley, let's not argue. I really must sleep."

Leah didn't want to overhear any more of the conversation. She stepped forward. "I'll take care of Kim," she said softly, putting her arms around the blonde woman who was beginning to cry.

For some reason Leah's action angered Wesley. "You can take care of her, can't you?" he said under his breath, teeth clenched. "You can take care of anything and anyone. Is that it? Leah the mighty can rescue a man with one hand, raise half a dozen children with the other. Nothing is too much for Leah, is it? She can look beautiful even in dirty dresses." He paused. "Go take care of someone else. I'll see to Kim."

With that he half jerked Kim away from Leah and led her toward the wagons.

Leah stared after them in stunned silence, sure that Wesley's outburst was one of the oddest things she'd ever heard. Did he expect all women to be like Kim? No work would ever get done if they all sat around and tended their hair. Surely Wesley must realize that. No doubt he was angry again because he somehow thought she wasn't being good to his darling Kimberly.

Angrily, Leah turned away. Why was she spending more time thinking about what Wes wanted when she'd just received a proposal of marriage? And why would Justin want to marry her?

Her head was aching when she went to bed and before long she was crying—and she didn't know why she was crying.

* * *

For the next three days it rained. The skies opened up and let loose a deluge that threatened to never end.

Justin drove the wagon, Leah beside him, through deep, sucking mud puddles. Rain poured over them and no hats or rain clothes could keep them dry.

Wesley had made a place for Kim inside the wagon and brought all her food to her. Twice Leah caught Justin smirking at Wesley, and Leah thought perhaps Wes was going to remove a few of Justin's teeth.

On the fourth day the sun shone weakly and flashed off the muddy land. In the evening it wasn't easy to get ready for the night's camp while walking around mud puddles as big as fish ponds.

Leah made her way between two deep mud holes to reach the wagon. They'd had to set up camp some distance away and now she was carrying heavy bundles and trying to balance on the little ridge between the mud holes.

Wesley stood by the wagon, watching her from under the brim of his hat. His buckskins were still wet in places.

Leah pulled a large bundle of food from the wagon and started toward the camp.

"Here," Wes said, holding out a bag she knew contained a skillet. "You'll need this."

Leah glanced down at her bundle, then returned to take the skillet.

"And this," Wesley said as he looped a horse's bridle over her shoulder.

"Maybe I should come back for some of these things," Leah said, looking at her shoulder and then at the narrow bridge of land she must walk across.

"You mean you can't carry everything at once?" Wes asked, one eyebrow arched.

"I guess so," she began, as Wes draped another bridle on her other shoulder.

"And this, of course," he said, putting a bag's drawstring over her neck so the heavy sack hung down her back.

"Is that all?" she asked in exasperation, her legs beginning to bow under the weight.

"That should do it. Oh, here's one last thing. Justin's hat." He settled the too-big hat on her head, nearly covering her eyes.

"I can't see very well," she mumbled, head back.

"That shouldn't bother you, should it? Nothing bothers Leah. Leah can do anything. Now, you'd better get going because people need those things." He turned her about, pointed her toward the narrow strip of land, and gave her a little push.

Leah was too busy concentrating on where she had to walk to think about what Wesley was trying to do to her. At the first step she took, the hat fell forward and more of her vision was blocked. To compensate she tilted her head back further and the sack dragging on her neck hurt.

She did quite well for about ten steps, then halfway across, her left foot sank into a soggy bit of ground, and when she tugged at her foot she began to lose balance. One of the bridles slipped down her arm, further upsetting her. She tried to shrug it upward, but just then her foot came loose.

For a moment she teetered on the brink, then suddenly she fell backward into the soft, oozing mud.

Blinking, she sat there, still clutching all her bundles. A fat drop of mud slid down her forehead, her nose, and as it came near her lip, Leah blew at it.

133

It was then that Wesley's laughter made her look up. He was standing on the dry piece of land and bending over her, his face a study in amusement. "It looks like somebody found something the ever-competent Leah can't do. You thought you could carry half the wagon and maneuver through the mud. It looks like you *can't*," he said with great glee.

Leah raised one arm, mud all the way up to her armpit, and tried to push her dripping hair out of her eyes. Justin's hat was half floating, half sinking down beside her. She had no idea what Wesley was talking about. Slowly she began to remove her bundles and put them on dry land.

"You couldn't even ask for help when you were falling," Wes said as he took the food bag from her. "If I hadn't been here you wouldn't have anyone to help you out of this mess."

"I wouldn't be here if you hadn't given me so much to carry," she said, removing the bag from around her neck.

"Did it ever occur to you, Leah, to say no?" He wasn't laughing now. "Why do you have to do everything yourself? Why don't you ever ask anyone for help?"

Leah looked at him and suddenly realized that she was sitting practically up to her nose in mud because he was trying to teach her some kind of lesson. Of course she needed help at times! But lately all she'd done was try to do her work and Kim's. She was trying to care for and protect the woman *he* loved.

Wes didn't see the look in her eyes change. Nor did he see her hands sink into the mud at her side. As he reached for the last bundle, Leah's arm flung out and threw a great gob of mud smack into Wesley's smiling face.

As he sputtered, spitting out mud, she started bombarding him with great handfuls of the nasty stuff. Moments later she stopped and he looked down at himself, covered with big splotches of mud. Leah, still sitting, looked up at him. "You think your Kim will greet you with open arms?" she said with a smile.

"Why you little—," he began, then took a flying leap at her.

Leah rolled away just as Wes hit, and he landed face-down in the mess. When he looked up, only his eyes white, Leah started laughing.

"Wesley." She gasped as she started to stand. "Here, let me help you up."

With a little grin, Wes lifted his muddy arm to Leah's extended hand, but when she took it, he pulled.

"No!" She gasped again before sliding back down, this time getting mud on the few clean parts of her body.

"You insufferable—," she began. "How could you do this? Look at me!"

"I am," he said with a chuckle. "I am." His eyes were on her dress front, which was plastered to her.

It was difficult, if not impossible, to retain one's pride while completely covered in mud. Leah was angry that Wes had caused her to fall, and now he was giving her lustful looks. She was sick of his leering at her. She was more than just a body.

With fists clenched, Leah pulled herself up and launched herself at Wes.

With laughter Wes opened his arms to her, and as she tried to hit him, he enclosed her in his embrace and began rolling with her.

"Stop it!" she screamed, beginning to try to kick free of him. "Wesley!"

"You can't do everything, can you, Leah?" He

laughed, tossing one of his muscular legs over both of hers. "Can you?"

She struggled against him, under him. "Of course I can't. I never said I could."

He was grinning down at her, his eyes and teeth white. "You sure are dirty."

"No thanks to you," she snapped, then her face changed. She couldn't help laughing; they must be an awful sight. "You're not exactly clean yourself." She stopped struggling as she looked up at him.

"Tell me something you can't do by yourself."

"What? Oh Wesley, can't you ask your idiot questions later? Let me up so I can take a bath."

His mud mask didn't move and when she pushed at him and he still remained immobile, she sighed.

"There are a lot of things I can't do."

"Such as?"

Leah had to think for a moment. "You've just seen me doing household chores. I've always done farm work so I'm good at it."

"I'm waiting," Wes said stubbornly.

"Hunting!" she said, pleased with herself. "I went hunting with my brother once and I got so scared he brought me home. We heard a bear at night and it frightened me. Now there! That's something I can't do."

"Anything else?"

"You are impossible. There's mud in my ears even! Please let me up. Oh, all right. I can't read, I can't write, guns frighten me, being away from people scares me. I hate men who care only that I'm a Simmons." She said the last with a great deal of venom.

"Guns, huh?" Wes said, seeming to ignore her last statement. Tightening his grip on her, he began to roll again.

"Wesley!" she exclaimed.

"Guns and hunting!" He laughed, turning over and over in the mud.

Leah could only cling to him and try to keep from drowning.

"Well lookee here!" came Sadie's voice over them. "If it ain't a couple of pigs wallowin' in the mud!"

Leah was sure her face was red under its coating of mud, but Wesley was grinning.

"I heard you ladies think mud is a beauty cream. I just thought I'd try it and Leah consented to show me how it's done. That's right, isn't it, Leah?"

"Release me, you oaf!" she hissed at him.

"Wesley!" came Kim's voice. "Whatever are you and Leah doing in the mud together? Did you fall?"

"I think I have," Wes said softly, to Leah alone, looking at her in wonder. He rolled off her to look up at Kim. "Leah fell and I jumped in after her." There was a tone to his voice that was almost a challenge.

"Oh," Kim said, blinking. "I don't guess a person can swim in mud."

Leah did not laugh. That was to her credit.

Wes slowly began to stand. "I guess we better get cleaned up." He held out his hand to Leah.

She wasn't sure whether to trust him again, but this time there was no laughter in his eyes, and she accepted his offered hand. He swept her into his arms and Leah didn't protest.

"Wesley—," Kim began.

"I have to take Leah to the river," he said blandly, walking past her.

There was something in Wesley's look that made Leah keep quiet. Behind them Sadie said, "Come with me, Kimberly, and I'll make you something nice to drink."

At the river Wesley left her alone, and when he walked back to camp he was frowning.

Kimberly brought Leah a towel and clean clothes.

"Leah," she said, puzzled, "I don't think a lady should get into a mud puddle with a man. I really don't think it's the proper thing to do."

"Kim," Leah said, "I certainly didn't do it on purpose. I fell."

"And Wesley was saving you?" Kim seemed to want reassurance.

Leah merely nodded.

"Wesley isn't as nice to me as he used to be," Kim continued. "Last night he was very rude to me and today he hardly spoke to me at all."

Leah paused in dressing. "What did you say just before he was rude to you?"

"I was talking about when we get married and I said I was looking forward to it and that I was glad I could wear white. I mean, with his first marriage, you couldn't—." She stopped at Leah's look. "I didn't mean anything about you, Leah. You can wear white when you marry Justin. No one in Kentucky will know the truth and I'm sure neither Wesley nor I will tell anyone."

Leah kept her back straight as she started back to the wagons. She completely forgot to ask what rude thing Wesley had replied to Kim's declarations of her virginity.

Chapter 12

Within the next few weeks they began to approach the new land of Kentucky. Instead of feeling excitement, Leah began to worry about how these new people would react to a divorced woman. When she was in Virginia, she'd wanted to leave behind a decent memory of at least one of the Simmonses. She didn't want people saying that a gentleman had married her but he'd had sense enough to get rid of her. The new land had seemed far away then.

But now she wished she'd gotten the divorce in Virginia. If she had, she could enter Kentucky as a free woman. Now she'd have to start her life here with an ugliness that would stain her as badly as her family had in Virginia.

As she rode beside Justin, she was silent. He still wanted to marry her even though he knew about her family. But would any man want her after they knew she'd been married and miscarried a child? Kim knew how important her virginity was and she hung onto it at all costs.

Regan and Nicole had said Leah was a lady, but Leah couldn't believe them. Kim was a lady. Everyone was polite to her. The man who loved her waited on her hand and foot. He treated her with respect, and even after this long trip she still retained her virginity. But with Leah, men were always lusting after her. Kim was right: no lady would roll in the mud with a man. Or throw herself at him and end up pregnant.

"What are you thinking, Leah?" Justin asked from beside her.

"Not thoughts one can share," she answered.

"I'd hoped you were thinking about your answer to my proposal."

"I was, in a way. There are some things you need to know about me."

"I'm not easily shocked. Leah, something is troubling you. Even if you don't return the love I have for you, I'm still your friend. You can tell me anything."

She was silent for a moment, wishing she could believe him. But if she told him now he'd never want to see or speak to her again. And she wanted these last few days of pretending that a handsome man wanted to marry her before he learned the truth and came to hate her.

"It isn't Wesley, is it?" he asked with some hostility in his voice.

She laughed at that. "Wesley Stanford is the last man on earth who might be interested in me. He's in love with Lady Kimberly and doesn't know anyone else exists."

"I wish I were as sure of that as you are."

Leah didn't answer him. She felt only her dread of

meeting new people and being branded as a brazen woman. She'd seen the way men in Virginia, who knew of her family, treated her. She wondered if she could bear it in Kentucky. Perhaps she should get the divorce from Wesley in his town of Sweetbriar, then leave there as soon as she was free. She just prayed that her reputation wouldn't follow her.

That night in camp everyone seemed to be subdued. Wesley kept his eyes on his plate of food, and Kim's eyes were red and swollen. Justin watched Leah while she mechanically went about her chores.

"I'd think you'd all be glad to be near home," Sadie said with a sigh, "but I've been to more cheerful funerals."

The next day Wesley paid a young man to ride ahead to his farm in Sweetbriar and tell the people that they would be arriving soon. Leah wanted to cry in frustration. Soon he'd have to tell people of their marriage and start divorce proceedings. Leah wondered if Kim would invite her to the wedding so Leah could see Kim's pure, white, flawless gown.

The wagons rolled closer to the border of Kentucky each day and everyone's mood seemed to grow more glum. Once, Justin angrily accused Leah of not accepting his proposal because she wanted all the men in the state pursuing her. Leah put her face in her hands and began to cry. Justin didn't make any more accusations after that.

Twice, Leah heard Wesley tell Kim he was too busy to get her whatever she wanted. Kim retreated to the wagon to sleep. By the time they reached Kentucky she was sleeping twelve hours a night and taking a three-hour nap every afternoon.

And Wesley didn't speak to anyone. He did his

chores, but retreated into himself, seemingly unaware that anyone else was near him.

"That young man is considerin' somethin' powerful hard," Sadie said as she and Hank took their leave. "I'm hopin' he's decidin' which woman he wants."

Leah just looked at her. "You're too much of a romantic, Sadie. Wesley has been in love with Kim for years. He's probably trying to force himself to wait until the wedding." She couldn't add that it'd be a long time before their wedding because of the inconvenience of Leah and Wes's marriage.

Leah hugged all the family good-bye and she was very glad that they'd never know the truth about her. They'd never learn of how she'd flaunted herself at Wes and he'd discarded her.

It was a silent group that trudged ahead toward Sweetbriar, Kentucky.

On the fourth day after Sadie, Hank, and their children had left, two men came galloping toward them. One was Oliver Stark, Justin's nineteen-year-old brother who worked for Wesley. The other was John Hammond, a tall, handsome man in his thirties with prematurely gray hair.

"The farm's doin' just fine," Oliver said, grinning at Wesley and his brother. "It sure took you a long time gettin' here."

"I didn't expect to see you here, John," Wesley said, extending his hand.

"The man you sent ahead said you had two of the prettiest women he'd ever seen with you. It looks like he was right," he said, looking Leah and Kim over.

Kim looked down at the ground. As usual, her eyes were red from crying.

"I'd like to introduce the ladies," Wes said, but Kim put her hand on his arm, her eyes pleading.

"Let me speak to Leah, please," Kim half whispered.

Wesley's jaw flexed, but he nodded and looked back at the men and began to ask questions about his farm.

Puzzled, Leah followed Kim to the back of the wagon. Something was upsetting her greatly. "Are you all right, Kim?" she asked, concerned.

"Wesley is being beastly," she spat out. "Once he makes up his mind to something, nothing will change it."

Leah couldn't believe she was being asked to comfort the woman who was to marry her husband. "I would think you'd be glad of that. He decided to marry you and *nothing* will change his mind, not even his marriage to someone else."

Kim gave her a hard look. "Sometimes he changes his mind. It takes him awhile to decide to do it but when he does, nothing will make him change."

"What in the world are you talking about? Oh!" Leah gasped as she slipped and nearly fell. The wagons were stopped on a narrow road on the side of a steep hill. Below them ran a stream with no trees in between.

"Watch out!" Kim said. "You nearly fell!"

Leah smiled. "It's not steep enough to be a danger. Unless the wagon fell on top of me, I guess."

Kim didn't reply to this. "Leah," she said slowly. "I need my pink hat. It's in that little brown trunk on the far side of the wagon. I'd get it but you're so much more agile than I am. Would you get it for me? Please?"

When Leah hesitated, Kim persisted. "You'll get rid of me soon and you won't have to help me out anymore."

Sighing, Leah agreed. Kim had been so upset lately that Leah couldn't refuse her request. Besides, anything that would postpone their arrival into Kentucky was good for her. She climbed into the back of the wagon and began looking for Kim's trunk.

When Kim returned to the men at the front of the wagon she was frowning. They were deep in conversation, not even aware of Kim as she stood by the horses on the side away from the steep drop. With one glance upward to be sure the men were busy, she slowly removed her bonnet, pulled out a four-inch-long hatpin, and with great deliberation stuck it into the horse's rump.

"Hey!" John Hammond shouted.

Kim turned frightened eyes toward the man, knowing he'd seen what she'd done.

But no one reacted to John's shout because instantly the horse reared, frightened the other horses, and the wagon began tumbling down the side of the hill.

"Oh damn!" Wes cursed, watching the wagon. Then he stiffened. "Leah! Where's Leah?"

Kim's eyes were locked onto John Hammond's and she couldn't speak.

Wesley didn't bother to wait for an answer as he ran down the hill after the wagon, Justin on his heels. Oliver and John followed quickly. Kim stood where she was in the road, not moving.

When the wagon stopped, leaving a trail of goods behind it, the horses screaming in pain, Leah was nowhere to be found. Wesley was throwing trunks and bags of food everywhere while Oliver cut the horses loose.

"Where is she?" Wesley demanded while Justin scanned the hillside, looking for her body.

"Kim is up there," came a voice beside Wesley.

Wesley turned to see Leah standing calmly behind him.

"What happened? How badly are the horses hurt? How much can be saved?" Leah asked all at once as she started to help Oliver with the horses.

"Damn you!" Wesley hissed, then the next second he caught her in his arms and kissed her so hard he hurt her.

"Wesley!" She gasped, pushing at him. "People are watching." She looked at Justin, who was scowling furiously, and John, who was watching them with great interest.

Wesley set her down and, for the first time in weeks, his face showed happiness. "Gentlemen, allow me to introduce my wife, Leah Stanford."

Only John saw Kim faint, and he was quickly up the hill after her.

Leah's knees gave way and Wes swept her off the ground. "Don't you have anything to say, honey?" Wes asked her.

Chapter 13

It took hours to clean up the mess of the wagon. One horse had to be destroyed and the other three were badly scraped and cut, but they'd heal in time. Some sacks of seed had burst open and most of the contents were lost, but few other goods were really hurt.

At the top of the hill, Kimberly was crying loudly while John Hammond tried his best to comfort her. Justin was very angry and threw goods about with force, never once looking at Leah or Wes. Oliver kept looking from one person to another while Leah, with shaking hands, tried to help sort the misplaced wagon contents.

But Wesley acted as if nothing at all was unusual. He was smiling, even humming at times, and telling everyone what to do.

"Leah, honey," Wes said, "hand me that little hatbox."

Obediently Leah picked it up, but as she looked at

him smiling at her she threw it at his face, turned, and ran toward the stream, tears in her eyes.

Wesley caught up with her, took her shoulders and turned her to face him. "What's wrong, honey? I thought you'd be happy when I told everyone the truth about us. It's what you wanted, isn't it?"

She moved away from him and tried to calm herself. "I knew it had to happen sometime, but when I heard you say it . . . You ought to tell your friends about the divorce and for heaven's sake, stop calling me 'honey.' "

"Divorce?" He looked puzzled. "Oh no, you don't understand. I've decided we should *stay* married. There won't be any divorce."

"I think I'll sit down," Leah said quietly before she almost collapsed onto the damp ground. "Could you explain all this to me?"

He grinned down at her confidently. "It's just that I've come to like you, Leah. I was pretty mad at first. Well, all right, more than a little mad and maybe I didn't give you much of a chance, but you'd ruined all my plans and all I could think of was losing Kim."

He hunkered down in front of her. "But on this trip I've come to know you. I thought I wanted a woman like Kim who needed me, but Kim needs a maid more than she needs a man. And besides, you need me, too. You're always trying to take on too much, always trying to do everything for everyone else."

"So you decided I needed you, too," Leah said softly.

"Yes. And besides, you're more fun than Kim. It took me a long time to make the decision but I decided we'll stay married. It just makes sense anyway and it'll cause a lot less trouble."

"And Kim?" Leah asked.

Wes looked down at his feet. "I used to think I loved her but I'm not sure I ever did. I'm not sure I've ever loved any woman. And I think Kim may be more interested in my money than in me," he said, his jaw clenched. "I've worked things out with her. She'll receive a handsome sum from me every month until she marries. She's pretty so I'm sure she'll have no trouble finding a husband."

He was quiet for a moment. "Aren't you going to say anything? I thought you wanted to marry me. That's why you seduced me that first time, isn't it?"

Leah stood and walked away from him. "I want to make sure I've heard you correctly. You don't love me and you've never loved Kim, but between the two of us you've chosen me because it's easier than a divorce and remarriage, and besides, I'm more fun and I need you to protect me from myself. Is that about it?"

He frowned up at her. "I guess so, but you make it sound awfully cold. I think we'll make a good team, Leah. Between the two of us we'll build a place bigger than my brother's and I know you're fertile so we'll have lots of children."

"And would you like to check my teeth also?"

He stood. "I think you're getting mad. Here I am giving you what you wanted and you're getting mad. Do you expect me to go down on one knee and declare undying love for you? I'm not sure I know what love is. I thought I loved Kim but now all I know is I've had enough of her tears and helplessness and I want something different."

She was breathing deeply to try to calm her fury. "And what happens to me when you decide you want more than just fun and my needing you? Will you go back to Kim or perhaps choose another woman?"

"Are you accusing me of . . . of being fickle?" he said.

She smiled at him. "As much as any woman trying to choose the right color of dress."

He took a step toward her and Leah backed away. "I don't want to stay married to you," she said. "I don't want your big farm and I especially don't want your children. You may have decided you like me but I do *not* like you. I will not build my future with a man who may run out on me at any moment. I don't want a husband who bases everything on a fun wallow in the mud. What if you and some other woman fall in a river? No! I cannot live with someone as fickle as you. Now I'm going to announce to everyone our intention to obtain a divorce." She turned on her heel, but Wes clamped a hand down on her shoulder.

"You will *not* make any such announcement," he said under his breath. "I've made my decision and I didn't do it lightly. I thought about this for a long time."

"And I don't make my decision lightly. I've known about our divorce always and I've come to accept it. We'll do the procedure in your town of Sweetbriar and after it's over I'll leave, maybe even leave Kentucky altogether."

His hand tightened on her shoulder. "You'd rather go through that than stay married to me?" he asked, astonished.

"I don't really have much choice. Maybe I can get away from my reputation as a loose woman but I'd never be able to live with a man who was so . . . so dishonest and changeable. I'd spend my whole life wondering from day to day if the kids and I would have a man to provide for us."

Wesley looked shocked. "No one," he said, "no one, man or woman, has ever hinted that I might not be trustworthy. I've never taken my responsibilities lightly."

"Tell that to Kim," she said, turning away again.

"Damn you!" he half yelled, grabbing both her shoulders and making her face him. "If you were a man I'd call you out for what you've said to me. But for you . . . you *will* remain married to me. You understand that? And furthermore, tomorrow we're going on a hunting trip, just the two of us, and we're going to act married. We're going to travel together, eat together—and sleep together."

She tried to twist away from him. "Get your hands off of me!"

"I'm going to put my hands all over that pretty little body of yours and you can damn well get used to it. You're my wife and you're going to start acting like a wife."

"I hate you," she said, seething.

"I don't bear you any great love at the moment either."

"I will *not* submit to you. I will *never* be your wife."

He dropped his hands from her shoulders and his eyes were steely hard. "I don't believe you have any choice in the matter. As my wife you're my property. Tomorrow morning at dawn you'll leave with me even if I have to tie you to the saddle. Is that clear, you stubborn little cat?"

"I'll do what you say because you have the legal right and the muscle to force me, but I'll fight you every step of the way. What you get from me you'll have to take and I guarantee you'll find no pleasure in the taking. Is *that* clear, you stubborn oaf?"

He tipped his head back and gave her a nasty little

smile. "You'll give to me, Leah," he said seductively. "By the time we leave the forest you'll be begging for me to touch you."

She returned his smile. "You think more highly of yourself than anyone else does. I don't beg."

He narrowed his eyes at her. "Let's put it this way: We'll stay in the cold, wet, scary forest until you *do* slip into my arms—and my bed—with a smile on your lips and an eager, warm, little body. So if you ever want to see a house or a soft bed again you'll give in to me."

She looked up at him in astonishment. "Do you forget how I grew up? Only recently have I even seen the comforts you've known all your life. I can hold out much longer than you can."

Wesley took her chin in his hand, forced her to keep facing him, then slowly he brought his mouth down on hers and kissed her sweetly. His lips were warm and moist and in spite of herself Leah leaned into him. He pulled away abruptly. "Can you hold out against me, Leah? Can you resist me while camped on some lonely mountainside when the cats howl and the bears come close to the fire? Just remember that I'll always welcome you to my bed."

She met his eyes with hostility, but his hand on her face felt good. She jerked away.

"Go and get ready for tomorrow's journey, wife," he commanded as he turned and left her.

"Of all the most ridiculous . . ." Leah muttered when she was alone. Virginal Kim wouldn't give him what he wanted, but he was sure a Simmons would. Maybe he'd begun to realize that Kim was never going to be a great bed partner, and since his upbringing as a gentleman wouldn't allow him to divorce merely because he wanted to try other women, he had decided to stay with Leah. She was a swamp rat and there was no need to treat her with any respect, no need to consider what she wanted as he would have with a lady like Kim.

"Men!" she said aloud. Wesley thought he could change women as he did clothes. Well, this woman was going to change his mind. He thought she'd seduced him the first time so he'd have to marry her. Even after all she'd told him, he still believed that. But maybe that was better than his knowing the real reason she'd walked into his arms. How could she have ever thought she loved him?

She straightened her shoulders because now she faced the ordeal of confronting the others. Both Justin and Kim were going to be very angry with her.

Slowly, reluctantly, she walked back toward the wagons.

The first sight that greeted her was Justin's fist plowing into Wesley's jaw. Quickly John Hammond and Oliver grabbed Wesley's arms.

"You could have told me from the beginning," Justin said loudly. "And putting Leah through hell! She doesn't deserve that. She was your wife, but she had to watch you paw Kimberly for months."

Pausing just below them on the hillside, Leah smiled to herself. It was good to hear someone defend her.

"Leah," Justin shouted, as he ran down the hill toward her. He held her at arms' length and looked into her eyes. "It's true, isn't it?" he whispered. "This is what's been hanging over your head all this time, isn't it? You could have told me."

As he started to pull her into his arms, Wesley's hand clamped on his shoulder. "That's my wife you're handling, Stark, and if you want to keep your face on that side of your head, you'll release her."

Leah stepped between the men before another battle started. "Justin," she said loudly, "legally, he is my husband and he has the right to change his mind as often as he pleases. Today he wants me, tomorrow I may be free again."

"Leah," Wes warned.

"I'm sorry, Justin. I wish I'd had enough courage to tell you before this happened. But I was afraid . . ." She looked down at the ground, unable to continue.

"I understand, Leah," Justin said. "It's him I blame for this. You don't deserve a woman like her, Stanford."

Wesley put his hand possessively on Leah's shoulder. "Deserve her or not, she's mine and I plan to keep her."

Chapter 14

Leah trudged along behind Wesley through the silent, roaringly loud forest. Her eyes kept darting this way and that, trying to see behind trees and bushes. A sound in the distance made her jump. Ahead of her, Wesley didn't even turn at Leah's sound.

In the morning he'd turned every time she'd given a little squeal of fright, then smiled smugly and turned back around. Leah swore she'd be quiet from now on, but she broke her vow constantly. Never had she been so far away from people. She'd grown up surrounded by brothers and sisters and the only time she'd left was to live at Wesley's plantation, where there'd been even more people near her. On the trip toward Kentucky, they'd never been out of sight and sound of many people.

Now for the first time in her life she was alone—or at least very close to it. The way she felt now, Wesley didn't count as a human being. Very early that morning they'd loaded goods into packs.

"Which horses do you plan to take?" John Hammond asked.

"We're going where a horse can't go," Wesley answered, slinging the pack on his back.

Refusing to comment or even look at Wesley, she put on her much smaller pack. She was swearing to herself that she'd show no fear.

Kimberly stayed close to John and it was unusual to see her up so early in the morning. Usually she stayed in bed until breakfast was cooked. Leah wasn't sure if Kim wanted to be near John or if he was insisting she stay there. But Leah was too caught up in her own problems to worry about Kim.

"Ready, Mrs. Stanford?" Wes asked.

Leah wouldn't look at him, but when he started walking, she was behind him.

Now they'd been walking for hours. Leah was tired, and long ago they'd left all sights and sounds of other people. Only she and the buckskin-clad man in front of her seemed to be left on the earth.

"Can you climb up there?" Wes asked, stopping and pointing.

Leah looked up at the steep climb to what seemed to be a cave opening. Curtly she nodded, but she wouldn't look at Wes.

"Give me your pack."

"I can carry it," she said, starting forward.

Wesley caught her pack and half pulled it from her back. "I told you to give me your pack and that's what I meant. You give me any more trouble and I'll throw you over my shoulder and carry you."

Still without looking at him, she slipped out of the pack and handed it to him. It wasn't an easy climb, especially in her long skirt, but every time she had difficulty, Wes was there with a hand freeing her skirt edge, steadying her at her waist, and once giving her a boost on her seat.

When she reached the top, she didn't thank him but stood on the ledge, flattened against the stone wall and peering into the blackness that was the cave. "Do you think there are any bears in there?" she whispered.

"Maybe," Wes answered unconcerned as he put their packs on the ground. "I'll have a look."

"Be . . . be careful," she murmured.

"Worried about me, are you?"

She met his eyes. "I don't want to be left here alone."

"I guess I deserved that," he half grunted, removing a heavy knife from the sheath at his side and a candle from his pack.

"Shouldn't you take the rifle?" she asked, aghast.

"Rifles are useless in close combat. How about a kiss before I enter?"

"I'm to reward you for putting us in the middle of nowhere in front of a bear's den? Maybe there's a whole family of bears in there and we'll both die."

His eyes twinkled. "If I could but die with your kiss on my lips . . ."

"Go on! Get it over with."

Wesley's face turned serious as he disappeared into the cave. "It's bigger than I thought," he said, his voice sounding hollow. "There're some Indian paintings on the walls and some signs of camp fires."

She could hear him moving in the cave and when he spoke again his voice sounded farther away.

"Doesn't look like there are any signs of bears. A few bones. Looks like lots of people have camped here."

For a few minutes he said nothing else and Leah

began to relax from her rigid stance and took a step closer to the cave opening. She could hear Wesley walking about and now and then see the flicker of his candle flame.

"Is it safe?" she called.

"Sure," he yelled back. "Clean as a whistle."

In the next few seconds everything happened at once.

Wesley said, "Uh oh," then bellowed, "run, Leah! Hide!"

Instantly, Leah froze right where she was, smack in the middle of the wide cave opening.

In a lightning flash of buckskin fringe, Wesley came tearing out of the cave, and inches behind him was a big old black bear, its fat rippling as it lumbered after Wesley.

The bear brushed past Leah so closely that her nostrils flared at the smell of it. But she could no more move than the rock behind her could.

The bear didn't seem to notice her at all in its pursuit of Wes.

Only her eyes able to move, Leah watched Wes tear down the hillside.

"Climb a tree, Leah," he yelled back at her.

Tree, Leah thought. What is a tree? What does it look like?

She was still wondering this when she heard a loud splash to her left.

"Move, Leah," she commanded herself. But nothing happened. "Move!"

When she did move, it was quickly. She ignored Wes's order to climb a tree and took off, running toward the sound of the splash. She stopped, chest heaving, by a little pool of water that was surrounded by rock. Everything was perfectly quiet. There was no sign of Wesley or the bear. Just the birds singing, the late afternoon sunshine, the smell of grasses.

The next thing she knew her ankle had been grabbed and she was being dragged downward. Instinctively she began to struggle.

"Stop kicking!" Wes's voice hissed—his voice alone, because Leah still saw no one.

When she paused in her struggles, Wes jerked her into the water.

"What—?" She gasped just as Wes put his hand on the top of her head and pushed her underwater.

Her breath held, furious, she saw him submerge and she glared at him through the clear water.

He pointed and she looked. There above them, sniffing the air, was the bear. Wes motioned for her to follow him underwater and she did.

He swam to the opposite side of the little pool and stuck his head up behind some hanging greenery. Leah came up struggling for breath and instantly Wes put his fingers to her lips.

With a sideways glance Leah saw the bear in the same place and she moved away from the animal, which happened to be nearer Wesley. His arms opened and he pulled her to him, her back against his front. She couldn't struggle because the sound might carry to the bear.

Wesley caught her earlobe between his teeth and began to nibble on it.

She tried to move away.

He released her ear and nodded meaningfully toward the bear.

She tried to tell him with her eyes that she almost preferred the bear's mauling, but Wes's grip wouldn't let her move.

He began to nuzzle her neck, his kisses trailing upward to her hairline.

The water was warm, heated all day by the sun, and it was relaxing Leah's tired muscles. As Wes continued to explore her neck and the side of her face, Leah leaned back into him, turning her head to give him freer access.

"The bear's gone," he murmured.

"Mmm?" Leah said, her eyes closed.

Wesley ran his teeth down the sensitive cord in her neck and Leah turned a bit in his arms. Her body felt as soft and liquid as the water surrounding her.

"The bear's gone," Wes repeated as the tip of his tongue touched her earlobe. "Shall we finish this on land? Of course maybe we could continue in the water. I'm certainly willing."

She whirled about, treading water. "How dare you—."

"How dare I!" He laughed. "Why do you keep lying to yourself, Leah? All I have to do is touch you and you're mine. Don't leave. Let's stay in the water. I've never—."

Leah, who was trying her best to make a dignified exit to the shore, turned to face him, her eyes flashing fire. "If you are planning to inform me of your previous conquests, please restrain yourself. I have *no* interest in what you have or have not done. And for your information, I react to *all* men who touch me just as I react to you. It's something all of us Simmons women are born with. I thought you knew that. After all, isn't your interest in me due to my whorelike nature?"

"Damn you, Leah!" Wes seethed, moving near her. "Why do you keep saying those things about yourself? I saw you with Justin. I'll wager he never touched you."

"Then you'd lose your money." Grabbing her skirt

she left the pool to stand on the bank, wringing out the wetness.

Wesley stood beside her, his big body outlined by his wet buckskins. "You'll give me what I want, Leah."

When she didn't look at him, he moved away. "We'll camp over there," he said, nodding.

As soon as Wesley was gone, Leah's shoulders drooped. With her wet skirt dragging behind her, she sat on a rock. She couldn't give in to him. She could not allow herself to do that. How many times had she already lost him? They'd made love and he'd tossed a coin at her and walked away. They'd been married and he'd left her alone, bruised and pregnant. And when he'd returned from Kentucky he'd refused to look at her, he'd said he wanted Kimberly and had again rejected Leah.

Three times, Leah thought. He'd left her three times and now she was supposed to trust him? Did he find pleasure in toying with her, watching her fall for him, then leaving her? Did he need that to make him feel like a man? To him it meant nothing more than a night's pleasure, but Wesley was something special to Leah. She'd loved him so deeply for so many years. When her father had beaten her she'd lain in pain and thought how someday Wesley Stanford would come to save her. When she'd lost their baby she'd cried, but she'd known there'd be other children—Wesley's children. But now that she knew what he was like she feared that he'd discard her as soon as she was pregnant. After all, her usefulness would be past.

And what about when they left the forest to go to Wesley's town of Sweetbriar? Wesley was willing to admit to a few close friends that Leah was his wife, but what if he wasn't willing to announce the fact before a whole town? No, a Simmons must be hidden in the woods, kept secret, not allowed into polite society.

Of course Wesley was a man and, as he pointed out every few minutes, Leah was a lusty woman. So he'd take her to the woods, play a nasty little game with her where she had the choice of his bed or months in the forest, and when she gave in to him, then what? Why of course, he'd return to his clean little farm and all he had to do was announce that she'd tricked him into marriage and that she was a loose woman and any judge in the land would grant a decree of divorce. Wes would be free and Leah would be . . .

Leah stood, taking a deep breath. Leah would once again be left with a broken heart. And there were just so many times a woman's heart could be torn apart and still heal. If she fell for Wesley again and he left her, she wondered if she'd be able to pull herself together for the fourth time. For her own sake, she had to resist him. She couldn't let him discard her again.

Through the trees she saw the flicker of firelight and knew Wesley had set up camp. With a shiver she started toward the fire.

"Coffee?" Wes asked, extending a steaming mug to her.

She shook her head and reached for the skillet Wes held.

"No." He pulled back. "You rest. I'll cook supper."

"Don't be ridiculous," she snapped. "Men can't cook."

"They can't? Well, my pretty little wife, you just sit there and I'll prove you wrong."

Leah sat, her eyes on her hands.

Wesley was frying bacon, moving it about in the

skillet and watching her. "Did I ever tell you about Paris?"

"Paris?" She looked up. "I've never heard of Paris, Virginia."

Wesley smiled at her. That wet dress of hers clung to her, but he knew that when it was dry it'd be loose and concealing. With a grin he remembered the low-cut dress she'd worn that night at the inn. She'd look good in Paris, wearing a pretty bonnet that set off her dark hair.

"Paris is across the ocean in a country called France."

"I'm sorry I haven't had the benefit of your education. My father didn't see the need to send his slave-children to school."

He ignored her. "One night about five of us had dinner in a private room." He stopped. "Perhaps I shouldn't tell you that story." He looked up at her. "Maybe you'd like to hear how my brother Travis courted Regan."

"Oh yes," Leah said. She'd love to hear about her friend.

"Well then, go and put on some dry clothes and while we eat I'll tell you the story."

Later they ate beans, bacon, biscuits, and coffee while Wes told, with much exaggeration, Leah was sure, an outrageous story of what Travis had done to win the return of his wife. There'd been hundreds of roses involved, an uncountable number of proposals on paper, and at last a circus in which, according to Travis, he had risked his life and had been the star of the show.

"*How* many roses?" Leah asked.

"Travis said thousands, but Regan always rolls her eyes, so who knows?"

"I've never seen an elephant."

"Travis brought back a wagon load of manure, said it'd make the tobacco plants grow twice as tall."

"Did it?" Leah asked, her eyes wide.

"Didn't do anything different that I could tell. Now that you've had your bedtime story, it's time for bed."

Leah braced herself and the flicker in Wes's eyes showed her that he saw her movement.

"I've made your bed over there," he said coolly. "I'm on the other side. If you get frightened, let me know. I'm a light sleeper." With that he tossed out the dregs of his coffee and went to his own pile of blankets.

Quietly Leah went to her own bed, grateful that he wasn't going to try to entice her to his bed.

For a long time Wesley lay awake, looking up at the stars.

He hated the way she jumped whenever he came near her. And her reaction was puzzling to him. She'd wanted to marry him. According to Travis she'd first gone to bed with him because she thought she loved him. So now she had him, he'd decided to stay with her, and she acted as if he were a disease she might catch. He didn't understand it at all.

Of course maybe he had been a little hard on her at first. It was just that he'd been so damned mad because he'd lost Kim, and Leah seemed to be one of those women he'd always detested, the kind of woman who needed no one and nothing. But as they'd traveled together he'd come to see that Leah needed a great deal. She needed someone to protect her from everyone who took advantage of her. Kim made Leah wait on her. Justin expected Leah to fall for him. And even Wesley had started relying on her. It was so easy to give a task to Leah because the word *no* wasn't in her vocabulary. She seemed to think she was the world's slave.

At first Wes had spoken to Kim about how much work she piled on Leah. Kim had been bewildered. She said Leah *wanted* to do all the work. Wes realized right away it was no use trying to talk to Kim. In fact, he began to realize he couldn't talk to Kim about anything. In the evenings he'd sit with Kim and want to tell her something about himself and he'd see her eyes dart around and more than once she'd jump up in the middle of a sentence. At those times, Wesley's eyes would dart to where Leah was leaning forward, listening intently to every word Justin was saying. And Wesley would think, she's *my* wife!

Wes wasn't sure when he began to be bored by Kim. Perhaps it was the time she screamed so loudly that everyone came running, thinking she'd been bitten by a snake. A honeybee had stung the back of her hand. Very calmly Leah had put baking soda on the sting and Wesley had led a shaking, crying Kim away to the wagon where she'd immediately gone to bed. Later Wesley had seen Leah trying to put something on the back of her own neck. It'd taken awhile to get her to show him what she was doing, but she'd leaned against some wild honeysuckle and had three bee stings on her neck.

"And you didn't say anything?" Wesley asked.

"They're only bee stings," she said, shrugging.

She wouldn't let him help her with the baking soda paste and so he left her, but after that he was much more aware of her.

And he began to ask himself questions.

Life on a farm was never easy, and contrary to what many people thought, he didn't have a great deal of cash. Half of Stanford Plantation was his, but the wealth of it was tied up in land. Only if it were sold would Wes get his money. Travis had agreed to pay Wes what he could, and whatever complaints he had about his brother, Wes never doubted Travis's honesty. So if Wes wasn't rich, couldn't afford an army of servants, what was he going to do with a wife who went hysterical at the sting of a little honeybee? Would Wes have to plow all day, then come home and take care of the house too? Would he have to bring Kim breakfast in bed each morning?

At one time, actually while he was living under the domineering rule of his brother, he looked forward to someone leaning on him. Kim didn't lean, she lay down most of the time.

And when he kissed her! Kim would say, "You may have two kisses tonight, Wesley." She'd purse her lips tightly and go *smack, smack,* then give a coy little laugh, as if she'd done something improper and highly suggestive, and move away from him.

For a while those prim little kisses and that suggestive little laugh had enticed him. He'd believed what she wanted him to believe—that when she let herself go she was going to be uncontrollably passionate. But somewhere along the way he'd stopped believing her. He began to imagine that even after they were married she'd still be saying, "You may have two kisses tonight, Wesley." Or maybe as her husband he would be allowed three.

Once, he'd tried to force her to some passion, but she'd pulled away from him, frightened, and when she recovered herself she chastised him as if he were a little boy she planned to spank.

He didn't try again after that—and he stopped taking his nightly dose of kisses, if they could be called that.

And the more he pulled away from Kim, the more aware he became of Leah. He became aware of her quiet efficiency, how she handled what could have become crises. And her generosity was unbelievable. Nothing was too much for her to do. She asked little of anyone but gave very much.

The longer they traveled together, the more Wes grew to like her. He wasn't sure exactly when he made his decision to keep her—perhaps it was a gradual one—but he knew he'd rather marry Leah than adopt Kim.

He'd wanted to tell Leah right away but somehow he sensed she might be a little reluctant to embrace him with open arms. He couldn't figure out why she might be, because he was, after all, giving her what she wanted, but who could understand women's minds?

So he'd thought about it a long time and decided he needed to get her into a situation where she had to depend on him—if there was such a situation. Leah was so infuriatingly competent that he wondered if he could make her need him.

Then when they'd had the mud wrestle—he smiled at the memory—he'd found out about her fear of the lonely forest. And so of course that was where he arranged to take her.

And just as he'd predicted, basing his guess on the odd workings of women's minds, Leah had turned stubborn when he'd told her she could stay with him. Give women what they wanted and damned if they didn't decide they wanted something else!

Now here they were, all alone, and Leah acted as if she couldn't stand him. If he lived a hundred years he'd never understand women.

But she'd come around. If need be they'd spend months alone in this forest; he planned to court her, woo her, win her. Maybe he could even get her pregnant again. Now that wasn't a bad idea at all. If she were swelled up with his child, surely she'd give him less trouble. They'd get back to Sweetbriar and his farm and there'd already be a child on the way.

Oh Leah, he thought, looking across the dying fire toward her, no woman could ever resist a Stanford man when he set his mind to winning her.

With that decision made, he turned on his side and went to sleep.

Chapter 15

Leah woke with a sense of dread. The forest was still and by the look of the moon it wasn't very late—but something was deeply wrong. Quickly she turned her head to look at Wesley. His eyes were open and there was warning in them. She obeyed his silent command and lay still while she watched him inch his rifle a little closer to his body.

"No need for that, mister," came a voice from behind Leah that made her go rigid. She'd never thought to hear that voice again; she had prayed never to hear it again.

"We're just travelers like you and the lady," the voice continued.

Leah lay still as out of the darkness came a tall, skinny body. In the moonlight she could see a bearded face.

Slowly, making every move count, Wesley sat up, the rifle never out of his hands. "Who's with you?" Wes asked in such a sleepy voice that Leah looked sharply at him, then noticed the alert look in his eyes.

"Jus' me and one of the boys. Mind if I have some of your coffee?"

The thin man didn't wait for an answer but knelt by the lukewarm pot. He didn't bother looking in Leah's direction.

He wouldn't, Leah thought with anger. Her brother Abe had never had much use for women unless there was ransom money involved. Years ago, after Abe had kidnapped Nicole Armstrong, he'd disappeared off the face of the earth, and none of the Simmonses had heard from him again. Now he was a great deal thinner, years older, but Leah had no doubt he was her brother, probably up to no good, and Wesley was right in staying near his weapon. But perhaps if Leah let her brother know who she was he'd leave them alone.

"I'll get you a cup," she said loudly, eyes on Abe's narrow back in its worn black coat. She wasn't sure, but she believed he tightened at the sound of her voice.

Moving quickly, she threw a handful of branches on the dying fire and urged it into a light-giving blaze. With slow deliberation, she poured him a cup of coffee and handed it to him across the flames.

He looked at her for only an instant and Leah wasn't sure he recognized her. After all, when Abe left she'd been only fourteen, and since then she'd grown into a woman and her manners and speech had changed greatly. But Abe's face hadn't changed much. It was still narrow, with close-set black eyes and a big nose that looked like some bird ready to attack from its perch on top of a dirty, scraggly beard.

"I'd like to see your friend," Wes said.

Abe turned to Wes, again ignoring Leah. "He's just a

boy, no harm in him, but if you want to see him . . . Bud, come on out here."

Leah was pouring another cup of coffee and nearly dropped it at the sight of the man stepping from the shadows. Or perhaps he *was* the shadows because he was by far the biggest man she'd ever seen. Both Wesley and Travis were big, powerfully built men, but this young man nearly dwarfed them. He was at least six feet eight inches, maybe taller, well over two hundred pounds. He wore baggy, coarse linen trousers tucked into tall black boots molded over giant calves. His upper body was bare except for a sheepskin slung over one shoulder, and his arms could only be described as massive. They more resembled sculptured tree trunks than arms. The man, truthfully not more than a boy, had a handsome, unsmiling face set on a neck that looked to be about the size of Leah's waist.

"Jus' one of the boys," Abe repeated, a chuckle in his voice.

"Coffee?" Leah managed to ask, her neck craning to look up at the big man.

"Bud likes to keep his hands free," Abe said, not allowing the *boy* to answer. "You folks just passin' through?"

"Hunting," Wes answered, still not moving from where he'd slept and not turning his back on the giant near him.

Abe creakily lifted his spindly little body, tossing the dregs of coffee on the ground. "We got to be goin' now. Thank you kindly, missus." He handed the empty cup to Leah and it was then she was sure he recognized her. His close little eyes bored into hers and swept down her dress, which was far better than anything he'd ever seen her wear before. "Come on, Bud," Abe said and started into the darkness, the silent giant moving noiselessly behind him.

Leah's head spun with thoughts, the first of which was that she was sure Abe was up to no good. Of course he'd never done anything honest in his life as far as Leah knew, so she wasn't surprised by this thought.

"What do you think they wanted?" Wes asked, watching her.

Leah jumped guiltily at the sound of his voice. She couldn't very well tell someone of Wes's class that the nasty creature was her brother and had probably meant to knock them over the head and rob them. Maybe he'd refrained because he had some family feeling. More likely he'd not harmed them because they were awake. Abe was a backstabber.

"I guess they were just traveling, like us," she said, then stretched exaggeratedly. "I certainly am tired. I'll be asleep again in minutes."

With great show, Leah rearranged her pallet, smiled merrily at Wes, yawned, and looked for all the world as if she went right to sleep.

Never in her life had she been more awake. Somewhere near them in the forest was her sly, devious, cowardly, thieving, treacherous older brother—and she knew he'd want payment from her for not causing them misery.

Every pore of her body seemed to be listening. She held her breath as Wesley, seeming to believe her words, settled down to sleep.

An hour went by and Leah's body began to ache. When was Abe going to make his move? She planned how she'd roll toward Wes and grab the rifle.

Another hour passed. She began to wonder if she really could shoot her own brother.

A noise from Wesley startled her, but it was only a soft snore followed by his turning over.

When Abe's signal came, a high-pitched whistle, Leah was past ready. Slowly, making no noise, she pushed herself out of the blankets and left the campsite. She didn't allow herself to consider the forest at night or remember that great, enormous man who trailed her brother, but she made her way over fallen logs, past frightening shadows toward the whistle that would repeat itself when she lost her way.

She traveled at least a mile before Abe oozed himself from behind a willow tree.

Leah jumped back, her hand to her throat.

"Scare you, baby sister?"

"Only as any other criminal would."

Abe looked almost hurt. "I thought maybe you'd be glad to see me I sure was glad to see you."

"Where's that creature of yours?"

Abe merely nodded upward to a space above her head.

Leah glanced to the side to see the shadow of a huge arm. Again she gasped as she turned to see the young man not ten inches from her. She moved away from the towering mass of him while he remained impassive.

Abe took her upper arm. "Don't mind Bud," he said, pulling her away. "He ain't too, you know." He tapped his head with his finger.

"I don't guess he has to be," Leah snapped as she jerked out of Abe's grasp. "When did you last have a bath?" She wrinkled her nose.

"Ain't you the fancy one! Last time I seen you you was dirtier 'n I ever been. I guess that was before you took up with the likes of the Stanfords."

Leah drew herself up rigidly. "I happen to be Mrs. Wesley Stanford."

"You!" Abe gasped, stepping away from her. "You, a Simmons, *married* to a Stanford?" He began to smile. "Hear that, Bud? My very own little sister thinks someone like a Stanford *married* her."

Bud gave no indication he heard Abe.

"I never knowed you was such a liar." Abe began to laugh. "All the Simmons women are whores but they're usually honest whores. Even Ma—Hey!"

He didn't finish his sentence because Leah administered a ringing slap to his laughing face.

"You little—," he began. "You want me to set Bud on you? He can tear bits like you apart with one hand. Bud!"

Bud didn't move and neither did Leah as she stared straight up at him, hoping he wouldn't see her trembling. Bud looked at her for a moment, then lifted his eyes to look into the forest's darkness.

"Well," Abe said, "maybe Bud's not in the mood tonight."

Leah released her pent-up breath. "Maybe he has a mother too and believes people *should* be slapped for saying bad things about their mothers."

"Hell, Bud and Cal ain't got mothers. Somebody carved 'em out of a mountain. Look, Leah, forget the pea brains. I got some business to talk to you about "

"Who is Cal?"

"I told you to forget 'em! Now listen, I didn't mean none of them things about you bein' a whore. I mean, even if you are it don't matter to me because all I want is your . . . your brain," he said brightly. "You allus was the smartest one in the family. Ma used to say it was too bad you was born a Simmons. You followin' me?"

"Only too well. I'm beginning to realize you want something from me."

"See?" He grinned. One of his incisors was rotting away. "I knew you was smart. And look at you too. Pretty as a lady and you talk all refined."

"You don't need to waste your flattery. What do you want from me?"

"I want you to join us."

"Us? Join you?" she asked in dread.

"You don't have to act like you're better 'n me. I got somethin' good goin' for me. I'm gonna *be* somebody."

Leah stood still and waited for him to continue. It wouldn't do to antagonize him further, especially not with the hulking man hovering over them.

"I want you to join Revis and me and the boys. We got a little deal goin' whereas we help ourselves to the people travelin' over the Wilderness Trail. I reckon you been travelin' with 'em and you know their ways better 'n us and since you're so smart you can plan things for us."

"Plan?" Leah whispered, beginning to understand. She'd heard, of course, of a gang of robbers preying on the westward travelers, but they'd never molested the Stanford party. "*You* are one of the robbers? Thievery is how you're planning to make something of yourself?"

"I ain't always plannin' to steal," Abe said righteously. "I'm puttin' the money away to buy me a little store—or I will put it away as soon as I pay off a few debts."

"Gambling, no doubt," she said. "And you think *I* would even consider becoming a part of your hideous den of thieves?"

"Don't you go callin' me names, you little whore. Ma and Pa know you're hidin' out with a Stanford?"

"For your information, both Ma and Pa are dead,

and I told you before that I am married to Wesley Stanford."

"Oh, yeah, and Bud here flies. Hey! How come if you're married to Stanford you two was sleepin' apart?"

Leah looked at her shoe. "It's a long story," she mumbled.

"Only one way a Stanford'd marry a Simmons. He got you pregnant, didn't he? And only them Stanfords would think they'd have to marry a slut—" He broke off. "Look Leah, married or not, the man don't want you. Anybody with any sense—even Bud here—would be able to see that. Why's he keepin' you in a woods, hidin' away with you?"

Abe's words were too close to how Leah actually felt. "I have to go. It'll be daylight soon," she whispered. "Wesley will miss me."

"He ain't gonna miss you. He'll be glad to get rid of a Simmons whether she's his wife or not. Come on with me now, Leah. Join us. We'll make you rich."

"Rich!" She spat. "Rich from stealing other people's goods? Those people on that trail have *worked* all their lives for what they have and you think I'm going to help you take it away from them? You make me ill! Worse than ill! I wonder if scum like you has a right to live!"

"Why you—," he said, before lunging at her.

But one silent step forward from Bud made Abe stop.

Leah blinked her eyes in astonishment and, with her heart pounding from anger and fear, she dared greatly and put her hand on Bud's bare forearm. "Bud," she said through a closed throat, "will you lead me back to my husband? I don't know the way."

Without a sound Bud slipped away into the trees.

"Don't try to bother me again or Wesley'll make you sorry," Leah said to Abe before following the shadow of Bud.

She slipped into her sleeping pad seemingly only minutes before Wesley woke. She did her best to conceal her nervousness from him, but every sound made her jump. Wesley mentioned her dislike for the forest and told her she had nothing to be afraid of.

"Men are the real danger," he said, eyeing her. "Take those two last night."

"What about them?" she asked nervously, then calmed herself. "They weren't dangerous, were they?"

"Maybe you should answer that."

"Me? Why me? How could I know anything about them?"

He was silent for a moment. "I just thought women were supposed to know these things, that's all. Women sometimes say they sense when people are good or bad."

Leah cursed herself for jumping at him. He didn't know the man from last night was her brother. He didn't know she'd sneaked away to talk with him. But she was acting so guilty he was going to guess something was wrong.

"Only rich women have time to guess people's motives. A Simmons like me has to take people as they are," she snapped at him.

Wesley seemed about to speak but changed his mind. "True to form," he muttered. "All right Simmons-Stanford, stay close to me." With that he began to plow through the trees quickly, leaving Leah standing.

"Damn, damn, damn!" she cursed as she followed him.

For most of the day he stayed very far ahead of her. Only now and again did she glimpse his buckskins.

Mostly she kept her head down and trudged along behind him, trying her best not to think of her brother Abe. Would he do something in revenge because she'd refused his request?

By twilight she was beginning to convince herself that Abe did have some family feeling and he wasn't going to retaliate. Still she kept a lookout behind every tree. She half expected to be kidnapped. That would be Abe's style.

A shot rang out, echoing off the trees and hills, reverberating all around her.

"Wesley!" she cried and knew with every fiber of her body that it was Abe who'd fired that shot. "Wesley!" she screamed and began to run.

Wesley's big body lay on the forest floor, silent, still, half sitting against the pack on his back. A great, gaping hole was in his chest.

"Wesley," Leah said with a gasp, dropping to her knees before him. "Wesley."

He didn't answer her but lay there completely still.

"He's still breathin'," came a voice over her head. "I didn't aim to kill him."

"You!" Leah hissed and launched at her brother.

Abe put his hands up to protect himself. "I told you I needed you and since you ain't got no family feelin's I had to do somethin'."

Leah stopped hitting her brother when she realized the stupidity of his words and turned back to Wesley. Bud was kneeling beside Wes, his big fingers probing at the wound.

"He *is* alive, isn't he?" she asked again going to her knees.

Bud nodded once as he removed a knife from his side.

"No!" Leah screamed, grabbing the big forearm with

177

both her hands. "Please don't kill him. I'll do whatever you want."

Bud gave her a quick, hard look before using the knife to cut away the torn part of Wesley's shirt.

"Them boys won't kill nothin'," Abe said in disgust, rubbing his arms where Leah had struck him. "Let Bud take care of Stanford and you come with me."

"I won't leave him," Leah said stubbornly. "I'll get you for this, Abe Simmons. If my husband dies I'll—"

"He ain't gonna die. I'm a good shot and it took me all day to come up with this plan. I figured you'd do most anythin' to keep from losin' all that Stanford money so I thought if maybe I laid him low you'd be willin' to do somethin' for me while he was healin'."

"You stupid—," she began. "How could you shoot someone just to get help with your criminal ways? Wesley, can you hear me?"

Leah was vaguely aware of the big man, Bud, as he began to feel Wesley's ribs. Leah was glad for the help as her eyes were full of tears of rage and frustration.

"Here," Abe said, grabbing Leah's arm and pulling her upright. "Let the boys see to him. They're good at doctorin'. You and me got some talkin' to do."

"I wouldn't talk to you if—."

"You want me to finish him off? It seems to me you ain't in a position to do much bargainin'. You already showed me you ain't got no real family feelin's so I don't know why I should care about you."

"You've never cared about anybody but yourself."

Abe stood still, glaring at her. "You tell me when you're ready to listen."

"Never, I—," A groan from Wesley made her turn back to him.

"Leah," he whispered, his eyes barely open. "Get

178

out of here. Save yourself." With that, his head fell to one side.

"No!" she cried. "He isn't—?" She looked up at Bud who shook his head once.

"You got a choice, missy," Abe said. "You help me and I'll let you take care of your rich boy, but you keep refusin' me and callin' me names and I'll let him rot right here. And you better make up your mind fast 'cause he looks like he's about to bleed to death."

Leah didn't take more than a few seconds to make up her mind. "I'll help you," she whispered, her hand on Wesley's cool forehead. "What do I have to do?"

Chapter 16

Leah looked down at Wesley's sleeping form. His wound was clean now and she realized it wasn't as bad as she'd thought, although he'd lost a lot of blood. He lay on a fairly clean bed in an old cabin that was hidden on the side of a mountain.

Slowly she moved from her seat on the side of the bed and took the pan of dirty water outside to empty it. Standing outside the door, silhouetted in the early dawn light like mountain guardians, were the young men, Bud and Cal. She'd been too upset about Wesley to know exactly when the brother had made his appearance, but now there were two of them, both massive, both silent, almost indistinguishable from each other. The brothers had carried the unconscious Wesley to the cabin, and without speaking a word they'd helped her wash and bandage him.

"He's sleeping," she said tiredly to the silent men, one on either side of the door. "In time I think he'll be all right."

"Told you he would be," Abe said loudly, making her jump as he slipped around the side of the cabin.

"Do you always have to sneak up on people?" She seethed at him, her eyes blazing.

"You've got to be the unfriendliest sister a man ever had. You gonna listen to me or we gonna fight over that rich man of yours?"

Everything in her hated having to cooperate with him. She'd do what he wanted in order to save Wes, but as soon as he was well, she'd get away from Abe. "What is it you want from me?" she asked belligerently.

Abe grunted but otherwise ignored her tone. "You don't have to do much to help out a member of your very own family. All I need you for is to do a little brain work. And maybe a little cookin'," he said under his breath.

Her head came up sharply. "So that's it, is it? You don't need me to help plan your robberies, all you want is someone to fetch and tote for you."

"Now Leah," he began, then stopped and gave her his rotten-toothed grin. "Sure, that's all we want. You come along and cook for us, do a little cleanin' and them other things women do. Ain't nothin' wrong in that, is there? There ain't nearly as many of us as all them kids Pa had."

Leah felt almost relieved. She'd hated the idea of having to plan robberies and although the running of the camp would be hard work, she'd rather do that than something directly bad.

Abe was watching her. "That makes you feel better, don't it?" he said as if talking to a kitten. "You just have to do a little cleanin', a little cookin', although these here boys eat a powerful lot."

"And what do I get in return?"

"You get to look after your rich husband." He looked down at his shoe. "Although maybe you better not tell Revis about him. Maybe it oughta be our secret," he said, ignoring the presence of the two young giants.

Leah glanced from Bud to Cal, but their faces were impassive. She wondered how intelligent the men were and wondered too if they realized how degrading Abe's treatment of them was. "Who is this Revis?"

"My partner!" Abe blurted with pride. "Him and me are in this together. We run the whole show."

"What happens when Wesley recovers?"

Abe grinned at her. "I'll tell Revis you run away, couldn't stand all the work. It's happened lots of times before. We sorta wear women out."

"You shot my husband to get a replacement cook?" She spat at him. "If cooks are so easy to come by and you have to rehire them so often, why did you have to *shoot* someone?"

Abe looked puzzled for a moment then smiled happily. "I wanted my sister near me. I ain't seen you in a long time."

Leah grabbed a long piece of wood from the wood-pile and started toward him.

"You hurt me, Leah, and you'll never find your way out of this forest," he half warned, half pleaded, covering his face with his arms.

She lowered the wood inches away from his head. "You dirty rotten blackmailer," she hissed before turning back toward the cabin and Wesley.

"You boys ain't no use at all," Abe said from behind her. "Wait till I tell Revis how you let somebody threaten me, nearly killed me she did. Revis'll have a few words to say to you two."

Leah took her time repacking her few belongings before leaving with her brother. She wished Wesley would wake up so she could tell him some story about where she was going, although she hadn't had a chance to come up with anything good yet. But he slept hard, his breathing deep and slow. There was a furrow of pain across his brow.

She sat beside him and touched his cheek. At this moment she couldn't seem to remember why she'd been so angry with him for the last few months. All she could remember was being a young girl and falling in love with him. Maybe it was Abe's presence that was reminding her of the nasty farm she'd grown up on. Thoughts of Wesley had kept her sane.

"You get through moonin' over him, you better come on. Revis'll want breakfast. He don't like the boys out of his sight for very long."

Quietly Leah leaned forward and kissed Wesley's sleep-softened lips. "I'll return as soon as I can," she promised him, then left the cabin.

Abe gave a squint toward the rising sun and said, "Let's get goin'." He was obviously beginning to get nervous.

The trail down the mountain was a maze through brambles and rocks. While they were fighting their way down, Leah tried to think. It would be to her advantage to find out all she could about this gang she was reluctantly joining.

"Where are Bud and Cal?" she asked, pushing a briar away from her face.

"They don't like walkin' with other people. They're too dumb to know people ought to stick together. Even Revis can't make 'em understand."

"Is this Revis ever able to control them?"

Abe stopped and turned to face her. "If you're thinkin' of gettin' the boys on your side against me, you can stop it right now."

Leah tried not to let him see that this was just what she'd been planning.

"Revis and the boys is brothers," Abe said smugly before turning around. "Some families stick together," he added.

"You mean there's another one of these 'boys'? There are *three* of these giants?"

"Naw, Revis is just regular size and not stupid or nothin' like the boys. They ain't real, blood-related, but Revis's ma got Bud and Cal from somewheres when they was babies. They was raised right alongside of Revis and that means somethin' to 'em."

Leah made a face behind his back, sick of his hints that she was disloyal.

They walked in silence for a while.

"Do Bud and Cal talk?"

Abe snorted. "Only when you pester 'em. I figure they got such little brains they don't have much to say."

"You think the more people have to say the bigger brains they have?"

"Sometimes you're too clever, Leah. I ain't so good with words, but Revis is. You try your words on him. And you be careful you don't start attackin' him with logs 'cause the boys protect Revis. I'd sure hate to see my own sister hurt."

"I'm sure you would," she said sarcastically.

"Ain't me got no family feelin's, it's you."

Leah didn't bother to make a reply.

In another few minutes they came into view of a little clearing with a ramshackle cabin, a woodpile, and a stream nearby. Leah stopped and looked down on the scene as an emaciated woman emerged from the back of the cabin and began loading her thin arms with logs.

"Who's that?" she asked.

"Verity," Abe answered. "She's our last, er, a . . . cook. She didn't hold up very long at all. It's them boys, always eatin' and eatin'," he added, his eyes slipping to the side.

Leah didn't question his story but kept her eyes on the woman as they went down the hillside. The woman didn't even look up. In fact, she looked too tired to care who walked into the clearing.

"Fix up some grub," Abe commanded the woman, his voice deepening.

The woman Verity didn't move any faster as she trudged into the cabin.

Bud and Cal appeared in the clearing as if they'd never left.

After only a moment's hesitation, Leah followed Verity into the cabin, went straight to the woman, and took the wood from her. "You sit down," she ordered gently. "I'll cook."

A flicker of surprise was Verity's only reaction before she went to a corner of the cabin and crouched on the floor.

"Not there!" Leah said, shocked. "Sit at the table."

Verity turned frightened eyes toward Leah and shook her head.

"Are you afraid of Abe?"

Verity shook her head.

"Bud or Cal?"

Again she shook her head.

"Revis," Leah whispered and saw the woman try to make herself smaller at the mention of the name. "I guess that answers that," Leah said, beginning to look into bags of supplies. "That *would* be the type of man Abe got himself into partners with," she murmured.

If there was one place Leah felt comfortable, it was in front of a cooking fire. All her life until she'd married Wes, she'd been involved with food—growing it, storing it, and cooking it. Now as she began to work, it was in the back of her mind that maybe a good meal would help get Bud and Cal on her side. She'd probably need any help she could get if this Revis was as brutal as Verity had indicated.

The supplies in the cabin were abundant, and after Leah found a woman's dress inside one of the sacks, she realized they were stolen. She refused to let her spirits fall. Bud and Cal had helped her with Wesley and she was going to repay them with a good meal, a very good meal.

"Can't you hurry up?" Abe demanded. "Revis might come back at any time."

"If you'd stay out of my way I could get done faster." She handed Verity a hard-boiled egg.

"She don't deserve nothin' to eat. In this group if you don't work you don't eat."

"Someone has worked her nearly to death. Now get out of here or I'll tell Bud and Cal you're interfering with my cooking."

To her surprise and delight, Abe's face lost some color and he immediately left the cabin. "Well, well, it looks like Abe is a little afraid of the boys." She looked toward Verity for confirmation, but the woman was greedily stuffing the egg into her mouth.

From start to finish it took an hour and a half to prepare a meal, the size of which astonished even Leah. "Bud, Cal," she called out the back door.

"You weren't gonna call me, were ya?" Abe whined as he pushed past her into the cabin.

186

The little interior consisted of a fireplace, a big table, five chairs, and some blankets in the corners. Scattered everywhere were bags of heaven-knew-what, Leah thought.

When Leah stepped back into the cabin she saw that Bud and Cal were already seated at the table, already beginning to eat. Leah sat across from them, Abe at the head. When she tried to get Verity to join them the woman cringed deeper into her corner.

"Don't bother her," Abe snapped. "She's scared of Revis. Don't know why, though," he added quickly. "Revis is a real nice man, ain't he, boys?"

Neither Bud nor Cal bothered to acknowledge Abe's question, but ate the food Leah had prepared. Their manners were good, much better than Abe's as he shoveled food into his mouth.

As Leah ate, she worried about Wesley. Would he rest? Would he try to get up and find her? Was he hungry? How was she going to find her way back to him?

"Eat up!" Abe commanded. "Revis don't like skinny women."

A little alarm went off in Leah's head. "Of what concern is my weight to your partner in crime?"

"Oh nothin'," Abe said hurriedly. "Just that Revis is a real gentleman and he likes pretty women."

She leaned forward. "No *gentleman* robs people for a living."

"Well said," came a voice from behind Leah.

Leah whirled about as Abe jumped up, knocking his chair over. "Mr. Revis," Abe said with a gasp, awe, respect, and some fear in his voice.

Leah wasn't sure what she'd expected, but the man standing in the doorway wasn't it. He was tall, broad-shouldered, slim-hipped, with black, curling hair. His dark, dark brown eyes were riveting. Set in a hand-some, square-jawed face, his eyes bored into hers as his lips curved into a sardonic smile.

Chills started to form on Leah's spine.

"This is her, Mr. Revis," Abe said. "This is my sister. Ain't she pretty? And she's real strong too. You ain't gonna wear her out in no month or two."

Leah couldn't look away from the man. There was something frightening about him, yet fascinating. She wet her lips.

Slowly, like a cat, the man approached her. He wore a black silk shirt, black wool trousers, and black leather boots. Gracefully he extended his hand to her.

Leah accepted and for a moment she thought she was back in the Stanford drawing room. She rose to stand before him as if he were bidding her to dance with him.

"She is indeed lovely," Revis said in his deep voice.

"I knew you'd like her, Mr. Revis. I just knew it. She's real willin' too. And she's got fire in her. She'll make you real happy."

Leah stood there holding Revis's hand while standing in the midst of the squalid cabin. Behind her were the quiet sounds of Bud and Cal continuing to eat. Slowly she began to hear her brother's words.

For a moment she looked from Abe to Revis and quickly it all became clear to her. Revis was no one's partner, least of all Abe Simmons's partner. And Leah wasn't there to cook, but she was there as some sort of human gift to this good-looking, charming villain.

She snatched her hand away. "I think there's been a misunderstanding," she began. "I came here to cook."

"Ain't she a caution!" Abe gave a nervous laugh. "My little sister knows lots about men, just loves men, and I can see she likes you a lot, Mr. Revis. Go on, Leah, give him a kiss."

Leah whirled on her brother, a snarl on her lips. "You said you wanted a cook but you expected me to whore for you, didn't you? Well listen, you piece of slime, I don't whore for anybody, especially not for criminals like this one."

Abe turned white. "Mr. Revis," he began, "she don't mean that. You know how all the ladies like you. She just thinks you'll like her better if she's a little hard to get."

"You—!" Leah gasped and lunged at her brother.

Revis's strong arm lashed out and caught Leah by the waist, pulling her to him. "Whatever the reason, I'm glad you're here," he said softly. "I like my women to have a little spirit." His free hand began to run up and down her arm. "I'll enjoy taming the tigress."

"Enjoy this then!" she exclaimed as she kicked him in the shins.

Whatever happened as a result of her action, she knew it'd be worth it for the look on Revis's face. Why did handsome men always assume women were going to fall for them? "No dirty thief is going to touch me," she said with bravado, but the next moment she was backing away from Revis.

"Get her, Mr. Revis. She's an ungrateful sister and she deserves whatever you give her," Abe shouted.

Revis's eyes were cold, hard, frightening as he advanced on Leah.

She backed around the side of the table, putting a chair between them. "Leave me alone," she warned. "I don't want you touching me."

"You're much too pretty for me to care what you want." Revis tossed the chair across the room.

Leah kept backing, her hands going across the shoulders of Bud and Cal who kept on eating. "Help me," she pleaded, but the young men ignored her.

"The boys obey only me," Revis said, advancing "Now why don't we stop these games and you come to me? I rule this little empire and everyone here gives me what I want. Or they wish they had," he added.

Verity began whimpering in the corner.

"Is that what you did to Verity? Force her?"

Revis gave a secret little smile. "When my women disobey me, I punish them."

In spite of herself, Leah shivered. If she ever got out of this she'd take a whip to her brother. Her eyes flickered toward Abe and in those few seconds, Revis was upon her.

He caught her arm and wrenched it behind her back forcing her close to him. "You have fire in you, my pretty," he whispered, "a fire that I plan to share."

"Stop it!" she cried, and there was more pleading in her voice than she intended.

Revis's lips went to her neck. "You'll learn to enjoy what I offer," he said silkily.

Leah could hardly think. It wasn't that she was responding to his hot mouth on her neck, but somehow she knew that if he got what he wanted from her, her life, and probably Wesley's, would be over. The only way she could save herself was to stop him.

She wasn't any match for his strength, but Bud and Cal were. If only she could get them involved.

"I don't like this public lovemaking," Revis whispered. "Come outside where we can be totally alone I'll show you the man inside this thief you're so frightened of."

"I'm not—," she began.

Revis's hand tightened on her throat, the thumb pressing into a pulse spot. "Perhaps you should be frightened. I like a woman's resistance."

190

"Because you can't find a woman willing to have you?" she spat up at him.

Revis raised one dark eyebrow. "Perhaps you should be taught a few manners. A little pain might make you less unwilling."

"She deserves it," Abe injected.

"Shut up," Revis said with a growl, his eyes never leaving Leah's face. "Did your stupid brother tell you about me? I take what I want and I use it until it's all gone. You can't resist me, can't fight me, because I always win."

With that his mouth took hers in a rough, fierce kiss.

When he was done, the light in his eyes told Leah he was sure she'd want him now. He was certain his kiss would make her fall down at his feet.

With a snarl, Leah spat in his face then turned her head away as he raised his hand to strike her.

"Bud and Cal," she said, "if you don't protect me, I'll never cook for you again."

The statement made Revis halt his hand in midair. Abruptly he released her, pushing her back against the cabin wall. His handsome face twisted into an ugly smile. "You think you can turn my brothers against me? Do you think that perhaps you can control what is mine?"

"No, I . . . I don't want you touching me, that's all. I don't want control." Something about him frightened her more than ever. Her hands clutched at the wall behind her as if she might be able to claw her way to freedom.

"You need to learn that I am the master here and no damn woman—." Again, he raised his hand to strike her.

But the blow never landed.

Bud's big hand lightly gripped Revis's wrist. "The woman will cook," Bud said in a soft, gentle voice, but there was no mistaking the command it held.

Revis's face was a study in astonishment. He started to speak, but as he looked from the men flanking him, making him seem small by contrast, his eyes went back to Leah and what she saw made her shiver. He hated her now and for a moment she almost wished she'd given in to him.

Revis twisted his arm from Bud's grasp, turned on his heel, and left the cabin.

For a moment all was silent. Then Verity began to cry loudly. Abe sat down heavily in a chair. "Oh Lord, but you've done it now, Leah. Revis ain't one you oughta make mad."

Bud and Cal looked at one another then quietly left the cabin.

With shaking hands, Leah began to clear the table.

Chapter 17

It was late at night when Leah finally was able to sneak away from the robbers' cabin. Revis hadn't returned, but his attack on Leah had frightened Verity so much that it had taken Leah hours to calm her. In her hysteria, the woman had started saying that Revis would come back and kill them all. Leah washed the frail woman and finally got her to sleep.

Abe started to tell Leah what he thought of her turning Revis down, but a few choice words from Leah made him leave the cabin. Most of the long day Leah spent cooking and at the noon meal she tried her best to thank Bud and Cal for helping her. The young men acted as if they didn't hear her. On impulse Leah kissed each one on the cheek.

"You ain't thinkin' about beddin' them dummies, are you?" Abe wailed. "You cain't turn down Revis for these goons."

"Abe," Leah said evenly, "I've just about heard enough from you. If you—."

Abe cut her off. "You make me or Revis too mad and I'll let him know about that rich boy you got hidden away. So think twice about threatenin' me."

Leah had not said much after that and Abe snickered in self-satisfaction and kept reminding her of little chores that needed doing.

It was night when she got everything cleared away and began the long walk to the cabin where Wesley was hidden. All the way up she invented a story to give him as to why she hadn't been with him.

She was very tired when she entered the cabin, but her heart was pounding. Would Wesley be all right?

She lit a lantern by the bed and breathed a sigh of relief when she saw Wesley sleeping peacefully. He opened his eyes immediately.

"Leah?" he whispered.

"I'm here now. I brought you some food. Can you eat?"

He was silent as he watched her. "Where have you been, Leah?" he asked softly as he eased himself into a sitting position.

"Don't sit up! Lie still and I'll feed you." She tried to stop him, but he brushed her hands away.

"I want an answer."

There was a command in his voice and suddenly it was all too much for Leah. She collapsed onto the edge of the bed, buried her face in her hands, and began to cry.

"Leah, honey," he began, reaching out to her. "I didn't mean to make you cry."

"I . . . I'm sorry," she said, sobbing. "I'm just tired and so many things are happening."

"What sort of things?" he asked, his jaw clenched. "Who shot me and why were you gone all day?"

Leah wiped her eyes with the back of her hand. Tired or not was now going to have to give the performance of her life. "Oh Wesley," she said. "It was such an awful accident. The men were hunting and they shot you by mistake. They helped me carry you here then left. I guess they were afraid you'd come after them when you recovered so they wanted to get away."

She took a deep breath. Now was the hard part. "After I got you here, a little girl appeared at the door. She begged me to come to her house. Her father was dead but her ma and six brothers and sisters were all down with the measles and there was only the girl to look after them. I felt that you'd be all right here alone since what you really needed was rest so I went with her. All day I've been cooking, cleaning, and nursing sick people."

She stopped abruptly and looked at him, her eyes begging him to believe her. She wasn't sure she could handle a fight with him on top of everything else.

Wesley's eyes bored into hers. Never in his life had he heard such a string of lies, yet she was begging him to believe her. There were circles under her eyes, her dress was food-stained. He knew no one lived in these woods, which was why he'd originally brought her to them. He also knew there was a nest of robbers here and if anyone tried to settle, they usually forfeited their lives.

Yet Leah was making up a story about a woman and seven kids living here. Right now he was too weak to get up and find out the truth about where she'd spent the day, and from Leah's look of fear she wasn't about to tell him what was really going on.

"That's just like you to take on other people's problems," he said, forcing a little smile.

"You . . . you don't mind?" Leah asked, holding her breath. Was he really going to believe her and not tear his wound open when he went searching for her?

"Leah," he said softly, "have I been such a tyrant that you'd believe I'd force you to stay with me and leave a widow and some children to die? Is that what you think?"

"No . . . I'm not sure I knew what to expect. You don't seem as badly injured as I thought. I was worried about you here alone."

And too scared of something to stay with me, he thought, but he took her hand and kissed the palm. "Can you stay or must you return?"

She dreaded the trip through the night down the mountainside, but she was afraid of remaining with Wes. Revis might start to look for her. "I have to return. Will you be all right?" She stood.

"I'll miss you but I'll survive. You go on and get as much sleep as you can. I'll just eat and sleep some more. My side hurts too much to do anything else." His voice was a study in tiredness.

"Yes," Leah murmured, and while she still had some energy she left the cabin.

"Goddamn her," Wesley muttered as soon as the door closed. What in the world had she gotten herself into? First she'd slipped off into the night to meet that good-for-nothing who'd visited their camp and all the next day she was jumpy as a rattlesnake. The next thing he knew he'd been shot, and while he was bleeding to death, she was fighting with that scoundrel.

Today Wesley had stayed in bed, eating food someone had left for him and waiting for his wife to return. And when he had seen her again, she'd looked ten years older and scared to death.

What the hell was going on?

Carefully, his hand on his bandaged ribs, he swung out of the bed. For all the blood he'd lost, the wound really wasn't that bad and he'd purposefully tried to get rid of Leah before she started wanting to inspect it. If she could lie, so could he, and his lie would be to tell her he was sicker than he was.

Outside he cocked his head and listened. It was easy to hear Leah thrashing her way down the mountainside. If she meant to do anything in secret, she was making a poor job of it.

As he started following her, he heard the sound of another person off to his left. It was a heavy person and Wesley guessed it was the big man he'd first seen in his camp. He was trailing Leah, staying just out of sight of her.

Soundlessly Wes slipped to the left, and as he traveled he picked up a large tree branch. With the size of the man, it'd take something heavy to get his attention.

Following the man and Leah, Wes traveled quite awhile before he halted above the cabin in the clearing. Silently he watched as Leah walked to the back, and in the moonlight he could see the thin man run to meet her.

The words of "Where the hell have you been?" floated up to him.

Wesley crouched on the ground, watching the scene, puzzled for a moment, wondering just exactly what Leah was involved in.

But the next moment he came upright because the stick he'd been carrying had someone's foot planted on it. He looked up into the eyes of the young giant he'd first seen yesterday. Instinctively Wesley drew his fist back, but someone behind him caught it. He swiveled about and saw a second giant.

Wes pulled his arm out of the man's grasp. "Either one of you touch my wife and I'll kill you!" he said, seething. He wasn't exactly in a position to threaten, but that didn't stop him.

"She is safe for now," one of the men said.

"Come back to your cabin now before you start to bleed."

Wes looked from one man to the other in the moonlight and suddenly he knew that what was going on involved great danger—and Leah was somehow caught up in it.

"My wife needs help, doesn't she?" he said, praying he could trust these two.

"Come to the cabin and we will talk," said one of the men.

Four hours later, Wesley was again alone in the little cabin. The lantern was out and it was dark in the room, but Wes was sure his anger was enough to provide half the world with light.

The two young men, Bud and Cal, had difficulty at first in talking, almost as if their voices had never been used very much. But, after some persuading and when they saw Wes's intense interest, they started talking as if they couldn't stop.

They didn't remember their parents but had been adopted by Revis's mother when they were three years old and already so big that people stared at them. Even as a boy, Revis had been a thief, yet he'd been charming too. While other people treated Bud and Cal as if they were freaks because of their size and their silence, Revis had been good to them. Revis's mother used the boys as an extra team of oxen, so when Revis suggested they travel westward, Bud and Cal had agreed.

Now they'd been living in the Kentucky forest for four years and even as good as Revis was to them and as much as they owed him, they didn't like the way he treated the women he brought to the cabin. A few times Bud and Cal had tried to help the women, but the women had screamed in terror, especially after Abe made up stories about the young men.

But Leah was different. She hadn't taken Abe's word that they were stupid and she'd been kind to them.

"Leah takes on everyone's problems," Wesley muttered. "Will you help her escape?"

Bud and Cal looked at each other. "She will not go without you. Abe says that if she leaves he will tell Revis where you are."

"Revis would kill you," Cal said flatly. "He does not like other men touching his women."

"Neither do I!" Wesley snapped before beginning to question the men about all of Revis's operation. Wes knew that thieves had been robbing the westward travelers for years, before Revis came west. All Bud and Cal knew was that Revis reported to someone called the Dancer and they knew nothing about him.

"I'd like to find out who this Dancer is," Wesley said thoughtfully.

The men rose. "We have to return now. Revis will be back. You just get well and we will watch out for your pretty lady."

"She is a lady, isn't she?" Wes said as they left.

Now he sat alone, thinking over what he'd just heard. He was impressed, very impressed, that Leah was risking so much to protect him. Thinking back over their marriage, he hadn't done much to make her love him. For just a moment he thought of Kimberly and wondered how she'd have reacted in the same situation. He was certain Kim would never risk her pretty neck or her cherished virginity to help anyone.

"I'll make it up to you, Leah," he whispered into the darkness. Right now he must leave Leah's protection to the boys, but when he was well and didn't think he might bleed to death at the least movement, he was going to protect her himself. And further, he was going to see if he could do a little more for her than just be a burden.

Chapter 18

Leah didn't sleep much that night. She kept having terrible dreams about all that could happen to Wesley alone in that cabin. Who knew what these woods held? That bear they'd seen could tear down the door and get him. Or even worse, Revis could find him and put a bullet through his heart.

When she woke, her head hurt and her eyes were swollen.

"You better stop lookin' like that," Abe said as she started breakfast. "Revis likes pretty women."

"I don't care what your Revis likes. I'll do what I please."

Abe leaned closer to her. "It better please you to please him or it just might please me to tell him the whereabouts of your rich lover."

With shaking hands, Leah returned to the skillet full of frying bacon.

It wasn't until after breakfast, when she'd cleared everything away and was starting the noon meal, that she saw Revis. He was leaning against the side of the cabin, trimming his nails with a long, thin-bladed knife.

ped, then put her chin up and walked past

ght her hair and wrapped it about his wrist, pu   er toward him. "So, the lady's too good to speak to the thief."

"Leave me alone! I don't want your attentions and I have work to do. Bud and Cal—."

He jerked her head back. "You'll regret turning them against me," he said, putting his lips near hers.

Leah saw him smile then felt a tug at her head. The next moment he pushed her away and held up a long strand of her hair in triumph. Leah's hand flew to the back of her head, feeling the ragged edge where he'd cut it. As she ran into the house, Revis's laugh followed her.

All day Leah worked herself nearly to the breaking point, cooking, cleaning, ignoring Abe's jibes, protecting Verity, who cried when any man came too near her.

And everywhere she looked, Revis seemed to be there watching her. He'd suddenly appear out of the forest or from behind the woodpile or he'd be standing silently in a corner of the cabin. He never got close enough to touch her, since after he'd cut away her hair either Bud or Cal was always close to her. Twice Leah caught Revis looking at the boys as if in speculation.

At sundown Revis disappeared and not long afterward Leah told Bud she was going to visit her husband. The big man nodded once and Leah wasn't really sure if he understood her or not. If she ever got time, she was going to find out if the young men were as stupid as Abe said they were.

"You better be back here afore Revis comes back," Abe warned, but Leah ignored him.

The lying was what was destroying her, Leah decided

as she trudged up the mountainside. She seemed to be telling everyone a different story. Wesley was lying alone in a cabin, no doubt cursing his luck at being stuck with a Simmons. He'd decided to stay married to Leah because she was more "fun," but where was the pleasure now?

When Leah opened the cabin door, Wesley knew he'd never seen a more forlorn-looking person. She looked so miserable he almost wanted to laugh. Ever since he'd known her no matter what was dished out to her, she fought back. He never felt guilty about telling her what he thought because if she disagreed, she did so loudly.

But the woman entering the cabin now looked as if she'd given up, as if she didn't want to bother with life's hardships any longer.

Immediately Wes knew there was only one cure for her misery: he was going to make love to her.

He held out his hand to her.

With a frown Leah ignored his hand. "I brought you some food."

"I'm not hungry. Come sit by me."

That's all I need, Leah thought, Revis after me during the day, Wesley pestering me at night. "I need to get back."

"Leah," Wes said with surprising firmness for one so ill. "Sit down."

She didn't really feel much like having a fight and besides, what could he do?

When she sat on the edge of the bed, Wes put an arm around her and drew her back so she was leaning against the wall. He nestled his big, warm body next to her small, rigid one.

"Chicken, potatoes, beans, cornbread," he said softly, looking inside the basket she'd brought.

With his free hand, he took the basket, leaned across her, and set it on the floor. That done, he didn't quite straighten up but kept lying half across her.

"I . . . I must go." She halfheartedly pushed at him.

"Leah," he murmured, trailing a finger down her cheek, "you aren't afraid of me, are you?"

"Of course not," she snapped. "I've got to go, that's all. I'm not afraid of any—"

She stopped because he kissed her, not just a simple kiss but a long, lingering, soft kiss that began to take the tiredness out of her.

"You were saying?" he said, caressing her cheek and neck with his big hand.

"Any man," she said, trying not to look at him. "I'm not afraid of any man, any . . ."

Wesley began kissing her neck in hot little kisses that were oh, so very nice.

"It occurred to me today, Leah, that even though you've been married for years and even had a baby, you've never been made love to."

She pulled away from him. "That's absurd. How can I have a baby if . . . I mean you . . . the night of the storm we . . ."

"My beautiful wife, I thought you were a prostitute and used you as such. Had I known that was our early wedding night I assure you I'd have acted differently."

"Differently?" she asked, curious. It was rather nice to be held by someone, to be touched and caressed.

"Wait a minute!" she said with a gasp. "You can't touch me. I swore you'd have to take whatever you wanted from me, that I'd never give in to you. Just because I'm a Simmons doesn't mean—"

"Shut up, Leah," he murmured, "and consider yourself forced." His lips took hers and held them—and held them until Leah's arms slipped around his neck and pulled him closer. With one arm he pulled her down into the bed, one thigh going over both of hers.

When he pulled away from her, he saw wonder in her eyes and Wes felt a wave of guilt that this woman was his wife yet he'd taught her nothing. Slowly, with great patience, he began to caress her body.

The dress she wore was dirty, stained, and very loose on her. With a practiced hand, he began to undo the buttons down her front.

"Wesley, I don't think . . ." Leah began. "Maybe we shouldn't . . . oh dear!"

His hand slipped inside her dress, his warmth going through her layers of underclothes. He kissed her again as he lifted her off the bed and slipped the dress from her shoulders.

As the dress lay about her waist, it was Wesley's turn to look at her in wonder. Never had he seen women's underwear like this. Nearly transparent fabric showed the rosy pink crests of her nipples, floated downward, and barely concealed her creamy skin.

Leah immediately turned a pretty shade of pink. "Nicole's dressmaker thought that since my outerwear had to be coarse, my underwear should be . . . should be . . ."

"Let's see the rest of you," Wes said eagerly, and before Leah could say a word he lifted her and removed four cotton petticoats to reveal lacy drawers that showed her long, firm legs to advantage.

"Leah," Wes said in a slightly shaky voice as he grabbed her to him and began to kiss her passionately.

Leah responded instantly. She'd never been taught

that she shouldn't enjoy sex, and as a result she acted
with as few inhibitions as a child. She began kissing him
back with enthusiasm.

Wesley, surprised for a moment, perhaps remembering Kimberly's rationing of kisses, smiled with pleasure
at his wife's response. His hands began a journey down
her body, and her warm skin, barely covered by the
silken fabric, excited him more.

While kissing her neck he began to unfasten the
buttons to her underwear.

Leah was losing herself to his touch. Her sexual
experience consisted of one quick fumble more than a
year and a half ago. This caressing was different and it
was sending the oddest feelings through her body. Her
fingers clutched at Wesley's head, entwining in his soft
hair.

She protested when he pulled his mouth from hers
and groaned with pleasure when his lips touched her
throat. When his lips encircled her nipple, she lay still
as one shock wave after another went through her.

"Wesley?" she asked in such a surprised way, her
head coming up.

He paid no attention to her but continued to make
love to her breasts.

Leah swallowed hard, her head rolled back, and she
arched her body upwards in an instinctive reaction.
Wesley's hard hands gripped her waist tightly as his hot
mouth moved down her body.

She grabbed handfuls of his shirt, caught buckskin
fringe in her mouth. "Skin," she murmured. "Let me
touch you."

Wesley came out of his clothes instantly and soon
knelt over her wearing nothing but a bandage across his
ribs.

Some part of Leah's mind told her she should be

concerned about his wound, but truthfully she didn't care if it tore apart—at least right now she didn't care. Her eyes trailed down to his swollen manhood and with no shyness she clasped it in both hands.

Wesley gave a deathlike groan and fell on her, kissing every part of her he could reach before climbing on top of her. He'd been worried she'd be afraid of him, but her eagerness was more than he could bear.

She arched to meet his first thrusts, threw her legs about his hips and pushed. Wes grabbed her and rolled to his back so she was on top. His hands on her waist, he guided her up and down, sometimes watching her, glorying in the look on her face, her expression of pure, undiluted pleasure.

When Wes could stand no more, he flung her to her back and with two blinding thrusts, brought both of them to a height of pleasure neither had experienced before.

Both lay together, locked in each other's arms, until Wes raised himself on one elbow and looked down at her. Her eyes were glazed, her mouth soft, her hair in sweaty curls about her face. There was wonder in Wesley's eyes: to think this hot little beauty was his very own wife, to have forever! Anytime he wanted her, she was his.

Leah opened her eyes and the look she saw on Wesley's face made her come back to reality.

"I have to go," she said abruptly.

He frowned because he didn't want her to go, but he knew she must. Right now the only way he could protect her was by letting her go, entrusting her care to the two large strangers. "Go then," he said with more harshness than he meant. It was difficult for his pride to allow what his common sense was forcing him to do.

Leah heard only the coolness in his voice and quickly

she began to dress. She didn't say a word as she slipped from the cabin into the darkness. But halfway down the mountain she sat down on the ground and began to cry.

She was never, never going to be a lady! Not all the cosmetics, pretty clothes, and hair rinses in the world were going to change her into a lady. She made vows of chastity, then at the first opportunity, she frolicked in the bed with a man who had done all manner of rotten things to her.

At each thought she cried harder. What would Regan or Nicole do now? No doubt Revis would see that they were ladies and he wouldn't even try to molest them. It was only because she was a Simmons that Revis wanted her. And now that she'd shown Wes she wasn't anything like a lady, he'd probably be glad to turn her over to someone like Revis who was her own type.

After a while she tried to collect herself and started down the mountain. Wesley Stanford might think she was of the same class as Revis, but Leah knew she wasn't.

The cabin was silent when she entered, except for Abe's snoring in a corner. There were no beds, so Leah took a place on the floor beside Verity, who often whimpered in her sleep.

The next morning Leah woke to the loud sound of Revis's boots on the floor.

"Get up all of you!" he said with a growl. "You," he said, addressing Leah, "where are the boys?"

Leah refused to be frightened of him. "Behind you," she shot at him.

Revis gave her an angry look before turning. "I got a wagon sunk in the mud about two miles down the road. You two go get it out and Abe, you lazy nothin', go help them."

"Yes, Mr. Revis," Abe said cheerfully. "Come on, you big louts, let's get to work. We'll have it out in no time."

Leah held her breath for a moment, afraid Revis would stay with her, but he left with the others. Breathing a sigh of relief, she started cooking breakfast. No doubt the boys would be even hungrier after a morning's exercise.

It was while she was reaching for a slab of bacon that hands caught her about the waist.

"They're gone now," Revis said into her ear.

She twisted away from him. "Don't touch me or—"

"Or what?" he half purred, advancing on her. "You can't get away from me."

Leah kept backing. "Why do you even want me?" she asked. "You're a good-looking man and you could have your choice of women. There must be women prettier than I am who are quite willing to have you." She backed into a wall.

He grabbed her arm. "Ladies like you always think they're too good for somebody like me. You think you're better than highwaymen."

"Ladies!" she exclaimed. "Abe is my brother. Do you think any *lady* could be related to that piece of filth?" Keep him talking, she thought. Maybe the boys will get back before he touches me.

"I'm not convinced he's your brother." Revis drew her to him. "What makes you stay here? Each night you leave here and go up the mountain. But you come back."

He smiled at her gasp.

"Did you know the boys follow you? And when I try to follow, one of those stupid brothers of mine stops me. What do the three of you do on top of that mountain?"

"You're disgusting. Now release me before they return."

"We have hours. I sunk that wagon in two feet of mud. They'll never get it out. And while they're wallowing, I'm going to have myself a lady."

"No." She twisted in his grasp.

"What's up the mountain, little sister? Shall we go have a look? Would you like to go with me and see what we can find?"

"No! I mean, why not? There's nothing up there except a little privacy. I need to get away from the stench of you and this hideous place."

"So why don't you leave? Why do you stay and cook and take care of that nothing that used to be a woman?"

Leah couldn't think of a quick answer to his question.

"Come on, lady, tell me."

"I promised to help my brother. He did something for me once and I owe him," she said in one breath.

"Abe never did anything for anybody. What are you hiding?"

Before Leah could answer, Bud appeared in the doorway, the lower half of his body covered in mud. Silently he walked across the room and put his hand on Revis's shoulder.

With a flash of hatred, Revis whirled on the young man. "You got it out already?" he snapped.

Bud nodded once.

Leah clutched at the wall behind her as Revis shot her a malevolent look before leaving the cabin. "Thank you," she whispered to Bud.

For the rest of the day Revis seemed always to be near her and that night she was afraid he would be able to follow her and find Wesley. She didn't dare make the trek up the mountain and risk discovery.

"Will you take this to him?" she whispered to Bud, holding out a food-laden basket, her eyes pleading.

He nodded briefly but said nothing. Leah wasn't sure how much she could trust the boys, but now she had to depend on them. "Don't let Wesley see you," she said. "He doesn't know that I'm . . . where I am."

Later Leah lay alone on the coarse blankets on the cabin floor and remembered the night before in Wesley's arms. Her husband wanted her because she wasn't a lady and Revis wanted her because he thought she was a lady.

"Men!" she hissed into the darkness and Verity, waking, crawled nearer to Leah.

"Ssh," Leah soothed as Verity began to whimper. "No one will hurt you."

But even as she said it, Leah knew she was lying. Revis obviously didn't like being thwarted and Leah knew he was going to do his best to hurt her.

Chapter 19

Leah woke to even louder whimpers from Verity and when she opened her eyes she saw Revis kneeling over the woman, caressing her arm. Verity began to inch away, her head sliding up the cabin wall.

"Leave her alone!" Leah said.

"Will you take her place?"

"No, but—."

"She's not like you, Leah," Revis said, using both hands to caress Verity's arms. "This one is easily terrorized. She doesn't have much of a mind now, but I could make her lose what she has. All I have to do is . . ."

He broke off as his hands went to Verity's throat.

"Stop it!" Leah commanded, grabbing his forearm. "I'll call Bud and Cal. They won't let you harm her."

"I won't harm her. All I'll do is let her see me. Wherever she looks that's where I'll be."

Leah knew instantly that what he was talking about would work. Verity had a very tenuous grasp on sanity as it was and with Revis intimidating her she'd not last long. "Why?" Leah whispered. "Why would you hurt her? She's nothing to you."

"Because I want something from you," Revis said. "I want you to take a ride with me."

This took Leah aback. "A ride? Where? And when you get me away from the cabin do you attack me?"

Abruptly, Revis moved his hands away from Verity and sat back on his haunches. "Maybe I've been a little too rough on you. Your brother'd spent an hour an' a half telling me how pretty you were and how willing you'd be to jump into my bed. So when you resisted me I thought it was an act, but when you used my own brothers against me . . ." He gave her a reproachful look. "I'm only human, Leah, and I guess I got a little angry."

Leah sat quite still, looking at him, her mouth half-open in astonishment.

"And I don't want to terrorize this young lady either, but I want to show you that I'm not such a bad person and I know the only way you'll come riding with me is if I blackmail you."

Leah looked at his handsome dark face, his eyes begging her to believe him.

Revis caught both her hands in his. "I know I'm a thief, but maybe you could help me find a way out. Just get to know me a little, Leah. Let me show you that I'm human. I swear by everything I cherish that I won't hurt you. I won't touch you at all. We'll just ride down the mountain a little way, talk some, look at the flowers. That's all. I swear to you."

"I . . . I don't know," she stumbled. "The boys wouldn't—."

"The boys can't know!" Revis snapped. "Now that you've turned my own brothers against me even they

don't trust me. If you and I go off together and com·
back and you've not been harmed maybe I can wi·
their trust again. Do you know what it's like to lose th·
people you love most?"

Leah thought she just might cry at that question
She'd lost everyone she'd ever loved. Even the ma·
she'd spent her childhood loving had turned agains·
her. "Yes," she whispered, "I know what it feels like t·
lose people."

"Then help me," he begged. "Give me a chance t·
prove to my brothers that I still deserve their respect
And let me show you the man behind the villain."

He grinned at her then and his smile, which she'·
never seen before, was charming. What could it hurt ·
she rode with him? And if she didn't he'd no doub·
keep his threats about terrifying Verity.

"Please, Leah," he said softly, squeezing her hands

"All right," she agreed. "How do we get away?"

"Right after breakfast slip into the trees. Tell one c·
the boys you need privacy. They'll obey you. I'll wa·
for you at the bottom of the ridge." He smiled again
"Thank you, Leah. This means a lot to me."

With that he stood and left the cabin.

While she was cooking breakfast, Leah though·
about Revis's words. Who was she to judge a perso·
when her own brother and father were criminals
Perhaps Revis wasn't all bad. Maybe some of him wa·
good. He did take care of Abe and his young brother
who were possibly too stupid to be able to take care c·
themselves. Maybe there were extenuating circum·
stances. Maybe there were reasons why he thieved
Maybe she *could* help him, show him there were othe·
ways.

By the time she'd cleared away breakfast, she wa·

actually looking forward to her ride. As she picked up the empty dishpan, Verity caught her arm.

"Don't go," Verity said in a hoarse whisper. "Revis is evil."

In spite of herself, Leah pulled away from Verity. She couldn't very well say what she thought, that Verity was frightened of her own shadow. Verity was afraid of Bud and Cal. No doubt she'd warn Leah not to be alone with one of those harmless giants.

"I'll be fine," Leah said patronizingly. "You just rest and when I return I'll bring you some flowers."

"Leah," Verity pleaded.

"Go rest," Leah half ordered and the light went out of Verity's eyes. Slowly the scared little woman turned back toward her corner.

Leah clucked her tongue for a moment over the woman's lack of courage, but she didn't waste time thinking about Verity. As soon as she started getting along with Revis, she could get Wesley out of the forest.

A half hour later she was running down the mountainside. It'd been quite easy to escape the boys and now she was looking forward to a morning away from work. When she saw Revis, she smiled tentatively.

"Come on." He half laughed. "Your horse awaits you, my lady."

At first Leah was so pleased to be away from her worries for a few minutes that she barely noticed Revis. It was hot and the air was hazy with mist—and it all looked beautiful.

"There's fire in you, Leah," Revis said beside her. "You'd be a good partner for a man."

"I'm a married woman," she said, patting the horse's neck.

"And where is your husband?"

"In Sweetbriar, Kentucky," she said quickly. "Are we going anyplace in particular?"

"Just down the mountain. Any man who'd let you out of his sight would be a fool. I could give you a silk dress."

She smiled at him. "I have several silk dresses, thank you. And I don't think my husband would want me to remain here." How she wished that were true!

"Is there nothing I can do to persuade you to stay with me?"

In spite of telling herself it didn't matter, it was very nice to be desired by this good-looking man. He thought she was a lady even though he knew she was a Simmons.

The woods began to thin as stumps showed where travelers had cut down trees.

"Isn't that the Wilderness Trail down there?" she asked, looking at the deep, permanent wagon ruts. "We'd better go back."

"No," he said. "There's a stream across the trail. I want to show you something."

"But if someone sees you . . . I mean . . ."

"I know what you mean, Leah," he said heavily. "Could I show you something now?"

"Of course." They were sitting on their horses in the middle of the well-worn trail and just a little way away was the smoke from a camp fire.

Out of his pocket Revis pulled a black silk handkerchief, and while Leah watched he tied it about his face.

She didn't like what she saw. She'd almost forgotten that he was a thief. "I think we'd better return."

"Not yet, my lofty princess," he said as he grabbed the reins of her horse.

The next minute they were thundering down the trail

216

toward the camp fire smoke, Leah barely able to hang onto the saddle. Once she screamed "No," but Revis paid no attention.

They burst like storm clouds into the clearing where two wagons sat. The settlers, each involved in some task about the campsite, looked up and froze.

Revis shot one man through the forehead.

Aghast, for a moment Leah couldn't move. Then, in one motion, she was off her horse and onto the ground, running toward the dead man. A woman near her screamed.

Revis rode his horse near to where Leah hovered over the man. "Get their goods, Leah," he said coolly.

"You animal!" she screamed and began to beat Revis with her fists.

Revis leveled his pistol and shot the woman beside Leah in the shoulder.

By now there were five settlers and two children standing by the wagons, looking in horror at the masked man and the people near him.

"If you don't obey me you'll have to choose who'll die next," Revis said as he pulled another pistol from his saddle.

The bleeding woman at Leah's feet began to cry.

"You have about ten seconds to obey me, Leah," Revis said.

"What . . . what do I do?" She knew that now only action counted and words were useless.

"Get that man's hat and fill it with whatever they have." He pointed with the pistol. "Any of you give my partner any trouble and I'll put a bullet through your head."

"I'm not—," Leah began but stopped. When she stood before the settler, he looked at her with hate.

217

"The Lord will see you burn for this," the man hissed at her as he handed her his hat.

"No, please, I—."

"Listen to him, Leah," Revis said. "All of you, want to introduce Mrs. Leah Simmons Stanford of Virginia and soon to be of Sweetbriar, Kentucky."

With shaking hands, Leah walked in front of the settlers as they put their watches and rings into the hat. One woman spit a great glob into Leah's face. Leah only halfheartedly wiped it away.

"Come on, Leah, honey," Revis said coaxingly. "We need to get back and these good people need to bury their dead."

At her horse she hesitated.

"If you stayed here they'd tear you to bits and if you don't go with me I'll kill two more. I think I'd like doing that," he said so that only she heard.

As if she were in a daze, Leah mounted her horse. Revis again took the reins and pulled her with him into the forest.

Just after crossing the Wilderness Trail, he stopped and pulled off his mask. "I told you I'd make you pay for using my brothers against me," he said. "In a few days everyone for miles will know about the lovely Mrs. Stanford who is a thief as well as a murderess."

"No," Leah whispered.

"And now, my pretty Leah, you have a real reason to stay with me. You leave my protection and the secrecy of our cabin and you'll be arrested and hanged by the neck until dead." With that he began to laugh. "You'll get used to it," he laughed. "On the next raid you'll know just what to do. And since you'll already be well-known, we won't have to cover that pretty face of yours.

"Let's go," he said, laughing. "Blood always makes me hungry."

He led her horse up the intricate, secret path to the cabin while Leah sat on the horse and knew her life was over.

Chapter 20

By the time Revis and Leah reached the cabin, Revis
was cursing her because she looked as if she were
living death. He didn't want any more women like
Verity, who'd never recovered from seeing Revis
shoot her husband. He wanted a woman who wasn't
afraid.

At the cabin he dismounted, leaving her still on top
of her horse. He stalked inside, threw some food into a
sack, and returned to his horse. Still cursing his luck
with women, he angrily pulled Leah from her horse and
stood her on the ground. Immediately she collapsed in
a heap, drawing her knees into her chest. She didn't cry
or make a sound; she just lay there.

With a sneer at her, Revis rode away.

Hours later, Abe found her there.

"Damn you, Leah, you're supposed to feed us! It's
time to eat and ain't nothin' cooked. And what're you
doin' layin' in the sun? You'll get burnt and then Revis
won't like you anymore."

Leah didn't move. Her eyes were open but she didn't seem to see anything.

"Leah?" He knelt beside her. "You been hurt?" There was concern in his voice. "You gonna talk to me or you rather just lay around?"

Tentatively he touched her forehead. Her skin was hot, but she didn't move at his touch. Frowning, he stood upright and gave a high-pitched whistle.

Quickly both Bud and Cal appeared from the forest.

"Look here at my sister," Abe said indignantly. "Either of you know what's wrong with her?"

Cal knelt by Leah, his big body shading her. Slowly he reached out a hand and touched her cheek. He looked up at his brother, seemed to get an answer to his silent question, and the next moment he lifted Leah into his arms.

"Hey!" Abe protested. "You can't do that. You leave her here. I'll take care of her."

Cal started toward the forest with Leah.

"You hear me, you overgrown piece of dog crap?" Bud planted himself in front of Abe.

"Here! Get out of the way," Abe commanded. "You can't take my sister off to who-knows-where. And that rich husband of hers ain't gonna want her if she's sick. She ain't got nobody but me."

For all Abe's protesting, he stayed where he was when both brothers disappeared into the woods.

Wesley was outside the cabin, shirtless, walking around, flexing and unflexing his arms, trying to get strength back into his side. He halted when he heard the footsteps coming up the path. Usually Bud and Cal didn't use the briar-covered path but came their own way through the underbrush.

Wesley slipped out of sight until he was sure his

visitors were indeed the boys. When he saw Cal carrying Leah, he ran forward.

"Is she hurt?" he asked as he took her from the young men. "What happened to her? Did that Revis—? I thought you two were watching her."

Leah lay limp in his arms, her eyes closed as if she were unconscious. He took her into the cabin and put her on the bed. He kept a bucket of water in the cabin and now he dipped a cloth in it, a cloth that had once been part of his bandages, and put the cool fabric on her forehead.

Leah groaned, turned to her side, drew her knees into her chest, and lay still.

"You two better start talking," Wes said, his eyes narrowed. "And fast."

Cal spoke first. "She told me she wanted privacy this morning and we gave it but after an hour we began to look for her."

"We followed horse tracks down the mountain and at the bottom we heard shots," Bud said.

"By the time we got there Revis had killed a man and shot a woman. He and Leah were riding fast back up the mountain. When we got to the cabin she was like that and Revis was gone."

Wesley walked away from the cot. "I thought all this Revis did was rob people."

"He kills people when he feels like it," Bud said with a stiff jaw.

Wesley banged his fist against the wall. "What a fool I was! How could I have left her there? I should have taken her away immediately."

"You would have bled to death," Cal said flatly.

Wes was quiet for a moment as he turned to stare at Leah. "No doubt she witnessed the shootings and that's what's wrong with her."

Suddenly he crossed the cabin in two strides, grabbed her shoulders hard, and lifted her to a sitting position. "Damn you, Leah!" he yelled in her face. "Why do you think you have to save the world? Why couldn't you have told me the truth? Why did I have to be so stupid as to believe you? I thought you'd be all right and now look at you. Damn you! Damn you!"

Wesley began shaking her and kept it up until Cal put his hand on Wes's shoulder. Abruptly, Wes stopped and saw there were tears in Leah's eyes. He pulled her to him fiercely. "That's it, sweetheart, cry all you want. You're safe now."

Bud and Cal silently left the cabin.

Once Leah's tears started, she couldn't seem to stop them. She clung to Wesley with all her strength and cried against his bare shoulder. When her body started convulsing, he made her drink water.

"Now tell me about it," he said patiently.

"No," she whispered. "No."

"Leah." He took her chin in his hand and tipped her swollen, red face upwards. "I never believed that cock-and-bull story of yours about the sick kids and I've always known about Revis and your brother Abe. Right now I want you to tell me everything that's happened."

"I have to stay here forever," she said, hiccupping. "They'll hang me."

"You're making no sense whatever. You saw Revis kill someone today, didn't you?"

She pulled away from him. "I *helped!* I held a man's hat and collected goods. I *stole!*"

She waited to see the shock on his face, but there was none.

"What did this Revis do to force you to steal? What did he threaten you with?"

Again Leah's eyes filled with tears. She had thought Wesley would believe she stole because it was her nature to do so. "He said he'd kill more people if I hesitated."

"Bastard," Wes said under his breath. "Anything else?"

She didn't want to tell him the rest. Never again could she live amid decent people. "Revis wore a mask," she whispered, "but I . . . I didn't."

"Oh," Wes said, glad it wasn't worse. "I'm sure they saw you were forced into it and that actually you were saving their lives."

"No!" she screamed and jumped off the bed. "You don't understand. Revis told the people I was his partner. He told them my name, that I was Mrs. Leah Simmons Stanford of Virginia, soon to live in Sweetbriar, Kentucky. He made me a criminal. He made me a thief. I can never leave here! If I do they'll hang me."

"Leah," he said in sympathy as he walked toward her and tried to pull her into his arms.

"Get away from me! Don't ever touch me again! You're the clean Mr. Stanford. Nothing like this would ever happen to you. They'd take one look at the Stanford name and know you're innocent but me, a Simmons, I'd—."

He grabbed her shoulders. "Stop feeling sorry for yourself. According to our marriage papers you're a Stanford too. Look, Leah," he said, calming himself. "All this isn't as bad as you think. There are courts of law and we'll hire the best lawyers. Bud and Cal can testify about how Abe forced you into Revis's camp and I'll bet someone today heard Revis order you to participate. There are ways to get out of this, even if you are accused. So stop saying you have to stay here."

Leah was sure she'd never wanted to believe anything as much as she wanted to believe this. "Do you think so?" she whispered. "Is there a chance?"

"More than a chance. Now let me see a smile because I'm sending you out of here right now."

"Here? You mean back to Revis's cabin?"

Wes's jaw hardened. "You're not going back to that place ever again. I'm going to send you down the mountain with Bud and Cal. They'll take you to Sweetbriar. I have friends there and if need be they'll hide you until I can get there and straighten everything out."

"But where will you be?"

"I have a little unfinished business yet. I owe somebody something. Now come on." He grabbed her hand and pulled her outside. "Bud and Cal'll take care of you and Revis won't be able to harm you again."

She pulled out of his grasp and squinted up at him in the sunlight. "Why aren't you going to Sweetbriar with me?"

"I told you, I have work to do."

Leah thought for a moment and then sat down on the ground, her arms folded.

"Just what is that supposed to mean?" He glared down at her.

"I'm not leaving here. You're up to something and I don't like it."

Anger surged through Wesley's entire body as he grabbed her shoulders and lifted her off the ground. "*You* think *I* am up to something?" He seethed into her face. "I have lain here helpless for days while you got yourself into one mess after another and you tell me you don't trust *me*? Leah, for two cents I'd turn you over my knee. When are you going to realize that you can't run the world singlehandedly? I could have gotten us out of this days ago if you'd only asked for my help.

But no, Mrs. Stanford has to do everything her own way. I've tried, Leah, I've tried really hard to be nice to you. You wanted to handle all this on your own so I let you. It was my own stupidity that kept me from realizing how much real danger you were in."

He dropped her to her own feet. "Damn you again and again! I don't know any man in the world who'd stand for what I've stood from you. You insult me, tell me I'm fickle then act as if I'm some helpless idiot you have to protect. You know what your problem is, Leah?"

She looked up at his furious, handsome face with wide eyes. "No. What's my problem?"

"You've always had control, that's what. From what I gather, you commanded that whole family of yours like you were some general, and on the trip here you took on everybody else's work and actually ran the whole trip."

Leah just stood there, blinking.

"My patience is all used up now and I've had enough of lying back and letting you have your way. Starting today you're going to be my wife and you're going to honor that part in the wedding vows that says *obey*. You understand me?"

"Maybe," she said, but at his look she changed her mind. "I understand you thoroughly."

"Good! Your first order is that you are leaving these woods right now. I'm staying here because I plan to find out more about who this Revis's boss is. And when I get ready I'll return to you and our farm but not before then. Is that clear?"

"Yes," she said thoughtfully. "Revis doesn't do all the robberies on his own?"

"Somebody else organizes them. Revis is nothing but a two-bit thief, not smart enough to run the business.

226

But he knows the identity of his boss and I want that information. Are you ready to go?"

"I'd like to know who'd do this awful thing, too."

"Good," he said impatiently. "I'll tell you when I get home." He gave a whistle. "Bud and Cal will take you home."

"Won't Revis miss them?"

"I have some plans." He glared at her. "None of which I plan to tell you. All I want for the next few months is to know you're safe. I don't need or want your interference in any of this. I'll clean out this band of thieves once and for all."

"All by yourself?" she asked aghast.

"You were planning to take care of Revis and me all by yourself. Did you think that Revis was going to shake your hand good-bye when you decided to leave?" His voice softened. "Here're the boys. Now give me a kiss good-bye."

"I don't like this," she murmured as he pulled her into his arms. "Won't you need some help?"

"Shut up, Leah."

She didn't say another word as his mouth closed on hers.

"I wish we had more time," he said against her lips.

Leah gave herself over to his kiss, losing all thoughts of Revis and his boss.

When Wesley pulled away from her she stared up at him because she knew she loved him. Actually, she'd never really stopped. He'd done some awful things to her and maybe she should hate him, but she didn't.

"And what's that look for?" He smiled down at her. "If I weren't so concerned about getting you out of here I'd take you back into the cabin."

She leaned into him, causing him to frown in puzzlement.

He smoothed a strand of hair back from her eyes. "I don't think I've ever noticed how pretty you are. Even after days of sleeplessness you're the prettiest girl I ever saw. Leah." He paused. "Thank you for what you did, for putting yourself in Revis's clutches in order to save me. It was . . . kind of you."

Pulling away from him, she thought she might just start crying again. "I'll see you in Sweetbriar?" she whispered.

Grinning, he kissed her lustily again. "I'm not about to tarry when I have you waiting for me. Now scoot." He turned her about and smacked her firmly on the seat.

An hour later, Leah was halfway down the mountainside with Bud in front of her, Cal behind—and already Leah was making plans.

Once out of Wesley's arms, she'd been able to think more clearly. If she went ahead to Sweetbriar as he'd told her to do, she just might face legal charges. Her only hope was to get someone to hide her and who was she going to ask? Kimberly? Justin?

And thinking of Kimberly, would Wesley return to pining for her if Leah wasn't around to remind him that she was alive? At night when he was alone, would he remember Kim's pretty blonde face rather than Leah's tearstained one? He just now had noticed that Leah was pretty, but would he *remember* it?

Tramping down the mountain, Leah kept thinking. Maybe if she had more time with Wes he might grow to love her. Didn't he already say he liked her? And wouldn't he need help with Revis? How was he going to find out all the information he wanted? And too, Wesley said he had a debt to pay, but didn't Leah owe Revis something for making her a part of his murders?

The more she thought about it the more she was sure she should return to help Wesley.

But first she'd have to escape Bud and Cal. As they walked, she began to look for a hiding place, a place to spend the night all alone in the big, lonely forest. She shivered.

"You would like to rest?" Bud asked from behind her.

"Oh no," she said sweetly, smiling up at the big man. "I'm just fine." Wesley, she thought, was worth the trial of being alone in the forest.

Chapter 21

Escaping the boys was harder than Leah had imagined, and hiding from them was even more difficult. She practically buried herself under leaves and shrubs, then held her breath as Bud and Cal walked all around her. After a nearly silent conversation, they separated and went north and south. Leah didn't move but stayed in her crouched position until her legs ached.

At sundown the young men returned and inspected the ground carefully. They seemed to know she was near them and wanted to give her time to emerge from hiding. But Leah waited until nightfall before she crept out of her hole. Bud and Cal were nowhere to be seen as she started up the mountain.

Every sound made her jump and after only a few yards, her spine was rigid with fear. It wasn't until after hours of struggling that she felt someone was near her. "Revis!" she exclaimed, then stood still.

"Bud and Cal," she said with a sigh. "I know you're there so come out."

As if they were part of the forest themselves, the young men emerged to stand beside her.

Perhaps she should have felt that she'd been caught, but she suddenly felt safer and was actually glad to see them. With a grin she looked up at them. "Now what happens? Do you take me screaming down the mountain? I warn you, I *will* scream. And kick, too," she added as an afterthought.

The men seemed puzzled by her. "Why do you want to return to Revis? Your husband wants you safe."

"And who will keep Wesley safe with both of you gone? And Revis will hurt Verity because there's no one to protect her and he'll probably beat Abe because I've escaped."

"You care for your brother?" Cal asked.

"Perhaps. I'm not sure. I do know I can't run away and let Wesley take on Revis by himself. Will you help me?"

Bud looked at Cal.

As Leah watched, the two young giants seemed to engage in silent communication. Abe had said they were brothers to Revis, but right now she wondered how close they really were.

"Do either of you ever ride with Revis on his robberies?"

"No," Bud said.

"Then why . . . ? Why do you stay with him?"

"He pays us for firewood and game and for watching his cabin to see that no one comes near."

Leah's curiosity was piqued. "Does he pay you well?"

"We have bought land in the town at the foot of the mountain. We are going to be farmers."

"The town . . . ? You mean Wesley's Sweetbriar? How much land do you have?"

They looked at each other. "It is now eight thousand five hundred sixty-two acres."

"Thousand?" Leah whispered. "The two of you own thousands of acres of land?"

"Wesley knows our land and says it is good. He said he will help us build a house and help us buy seed and tools."

Leah couldn't help laughing. According to Abe the boys were stupid, but in truth they were smart enough to make themselves rich. "When are you planning to leave Revis?"

"We owe him something. He helped us when we were children," Cal said. "But our debt is close to being paid. We will leave soon."

"And now you have a new protector. Wesley will help you as much as you need. And if you'll help me now I'll . . ." She couldn't think of what she had to bargain with. "I'll cook for you. While you're building your house and barn I'll give you meals."

For the first time ever, in the moonlight, she saw the men smile, and they looked even younger. Their size made them frightening and she guessed they were used to stares and odd remarks, but she was rapidly growing fond of them.

"On the way down here," she said slowly, "I saw a patch of wild strawberries. Have either of you had strawberry cobbler with a thick crust on the top, little holes cut in it with hot strawberry juice oozing over the crust? Or maybe you'd like something called chicken in a coffin. It's a chicken baked with—."

Bud cut her off. "What do you want done?"

"We do not murder people," Cal injected.

"No! I didn't mean—." She saw they were teasing her. "Does Revis know what the two of you are really like?"

Cal's face hardened. "Revis thinks we are his, as his mother did, but Revis does not treat us like slaves. We make him pay us well for what we do. You should not return to him."

She wanted to explain things to him. "Cal," she said quietly, "if Bud were in trouble would you risk your own safety to help him or go somewhere safe? Wesley is the man I love and I believe I can help him."

"I would die for my brother," Cal said, "and he for me. We will help you."

"We will take you back to Revis and when your man returns—."

"Returns! Where did he go? What's he up to?"

"He did not tell us. He said only that he would be back in two days. You can stay at Revis's cabin until then or we will hide you in the woods."

"I'll go back to Revis. At least there I can help Verity and see that everyone is fed. Shall we start walking?"

Bud looked down at his foot. "Perhaps we should wait until morning, when there is light."

"But I'd like to get back in case Wesley . . ." She stopped. "I guess we can't pick strawberries at night, can we?"

"No," Bud said with a smile.

"What did you boys eat when you were growing up?"

"Gray things," Cal said grimly. "Big bowls of gray."

Leah tried not to laugh at his bleakness. Someday perhaps they could visit Stanford Plantation and see the vast quantity and variety of food there. And too, they might like to meet Clay Armstrong's pretty young niece.

She sat down. "I guess we could get some sleep." Without another thought she curled into a ball on the damp ground and went to sleep. One thing about having guardians half the size of a mountain, it made one feel safe.

Leah had just finished putting another meal on the table in the little cabin, but she hesitated calling the men in to eat. Wesley had just arrived, sunlight flashing off his buckskins, his face serious as he talked to Revis. Leah could see the tension in the cruel smaller man; Revis's shoulders were hunched together as if he expected a blow any minute.

Over the past few days Leah had stayed close to Bud and Cal. She was amazed at how deep her hatred of Revis went now. Again and again she saw him kill the settler and shoot the woman. Once he tried to sweet-talk her into believing he'd done it out of his growing love for her, but Leah knew he'd murdered the travelers because he couldn't abide being turned down.

The closer Leah stayed to the boys the more she liked them. They were silent while Abe spoke to them and of them as if they had the intelligence of the floorboards. A few times she caught Bud's eyes twinkling.

Revis brought a load of fresh eggs and cream to the camp and Leah made a big custard covered in burnt sugar. But before she'd allow Bud or Cal to have a morsel, she made them tell her what they knew about Wes. They knew only that Wes was pretending that he was from the Dancer and would work with Revis.

"I'm sure Revis will welcome him with open arms. He'll just love sharing his command," Leah had said with disgust.

Now Wesley was outside explaining something to Revis, and Leah's throat was dry in anticipation of how angry he was going to be with her. Maybe she should have obeyed him and gone to Sweetbriar, but then she'd had another look at him. Neither Kimberly Shaw nor any other woman was going to get him if she could help it!

"Abe," Leah said as she saw her brother walking toward Wesley. Abe would tell Revis who Wesley was. She was almost to the door when she heard Abe say, "Who's this, Mr. Revis?"

Leaning against the door, Leah breathed a sigh of relief and smiled. Somehow Wesley had taken care of Abe. What in the world had Wes promised Abe to make him go against his precious Mr. Revis?

Now the only unaccounted problem was Leah. She smoothed her hair, her dress, and tried to brace herself. She hoped he wouldn't be too surprised to see her.

She was bending over the fire when he entered the cabin.

"And who is this pretty bit, Revis?" Wesley drawled. "I heard you had all the comforts up here but I didn't know about this one."

Slowly Leah turned to face him. There was no surprise on his face, but his eyes were shooting fire.

"Leah's mine," Revis said in a hard voice. "I don't share her and there's no question of who she belongs to."

Wesley, with a slow smile, stepped nearer Leah. Only she could see his face and what she saw there made her step backward. His anger made her afraid.

"Wesl—," she began.

He grabbed her about the waist, pulling her to him. "Watch out, pretty lady, you're about to step into the fire. My name's Wesley Armstrong, what's yours?" His eyes were warning her and threatening her all at the same time.

Over his shoulder she could see Revis as his dark face

turned darker. Here was something she hadn't considered. If she showed Revis she preferred Wesley, would Revis slip a knife into her husband's ribs?

"Unhand me, you filthy thief," she said loudly and watched the confusion in Wesley's eyes. "None of your kind will ever touch me." Taking advantage of Wes's astonishment, she pushed away from him.

Wes began to recover himself. "I think I'd like to have this little filly, Revis," he said smugly. "Maybe we can work out a deal."

"Leah is mine," Revis repeated, teeth clenched.

"Maybe the lady should choose." Wes smiled as he confidently advanced toward her. "Maybe you have trouble with women, but I don't. Come here, wench."

"Wench!" Leah said with a gasp. Perhaps she did love him, but this wench business was a little too much. To her right was a bowl of cornbread batter she had just mixed. With a little cat smile forming on her lips she lazily lifted the bowl, then with a quick motion tossed the contents into Wesley's smiling face. While he stood there flinging globs of batter off his face, Leah turned to Bud and Cal. "This overdressed peacock is the same as the other one. If he gets too near me I'll serve you raw bacon for breakfast."

Out of the corner of her eye she saw Revis give a satisfied grunt, turn on his heel, and leave the cabin. Now all she had to deal with was Wesley's rage. "Wench indeed," she snapped before moving out of Wesley's reach.

Before he left the cabin to wash, he didn't say anything to Leah, but the look on his face made her swallow hard.

"Do you think he will beat you?" Bud whispered.

"Would you let him?" she asked, aghast.

"You were mean to him," Cal answered.

"Be quiet and eat," she said, and only then realized they were laughing at her. "I hope you realize it was *your* cornbread I dumped on him. Maybe next time it'll be the apple tart I'm baking for supper."

"We will not let him beat you!" Bud and Cal said, eyes wide, then they grinned at her. "You sure are an exciting woman, Leah."

"I hope Wesley agrees with you," she said heavily before turning back to the fire.

As the sun began to set and Leah was once again loading the table down with food, Wesley entered the cabin. If he looked at her, Leah didn't see because she was afraid to turn in his direction. She knew he didn't understand why she'd turned him down. No doubt he thought he could protect her better if she were *his* wench.

Still playing her role, she stepped completely out of his reach when she put food on the table. She could feel the eyes of both Revis and Wesley on her.

"So you know of this rich wagon?" Revis was saying to Wes. "The Dancer sent you to lead for this one job?"

Wes looked around the room at Bud, Cal, Abe, Verity, and Leah. "Perhaps we should talk later."

Revis gave a slow grin. "Bud and Cal are my brothers. Abe wouldn't talk, would you, Abe?"

"No sir, Mr. Revis," Abe said with his mouth full. "Secrets are safe with me."

"And Verity is too frightened to tell anything," Revis continued.

"And the pretty one?" Wesley asked.

"She's mine and she can't leave," Revis said in a hard voice. "Now tell me what you were sent here to tell me."

237

...h served food, Wesley mapped out a plan to ... pair of wagons that looked as if they belonged to ...ers but were in truth carrying gold.

"The Dancer always knows of these things," Revis said as he leaned back in his chair and lit a thin cigar. "And tell me, how's he doing? He looked fit the last time I saw him."

"You know the Dancer," Wes said. "He's healthy as always. He mentioned the last time you met, at his house."

"At the party, yes."

"He seemed to be angry about you and a young woman."

Revis smiled. "His daughter, actually. Didn't he mention that the young lady who was so taken with me was his beautiful daughter?"

Wesley grinned, too. "The Dancer failed to mention that little detail. Now if you'll all excuse me I think I'll tramp up the mountain to that pond I saw and take a bath."

He stopped in front of Leah and ran a finger down her cheek. "Perhaps you, pretty lady, will join me."

She gave him her sweetest smile. "I will indeed have to bathe now that you've touched me, but I'll not bathe with you. That would defeat the purpose, wouldn't it?"

She felt a little guilty at the look on Wesley's face and at the way his hand dropped as if she were something he no longer wanted to touch. The cabin was silent as he left, except for a soft chuckle from Revis.

Later only Bud and Cal were still in the cabin, still eating at the table.

Leah removed her apron. "I'm going to Wesley. Will you see that Revis doesn't come near us?"

Bud looked at his plate. "What is for supper tomorrow night?"

"Are you blackmailing me?" She smiled at them. "Do a good job tonight and I'll show you what I can do with that brace of doves you brought in." With only a bit of hesitation she kissed each one of them on the forehead. "Good night, my lovely princes."

With that she was out the door and running through the dark forest, up the trail to the cabin where Wesley had stayed. Above that was the pond. The whole time she traveled, she tried to come up with a way to cool his anger. The more she thought about it the more she was sure that she should let her body do the talking.

She stood on a little rise for a moment, looking down at the pond, at Wesley's long body swimming lazily about. The moonlight gleamed on his dark skin.

This wasn't going to be nearly as difficult as she'd thought. Coughing a few times to get his attention, and when she was sure he was looking at her, slowly, she began to unbutton her dress. Easily, the stained, sturdy garment fell to the ground and what was left was a semitransparent chemise.

She walked toward him; he was treading water, watching her, the fabric clinging to her thighs with each step, and when she reached the foot of a tall tree she paused. Eyes locked with his, she unfastened the chemise and let it fall.

The last layer of clothing was a pair of drawstring pantalets, so sheer they left nothing to the imagination, and short, soft silk stays.

When Leah was a child, to escape her father's wrath she'd learned to be very good at climbing trees and now, with agility, she pulled herself onto a long, heavy branch that overhung the pond. Balancing herself, she walked about halfway out. Then, looking down at Wesley, she removed her stays and dropped them to the ground, freeing her full breasts to the moonlight. Next

239

she removed the clinging pantalets and tossed them down.

Nude, she didn't look at her husband, but very calmly walked to the end of the branch, balanced for a moment, then made a perfect dive into the cool water, not two feet from him. When she came up, he caught her arm.

"Lord, woman," he more breathed than said, "you do know how to get a man's attention."

Without another word he pulled her out of the water, half dragging her so that her legs floated out behind her, and led her to the shore. "Leah," he whispered as he pulled her into his arms, their wet bodies sticking together as if they were one.

With hands on both sides of her face, he kissed her hungrily and Leah put her arms about his neck, knowing that this moment was worth all his anger.

His hands moved down her wet back, playing with the damp tendrils of her hair as his lips caressed her face, kissing her eyelids, her cheeks.

Suddenly he pushed her away. "Here, let me look at you."

Color rose to Leah's face. Perhaps he wouldn't find her pleasing.

He held her hands, pulled her arms out to the side and let his eyes travel down her body. "When we get home I want to keep you in my house just as you are now. I'll never let you wear any clothes."

"Oh Wesley," she said in a girlish giggle. "I'd freeze in the winter."

"Not with me to keep you warm," he said as he pulled her to him and began to nibble her neck.

Leah shivered, chills running up and down her spine and down the backs of her legs. The movement caused Wes to pull her closer, and when he kissed her again she felt fire run through her and attempted to move closer to him.

With a soft, seductive smile, Wesley pulled her down to the ground, but when Leah started to touch the grass, Wes moved her to the top of him. "That skin of yours shouldn't touch the hard ground. Just touch me, my pretty wife." With that he lifted her and set her down on his maleness.

With a gasp Leah began to move atop him, undulating to the delicious rhythm that began coursing through her body. Wesley caught her hips in his powerful hands and helped her move. And when she felt her body reach a crescendo, she fell forward, wrapping her arms about his neck, pulling him ever closer while his hard thrusts made her feel as if she were drowning.

"Wesley," she cried as her body convulsed against his.

He held her so close she felt as if she might break.

Then suddenly he pushed her off him. "You certainly changed your tune. Are you sure you wouldn't rather be with your lover instead of your husband?"

With a deep sigh, Leah rolled away. "Why is it that men are so agreeable when their male member is standing upright and so disagreeable at other times?"

Wesley made a noise that was half laughter, half shock. "Where are you off to? Back to Revis? What's he like when his male member—?" He stopped because Leah swung around to glare at him, and since her beautiful nude body was still a highly unusual sight to him, all he could do was gape.

"Just because I'm a Simmons and you're a lordly Stanford doesn't mean I jump into bed with every man who asks me, and if you ever again insinuate that I've been to bed with Revis, of all people, I'll never speak to you again. *Or* let you make love to me. Is that clear?"

He stood, catching her shoulder just as she reached her clothes on the bank. "I'm sorry, Leah. I guess I was just mad about today. The boys told me how you've kept away from Revis. But why the hell did you turn me down this morning? If Revis knew you were mine he'd think twice about touching you. Now I can't protect you, at least not openly. Your little stunt of dumping cornmeal on me cost us a lot."

"I knew you wouldn't understand," she said heavily. "I refused Revis because he's a thief and I'm a married woman, so how would it look if you, another thief, walked in and I fell into your arms? Wouldn't he be suspicious?"

"Well, I am . . ." Wesley said.

"You're what?" she demanded. "My husband? We don't want Revis to know that, do we?"

"No, I meant I'm . . . I'm a lot better looking than Revis and it would make sense that you'd want me and not him."

"Oh Wesley," she exclaimed, beginning to laugh.

"You don't think so?" He was indignant.

Still laughing, she put her arms around him. "Yes, I do think so. I honestly believe you're the best-looking man I've ever seen."

He held back from her. "Better than Revis?"

"Much."

"And my brother Travis?"

"By far."

He grinned at her for a moment before beginning to kiss her.

As difficult as it was, she pulled away from him. "We can't stay. Revis will want to know where I am. If we're both gone he'll suspect something."

"I can handle Revis. I'll tell him the better man won the lady."

"No," she said as her fingers played along the muscles on his chest. "Please don't do that. You don't know him. He's evil. One night you'll be sleeping and he'll slip a knife into you. Please," she begged.

With a little frown, he caressed her cheek. "What happened to the little cat who was spitting at me on the way up this mountain? Where's the woman vowing to never give me anything but what I took?"

She pushed away from him. The last thing she wanted to do was tell him she loved him. When and if they ever got off this mountaintop and he abandoned her, she wanted to have some of her pride left. And when he walked out she wanted to be able to tell him she didn't care, that he'd given her a few hours of bed pleasure and that was all she'd wanted.

She twisted away from him. "Of the two of you, you're safer. If I stayed with Revis I might end up like Verity, and besides, you said you and your money could get me off from the murder charges."

"Is that all I mean to you, Leah?" he asked quietly. "I'm someone whose money you can use?"

She tried to keep her voice from shaking. What was she supposed to say, that she thought she might lie down and die if anything happened to him? "We were married because you thought we had to be. *I* was nearly unconscious. I wanted to end the marriage but you refused to oblige me, so legally we're still attached and because of that and because it was my brother who shot you, I joined Revis's gang in order to protect you. After all this is over I think my duty to you is finished."

"Duty?" he said. "And what about this?" His eyes roamed down her nude body.

She gave him a lusty grin. "We Simmons women enjoy a tussle with a handsome man. I wouldn't bed Revis because I think he may be a man who likes pain."

He moved away from her. "God, but you're a cold-blooded woman, Leah. I guess I should feel privileged that you didn't leave me to bleed to death after your brother shot me."

She wouldn't answer him because all her concentration was on not crying. How much she wanted to tell him she loved him and have him tell her the same thing. But if she told him, he'd probably only laugh at her and say that of course someone of her class would love someone of his high station in life. No, it was better to keep her pride, if not her heart.

"I have to go now," she said, turning and beginning to pull on her clothes.

"Yes, do go," he said as he walked away from her.

Leah gave way to silent tears then. The fragile bond between them had been broken.

Chapter 22

Leah didn't sleep much that night, but she cried some, hugged Verity some, and was generally miserable. She wished with all her might that she'd never even met Wesley Stanford. If she'd only listened to her sister and not walked out after him that night at the tavern and leaped on him like a starved animal, she wouldn't now be in the midst of a den of thieves. Or be walking off the end of tree branches without any clothes on and making a fool of herself. Or spending hours in the strong arms of the man she loved.

"Damn!" she said aloud as she tossed the blanket off and rolled away from Verity.

"It's time to get up," she said. "And today you're going to help me cook," she said on impulse. Perhaps work could give Verity a little of her self-respect back.

While she was cooking breakfast Wesley entered the cabin, but he didn't speak to her. In fact he was so cool there was a definite chill in the air.

"Would you like some breakfast, Mr. Armstrong?" she asked.

"Not from you," Wesley snapped just as Revis entered the cabin.

Leah saw the scowl on Revis's dark face and knew he was considering Wes's attitude. "This one's not as smart as you, Revis," Leah said smoothly, setting a platter of bacon on the table. "He thought he could have me for the asking and he doesn't take kindly to being told no. Breakfast is ready."

Twice during the meal Leah saw Revis watching Wesley, and to distract him she leaned over his shoulder as she set dishes on the table. Revis must hate someone else coming into his territory and he would hate Wes more if he thought the newcomer was succeeding where he'd failed.

"When is this job of yours, Armstrong?" Revis asked.

"Tomorrow morning. They'll be four miles down the mountain by then."

"And what makes you so sure about how fast they're traveling?"

"I have my ways," was all Wesley would answer.

It was later, as Leah and Verity were clearing the table, that Abe came to his sister.

"You two have a lovers' quarrel?" he hissed into her ear.

"Revis and me?" she asked, pretending not to understand.

"You and that Stanford fella. You two was lookin' sparks at each other all mornin'."

"I never looked at him," she protested.

"Not when he was lookin' at you. And he watched you ever' minute. Leah, you two lovebirds is gonna ruin ever'thin'. I ain't never gonna be respectable if you

246

two get killed. And Revis'll kill you both when he finds out you're playin' him for a fool."

"What did Wesley promise you if you helped him?"

"None of your business. Me and him got a business deal goin'. As soon as he finds out about the Dancer we're leavin'. All of us. That is, if he'll still have you. You oughta watch yourself, Leah. You ain't never gonna get a husband like that again."

"I thought you hated all the Stanfords."

He gave her his rotten-toothed grin. "I don't hate anybody what promises to share his money with me." He leaned closer to her. "You don't think he's lyin', do you? He'll do what he says, won't he?"

"Yes, I'm sure he will."

Later at the noon meal Wesley didn't appear, and when Leah could, she asked Cal where he was. After telling Cal where she was going, she again asked him to keep Revis away. With a sackful of food she trudged up the hill to where Wesley was chopping wood.

For a moment she stood watching him, looking at the sweat gleaming on his muscular back, and found that her own palms were sweaty. But all lust within her died when Wes turned and saw her, his face angry.

"I brought you something to eat," she said with a dry throat.

Slowly he put down the ax and came toward her.

Instinctively she backed away.

"I'm not going to attack you if that's what you're afraid of."

"I'm not. I came to tell you something. Abe said that you and I . . . this morning . . . I mean, he was afraid that Revis might begin to suspect something about us."

"Such as that you and I were rolling about in the bushes and then we had a quarrel?"

She looked up at him for a moment, watching as he

took a seat on a tree stump. "Did you *want* Revis to believe that?"

"Of course. Why else would I have been acting sulky and angry?"

"Acting?" She sat down on the ground, not far from his feet. "I don't understand anything."

"Something I learned from my brother was that it's best not to let women in on your plans. I was hoping, after I learned you had stupidly returned to Revis's camp"—he gave her a look of reproach—"that you'd do the sensible thing and pretend to fall madly in love with me at first sight, but I knew that'd be too much to ask from a woman. Especially you, Leah. You have the most contrary mind I ever saw. Every time I give you what you want, you change your mind. You wanted to marry me and when I did, you changed your mind."

She started to defend herself, but he waved her words aside.

"That's neither here nor there except that I wanted you safe in Sweetbriar and when you wouldn't go there I hoped to be able to protect you here. But you always seem to know exactly how to do the opposite of what I want."

"I couldn't go with you when I'd turned Revis down. He would have—"

"If you tell me again that Revis would kill me, I may strangle you. Leah," he said, calming himself, "do you think I am so little of a man that you have to use your own sweet little body to protect me? I've told you I wasn't going to let you control things and damned if you don't just keep on trying to control everything and everybody. If I tell you to walk left, you walk right. Not only do I have to concern myself with Revis and the Dancer, but I have to worry about what you're going to

248

do next because you think you're the only smart one in the world. Except for Revis," he added with a hurt look in his eyes. "For some reason you think this Revis is so smart he could kill me without me even knowing about it."

"It's not that he's so smart, but he's so evil. You're not. You're good and kind and—"

He was looking at her with his head to one side, a hunk of cornbread halfway to his mouth. "Last night you said I was the best-looking man you'd ever seen and today I'm good and kind. Are you falling in love with me, Leah?"

"Never!" she exclaimed, but her face turned pink.

"Too bad," he muttered.

"What kind of plans do you have?" she asked quickly, to cover her confusion.

"To be honest, Leah, I'm afraid to tell you the truth. If I told you what I want to do you might decide it was too dangerous for me and do something that would be the opposite. Of course I could tell you the opposite of my plans and then by sheer accident you might end up helping me."

"Why you—!" she spat at him as she rose.

He caught her thigh in his hand and pulled her to him, her mouth near his. "How come you said all those mean things to me last night when you really think I'm good and kind?"

"How come you only believe the good I say about you and not the bad? Have you *ever* listened to me?"

Releasing her, he looked back into the bag of food. "Not much I don't, because to tell the truth, Leah, you don't make much sense to me. You're always leaping—or diving—into my arms and then saying the damnedest mean things to me. It just seems to me that if you *really* didn't like me you wouldn't be taking off your clothes in front of me as often as you do."

Leah had absolutely no reply to his words. Quietly she sat down again. "What plans do you have for Revis?" she whispered.

"I want to make him mad," Wesley replied simply.

"And you're using me to make him mad?"

"I was planning to, but now it's so hard because you fight me all the time. I have this fear of coming to a showdown with Revis, telling you to get behind me and you throwing yourself between us saying something real dumb like, 'You'll have to shoot me first.' That gives me nightmares, Leah. I wonder if maybe if I said, 'Get between us, Leah,' you'd stand behind me. But I'm not sure that'd work either. Lord, but you are a problem."

"So how have you changed your plans?" she asked meekly.

"I've just had to be calm. I'm afraid to provoke Revis and get him to talking because I'm afraid of what you'll do. Bud and Cal have tried to get you away a couple of times but you stick beside either Revis or me, like you've got to protect both of us. Or maybe it's just to protect me from Revis since you seem to think he's perfectly able to protect himself and I'm not."

"I didn't mean . . ." she began. "Have I really been awful?"

"Worse. Have you ever even heard the word *obey*? Did you maybe learn that it meant do-the-opposite?"

When she looked up at him she saw he was smiling at her. "Maybe I could learn."

"That's what Bud and Cal said, but I think you've got a head made of iron and the last thing I want to do is risk that pretty little head."

"So I've fouled up your plans and made it impossible for you to find out who the Dancer is, and also maybe put your life in jeopardy because I might interfere with your protecting yourself."

"That's about it." He was now eating a piece of peach pie. "But you sure have made the last few days interesting. You pour cornbread batter in my face, you dive stark naked into my baths, you yell at me so furiously all the best parts of your body start bouncing. I just wish I had time to enjoy all this properly without worrying about Revis."

She turned away to hide her pink face. "So now what do you plan to do?"

"I'm trying to figure it out. I tried to talk the boys into carrying you away, but they agreed that all you had to do was mention something like strawberry pie to them and they'd do whatever you asked."

She started to laugh. "What if I swear to obey you? Would that help?"

"You swore before a preacher to obey me, but it went in one ear and out the other."

"But this is important!"

"And being married to me isn't?" he snapped.

She wasn't going to answer that. Obviously if she told him it was he who hadn't wanted their marriage, he'd never listen to her. Or probably he'd twist it around and hear her saying something good—or maybe he'd only watch the "best" parts of her bounce. "I promise that I'll listen and obey. If it's a good plan," she added.

"Not good enough," he said, licking his fingers. "I want total obedience and I'll take nothing less. I don't care if you think my plan is stupid, dangerous, or what. Either you agree to obey or I'll leave you in the woods tied to a tree."

251

"You wouldn't," she half laughed.

His eyes were deadly serious. "Try me."

"I don't think I shall," she said with some nervousness. "I swear to you that I'll obey your orders. Now will you tell me?"

Wesley was still reluctant to tell her and she found that what he really wanted were kisses of persuasion. Leah, for all her seeming abandonment of the night before, was shy with him. He was and he wasn't her husband. He was hers only as long as they stayed hidden in the woods.

He told her his plan and she was astonished by it. Wesley had contacted Justin and Oliver Stark and John Hammond to ask for their help. They were to load two of Wesley's wagons with valuable goods and Revis was to steal from them.

"You'll be stealing what you already own," Leah said.

"Better that than some innocent victim. I hope that once Revis knows I'm an actual thief, he'll trust me more."

"Wesley," she said, pushing out of his arms, "how did you know the Dancer has a daughter and how did you know about his house?"

"I didn't. I just guessed. Revis likes to think women want him so I played on his vanity."

"Wasn't that a little dangerous? Suppose he was testing you too?"

"He has no reason to suspect me and he's never been out from under the watch of Bud or Cal so he couldn't have contacted the Dancer. Now stop worrying and give me another kiss."

Later, as Leah was rolling out pie crust, she thought over her conversation with Wes. For all his bragging, Wes still might need help tomorrow. But how in the world was she going to persuade him to let her go with him?

Revis solved her problem. At supper he said either Leah went too or there would be no raid.

"What the hell do we want with a damn woman?" Wesley exploded.

"I don't trust her. I won't leave her here unguarded. She sneaks around these woods too much as it is."

"So what? Let her go. Maybe these wagons will have more women. You can pick one of them. Surely one of them will like you more than this one does."

"That's why I want her," Revis said, watching Leah's stiff back. "She goes or there's no raid."

Before Wesley could say a word, Leah stepped between them. "I've already been publicly branded a thief, I might as well go again. Besides, maybe I can find a new dress."

Abe looked at her with his mouth hanging open, Bud and Cal continued eating, and Wes refused to look at her while Revis studied her through a haze of cigarette smoke.

That night, as Leah was emptying dirty dishwater, Wes caught her by the waist and pulled her into the shadows.

"Tomorrow, watch me. I'll give you signals as to where you're to stand. Don't even get off your horse. There shouldn't be any shooting but if there is, even if it's only someone dropping his gun, you head your horse due east and go as fast as you can. Are you listening to me, Leah?"

Suddenly he grabbed her head and pulled her close to his shoulder. "I just wish you were more sensible than you are. Please don't do anything heroic. Under no circumstances do I want you to do anything noble. Don't try to save anyone's life or lead the robbery or anything else dumb like you usually do. Stay on your horse, stay calm, and run if there's any danger. Do you understand me? Will you obey me?"

"To the letter. I'll not put anyone in jeopardy."

"Now, I have another plan. As we ride away, just as we get into the trees, I want you to quickly turn your horse around and go back. Sssh," he said, putting his fingers to her lips. "It's all arranged. I saved it 'til now to tell you because I wasn't sure if Revis would demand that you go with us or not. Justin will take care of you and see that you get to Sweetbriar."

"But Revis will know that you're in on this if you don't come after me."

"That's my worry, not yours," he snapped. "I just want you to obey. Now what are you going to do?"

Quietly she repeated his instructions. "You'll protect Verity? Please don't let Revis hurt her."

"If you obey me, I'll take care of Verity, even if I have to drag her into my own bed."

Leah stiffened. "Perhaps such a drastic measure won't be necessary."

"I guess that's as close to a jealous fit as I'm going to get. Kiss me, then go in and sleep. We'll leave early in the morning."

"Yes," she whispered. "Yes."

Chapter 23

Morning came much sooner than Leah wanted. All night long as she tossed and turned she had the feeling something was going to go wrong. Deep inside her she knew that something awful was going to happen today.

With heavy eyes, she prepared sacks of bread and cheese to take with them as they began the trek down the mountain. Only Verity was to remain behind.

Wesley emerged from the woods riding a huge roan stallion, followed by Bud and Cal on equally large black stallions. The horses pranced and snorted as if in anger, while their masters easily controlled them.

"We ride," Wesley said as Leah mounted a sedate chestnut mare.

All down the long trail Leah's heart beat faster and faster. Twice she caught Revis looking at her and again she knew that something was about to happen. Any man who could kill merely to insure that a female he wanted couldn't run away would not follow another man's lead so easily. And Revis had been very quiet about Wesley's entering the group.

By the time they reached the bottom and sighted the wagons, Leah could barely sit in the saddle. Once Wesley gave her a sharp look of warning to which she nodded curtly in acknowledgement, but otherwise he paid no attention to her.

Revis, Wesley, and Abe, flanked by Bud and Cal, approached the wagons as Leah held back. She watched them pull masks over their faces and saw them level guns at the drivers. She saw Justin get down from the seat, and from the second wagon came John Hammond, walking slowly, both with their hands up. On the wind she could hear Wesley giving orders to Oliver Stark to remove goods from the wagon.

In many ways it was like a play. She knew all the actors, yet some of them were pretending not to know each other. They were doing unreal things such as wearing masks and threatening each other. Perhaps she should be enjoying the charade, but each minute her heart increased its pace.

What was wrong? What was wrong?

Revis gave a low whistle in Leah's direction and when she looked at him, he silently motioned her to come nearer. Purposefully she didn't look at Wes. He might signal her to disobey Revis and she didn't want Revis to turn on Wesley.

As she nudged her horse forward something in the trees caught her eye. It was just a flash of a shiny glint. At first she ignored it, but as she stood beside Revis, looking down at Justin, she realized she had just seen the sun flashing off a gun barrel.

"You'll never get away with this," Justin was saying in a convincing manner.

Leah hardly heard any of what was going on around

256

her. She wondered if there was more than one gunman hidden in the trees. Were they Wesley's men and he just hadn't told her about them or were they Revis's men?

Wesley was giving orders, John was obeying, and Justin was arguing while Leah was trying to think. Secretly she jammed the stirrup into her horse's side, making it jump. While she looked as if she were trying to gain control, her eyes searched the tree line. There was concern on Wesley and Justin's faces, but Revis watched her with the unblinking gaze of an eagle. He watched her eyes.

They're his men, Leah thought. Those men belong to Revis.

"Whoa girl," Leah said, patting her horse's neck and leaning forward to adjust her stirrup. One of the glints in the trees moved.

"Cover me," Wesley said to Revis as he dismounted.

Revis nodded once and leveled his pistol at Justin while Wesley and Bud began to load goods onto the horses. Abe sat on his horse, his eyes darting around.

He's as nervous as I am, Leah thought.

When all the goods were loaded, Leah knew that what was going to happen would start soon.

Revis dismounted.

"Let's get out of here," Wesley said.

"I want to see inside those wagons for myself."

"Are you saying you don't trust me?" Wesley threatened.

"I don't trust anybody."

It seemed to Leah, that Revis made what was a strange move in the way he stepped between Wesley and the wagon. As he moved, Leah's head instinctively came up and again she saw a glint in the trees.

Without another thought she raised both legs and slammed her heels into her horse's side and went charging straight for Wesley. Complete confusion erupted.

Wesley jumped out of the way, was knocked down by the rump of Leah's horse, and as he went sprawling in the dirt three shots were fired.

All of them hit Revis in the chest.

Bud grabbed the reins of Leah's horse as Leah half jumped from the animal. "Wesley, are you hurt?"

He gave her a very odd look, his mask about his neck. "No." He looked up at Justin, who was bending over Revis.

Justin shook his head.

With a frown Wesley went to Revis and held the dying man's head in his lap.

"You thought you were so smart," Revis whispered. "You thought I'd believe you. I knew you were the one she visited. She turned everyone against me, even my own brothers."

He stopped to cough. His chest was soaked in blood seeping from the three wounds.

"Who is the Dancer?" Wesley asked. "Do something good in your life and tell me who he is."

Revis gave a bit of a smile. "I thought that's what you wanted to know." He closed his eyes for a moment, then opened them to look from one face above him to another.

"Macalister," he whispered. "Ever hear of Devon Macalister?"

"You're lying," Wesley said.

Revis started to speak but coughed again and fell dead in Wesley's arms.

Gently Wesley lay the dead man on the ground and rising, his eyes caught Justin's. "He was lying."

"Yes," was all Justin said before turning away.

Wes's eyes caught Leah's and he took her hand, leading her toward the trees.

"But what about the gunmen?"

"I'm sure they're long gone." He stopped, facing her. "You saved my life. Those shots were aimed for me. Thank you."

She turned pink under his praise. "You aren't angry that I disobeyed you?"

"Just this once I'm not. We're both free now. We can go home."

Pulling away from him, Leah walked farther into the woods. *Home* meant Sweetbriar, Kentucky, a place where she might or might not be wanted as a criminal. A farm waited for her there with a magnificent barn and a run-down house that Wesley had told his brother he couldn't bear to repair because he hated the idea of working on it for someone like Leah. Kimberly with all her charms and her prettiness waited for them at *home*.

"What's bothering you?" Wes asked, his hand on her shoulder.

"Do we have to go right now? I mean couldn't we have a little time here?"

"Just the two of us? No Bud and Cal? No Revis or Abe? No Verity?"

"Yes, just a day or two. I know you want to get back but—."

"But I'd much rather frolic in the woods for a few days with my pretty little wife. Right now I owe you a great deal. Don't you want something from me that's a little more difficult?"

She wanted so many things from him that she couldn't say a word. She couldn't very well just ask for his love, but she knew she had to earn it. In the woods she could be herself, but as soon as they reached

Sweetbriar she'd have to try to live up to the Stanford name.

"No," she answered. "All I want is to stay here for a while."

With a soft kiss Wesley told her he was glad to give her what she wanted.

It took hours to sort out everything in the cabin on the mountainside. When Verity heard of Revis's death, she stood fully upright, not slumping as she had. She walked out of the cabin with Leah, who escorted her to Justin's wagon. She didn't seem afraid of the other men as Leah feared she would be. Softly Verity asked to see Revis's body, and when the sheet was pulled back she smiled and stood even straighter. She then proceeded to tell Justin about some of her relatives in the East.

Revis's cabin was ransacked and all the goods, except for a sack of food, were removed.

"Find the owners of the jewelry if you can and distribute the food to whoever needs it," Wesley told Justin.

As they were stacking goods, Justin caught Leah's arm. "Is he good to you? You look different."

"He *is* good to me," Leah said with some surprise. "I don't know what will happen in Sweetbriar when he sees Kim again, but—."

"Kim?" Justin said, his head coming up. "Didn't Wes tell you that she and John Hammond were married a few days ago?"

"No," Leah said, trying to catch her breath. "No one told me."

It was dark when the overloaded wagons were ready to leave. Leah stood by Wesley and waved good-bye, giving John an especially hearty send-off. She was very happy when they were gone at last.

"Something certainly put a sparkle in your eye. It

wasn't Justin, was it?" Wesley asked, one eyebrow raised.

"You didn't tell me Kimberly was married."

"I guess it slipped my mind." He shrugged. "Let's go up the mountain and see who can get out of their clothes the fastest."

"And what do I get if I win?" she said with a laugh.

"Me and my male m—."

"I understand," she interrupted. "What are we waiting for?"

For three days they did little else but make love. They didn't talk about themselves or anyone else, and Leah refused to think of what awaited her in Sweetbriar.

The cabin that had been so full of hate and fear was now full of laughter and teasing. They chased each other about the table, made love on the table, under the table, and once half on a chair, half on the table.

On the morning of the fourth day she knew it was over. As she curled against Wesley's nude body she felt the tension in his muscles.

"I'll start packing," she said, but he caught her to him before she could move away.

"I've never enjoyed myself more in my life, Leah," he whispered, hovering over her lips. "Even the time with Revis was almost enjoyable because you were here."

She held her breath, praying he would say he loved her, but he rolled away and sat up.

"But the honeymoon's over because we need to get back. I've got crops to put in, animals to feed, people to set to work and—."

"And a wife who's known as a thief," Leah said flatly.

"We'll fix that," he said, brushing her words aside. "The Dancer is more important."

"Why did you say Revis lied when he told you wh
the Dancer was?"

Wesley stood, his big body beautiful in the hazy earl
morning light in the cabin. "Devon Macalister is m
friend, a very good friend of mine, and it's going to g
against everything I believe to prove he's the leader c
thieves. And yet"—he paused—"he does have acces
to knowledge and he does know the woods.

"Goddamn it!" Wes suddenly bellowed, and hi
mood changed from that of a lover to one of broodin
silence.

Leah had her own grim thoughts. It was easy fo
Wesley to dismiss her fears, but Leah couldn't. Sh
kept seeing the hatred in the eyes of the woman Revi
had wounded. Would that hatred be in other people'
eyes?

As they went down the mountain, they were quietl
occupied with their own dark thoughts.

Chapter 24

Leah stood on the hill, reins trailing behind her, and looked down at what her husband said was her new home. It wasn't Stanford Plantation, but it was large and sprawling, with two barns, three sheds, acres of cultivated fields, and an L-shaped log cabin.

"There's a spring not far from the house," Wesley was saying, "and I'll put in a kitchen garden for you this week." He paused. "Do you like it, Leah?" he asked quietly. "It's not the house Travis gave his bride, but I'll add onto it soon, I promise."

Turning, she smiled at him. "It's better than I'd ever hoped for. I like it very much."

"I had Justin and Oliver make some repairs on the house."

She looked away because she didn't want him to know she remembered that he'd said he couldn't bear even sleeping in the house because she was to live in it and not Kim.

They mounted their horses and as they rode onto

Wes's land three dogs came out to greet him. Oliver Stark, his sleeves rolled up, came from the barn.

"Am I glad to see you! I've got a horse foaling and it's breech. Know anything about horses?"

Wes was on the ground and following Oliver in seconds. "The house is yours, Leah," he called behind him.

For a moment Leah sat there studying the house with its deep, columned porch. Hers. Her very own house, her very own husband. Months ago in Virginia she'd imagined this time. She'd hoped Wes would be in love with her and she'd thought of how he'd carry her over the threshold and they'd be the picture of wedded bliss.

But the actuality was that she was to enter alone, her husband might or might not be in love with Kimberly, Leah was publicly known as a thief, and Wes was not by any means in love with his wife.

"Good morning."

"Good morning."

Leah looked to each side of her horse to see identical twin boys, big, strong, sturdy boys of about seventeen with handsome faces, dark skin, and brilliant blue eyes.

"I'm Slade," said one, eyes twinkling.

"And I'm Cord Macalister. Welcome."

"We work for Wes. Actually we keep the place going better when he's not around," said Slade.

"Wes has an awful habit of interfering with us. Would you like to see the house?"

"Or the fields? Or the town? Sweetbriar's not much but it's what we have to offer."

"Can I help you down?"

"I'll help too."

"Wait a minute!" Leah laughed. "You're going too fast for me. Yes, I'd like to get down, and yes, I'd like to see the house, but no thank you, on the town. At least not today."

Cord walked around the horse to stand beside his brother and they were indistinguishable from each other.

"Allow me," Slade said, arms extended.

"And me," Cord added.

Their humor was infectious and Leah allowed herself to be helped down by both young men and they did it with ease and grace, as if they often, together, lifted women from horses.

"It's not much," Cord said. Or was it Slade?

"But we did the best we could. Justin told us so much about you that we wanted to make the house nice."

"Bud and Cal had a few things to say about you too."

"You met them then? They're safe?" Leah asked.

"Safe!" Slade snorted. "Except that at first we thought they were breeding bulls and almost put them out to pasture, I reckon they're safe enough."

Again laughing, she started toward the open cabin door.

"Wait a minute, aren't new brides supposed to be carried over the threshold?" Slade asked.

"By their husbands they are," came a deep voice from behind them.

They all turned to see Wesley.

"You two weren't planning to volunteer to carry *my* wife, were you?"

"No sir," both boys echoed with wide eyes. "Never even crossed our minds."

With a laugh and a shake of his head, Wes came forward. "Get out of here and get back to work—and stop flirting with my wife," he shouted as they scurried off, after they'd given big winks to Leah.

ice boys," Leah said.

"Huh!" Wes said with a snort. "They're the bane of this town. Every woman they see falls in love with them, and then spoils them. Their father and I are the only people who give them any discipline. Now, about that carrying." Bending, he swept her into his arms.

"You know how this custom started, don't you? The Romans captured their brides and had to forcefully carry them into their houses. Are you a reluctant bride, Leah? Am I going to have to drag you into my bed tonight?"

She took him seriously. "I'm afraid not. When it comes to . . . *that,* I don't seem to have much resistance."

With a chuckle he kissed her long and lingeringly as he carried her inside the house. Still holding her, he seemed to be wanting some reaction from her.

To Leah, the cabin was very nice. It was large with simple, plain furniture, glass windows, a big stone fireplace, a hallway to the left, and her beautiful loom set not far from the fireplace.

"Bedroom?" she asked, nodding toward the hallway.

"With a great big featherbed. No expense has been spared when it comes to that room."

She smiled up at him. "It's a very nice house. I like it very much."

"You're not disappointed that it isn't like Travis' house?"

"No," she said honestly. "I was born in a swamp and this house suits me better than that mansion of Regan's."

"Mmm," he said, frowning. "I'm not sure I like my house being compared to a swamp."

Before she could answer he kissed her again, then set her down. "I'll have to go see about my foal. Anything you need, tell Oliver or, if you must, go to the twins. I'll have to double their work load to keep them away from you. Trouble is, they pretend to be each other and I never know who's working and who's not. See you later."

With that he was out the door.

As she looked about the place realizing it was hers, Leah told herself everything was going to be all right. Wesley would grow to love her because she was going to be a good wife to him, Kimberly would have no power over him, and everyone everywhere was going to live happily ever after.

With a smile she set about making the cabin more completely hers. It was larger and far cleaner than the shack in which she'd grown up with her enormous family.

In the bedroom were her trunks of clothes that Nicole had given her. Pulling a gown of lavender silk from the trunk, her rough hands caught on the fine fabric.

"First things first," she said aloud. Before a clean house and food on the table, Wesley would come home to a sweet-smelling wife with creamed, perfumed skin. In the kitchen she began searching for the ingredients for the creams and lotions Regan and Nicole had taught her to make.

It was hours later when her skin and hair seemed to be somewhat restored after the time in the forest. The roughness and redness of her hands were gone and her hair was gleaming in soft waves as she sat on a stool before the fireplace to dry it. It was nearly sundown, there was no meal prepared, and she hoped Wesley wouldn't be angry. To encourage his good humor, she wore a semitransparent dressing gown without a stitch on under it.

When Wesley walked in the door he paused, hat in hand, and stared at her. The firelight showing through her gown made her look as if she had a delicate layer of fairy cloth over her beautiful body.

Unnoticed, his hat fell to the floor as he advanced toward her and pulled her into his arms, her thick hair tangling around his forearms.

"I didn't cook anything," she whispered as his lips descended.

"And I don't plan to wash," he replied. "If you can overlook me, I'll forgive you."

He kissed her then, pulling her to him as if he were starving.

Leah clung to him. He'd been working in the fields and his clothes were damp with sweat, his hair curling about his neck. Her fingers went up his neck to intertwine in the curls.

Wesley began to kiss her throat as his hands ran over her arms. Her body was hot from being near the fire and with his sweat and her heat, they nearly sizzled upon touching.

Wesley swept her into his arms, carried her into the bedroom, and carefully laid her on the featherbed.

"Take that off," he commanded in a low, husky whisper as he stood back from her.

The fading sunlight streamed through the single window, making a golden haze of light in which Leah knelt on the bed, the deep mattress fluffing about her. Slowly she undid the little silk ties that held the gossamer garment together. Then, raising her head to meet his eyes, she languidly slid the silk off her shoulders but managed to keep most of her body hidden. For a moment she held it in front of her, concealing herself from him.

"And now you," she murmured, toying with the silk.

With a crooked grin, Wesley stripped himself of every stitch of his work clothes, flung them to a corner, and made a leap for her.

Leah, not expecting this sort of exuberance, squealed and rolled out of his way. The silk gown stayed on the bed, caught underneath Wesley.

"Pretty little thing," he said as he pulled it from under him, then tossed it to the floor. "Come here," he commanded.

Leah stayed against the wall, her arms held demurely so most of her was covered.

"No," she said easily. "I worked all day on smelling good and now you expect me to roll around with some sweaty, unclean man. Ladies don't—."

He caught her ankle, pulled her down into the bed, and dragged her toward him. "I guess we'll just have to make you smell a little less sweet." With that he pushed her down into the feather mattress and covered her clean body with his dirty one, rubbing against her, smearing her with his sweat.

"Wesley!" Leah gasped, and she knew nothing had ever felt as good as this man. "Wesley," she said again, her eyes shut.

He smiled at her then and began to kiss her body, starting at her neck, his lips grazing her breasts, moving down to her stomach, his big hands toying with the muscles by her hipbones, his tongue licking around her navel. His hands parted her thighs, rubbing the inner recesses as his lips followed his hands.

Working his way downward, he reached her feet and with his tongue caressed the little pads of her toes.

Leah was almost crying with desire by the time he made his way up her body again. He hovered over her lips for just a moment.

"Is the answer still no?"

"No," she murmured, then her eyes flew open. "I mean yes. Oh Wesley." She sighed and pulled him closer as her legs began to rub up and down his.

He made love to her with tenderness, so slowly she was frantic for him when he finally pulled her to him and with hard thrusts brought them both to a peak of ecstasy.

They lay together, wrapped about each other, their skin sticky and wet.

"You planning to feed me?" Wesley murmured against her shoulder.

With a laugh, Leah pushed at him. "I guess the honeymoon is over. But first we wash."

As he rolled off her, Wesley sniffed. "You should wash. You smell like you've been out in the fields all day."

"You!" she exclaimed, starting to pummel his chest.

"I sure do love the way you bounce, Leah. Now stop trying to entice me and go fix me something to eat."

"And if I don't?" she challenged.

"I'll do something else with that bare little bottom of yours, such as smack it." His threat lost meaning as he began to kiss her, and she snuggled against him.

A loud knock on the door made her pull away. "Who do you think that is?"

"Probably Bud and Cal. Seems you promised to cook for them."

"When? Oh yes, when they were going to take me back to Revis's cabin. But tonight I haven't cooked anything."

Wesley moved to the side of the bed. "I'm sure that if you just explain to them that you spent the day making yourself pretty in order to seduce me, they'll understand."

"I could tell them I dumped dinner over your head. They'd understand that even more."

The knock sounded again.

"Come on, get dressed," Wes said as he pulled on his pants. "You can fry up half a hog and that'll do fine. You know, I think I like making love to you in a bed." With that he left the room and moments later Leah heard him talking to Bud and Cal.

Hurriedly she dressed, pulled her hair back from her face, and went to join them. It was obvious that the big men were so glad to see her that they weren't going to mind too much about food.

While Leah fried ham and potatoes, boiled water for corn on the cob, and mixed cornbread batter, they all talked. Bud and Cal slowly told about their farm, about the animals they planned to buy, and what kind of house they'd build.

"Perhaps you should build two houses," Leah suggested, "in case you get married."

Bud and Cal looked at one another. "No women would marry us. Women are afraid of us."

"I'm not," she said, a hand on each big shoulder, "and I'll bet Sweetbriar is full of women who'll fall in love with you."

"If Abe can do it, so can you," Wesley said, his mouth full of corn.

Bud and Cal slowly broke into big grins.

"What about my brother?" Leah asked, filling their plates with food.

"I forgot you were here 'working' all day," Wesley said, his eyes smiling at her. "You haven't heard about Abe."

"Will *someone* please tell me?"

"You do the honors, Bud," Wes said. From the

sound of his voice he seemed about to burst into laughter.

"Abe fell in love," Bud said softly, his attention on his food.

Leah sat down. "Is that true?" she asked Wes.

"As far as anyone can tell," Wes answered. "He took one look at Miss Caroline Tucker and fell in love. Two days later he asked her to marry him."

"Marry him? This is my brother Abe you're talking about? No mistake? Abe never loved anyone but himself in his whole life."

"He does now. Pass me the potatoes, Cal," Wes said. "You boys don't know how lucky you were to get anything to eat."

"What's the rest of it?" Leah asked. "There's something you're not telling me about my brother. What's Caroline Tucker like?"

Wes nearly choked on a piece of ham. "Describe her, will you, Bud?"

"'Bout my size," was all Bud answered.

Leah digested this. "My brother fell in love with a woman the size of one of you?" she asked in disbelief.

"Shorter than us," Cal said.

"Wesley!" Leah threatened.

"I wasn't there but Oliver said that your brother arrived in town, took one look at the . . . ah, very large Miss Tucker, and fell in love. He said something to Oliver about she'd never been hungry and I guess he liked that idea. He followed her around town until she asked him to dinner with her parents and sometime during the meal he stood up and asked for Caroline's hand in marriage. He told them he had been a thief and had done some bad things in his life but with Caroline's help, he was going to become a new man."

"Gracious!" was all Leah could answer, completely astonished by this news.

They finished their meal, Wesley removed pipes from a wall cabinet, took one, and handed the other two to Bud and Cal.

As Leah cleaned up, she thought of how pleasant this moment was. She still glowed from Wesley's lovemaking and behind her were people she cared about. After Bud and Cal left, Leah and Wes gave each other baths out of basins of hot water, and ended up making love in a leisurely manner on the floor before the fireplace.

When they went to bed, it was to snuggle comfortably in each other's arms.

Hours before daylight the next morning, Wesley was up and out of bed while Leah started the day's chores and had her first real look at the outside of her new home.

The number of animals on the farm was impressive. About a dozen geese lived under the porch and set up a racket whenever anyone walked past them. Thirty ducks waddled around the yard. Behind the house was a well-built, completely fenced chicken house, and Leah went inside, her apron full of crushed corn. To her left she could hear hogs grunting and behind her was the bleating of sheep.

"Wool," she said, smiling. Wool to be spun for weaving on her precious loom.

Still smiling, she left the chicken yard but her smile disappeared instantly. Wesley was coming toward her and in his arms was the unmistakable form of Mrs. John Hammond—Kimberly.

Chapter 25

"I think she's fainted," Wesley said with concern.

"Did you ask her to?"

"Leah," Wes warned. "I'm taking her into the house. She may need help."

"I'm sure she does," Leah said under her breath, but she followed him.

"Just put her on the bed," Leah directed, "and you can go back to work. I'll take care of her."

"She scares me to death when she does that," Wes said with a frown. "You think I should get a doctor?"

"She'll be fine, now please go."

Reluctantly Wesley obeyed her.

"He's gone," Leah said. "You can open your eyes now."

With a bouncy little smile Kim sat up on the bed. "How nice! A featherbed. You look so pretty, Leah." Her face changed. "I don't have time anymore to look pretty. Just look at my hair. Dull as mud."

"What do you want, Kimberly?" Leah asked flatly.

"What did you think your fainting was going to get you from Wesley?"

She looked up at Leah with sad eyes. "I never intended to faint, but Wesley always did love it so. John just hates for me to faint. He says such awful things to me that I've just about stopped."

"Chalk one up for John," Leah murmured.

"But Wesley just loves fainting women. Have you fainted for him?"

"No, Kimberly," Leah said patiently. "I really need to get to work. I have breakfast to cook and other chores to do and—."

Kim suddenly buried her face in her hands and began to cry. "Oh Leah," she wailed, "you aren't even glad to see me. After the way you ruined my whole life I'd think you could spare a little sympathy for me. I got married and you haven't even asked me about it and you're really the best girlfriend I ever had."

Waves of guilt spread over Leah as she sat on the bed and took Kim into her arms.

"How was your wedding, Kim?"

Kim began to sniff. "Just awful! Just dreadful, awful, terrible, that's how it was. The only people there were an old skinny man named Lester and his wife and John and me. No one else came to see my pretty dress, no one even wished us happiness."

She looked up at Leah. "It was the dress I would have worn to marry Wesley if you hadn't taken him away from me. Oh Leah, I still don't understand why you did that. Wesley was all I had except Steven, and he never liked me."

"Kimberly," Leah began, not knowing what to say.

Kim moved off the bed to stand before Leah. "Look at this awful dress. It's *brown!* Did you ever see me wearing brown before? John says it's better for all the

275

chores he makes me do. And look at my hands! They're
red and raw. Oh how I wish you'd never taken Wesley
away from me."

"If you had Wesley, you'd still have to work. I don't
have any servants and right now I have to cook."
Sweeping past Kim, she left the bedroom to go to the
fireplace.

Kim followed her. "But at least Wesley wouldn't
make me do the things at night that John does."

Leah gave a quick glance skyward. "All men expect
'night things' and Wesley is no exception."

"But is Wesley so . . . forceful?"

"Yes! Here, sit down and peel this potato."

"I can do that," Kim said brightly, taking the potato
and a chair. "Are you mad at me, Leah?" she asked
after a moment.

"What do you care?" she snapped, then calmed.
"Kim, I'm trying to be patient. I'm sorry Wes felt he
had to marry me. I certainly never set out to harm
anyone and if you'll remember, Wesley is the one who
decided we should stay together so maybe you should
be angry with him."

"Oh well, men," Kim said blandly, peeling the
potato. "Wesley liked you better because you're so
exciting. All sorts of things happen around you. I'm
sure Steven was drowned because he was showing off
for you, and Justin fell in love with you, then Wesley
decided you are more interesting than I am. And you
are, Leah. The only interesting thing I do is faint and
my husband doesn't even like for me to do that. So,
see, it really was all your fault. Do you plan to keep
Wesley or can I have him back someday?"

"Kimberly," Leah said slowly, "you're talking about
dissolving two marriages. You can't do that very
easily."

"I don't know. Wesley's friend, Clay, was married to Nicole, then married to someone else, then married to Nicole again. I really truly don't like John much."

"Then why did you marry him?"

She paused in her peeling. "It was the oddest thing, but after Wesley chose you over me, I felt as if I weren't pretty anymore. I know that's silly, but I almost felt ugly and then John asked me to marry him and that made me feel pretty again so I said yes. I just didn't realize men could be so different. Wesley was always so nice to me."

"But John is mean because he makes you work and do things in bed?" Leah had almost cooked a whole meal while Kim was peeling one potato.

"More or less," Kim said, but before she could say more, the geese outside set up a racket, the door opened, and in came Wesley, followed by Oliver and the Macalister twins.

"I think I forgot to tell you that the hands eat breakfast with us since they've already put in a few hours' work."

Leah only had time to shake her head at him before she began throwing more eggs and ham into skillets.

Kimberly acted as if all the men had come to see her; she preened under the twins' flirting with her and prettily complained to Oliver that his brother Justin was quite unpleasant to her.

"Oh, that was nice," Kim purred when she and Leah were alone again. "It's never nice like that at my house. Leah, John's going to be gone all day. Could I stay with you? I'll help you do what you need to do and later maybe you can put something on my hair to make it nice and shiny like yours."

Leah knew Kim would be a nuisance all day, but she didn't have the heart to refuse her request.

"You may stay," Leah said and was rewarded with Kim's arms about her neck.

"Thank you so much, Leah. It's so good to have a friend."

They spent the day together, Kim chattering constantly about her former life of dances and handsome young men while slowly doing the chores Leah gave her. She didn't complain anymore about Leah's "taking" Wesley from her, nor did she again mention her husband John.

Surprisingly for Leah, Kim turned out to be good company. She was slow at doing things, but once she understood what was to be done she was willing enough, and in the afternoon they laughed a lot together while Leah washed Kim's thick blonde hair.

Toward evening when Kim had to leave there were tears in her eyes. "No other woman has ever been nice to me," she cried softly. "They were all like Regan, so unkind, always mean to me."

Leah was silent, accepting the compliment but not trying to explain exactly why women disliked Kim so much. Perhaps it was the way she treated women, as if they didn't or shouldn't exist. "Please come again," she said sincerely when Kim left. "I enjoyed myself."

At supper Wesley calmly announced that in the morning Leah, Bud, and Cal were going into Sweetbriar with him.

Three faces suddenly showed fear.

"It's just a quiet little town," Wes said with some disgust. "Nothing's going to hurt you. Except for what Abe's told people, no one knows what happened in the mountains. Neither Justin nor Oliver nor John has said a word so you're all safe."

"What about the woman who Revis shot?" Leah asked quietly. "He told all those people who I was and where I lived. I've had one safe day here, but it won't last if I go into town."

"That's absurd, Leah!" Wes said explosively, then clenched his jaw. "And what about you two?"

Bud looked at Cal. "We will stay here with Leah," Cal said softly.

"Damn all of you!" Wes shouted, jumping up and knocking over his chair. "I'll not live with a bunch of cowards. You're going with me in the morning even if I have to drag you."

No one laughed at the idea of Wes or any man trying to drag Bud or Cal someplace, but the three of them looked into their coffee cups and nodded.

"That's better," Wes said. "I have to see to the cows." He left the cabin, obviously still angry.

"We did not like Revis," Cal said, "but we liked staying away from people. People are afraid of us."

Leah didn't want to think of all the things that could happen tomorrow. Wesley could cause trouble with this man who Revis had said was the Dancer—Devon Macalister; Bud and Cal could be laughed at and get their feelings hurt, and she . . . she didn't want to think of that.

Her head came up and she really looked at Bud and Cal. She was used to seeing them bare-chested, wearing sheepskin and leather, but perhaps if they wore shirts people wouldn't be as likely to laugh at them.

"Do you own any shirts?"

"Shirts do not fit us," Bud answered.

"Of course," Leah said, rising and looking at the kitchen yet to be cleaned. "If you'll help me tonight, I'll make both of you shirts. I think I can have them ready by tomorrow morning."

Slowly it began to seep into the young men what Leah planned to do, and their eyes started to shine.

"Do you think you can wash dishes without breaking them?"

Bud gave her an indignant look. "We have repaired robins' broken legs; we can do your dishes."

Wesley returned to see Bud and Cal doing women's chores and Leah cutting huge pieces from yards of heavy blue cotton. With a smile, because he knew something had happened, he asked if he could help.

Leah didn't get to bed until three in the morning. The shirts were done except for the buttonholes, but she figured the boys could wear them unsewn for one day. Tired, she crawled into bed beside Wesley and he sleepily pulled her to him.

"All done?"

Yawning, she nodded.

"Next time you adopt somebody I hope they're smaller than those two. I have to work three hours longer every day just to feed them. Couldn't you adopt stray cats instead of stray people?"

Leah wasn't listening to him because she was already asleep.

With a smile he pulled her closer and went back to sleep.

For Leah, daylight came much too early. She was so nervous she cracked an egg directly into the fire, completely forgetting to use a skillet, and Bud and Cal, who'd come for breakfast, were so jittery they each ate only four pork chops, six eggs, half a loaf of bread, three fried apples, and a partridge. A pittance.

"Hope neither of you faints from hunger today," Wesley said as Leah cleared the table, but no one responded. Oliver, Cord, and Slade went to work while Wesley packed the wagon with food for the noon meal. He was determined to spend the whole day in Sweetbriar and show the three of them that things weren't as bad as they thought.

Leah and Wes sat on the wagon seat on the ride into town while Bud and Cal sat stiffly in the back, their eyes glum.

Sweetbriar wasn't very large; a few houses, a livery stable, a general store, a ladies' clothing store, a blacksmith shop, a few more shops here and there. Nothing that looked especially frightening, but the eyes of the people milling about were all on the newcomers.

"They're watching us," Leah whispered.

"Of course they are," Wes snapped. "They've never seen you before."

As they stepped down from the wagon a woman in her fifties came toward them and Leah drew back, but Wesley pushed her forward.

"You must be Leah Stanford," the woman said, smiling. "I've heard so much about you from Abe."

"Abe?" Leah said stupidly.

"I'm Wilma Tucker and maybe you haven't heard, but my daughter Caroline is engaged to your brother. We're all going to be family. My son Jessie—he's a senator now," she said proudly, "he's coming back for the wedding. Floyd and me are real proud of your brother and you don't look a thing like him."

Leah began to smile and at the same time she started to relax. "I haven't seen my brother for a while but Wesley told me about the wedding. May I introduce some friends of mine?"

Bud and Cal were still sitting on the edge of the wagon. With a glare Leah motioned for them to rise.

"My goodness," Wilma said, looking up at them. "How nice and big you are."

"This is Bud and Cal . . ." Leah had no idea what their last names were, but as she looked at them they were smiling down at Wilma. Obviously they liked the woman because she wasn't afraid of them.

"Haran, ma'am," Cal said softly.

Wilma smiled. "Oh yes, you bought the land near Wesley's. Abe was saying—. Oh, here's my daughter now."

Leah was glad she was prepared for the sight of Caroline Tucker. Caroline seemed at least as wide as she was tall, with a pretty, freckled face. Perhaps she appeared outrageous, but Leah found herself liking Caroline right away.

"You're Leah," Caroline said, holding out a fat little hand. "Abe said you were the prettiest woman in the world."

"Did he?" Leah was genuinely pleased.

"I was supposed to meet him today, but I haven't seen him anywhere."

With a jolt, Leah realized she was imagining Caroline and skinny, angular Abe in bed together. She really hoped Caroline didn't get on top. Leah straightened herself. "I haven't seen him since we arrived."

"I just saw him," Wes said as he was looking over the leather harness. "He was going into that white house at the end of town."

"That's where Lincoln Stark is living!" Caroline said angrily, stamping her surprisingly small foot. "Abe is gambling again. He promised he wouldn't. Oh Ma!"

Before Wilma could say a word of caution, Caroline was hurrying down the street toward the white house.

Obviously Wilma was embarrassed. "Abe really did promise," she said meekly. "And Caroline does have a mind of her own, and I think she really does love Abe and—."

She stopped because the loud slamming of a door was like a shot fired, and seconds later came the

282

muffled sounds of shouts from the little house. The five of them were silent as they heard what sounded like furniture being tossed about, and then a stool came flying through the window.

"I guess I'd better go see what's happening," Wesley said, looking at Wilma, who was beginning to look frightened.

"I hope Caroline isn't hurt," Wilma whispered, and all of them began to follow Wesley as he advanced on the house.

Just as they reached it the door flew open and a deck of cards came flying out, catching the wind and fluttering like big snowflakes.

"Ain't no woman gonna tell me—," came Abe's voice. "Here! You watch out! Don't you hurt Lincoln again! Caroline, I'm warnin' you!"

Wesley tore up the two porch steps to the open door, looked inside for a moment, his mouth open in astonishment, then began backing down as his face split into a grin.

"She all right?" Wilma asked.

With the beginnings of some deeply felt laughs, Wesley just nodded toward the door.

Within seconds, Caroline Tucker emerged with Abe's thin body slung across her left shoulder.

"Put me down, you goddamn, overgrown horse!" Abe bellowed into her back.

"Hush up, Abe, my ma's lookin'."

Immediately Abe quieted, and as Caroline walked down the stairs she paused before her mother. "He'll never gamble again, Ma," she said solemnly.

"That's true, Miz Tucker," Abe said. "Caroline done showed me the light. Leah! That you just standin' there?" he hissed from his upside-down position. "You fergit I'm your brother? You oughta help me."

Leah was trying very hard not to laugh. "Hello, Abe. Fine day, isn't it?"

After giving his sister a dirty look, he began caressing Caroline's backside. "Caroline, honey," he said sweetly, "you oughta have more respect for me than this."

"I think I'll take Abe home now, Ma," Caroline said. "And I'm going to have a word with Doll Stark about that boy of his leading my man into sin."

"Me?" came a voice from behind them. Standing on the porch leaning heavily against the rail, was a pleasant-looking young man—or had been. Now one eye was about to turn black, and blood was pouring from his nose. Holding an already soaked handkerchief to his nose, he glared at Caroline. "That precious Abe of yours started this game. It weren't *my* fault."

"Hah!" Caroline snorted, her nose in the air as she walked away regally, bearing Abe across her shoulder.

Abe's words floated to them on the wind. "You sure were pretty in there, Caroline. I sure liked the way you punched Lincoln all them times. You sure we gotta wait for the weddin' 'fore we—?"

"Hush, Abe," Caroline commanded. "Don't talk dirty."

"Yes, sweetheart," Abe said, his hands moving up and down the backside of her.

Wesley was the first to erupt as he removed his hat, slapped it across his knee, and broke down with laughter.

Leah wanted to stop him for fear of offending Wilma, but Wilma put her arms out and fell against Wesley, the two of them barely able to stand for laughing so hard.

"They been like that ever since they met," Wilma said between gasps. "Abe seems thrilled she wants him."

"And Caroline's wild happy 'cause somebody wants her," Wesley finished. "They are a pair."

"I'm bleedin' to death and you two are fallin' apart laughin'," Lincoln Stark accused.

Leah, still so shocked by the whole scene she couldn't yet laugh, looked at Bud and Cal and saw they were grinning from ear to ear, so she went to Lincoln. "Let's go in the house and I'll see if I can get the bleeding stopped."

It was sometime later when Wesley came into the house, still smiling. "There are some people out here I want you to meet. They're the twins' parents, Linnet and Devon Macalister."

The Dancer, Leah thought, washing out the bloody cloth she'd been holding to Lincoln's nose. Now was when she'd be exposed as a thief.

Chapter 26

As Leah left the little house she prayed that Wesley wouldn't let his temper show, that he'd be cautious and not blurt out what he felt about a man who'd planned robberies for years. But what greeted Leah was not what she expected.

Wesley was talking to the man as if they were the best of friends, smiling at him, his eyes alive. Macalister was tall, lean, dark-skinned, and very handsome. His black hair had bits of gray in it and his eyes crinkled against the sun, all of which added to his sharp good looks. Beside him was a pretty little woman with a delicate-featured face, big eyes, dark blonde hair and a curvy little body. She didn't look a day over twenty-five, but she had to be quite a bit older if she was the mother of Slade and Cord.

"You must be Mrs. Stanford," said the woman in a pretty, crisp accent. "I'm Linnet Macalister. And this—," she pulled a little girl from behind her skirts, "this is my youngest daughter, Georgina. I believe you've met my sons."

Instantly Leah liked this lovely woman and she wondered how much Linnet knew about her husband's illegal activities.

The little girl gave Leah a shy smile, then ran to her father, tugging on his pants leg until he picked her up.

"Leah, honey," Wesley said, "come here. I want you to meet Mac."

Right away Leah knew it was going to be difficult to dislike Devon Macalister. "How do you do, Mr. Macalister."

The man looked at his wife as if sharing some private joke. "Mac will do," he said in a deep, pleasant voice. "Wes says you like to weave. Lynna has some patterns for weavin', and Miranda spins wool."

"Miranda's our eldest daughter," Linnet explained. "This morning she was visiting Corinne Tucker's eldest daughter and she should be back fairly soon. Perhaps you and I could leave the men to their talk and I could show you Sweetbriar."

"That's very kind of you, but I'd hate to take so much of your time." Truthfully Leah wanted to sit in the back of the wagon with a blanket over her head. That way she'd be sure no one recognized her.

"Go ahead," Wesley said. "Linnet knows everybody a lot better than I do." He gave her a hard look of warning that only she could see.

"What about Bud and Cal?" she asked quietly. She felt much safer with the men near her, as if they could protect each other.

With a sigh Wes looked down at her. "The boys will go with us, and Mac and I will protect them with our lives. If any children hurt your boys we'll string the kids up right there. No trial or nothin'. And if any—."

"Stop it!" she hissed, but she was smiling. "They're just . . . you know."

"Delicate," Wesley said seriously. He leaned back toward Mac. "She's talking about those two bulls over there. Leah's afraid somebody will laugh at them and hurt their feelings."

Mac gave a snort of disbelief.

"You just go with Linnet," Wesley said, "and I'll meet you at Mac's store about noon." Bending, he gave her a quick peck on the cheek. "And we'll take care of your boys."

Leah felt a little lost when Wesley and Mac, followed by the towering Bud and Cal, walked away, but Linnet soon put her at ease.

"Everyone in town is dying to meet Wesley's new wife. We've known Wes for years and seen him work hard on his farm, so of course everyone is curious about who he was doing all the work for," Linnet said. "I wouldn't be surprised if nearly everyone in Sweetbriar came to town today just to see you."

With a laugh at Leah's grimace, Linnet continued. "You'll have to get used to this town. There's no such thing as a secret to them. It's not that they're nosy, just that they're . . . concerned, I guess. When I first came here twenty years ago—."

"Twenty years!" Leah said in disbelief. "You don't look much over twenty now."

"How kind you are. My eldest daughter is nineteen. Here comes Agnes Emerson. Her husband died a few years ago and now her son Doyle runs their farm."

What followed for Leah was a confusing array of names and faces. There were people who'd only been in Sweetbriar for a year or two, but that special light in Linnet's eyes was reserved for the parents and children of people who, Linnet said, had been in the town for years. Leah found it impossible to keep all the people straight. She met Nettie and Maxwell Rowe and was told their youngest daughter, Vaida, was the town schoolteacher and their eldest, Rebekah, was married to Jessie Tucker who was now a state senator.

"Everyone seems to be very proud of this Jessie Tucker," Leah said.

Linnet smiled. "Jessie would inspire pride in the people around him no matter what he did. How many of the Starks have you met?"

"Quite a few," Leah said with a laugh. "How many are there?"

"New ones every year. Gaylon Jr. went to Boston last year to attend school. He's a very intelligent young man and we all hope he'll become governor or even president."

As they walked through the town, stopping in stores and meeting people, Leah became aware of the strong sense of community. In Virginia, no matter how many times she reminded herself that she had become a Stanford, she still thought of herself as a Simmons. The swamp seemed to pull her toward it, and Regan and Nicole, for all their kindness, always seemed as if they'd been created in another world that was far removed from Leah's.

But here in this little town with all the people wearing clothes of homespun cotton or wool, often patched garments, she began to feel as if she belonged. In spite of what Wesley had accused her of, of wanting Stanford Plantation, Leah had never wanted to be rich. Her dreams had been about safety, a place where she was sure she wasn't going to be beaten. Stanford Plantation had been safe, but the delicate dishes, the silk clothes that made her constantly worry about tearing them, the manners she had to memorize, all the things that came naturally to Regan and Nicole, all made Leah nervous.

This town was safe and it wasn't formal. Most of the people she met slurred their words and made no pretense at talking in the way Nicole had taught Leah, a way that was sometimes difficult for Leah to remember. Linnet, for all her plain cotton dress, seemed to exude a ladylike air that reminded Leah of Nicole.

Linnet's daughter Georgina soon lost her shyness when she saw an older woman walking beside twin girls, and Georgina ran ahead to meet them.

"That's Justin and Oliver's mother, Esther," Linnet said with some sadness in her voice as they approached the woman. "Doll's nearly worn her out with having so many children. The twins are her granddaughters. Their mother, Lissie, died in childbirth."

Leah was introduced to Esther Stark and the six-year-old twins, and afterward Linnet led Leah to the Macalister store. "It's grown some in the last few years," Linnet explained, "and now I do the bookkeeping so Devon has more time off. It's all worked out quite well," she said in a dreamy way that seemed private to Leah.

Before the empty fireplace sat an old, thin man, idly whittling on a stick.

"This here the new one?" the man asked.

"Allow me to introduce Doll Stark," Linnet said. "This is Mrs. Leah Stanford."

Leah nodded to the man, all the while remembering everything Justin had said about his father.

Doll looked at Leah for a long moment and seemed to sense her dislike of him. "I think I'll go see to some things," he said, rising.

When they were alone in the store, surrounded by

shelves of merchandise, Linnet spoke, a small frown on her face. "He's a very lonely man now since Phetna and old Gaylon died." At the puzzled look on Leah's face, she explained. "After Devon and I were married, Doll used to sit in here with his friends, Gaylon and Phetna, but when they died, most of the life went out of Doll. Devon has been trying to find someone to sit in here with Doll but no one nowadays seems to have quite such a capacity for inactivity. Perhaps it's all the travelers passing through here. Everything seems so much faster now."

Leah could hear all the love in Linnet's voice and it was the same as hearing another side to the story. Justin despised his father for his laziness while others loved Doll for it.

It was while they were inside the store that they heard a woman's screams outside.

"That's Miranda," Linnet said with a gasp and started running.

Outside, tearing down the main street, was a runaway team of horses pulling a wagon that lurched drunkenly from one side to the other. On the seat, trying her best to hold on, was a pretty young girl with wild, frightened eyes, hair flying about her face.

"Devon!" Linnet screamed as the wild wagon ran past Leah and her. The next moment the two women started running after the wagon, Linnet's face a mask of terror.

Neither Mac nor Wesley was in the street to see the wagon, but Bud and Cal were. It was amazing that men so big could act so quickly. As if they'd planned their actions together, Bud ran to the back of the wagon while Cal spurted ahead to the front.

Bud jumped on the back of the wagon and agilely

291

made his way to the seat and the frightened girl. With one hand he caught her about the waist while steadying himself with his powerful legs wide apart.

Miranda, with a little scream when Bud first touched her, turned and clung to him, instinctively trusting him with her life.

Meanwhile Cal ran in front of the horses, grabbed the harness, and used his big body to create resistance. For a few seconds he was pulled under, his heels tearing into the dirt, then the horses began to slow and Cal gained control.

Mac and Wesley walked out of the feed store to see Bud standing in the back of the wagon, Miranda clinging to him with all her might, while Cal gathered the loose reins and secured the horses.

"Miranda," Mac said breathlessly, and in one step was at the foot of the wagon. "Come here, princess." He held up his arms to her.

Miranda, obviously shaken and still frightened, looked from her father to Bud, who still held her; she closed her eyes and remained where she was.

"What—?" Mac began, but Linnet put her hand on her husband's arm as Bud walked to the edge of the wagon.

Cal put up his arms for Miranda.

"Two," was all Miranda whispered before sliding into Cal's massive arms and snuggling against him.

Everyone around this trio could do little more than stare. Leah wondered if young Miranda was always so forward, and she also wondered why the boys had said people, especially women, were afraid of them. This young lady certainly didn't seem afraid of them.

"Miranda!" Mac said sharply as she gazed up into Cal's big brown eyes.

With seeming reluctance Miranda turned to her father.

"Are you all right? You're not hurt anywhere?" Mac asked, stiff-jawed.

"No," she said slowly, making no attempt whatsoever to leave Cal's arms. "I'm quite all right." When Bud stood beside them she reached out her hand to his.

They were a striking trio, Miranda so small, Bud and Cal so large, the three of them wrapped together, unaware of anyone outside their tight circle.

"Miranda," Wesley said, laughter in his voice, "may I introduce Bud and Cal Haran."

"You're Cal and you're Bud," she said softly and was rewarded with a nod from both of them. "Thank you for saving my life."

Before a word could be said Miranda astonished them all by climbing onto the wagon underpinnings, slipping her arms about Cal's neck, and kissing him thoroughly. Again Linnet put her hand on her husband's arm while Miranda moved to Bud and kissed him too.

Moving back, Miranda put her hand on each big shoulder. "Come with me and I'll fix you something to eat."

Together they walked away, leaving an astonished group behind them.

"Well, that should kill the romance." Wesley broke the silence. "As soon as she finds out how much those two eat she'll run from them."

"I don't like it, Linnet!" Mac said explosively. "I don't like it at all. She's never acted like that before. How come you raised a daughter that'd act like that about two strangers?"

Quite calmly, Leah thought, Linnet ignored he[r] husband's temper. "I'm afraid it must run in my family[.] I believe your daughter has just fallen in love."

"In love!" Mac snapped at her. "She doesn't eve[n] know them. Sometimes, Linnet, you say the—."

"Devon," Linnet said sweetly, "may I remind yo[u] that I fell in love with you when I first saw you? Wh[y] should your daughter do any differently?"

Mac stiffened. "There's a lot of difference betwee[n] me and those two! I was rescuing you and—." Th[e] anger suddenly went out of him. "Which one do yo[u] think she's in love with?" he asked heavily.

With a sigh Linnet looked toward their store. "[I] hope I'm wrong but it looks as if she wants *both* o[f] them."

Before Mac could speak, Wesley slapped him har[d] on the shoulder. "Congratulations, Mac. Two sons-in[-] law at once. And believe me, you'll need all th[e] supplies in your stores to feed them."

Mac cast Wes a black look. "No daughter o[f] mine—," he began but stopped with a look of disgust[.] "Women!" he said between clenched teeth. "Come on[,] Lynna, let's see what she's up to now."

Glumly Mac escorted his wife toward their store.

Turning, Leah smiled up at Wesley. "I don't know i[f] that solves something or starts new problems. Bud and[d] Cal certainly did seem to take to Miranda, didn'[t] they?"

"Are you jealous?" he asked, half-serious, half i[n] jest. "From now on you may not be the only woman i[n] their lives."

The sunlight on his face, his eyes shadowed by hi[s] broad-brimmed hat, made him look especially enticing. Her eyes went to his lips.

"Leah," Wesley said huskily. "You're singeing my eyebrows."

Embarrassed, she looked away.

A crowd of people had gathered when Miranda's wagon had torn down the street and many people had stayed, chuckling, to watch Miranda reward her saviors, but now they were moving away.

"That's her!" gasped a heavyset woman, looking straight at Leah.

Leah froze where she was. Never would she forget that woman's face. When Revis had shot her husband, the woman's hatred had gone to Leah's heart.

"She killed my husband," the woman said loudly, and the next moment she was advancing on Leah with hands made into claws.

"Murderer!" the woman screamed. "Murderer!"

Leah didn't move but waited for the woman, almost as if she deserved what she got.

Wesley put himself between Leah and the enraged woman. "Don't," he said kindly.

"She killed him!" the woman screeched. "He was all I had in the world. We were gonna build a farm together. Now everythin's gone because of her." Still screaming, she began to kick Wesley, hitting him with her fists.

"Get in the wagon, Leah," Wesley said calmly. "Go! Now!" he commanded when she didn't move.

Leah tried to keep her chin high, but it wasn't easy because she could feel the eyes of everyone in town on her. Stiffly she climbed into the wagon, her eyes straight ahead.

After a few moments Wesley sat beside her and without a word to her clucked to the horses to go.

Leah didn't blame him for not speaking to her. And imagine, she'd just started to think that Sweetbriar might be safe. What little safety there had been was now gone—as were her chances for gaining her husband's love. No Stanford could love a woman accused of murder.

Chapter 27

With his shoulders hunched and his hands in his pockets, Wesley stood in the Macalister store, listlessly ordering supplies. It was raining hard outside.

"Think it'll flood?" Doll asked.

"I don't know," Wes replied glumly.

"Sure ain't no sunshine in here," Doll complained. "What happened to that wife of yours?" Doll looked at Mac. "I ain't seen her in weeks."

Mac's head rose above the counter. "She's cookin' for them two bears," he said with anger. "That is when my daughter ain't cookin' for 'em. Wes, I ought to wring your neck for bringin' them two here. Miranda cried all night last night sayin' she wanted *both* of 'em and damned if her mother didn't act like she thought it was a goddamn fine idea."

He went to the back of the store for a moment and returned with more goods. "Anythin' else?"

"You know anything about women?" Wesley blurted.

Doll gave a derisive snort.

After a glare in Doll's direction, Mac said, "Before I met Lynna I knew lots about women but ever' year now I know less. You got problems?"

"He's married, ain't he?" Doll said. "Then he's got problems."

Wesley leaned against the counter, looking at his boot toe. "I used to think I understood women too, but I don't. I thought that if you had a wife and you were kind to her, didn't beat her, gave her a good home and pretty dresses, she'd be happy."

"But yours isn't happy," Mac said. "They want love too."

Wesley stiffened. "She couldn't have any complaints there. I keep her pretty busy."

Doll gave a chuckle.

"No," Mac said, "that ain't enough for a woman. She wants you to love her. I don't know how to explain it. You just know when you love her."

"Oh that." Wes waved his hand. "I fell in love with Leah a long time ago. She's got more courage than anybody I ever met."

"So what's your problem?" Mac asked.

"You remember a month ago when that woman accused Leah of murdering her husband?"

Mac grimaced. "That's the day Miranda met those two boys of yours. I ain't likely to forget it. But I thought you got all that straightened out."

"I thought so too. I found two people who'd been there when Revis killed the woman's husband and they heard Revis threatening Leah. So I took the two to the woman but she wouldn't listen, just kept screaming about Leah. There wasn't anything I could do about her so I took the two men around town and let them tell everyone in Sweetbriar the truth about Leah."

With a nod, Mac agreed. "Sounds sensible to me. So what's wrong with your wife?"

Wesley sat on top of a cracker barrel. "Leah has more courage than anyone," he repeated. "In Virginia she used to tell me off about every two days and later I was shot and she put her own life in jeopardy to save me, who she kept saying she didn't like very much. Of course she didn't mean that. Leah's crazy about me," he added quickly. "Nothing ever seemed too much for her, but this woman screaming at her has changed Leah. All she does now is chores and sit at that blasted loom of hers. And the least little thing makes her cry."

"Is she breedin'?" Mac asked. "Women get funny at that time."

"I don't think so. I've asked her twenty times what's wrong and she just cries and says she'll never be respectable now."

"I guess you told her about the two men, didn't you?"

"Sure," Wes answered. "I even brought them to the house, but Leah said their word didn't matter because the woman thought Leah'd killed her husband. Everybody in Sweetbriar knew about Revis's robberies and I told a few women about how Leah joined the gang because I was wounded and they believed me. Nobody in town is against Leah except that one crazy old woman, but Leah just plain won't believe me. She won't come to town, won't see anybody but Kimberly and Bud and Cal."

There was quiet in the store for a few minutes, only the rain beating down on the roof.

"I never did like those Hayneses," Doll said quietly.

For a moment Mac looked startled, and it was awhile before he spoke. "You ever think maybe somebody's payin' this woman to keep to her story about Leah?"

299

"Paying her? To lie about Leah? Why?" Wesley wa bewildered. "What could anyone gain by making th town think Leah's a murderess?"

Mac walked out from behind the counter. "I know what you've told the townspeople about this Revis and I know you only told 'em because of Leah, but I think you left out a lot."

Wesley set his jaw. "Maybe you ought to tell me wha I didn't say."

"Maybe you didn't hear," Mac continued, "bu about four years ago several of us men went into th woods and cleared out the whole nest of robbers. I was . . . successful, but Lyttle Tucker and Ottis Water were killed. It wasn't long before the nest was fille again, only this time all the women of Sweetbria marched on us and said they'd leave us if we went afte the robbers." There was anger in Mac's eyes. "Some times the women of this town don't rightly act lik women should."

"I liked it better when my woman disobeyed me," Wesley said sullenly. "If I'd wanted somebody who obeyed me I'd have married Kimberly."

"Linnet don't even know how to obey," Mac snapped. "Sometimes I think she stays up nights thinkin' up ways to do what I don't want her to do."

"Leah used to do that but—."

"'Fore you two get so hot for your women you have to run home to 'em for a little lovin', why don't we ge back to the Haynes woman and her callin' Mrs. Wesley a murderer?"

Mac ignored Doll's first remark. "The Hayneses ain' been here long and we've had some trouble with 'em with stealin' and the like. This woman that accused Leah was a Haynes before she married and now that she's a widow she's livin' with 'em."

He paused. "A few of us men speculated some on how come that den of robbers is always filled and they always seem to have new leaders ever' few years. Even if you kill the leader, a new one comes back real soon. There ain't been no robberies since this Revis was killed, but I'm expectin' any day to hear of one."

Wesley was cautious. "How do you explain the leaders being replaced?"

"There's somebody behind all the robberies, somebody that don't live in the woods that's plannin' them all."

"And who is he?" Wes asked quietly.

"How the hell would I know?" Mac snapped. "You think he'd be free if I knew who he was?"

Doll turned around in his chair to look at Wesley. "Mac," he said slowly, "that boy knows more'n he's tellin'." With that he turned back around.

Mac gave Wesley a hard look. "That true? You in here fishin' to see what we know?"

Wesley began to get angry. "I'd never heard that the men of Sweetbriar had ever cleared out the robbers."

"You think we hear about other people's misery and just sit on our asses doin' nothin' about it? Is that the kind of people you think we are? I lost Lyttle Tucker in that fight and he was one of the best friends I ever had."

Doll came out of his chair. "Goddamn you, Macalister! I thought that once you got some gray hairs you'd calm down. But you ain't. You're just as hotheaded now as you always was. I don't know how that sweet little Lynna puts up with you."

"She puts up with me just fine!" Mac yelled. "Better'n anybody can put up with you, old man."

"Stop it!" shouted Linnet from the doorway, rain dripping off her. "I could hear you two shouting outside even in this downpour. Hello, Wesley. I haven't seen you for weeks."

Mac, rigid with anger, went behind the counter.

"Hello, Linnet," Wesley said softly.

"Wesley," Linnet said pleasantly, "would you please tell me what's been going on in here?"

"I don't know if I should . . ." Wes began.

"Tell her," Mac snapped. "Cain't nobody keep a secret from her."

Briefly Wesley told her about Leah's refusing to leave the farm, about her unhappiness, and then about what he'd done to clear her name. Then he told of what had led up to the argument.

Linnet thought for a moment. *"Do* you know something about the robbers?"

Wesley wasn't going to tell Mac that Bud, Cal, and Abe had been part of the robbers, not when Miranda might marry Bud or Cal. "There is a leader," he said quietly. "All I know is that he's called the Dancer."

"You have no idea who he is?"

"I was given a name, but it was a lie." The last thing Wes wanted to do was tell Mac what Revis had said. Mac's temper was explosive enough over little things, but what would it be over this?

"What was the name?" Linnet asked.

Wesley hesitated.

"You can be sure it won't go beyond these walls."

"I knew right away it was a lie. When Revis was shot he gave us a name, but none of us believed it. And besides, Mac, you spent two years in North Carolina. It couldn't have been you."

The silence in the room was deafening.

"Me?" Mac said, then slowly he began to smile. He walked over near Doll. "You hear that, ol' man? I'm supposed to be the leader of these outlaws. I'd like to know when I'm supposed to get time what with all the kids I've got, and what did I do with the money? Miranda wants a new dress once a week and I can't give her one."

He seemed to be highly amused by the whole idea.

"Seems mighty peculiar to me that a man that's dyin' would tell a lie," Doll said.

Wesley was sure Mac would start yelling at Doll again.

"That *is* odd," Linnet said. "What do you think, Devon?"

"He was scared," Mac said flatly. "Maybe this Revis has some kinfolks and if he gave away who the Dancer was, this Dancer would kill 'em."

"I hadn't thought of that," Wesley said. "I just never believed what Revis said about you."

"But you did ask around enough to know Mac was in North Caroliny and *couldn't* be this robber," Doll injected.

"So why does the Haynes woman still say Leah is a murderer?" Mac asked.

"Because whoever the Dancer is, he's afraid Leah knows something. Did Leah know Revis very well?" Mac answered his own question before anyone else could speak.

"Not the way you mean," Wesley snapped. "But—" He came off the barrel. "Revis could have bragged to the Dancer. Revis was a loner, skulked about the woods all the time, nobody ever knew what he was thinking, but he liked Leah. From what I gather he killed the Haynes woman's husband just so he could force Leah to stay with him. He seemed to terrify most women and Leah . . . Leah doesn't usually scare too easily."

"I once lived in a town," Linnet said softly, "where if

one of the residents had been accused of murder the other townspeople just might have hanged her. Sweetbriar isn't like that," she said proudly, "but even our town can be pushed too far. Some of the newer residents are saying you may have paid those two men to say Leah was forced into the robberies."

"Just tell me who they are and I'll break their lying bodies in two," Wesley said as he spat.

"That won't do any good," Mac said. "I think we've got to find out who the Dancer is."

"Must be somebody pretty close or he wouldn't be so worried about your missus," Doll said.

"So how do we find out who he is?" Linnet asked. "We can't just ask people."

Mac locked eyes with Wesley. "There's only one way: by making him show his hand again."

It took Wesley a moment to understand. "You want to use *my* wife as some sort of pigeon for this Dancer to shoot at? You expect me to expose Leah to the whims of a thief and a murderer? Not on your life, Macalister."

"Nobody's askin' you to——," Mac began angrily.

"I think you should ask Leah," Linnet said. "She should be given a choice. Right now she's miserable because she's been accused of murder and she has no way to clear her name. If the real culprit is found only then will she be free."

"Absolutely not," Wesley said firmly. "I don't care if Leah never leaves my house again. I won't let her expose herself to a murderer. If the Dancer thinks she knows something, he may try to kill her. I will not let Leah out of my protection."

"Then you're forcing her to a half-life," Linnet said with passion. "All the Dancer has to do is keep paying that dreadful woman to spread her stories about Leah,

304

and if Leah merely stays home and cries, never defends herself, it won't be long before people begin *believing* Leah is a murderer."

"Yep," Doll said. "People will say where there's smoke there's fire, and in a few months they'll all agree that there must be somethin' behind your little wife's misery. They might say maybe she's stayin' home 'cause she feels guilty."

"Wesley," Linnet said, her hand on his arm. "You must talk to Leah about this. It's really her decision."

"As long as she's my wife—."

"Hah!" Mac interrupted. "If you want her to act like a wife oughta, you better hightail it out of this town right now. It's my guess that if you won't tell her, Lynna will."

"Is that true?" Wesley asked, eyes wide.

"It had crossed my mind," she said, giving her husband a stern look when he smiled at her.

"Maybe we could go—," Wesley began.

"It'll follow you wherever you go," Mac said. "The only way you can settle this and really protect your wife is to find out who the Dancer is. And the only way I see of doin' that is to have Leah show her face. Maybe she knows somethin' she don't remember. Maybe the Dancer wants her out of the way 'cause of that. Maybe the Dancer lives a hundred miles from here and that Haynes woman just wants to pretend she's important. Who knows? But the only way you're gonna find out is if Leah leaves that house of yours and we see what else the Dancer does."

"Seems to me," Doll said, "that maybe there's somethin' else this here Dancer wants 'cause he could have murdered your woman right away. What's he got to gain if he makes her look like a murderer?"

"Freedom," Wes said slowly. "If he can make someone else look guilty no one will suspect him. Even if he makes a slip now and then, people won't notice because they'll remember Leah as the guilty one."

"Remember?" Linnet whispered.

Wesley's eyes turned dark. "I won't let her out of my sight," he said under his breath. "If I have to take her to France to live, I will. She'll never be in danger if I can help it, and if any of you hint to Leah about any of this, I'll make you sorry." With that he left the store.

Chapter 28

Leah was slowly braiding Kimberly's long hair.

"I'm so looking forward to the dance tonight," Kim said. "I'm going to wear my rose silk dress with the lace shawl. It's the first time in months that I've been anywhere. Except here, of course. John makes me stay home the rest of the time. What are you going to wear tonight, Leah?"

Leah turned away toward a basin of dirty dishes. "I'm not going."

"Not going! Oh Leah, you must go. Everyone will be there. Even Bud and Cal are going." She laughed. "I hear Miranda Macalister has made both of them new shirts and everyone is dying to see if she can dance with both boys at once. It's going to be such fun! I know you have pretty clothes, Leah, so there's no reason for you to stay home."

"I have been forbidden to go," Leah said with suppressed anger.

"Forbidden?" Kim was aghast. "But who—? Yo mean *Wesley* said you couldn't go?"

Leah's hands clutched a plate beneath the dirt water. "I thought perhaps it was time I left the hous and faced the outside world, but my husband wouldn' hear of it."

Kim looked as if she'd just heard the most tragi story of her life. "But why, Leah? Wesley is th kindest, gentlest, most considerate man alive. Ho could he forbid you to go to a dance?"

"I have no idea. He refused to discuss the matter. H just said he didn't want me surrounded by so man people."

"I'd rather be surrounded by people than hom alone with John," Kim said. "Surely Wesley gave yo some reason."

Leah turned toward Kim, fighting back tear "Maybe a Stanford doesn't want to be seen with Simmons who's been accused of murder. Perhaps m husband can't bear people knowing what kind of wif he has."

"Oh Leah," Kim whispered as she put her arm around her friend. "Sit down and let me make yo some tea."

Obediently Leah sat down, her shoulders shakin with a combination of grief and despair.

"That's not very nice of Wesley," Kim said though fully, sitting down at the table and forgetting about th tea. "When I first met you I dreaded having to trave with one of the Simmonses. Steven kept saying th most awful things about you. He bragged about how h was going to . . . well, do things to you as soon a Wesley turned you over to him. He said all yo Simmons women loved, you know . . . sex."

Leah was looking at Kim with horror.

"I believed him," Kim continued, "for a long time, but you were always so kind to me when other people weren't and as far as I could tell you weren't running into the beds of all the men like Steven said you would. I almost understood when Wesley said he wanted to stay married to you. But I was very, very angry." There was an apology in her voice.

"What did Wesley say when he told you he wanted to remain married to me?" Leah asked softly.

"Actually, he was very kind, although I didn't think so then. He said it'd been a hard decision for him to make but he really thought he ought to stay married to you."

"He ought to, huh?" Leah muttered. "That's all?"

Kim smiled. "He said he'd always love me because I was his first love, but he had to do what was right and he'd married you and he planned to honor his wedding vows."

Leah stood. "Those Stanfords are good people aren't they? They believe in honor and loyalty to the core. Even when it means doing something as disgusting as remaining married to a bit of swamp scum who forced him into marriage in the first place. Of course there are compensations. Women from my station in life make great bed partners and farmhands, and if they get in trouble while protecting a Stanford then the women can be hidden away, not allowed to go out in public, just stay home, cook and clean, and warm his bed at night—or in the day. Women from the Simmons family are easy to persuade."

"Leah," Kim said with a frown, "that may all be true, but when Wesley told me he was going to stay married to you, I felt that he *wanted* to, not that he *had* to. Wesley can be awfully stubborn and he won't do what he doesn't want to do."

"Oh, he wanted to stay married to me, all right," Leah said with anger. "Where else was he going to find a worker and a sex partner? He took me to town once to introduce me, but he hasn't let me go out in public since. And tonight he doesn't want to be embarrassed by somebody like me."

Kim frowned harder. "I don't understand. I thought you didn't *want* to go into town."

"For a while I didn't, but for the last two weeks every time I've mentioned facing the townspeople, Wesley's given me a dozen reasons why I should stay home. And tonight he's forbidden me to go to the dance."

"I was so hoping you'd be there," Kim said. "In fact, I even brought you a present." Out of her pocket she pulled a little package wrapped in a scrap of fabric. "I thought it would look quite nice on your green dress."

Slowly Leah opened the bundle to see a brooch, gold filigree, edged with a hand-painted miniature of a woman on the ivory oval. "Who is she?" Leah whispered.

"I don't know. It's very old, don't you think? And the green dress in the picture just matches yours. I so wish you were going tonight."

"I am," Leah said suddenly, astonishing herself. "Wesley Stanford may think he can hide me away, but he can't. He may think a Simmons has river mud for blood, but we don't."

"I'm not sure you should do that, Leah. Wesley can get awfully mad sometimes."

"Wesley Stanford doesn't even know the meaning of anger. I'm not going to sit here in this house for the rest of my life and feel sorry for myself. I didn't participate in those murders and that woman can tell everyone from now until doomsday that I did and it won't make it true."

"I think I'm glad you feel this way, but Wesley said you couldn't go and—." She brightened. "Maybe if you cry and tell him you'll just die if you don't go he'll say yes, then you won't really be disobeying him. Or maybe you could faint! Wesley does love—."

Leah gave her a stern look. "I'll not beg and I'll certainly not faint. No, first I'm going to get Wesley to go, then I am going to turn up at the dance. I can hardly wait to see his face."

"Neither can I," Kim said grimly. "I think I'd fall down dead if anybody got as mad at me as Wesley's going to be at you."

"It'll be worth it just to show that arrogant man that he can't keep me locked away from the world as if I were something nasty he had to hide. And you, Kim, are going to help me."

Kim paled. "No, Leah, Wesley scares me."

"I thought you said he was kind and gentle."

"Only when he gets his way. Really, Leah, I couldn't possibly help you."

Leah sat down across from Kim. "All you have to do is send him a note tonight saying you need help. Lately Wes has been hovering over me, but he'll leave the farm to go to you. You're the only one. And while he's gone I'll go to the party. You can write another note for me to leave Wes saying I've gone to the dance. When he gets to your house he'll find you and John gone, come back here, find the note, and probably come to the dance. Or maybe I'll come home with someone else if he doesn't want to come to the dance."

"Do you think Wesley will beat you when you get home?" Kim asked seriously. Her eyes widened. "Do you think he'll beat *me?*"

"No, of course not. I expect he'll be mad, but I hope to show him that I won't embarrass him in public. Nicole had a man teach me how to dance, and my clothes aren't exactly what someone from the swamps would wear. Maybe when Wesley calms down he'll realize I'm not something he has to hide away."

"Oh Leah." Kim put her head in her hands. "I'm just awfully afraid of doing this. Somehow it doesn't seem right. Wesley doesn't act as if he's ashamed of you, in fact he seems to like you a lot. Couldn't you write the notes yourself and then I could be innocent? I can say I knew nothing about anything. I'm good at lying. It's easy for me."

"I can't read or write and if I have someone else deliver the messages, then they'd be involved, and besides there are only men around here anyway. They'd all take Wesley's side. Please Kimberly. Please."

There were tears in Kim's eyes—tears of fear—when she nodded agreement.

As Wesley rode back to his farm he imagined all the things he was going to say to Kimberly the next time he saw her. What great crisis had happened to make her write that frantic note to him? No doubt John had dared to suggest she get off her spreading backside and do some work, and in anger she'd written to Wesley. And Wes, like a fool, had gone rushing after her, ready to rescue her, ready, if needed, to punch a good man like John Hammond in Kimberly's defense.

Yet when Wes got there the house was empty and a hand said John and Kim had left for the dance an hour ago. All Wes could think of was that he'd left Leah alone in the house, unprotected except for the hands, and for all Wes knew, one of them was the Dancer. Right now he trusted no one. He'd even begun to suspect Bud and Cal. Yet here he'd left his wife alone, drooping about the house, feeling poorly, tired, overworked—and possibly the victim of a plot against her.

"Leah," he called before he'd even dismounted. Slamming into the house he tore through it, shouting, "Leah!"

The emptiness and silence of the place made his heart pound. He ran outside to the outhouse, to the chicken coop, calling repeatedly for her.

"Where's Leah?" he shot at one of the Macalister twins.

"I thought she was in the house."

"Damn," Wes cursed, running back into the house, and there he saw the paper on the table.

Dear Wesley,

Leah can't read and even though she's telling me what to write, I'm going to tell you the truth. It wasn't very nice of you to forbid Leah to go to the dance. Just before she got mad at you, her feelings were hurt. So, she made me write two notes for her so she could go. It wasn't really my fault, Wesley. Please don't be mad at me.

With love, Kimberly

P.S. Leah is really very nice and she isn't at all some nasty thing from the swamp. Please don't hit her.

"Hit her!" Wesley said with a gasp. "Oh Lord, you stupid women. I may beat you black-and-blue, Leah. That is, if you're still alive," he whispered.

313

Crumbling the note, he left the house in a few easy strides and mounted his horse, setting off for town at a gallop.

Leah was nervous by the time she reached the Macalister store where the dance was being held. It wasn't exactly proper for her to arrive unescorted.

"Leah!"

Justin Stark was standing outside and now he hurried forward to help her from her horse.

"So where's that husband of yours who keeps you locked away from us? He didn't let you out of his sight, did he?"

"Wesley . . . had some work to do. If he finishes he'll be along later." As she spoke, Leah's eyes went to the side.

Justin caught her arm and pulled it through his. "I won't question that. It's Wes's loss and our gain. Come dance with us and let me show everyone I have the prettiest girl in the state on my arm."

The inside of the store had been cleared and was lighted with what looked to be every lantern in town. Four fiddlers occupied one end of the big room and one side had a long, long table weighted down with food.

"I should have brought something," Leah murmured.

"Your own pretty self is enough."

"Leah!" Kimberly exclaimed from beside her. "You're here. Did Wesley—?"

"Would you please excuse us?" Leah said to Justin as she led Kim to a corner.

"Did you see Wesley? What did he say? Was he really mad?"

"Kimberly," Leah said slowly, sniffing. "Have you been drinking?"

"Just a tiny bit. Not even enough to count. Justin's father makes this wonderful stuff that relaxed me with one swallow. I've just been so nervous and John is hardly speaking to me. Don't you think Justin looks nice tonight? But then so do all the men. Every man looks good except my husband."

"Kimberly, I want you to eat something right away and for heaven's sake, stop talking!" With some force Leah led Kim toward the food-laden tables.

"Leah!" Linnet Macalister said, looking at Leah as if she were a ghost. "I didn't think you were going to be here."

"What a pretty dress," Agnes Emerson said. "Is that a picture of your mother?" she asked, referring to the brooch Leah wore.

"It was a gift from a friend of mine. Could I get a plate of food for Kim and maybe someone would see that she eats it? I need to talk to Doll Stark for a moment."

Agnes took one look at Kim and understood immediately. "I hope you say a few words to Doll for me too," she called after Leah.

Doll sat in his usual place before the fireplace, except that now his chair was turned to face the dancing people. Lester Sawrey, sitting next to Doll, punched the older man when he saw Leah coming.

"Yes, ma'am," Doll said. "What can I do for you?"

"I want to ask you not to give Kimberly Hammond any more of whatever you gave her."

"That little lady sure can drink," he said in wonder. "Thought she was gonna drain the jug."

Leah glared at him.

"Where's that husband of yourn?" Doll asked. "I didn't think he'd let you come to this shindig."

Still refusing to answer, Leah just looked at him.

"All right," Doll said heavily. "I won't let her have no more. Sure seems a shame to me, though. That little lady has capacity."

"Mrs. Stanford?"

Leah turned to look at John Hammond. He was a good-looking man with beautiful gray hair. "May I have this dance?"

After a quick look to see that Kim was sitting down and eating, Leah took John's arm.

Her dancing lessons hadn't prepared her for the energetic country dances, and when they were finished she was fanning herself with her hand.

"How about a breath of air?" John suggested, his eyes twinkling.

"Yes, I need it," Leah said with a laugh.

Outside with the stars winking overhead, the cool, fragrant night air about her, Leah was very glad she'd come to the dance. And to think that Wesley had forbidden her to attend.

"Penny for your thoughts."

She smiled at him. "I was just thinking that I'm glad I came."

"I am too," John said seriously. "I've wanted to talk to you for a long time. Actually, I wanted to ask your advice. You see, I know Kimberly is very unhappy, but I honestly don't know why or how to make her happy. I've tried my best to be as patient as I know how. When I come in from the fields, supper isn't ready, and it's taken me weeks to teach her how to fry eggs for breakfast. I've done everything I can to be lenient with her, to understand that she's not used to so much work, but no matter what I do, she still seems to resent me. You must believe me, Mrs. Stanford, I love my wife, and if I could afford servants for her I'd gladly hire them, but I can't. I know the two of you are friends and I thought maybe she'd said something to you. Could you please help me?"

Leah wasn't sure, but there seemed to be tears in his eyes. Damn Kimberly! she thought. Her laziness was causing this gentle man a great deal of misery. "She hasn't said much to me," Leah lied.

"But anything could help," John said in desperation. "She won't talk to me and if I just knew exactly what she complained about maybe I could fix it. I do want to make her happy."

"I guess marriage in general is difficult for her," Leah said slowly. "She's not exactly in love with work."

John smiled. "How kind you are. But there's nothing . . . specific about our lives together that she complains about?"

"John," Leah said, putting her hand on his arm, "I really wish I could help you. Kimberly is my friend, but I'm aware that she must be difficult to live with. I'll talk to her and try to find out whatever I can. I want both of you to be happy."

"Please try to convince her that I love her," John pleaded.

"I will. Now, shall we go inside?"

With a grin John offered her his arm. "You must have heard this a dozen times already tonight, but you look lovely. That green sets off your eyes. Is the miniature on the brooch of your mother by chance?"

Leah gave a little grimace as she thought of her mother's never having worn a silk dress in her life. "Actually, Kimberly gave me the brooch. Perhaps it's a picture of someone in her family."

"Ah yes, perhaps I've seen the brooch before and don't remember it. It was nice of her to give you a gift, wasn't it? Perhaps she'll tell you the history of the woman in the painting and you can tell me. It looks like the only way I can find out about my own wife is through a third party."

Leah's heart went out to him and she felt like smacking Kimberly for mistreating this sweet man. "Excuse me," she said when they were inside, and she went directly to Kim.

"You were talking to John," Kim said belligerently before Leah could speak. "Did he ask about me?"

"Yes he did. That poor man is working very hard to make you happy and you've been very unkind to him."

"Leah," Kimberly began, but suddenly John was in front of her, his hand extended.

"Dance with me?" he asked with longing in his voice.

Kim's face lost some of its color. "Yes," she murmured and took his hand.

As Leah watched they joined in with the others, but every time Kim came in contact with John, her face fell until by the end of the dance Kim was no longer smiling.

"You can't stay here against the wall all night," Justin said from beside her. "I expect any minute for that husband of yours to come roaring through the door and take you away from all of us."

"I'm afraid I expect that too. Do you think we could get some food instead of dancing? I think my dancing mood has fled."

"Could it have to do with John and Kim? You've been watching them and frowning for minutes."

"I don't guess I like to see anyone unhappy."

318

Justin snorted. "Kim would make anybody unhappy. I pity John for having to live with her. Uh, oh. I think a storm just blew in."

Coming toward them with the full force of a gale was Wesley, his cotton work shirt damp with sweat, his hair plastered about his face.

Chapter 29

"Come with me," Wesley said through clenched teeth as his fingers bit into Leah's upper arm.

"If you'll pardon me," Leah said politely to Justin just before Wesley gave her arm a quick jerk.

All the way across the floor Leah tried to smile and nod at people, tried to act as if she were merely on her way outside with her husband and he wasn't half dragging her. But inside her anger was reaching the boiling point.

"Get on my horse," Wesley commanded as soon as they were outside.

"So you can save the rest of your reputation? Let me tell you, Wesley Stanford, it's too late! Everyone has already seen me, already knows that his majesty, Mr. Stanford of the magnificent Stanford Plantation, has a wife from the swamps of Virginia. And you know what, no one was repulsed, not one person wiped off his hands after touching scum like me."

"Have you gone crazy, Leah? I don't know what you're talking about."

"I'm talking about being a Simmons, that's what. I'm talking about your being ashamed of me and not wanting me to be seen in public."

"Not wanting—." He shook his head at her. "I still don't understand you, but let's go home and discuss it."

She backed away from him. "Go home and no doubt climb into your bed, is that it?"

"I wouldn't mind," he said with a grin.

"You—!" She made a fist and punched him in the stomach.

Wesley didn't move. "What in the hell's got into you?"

"You forbid me to go to a town dance because you think I have to be kept at home chained to your bed and your kitchen and you ask me what's wrong? You may think only rich people have feelings, but I assure you that I have my pride, even if I am a Simmons."

"Women!" Wes said under his breath. "Leah, I'm not ashamed of you. I don't know where you get such dumb ideas. You're beautiful and tonight you're no doubt the prettiest woman here, but right now I just don't want you around so many people."

"Because I don't know how to behave? Because I might not live up to the Stanford name?"

"Good God! It's your name, too. Just one day of my life I'd like to really understand a woman. Just any woman will do. Leah, will you *please* come home with me right now?"

"Why?" she asked angrily. "Why do you want to hide me?"

"I don't want to hide you . . . well, maybe I do." Smiling seductively, he moved closer to her. "I can make our own party at home."

"The only way I'll go with you is if you carry me kicking and screaming, and that could further damage your reputation."

Wesley turned away from her for a moment, and when he looked back his face was a study in confusion. "Leah, I honestly don't have any idea why you're so upset. I didn't ask you not to come to this dance because I'm ashamed of you and don't want to be seen with you. Far from it. I'd like nothing better than having you on my arm. But right now there are reasons why I'd rather have you home where I can be near you."

"What reasons?"

"I can't tell you and for once you're going to have to trust me."

She gave him a nasty little smile. "I don't have to guess why you want me to go home with you. I *know*. You said you hated the whole idea of being married to somebody like me."

"*I* said that?" Wes exclaimed. "When?"

"You told your brother Travis that, and Regan and I heard you."

Just then two overheated dancers came outside, so Wes grabbed Leah's arm and pulled her into the shadows, imprisoning her between his legs. "All right, you little wildcat, you're going to listen to me. First of all, I'm sick and tired of your telling me I'm this century's biggest snob. *You* are the snob, Leah. You're much more concerned with where people grew up than I've ever been. Yes, I did tell Travis I hated being married to you, but not because I couldn't bear living with a lowly Simmons."

"Hah!" Leah tried to look away but Wes pulled her face back around.

"I wanted a woman who needed me and as far as I

could tell Kimberly needed me worse than any man's ever been needed. So here I was wanting a woman like Kim and instead I got one who could run a farm, raise kids, deal with a crazy father—you, Leah, didn't seem to need anybody or anything. You made me feel useless."

"Me?" she whispered. "How could you feel useless?"

He put his nose to hers. "Because you never ask me for a goddamn thing," he said with feeling. "You join robbers and never even mention the fact to me. Remember last week when the chimney half fell down? You fixed it by yourself. I wouldn't even have known about it except Oliver saw you hanging onto a ladder and setting stones. You could even take the ugly woman I married and make her into the beauty you are now."

Pausing, he smoothed her hair back from her face. "It took me a long time to realize that you need me more than Kimberly ever did. Kim will always land on her feet, but you, my little wife, can get into trouble on your way to the outhouse."

Leah was trying to digest this information. "But Kim's a lady and I'm—."

"You're my wife and as I've told you, you're a Stanford now, so if I'm royalty, you are too."

She pulled away from him. "Then if you aren't ashamed of me, why don't you want to be seen with me at the dance? Why do you want to keep me hidden on our farm?"

The last thing Wesley wanted to do was tell Leah about a possible plot against her. No doubt Leah would stay up nights figuring out how to get involved. "You have to trust me. You have to believe that I want what is best for you."

Leah walked away into the moonlight. What he said about Kim's needing him made sense; in fact, Kim had even hinted at that. She sensed that Wesley wanted her to faint, wanted her to be helpless, and Kim had obeyed him. But Leah had just done what had come naturally to her. Could it be possible that she also made other people feel useless?

Wesley didn't speak of love, but maybe love wasn't far away if he didn't resent her being a Simmons. What was really amusing was that Leah had worked so hard not to be a burden to Wes. When the chimney had fallen, she'd first sat down and cried. Then with determination she'd repaired it herself merely because she didn't want Wesley to think she was helpless.

She turned back to him. "If I faint for you, will you sweep me into your arms and carry me to your bed?"

The look on Wesley's face was reward enough for her jest. Without a word he came to her, lifted her, and held her close to him. "Sometimes it amazes me how much I've come to love you, Leah," he whispered. "I just wish you wouldn't yell at me so often."

Leah's impulse was to push away from him because she wanted to see his eyes when he told her, this first time, that he loved her. Instead she snuggled against him. "Maybe now that I know you love me I won't be angry quite so often."

He walked with her to his horse and lifted her into the saddle. "I've sure told you often enough. It's about time it sank in."

Above all Leah didn't want to start another argument. "I guess I just didn't hear you say it the other times. Oh Wes," she said when he was mounted behind her. "I have to get my shawl."

"I'll get it tomorrow when I get your horse."

"Good heavens, no. That shawl cost Clay a fortune. It came all the way across the ocean. I'll just be a minute."

"You stay right there," he said down to her. "I'll go with you."

Leah giggled. "Can't stand me out of your sight?"

"Something like that," Wes said seriously.

Quietly Leah stood outside and waited for her husband. It wasn't easy for her to think of trusting him, but perhaps he did have a reason for not wanting her to attend the dance. It could be that he was jealous, which gave Leah a little sense of delight. If it were true that he did love her it would make sense that he was jealous. Leah certainly had been jealous of Wes and Kimberly.

Suddenly she remembered that she'd seen Corinne Stark wearing a shawl very much like hers. Wesley would never find the right one by himself.

Inside the brightly lit store everyone was dancing and laughing. Kim stood against the wall, her eyes downcast while her husband John stood near her.

As Leah searched the room, the music stopped and the laughing dancers halted. It was in this comparative silence that the woman screamed, and when Leah turned in the direction of the scream, the woman, whom she'd never seen before, was pointing at her.

"That's my aunt's brooch," the woman screeched at Leah. "You stole it from her!"

Aghast, Leah put her hand to her breast. "No," she whispered. It was like the repeat of a nightmare.

Instantly Wes was beside his wife, putting his arm about her in a protective gesture and leading her outside. "Leah," he whispered once they were outside. "Justin's going to take you home. I'm going to stay and find out what I can about this. Do you understand me?"

Numbly Leah nodded as Wes handed her up to Justin.

"Take care of her," Wes said. "I'll send word as soon as I can, but right now I want to stop this once and for all." His head came up sharply as Kimberly came outside with John. Kim was crying softly.

"Go on, get out of here," Wes said to Justin.

Leah didn't think much on the way back to the farm and only when Justin pulled her from the horse and led her inside did she realize how cold she was. She began to shiver.

Justin led her to a chair and then pulled her into his arms. "It's all right, sweetheart. Wesley will find out what's going on. No one will believe you stole the brooch."

Leah couldn't cry but just leaned stiffly against Justin.

"Where did you get the brooch, Leah?" he asked, stroking her arm. "Leah!" he commanded when she didn't answer. "Where did you get that pin?"

"Kimberly gave it to me," Leah whispered.

"Damn that selfish little bitch!" he said with a growl as he tossed Leah back against the chair and began to pace the room. "I could see her being involved with robbers. She has the morals of a whore. Pardon me, Leah, but she does. She'd sell herself or anybody else to get what she wanted. Do you think John has any idea what he married? Poor man, he probably thought there was a woman inside her pretty frame.

"Leah," he said, kneeling before her. "I'm going to see what I can find out from Kimberly. Maybe between John and me we can talk some sense into her. Wes'll probably be back soon, just as soon as he finishes talking to that woman at the dance. Oliver's in the barn. Do you think you'll be all right here by yourself?"

Absently, Leah nodded. She wanted to be alone; she didn't want anyone to see her shame.

He kissed her forehead. "Just stay here and wait for Wes. Don't go anywhere, promise?"

Again she nodded and Justin left her alone.

Leah had no idea how long she sat there because time seemed to have no meaning. Her thoughts wandered to the fact that the fireplace needed cleaning. The sun was beginning to rise when she stiffly got up from the chair and began the filthy task of cleaning it and as much of the chimney as she could reach.

Behind her the door burst open.

Slowly, disinterestedly, Leah turned to see Kim, her eyes bright, her hair tumbled about her shoulders, her muslin dress grass-stained.

"Oh Leah," Kim said breathlessly. "It was heavenly, absolutely heavenly. It was the most wonderful experience of my life. What in the world are you doing? Leah, look at you! You've absolutely ruined that beautiful dress."

Kim went forward, but as she reached Leah she pulled back. "I don't think I'll touch you. Stand up right now and get that dress off. And while you're washing I'll tell you about the most wonderful night of my life."

Kimberly gave Leah cold water to wash in because Kim wasn't about to lay a fire in Leah's bare fireplace. "Wash your ears, too," Kim commanded as Leah stood in her underwear. "It was so silly of you to ruin your dress. Oh well, that's enough about that. Leah," she said slowly, "Justin and I made love last night."

That was the first thing that had gotten through to Leah. She paused in her washing. "You and Justin?"

"Isn't it so hard to believe? It seems that Justin has hated me from the first moment he saw me. Men don't usually hate me, but Justin did, and last night he was just furious, but later . . . Oh Leah, it was sheer heaven."

"Kim," Leah said. "Tell me everything from the beginning. Where did you get the brooch you gave me?"

"Well, that," Kim said with a sigh. "I guess things started a long time before last night."

"I have all day," Leah said firmly. "Would you like some breakfast?"

"Breakfast? I guess so even though it's afternoon, but lovemaking does make you hungry."

Minutes later Leah was washed, dressed, and cooking. "Start," she ordered Kim.

"I guess it started with Steven. He said there were two kinds of women: ladies who didn't enjoy it and women who did."

"Kim, why don't you tell me about the brooch?"

"I will, but everything's tied together. Oh Leah, you have to swear you won't hate me when I tell you all this. You're the best friend I've ever had and some of the things I've done—."

"I swear I won't hate you unless you keep delaying the story."

"As I said, Steven made me think that ladies had to behave all the time so when Wesley and I fell in love—and I really did love him—I never let Wes kiss me very much. You see, I very much liked Wesley's kisses, but I was afraid that if I showed him that I liked them he would think I wasn't a lady and wouldn't marry me. Oh Leah, it was hard at times to push him away. Wesley's kisses are so nice. They're—."

"Could we skip this part of the story?"

"I guess so. Leah, this is the part I don't like. When Wesley told me he was going to stay married to you, I

328

was very, very angry. Actually, I was furious. It seemed so unfair because I'd always been holding back and being a lady while you and Wesley sneaked out at night and delivered food—oh yes, I knew about that. And, too, you'd wrestled in the mud. You hadn't been a lady at all but you'd won the man."

Pausing, she looked at Leah pleadingly. "I was so angry that I stuck a hatpin in the horse and made the wagon fall down the hill. I thought you were inside. Oh Leah," she wailed, burying her face in her hands. "I hated you so much I wanted to kill you."

Leah put her arm around Kim's shoulders. "I had a sudden call of nature and left the wagon, so you didn't hurt me. Maybe in your place I'd have done something similar. Here, now, eat your eggs and tell me what happened next."

"John Hammond saw me stick the pin in the horse and when I fainted—it's the one and only time I ever really did faint—he told me he wouldn't tell anyone. But later . . ."

She took a big drink of milk. "He really is a dreadful man, Leah. He said he'd tell everyone what I'd done if I didn't marry him."

"He blackmailed you?" Leah asked, aghast, as she sat down across from Kim. "But why? Why would he want to force you to marry him? He must have known you'd resent him."

"I asked myself that over and over. I didn't like him much for making me marry him and I did everything I could to make him regret marrying me." She smiled at a chunk of buttered bread. "You want to know a secret, Leah? I can cook. I never let Wesley know because Steven said real ladies didn't cook and when we were traveling you always seemed to want to do everything by yourself."

"I made you feel useless?" Leah asked softly.

"You could probably make any six people feel useless, but anyway, to punish John I refused to do anything at all. He was . . . very unpleasant at night and I didn't really know about lovemaking until Justin—."

"What about the brooch? Doesn't that come before Justin?"

"Oh yes. It was very boring in John's house, what with him gone all day, and since I refused to do anything I was supposed to do, I had trouble occupying myself. Except that John has this study, which he keeps locked, and right after our marriage he told me never, never, never was I to go in there."

"So of course you did," Leah said with a smile.

"Every day. It didn't really matter because I didn't care if he caught me or not because I'd already sworn to spend the rest of my life with him, so what more could happen to me? It took some searching, but I found the key, used it every day, searched the room, and returned the key."

"What were you searching for?"

"For whatever he had hidden in there that he didn't want me to see. I couldn't find anything until I found his hidden closet."

"Hidden?"

"Behind a bookcase. It was all I could do to move that case. Anyway, inside this closet were some very pretty things like jewelry and pretty little boxes and some books. It made me so angry because I thought he was hiding these things so he wouldn't have to share them with his wife."

"You *thought* this? You've changed your mind?"

"Leah, I couldn't wear any of the jewelry, but I thought someone else could. John wouldn't yell at

330

someone else as much as he would at me. And besides, you're so good at yelling back at men. You scream at Wesley all the time. I never could understand that, Leah. You said terrible things to him and I was always nice, yet he wanted to stay with you."

"What about the brooch?" Leah repeated.

"I thought it was a miniature of one of John's relatives and I knew it'd look good on your green dress and it did until you ruined it by playing in the soot. All right!" she said at Leah's narrowed eyes. "The next thing I knew, that silly woman was screeching that you'd stolen John's brooch. John grabbed my arm, said some terrible things to me, and pulled me out of the dance. Oh Leah, I was so scared."

"Then what happened?"

"John didn't speak to me all the way home and at the house he locked me in his study and I heard him ride away."

Kim's eyes turned misty with a faraway look. "Then Justin came to my rescue."

"Rescue?" Leah asked. "Wasn't he a little bit angry at you?"

"Oh goodness yes. He was raging! Shouting all sorts of things to me and calling me the most awful names. I'd always known he wasn't exactly enamored of me, but I had no idea he detested me. While he was shouting at me, and once he put his hands around my throat, I kept trying to show him the bookcase where the hidden closet was. It took a long time to get him to listen to me, but he finally helped me move the bookcase."

"And Justin saw all the things inside?"

"More than that. While we were inside, John came home."

"Kimberly! Where's Justin now?"

"I'm getting to that. You see, Justin didn't have any keys and all the doors in our house have locks, not like your house at all, and John had locked every door so Justin had to break in a window and the study door to get to me. Justin and I hid in the closet, wrapped in each other's arms"—Kim sighed—"while John walked through the house. When we heard him leave and ride away, Justin said, 'Let's get out of here.' So we went outside, way into the woods, and it was dark and Justin wanted me to tell him everything that was in the closet because he hadn't been able to see anything because John'd returned and we had to pull the bookcase shut. So"—she paused for breath—"I was talking and suddenly Justin got real excited and began to kiss me. I was so tired of holding back with Wesley and even with John that I just let go and the next thing I knew we were making love. It was so, so wonderful, Leah. I never dreamed—."

"What did you say that made Justin kiss you?"

"It was something very ordinary. What was it? Oh yes. At the dance last night John'd said he wasn't a good dancer and I told Justin that was a lie because I'd found a paper in the closet that said he used to teach dancing in St. Louis."

"Kimberly," Leah whispered, "where is Justin now?"

"He said he'd seen Wes and Wes was on his way to Lexington to see what he could find out from the woman who used to own the brooch, and Justin said I was to come to you and we were both to go stay with Bud and Cal, and Justin was going to wait for John to return."

"Kimberly," Leah said with as much calm as she could muster, "I think Justin may be in trouble."

"Probably." Kim smiled. "John's going to be very

upset when he finds out I'm leaving him, but now that Justin loves me . . . I did tell you that Justin said he loved me, didn't I? He even said it with a prayer. He said, 'God help me, Kimberly, but I think I'm in love with you.' Isn't that sweet?"

"Get up, Kimberly," Leah commanded. "Leave the dishes where they are. We're going to get Bud and Cal and then we're going to try to help Justin. Wait! We have to leave a note for Wesley."

"Oh no! Not me," Kim said, backing away. "Justin made me tell him all about the last letter I wrote Wes, and Justin said it was his guess that Wesley was keeping you from the dance so he could protect you. If you hadn't made me send for him, none of this about the brooch would have happened."

Leah advanced on her. "If *you* hadn't tried to kill me you wouldn't have been forced to marry John. And if *you* hadn't been so nosy you wouldn't have found the Dancer's cache. And if *you—*."

"I understand, Leah." She brightened. "If none of this had happened, I wouldn't have known Justin loved me and we wouldn't have spent last night together. Oh Leah, marriage to someone like Justin must be heaven."

"You can tell me all about it later," Leah said, removing paper, quill, and ink from a drawer. "Now write what I tell you."

Dear Wesley,
I hope this letter doesn't make you as mad as the last one did, but this time I am innocent because I don't even know what Leah's talking about. She said to tell you that my husband, John, used to give dancing lessons and that Justin, the man I love now, knows everything and since you're not here Leah

*and I are going to ask for help from Bud and Cal
before we visit John and Justin.*

*I think that if I understood all this I'd be fright-
ened.*

I hope you had a pleasant trip to Lexington.

> *Very sincerely yours,*
> *Kimberly*

"Did you write what I said about asking for help?"

"Right here," Kim said, pointing. "Leah, what are
we going to do if Bud and Cal aren't home?"

"Justin needs help," Leah said stubbornly.

Kim swallowed hard. "I was afraid you'd say that."

Chapter 30

Devon Macalister helped his wife from her horse. "Anybody home?" he called into the empty-looking Stanford house.

"Wesley said Leah was staying here with Justin looking after her," Linnet said. "You don't think something's happened, do you?"

"Something's wrong," Mac said, looking about. "It's too quiet and why the hell is that cow bawlin'? Lynna, I want you to stay right here while I find out what's happenin'."

When Linnet saw him disappear into the barn, she entered the house. There were dirty dishes on the table and everything looked as if someone had left in a hurry. But there didn't seem to be any signs of a struggle.

As she was leaving she saw the note on the table, half hidden under a plate.

Mac burst into the cabin. "I thought I told you to wait outside," he snapped. "This whole place is empty.

335

None of the cows've been milked, the other animals need feedin'. What you got there?"

"I think Leah and Kimberly may be in trouble," she whispered, then read aloud Kimberly's note.

"So, John Hammond's the Dancer," Mac said thoughtfully.

"Devon," Linnet whispered. "Bud and Cal were coming to our house today. They won't be there when Leah and Kim arrive."

"Surely those women wouldn't go after somebody like the Dancer all by themselves, would they?" Mac asked in disbelief, but he didn't give his wife time to answer. "You get on your horse and ride back to town as fast as you can. Get somebody to go after Wes and somebody else to tend to this place. And *you*—" he threatened, "stay in Sweetbriar. I don't like what's goin' on at all."

"Devon," Linnet began, "perhaps you should get some help before you—."

"No time," was all he said before he gave her a quick kiss and was out the door.

It was just growing dark by the time Kim and Leah reached the Hammond house.

"Are you sure you should do this alone?" Kim whispered as Leah dismounted some distance from the house. "Justin seems awfully strong and brave and maybe he knows what he's doing."

"Get down and be quiet—and I'm not alone. I *did* ask for help," she said defiantly. "And I have you."

"I don't really think it's the same," Kim said as she dismounted.

After tying their horses out of view of the house, they stealthily began to make their way toward it. From the glow through the windows, every candle and lantern in the house must be lit.

When the shot echoed through the cool night, Leah and Kim looked at each other for a moment before Kim turned back toward the horses.

"Let's go!" Leah commanded, grabbing Kim's arm and pulling her toward the brightly lit house.

They ran across the yard to crouch by a window. Inside everything looked perfectly normal, with no one to be seen. "Where's the room with the hidden closet?" Leah whispered.

Kim, obviously too frightened to speak, managed to point to a far window.

Leah, holding Kim's hand, made her way down the side of the house, crouching all the while to keep her head below the windows. Cautiously she raised herself up to peer inside the house. What she saw made her gasp. On the floor, lying in a pool of blood, lay Justin, dead still.

Leah slid back to the ground. "Justin," she managed to whisper.

Immediately Kim stood up to look, and just as quickly she bent down again. "I think John may have seen me," she said.

"We have to hide," Leah said, looking about the unfamiliar farm. "Where?"

"Follow me," Kim said, standing and raising her skirts, running with extraordinary speed toward the forest.

Leah followed her friend, running until her heart was pounding hard.

Once inside the forest Kim kept going, jumping over fallen trees, pushing aside briars and brambles with ease.

"Wait, Kim," Leah urged. "Stop for a minute."

Reluctantly, wild-eyed, Kim obeyed.

"Where are we going?" Leah asked.

"Into the forest," Kim answered.

"Yes, but where? Surely you have a destination i[n] mind."

"The forest," Kim repeated, puzzled, frowning a[s] she panted from her run.

"But—," Leah began, but she didn't finish because [a] shot rang out and landed in a tree behind her, missin[g] Kim's head by inches.

No one had to tell either woman to start runnin[g] again, and Leah didn't care where they were headed.

They ran until their legs and lungs ached, and Lea[h] caught Kim's arm. "We have to stop and rest. We hav[e] to figure out where we are and head back towar[d] Sweetbriar."

"I don't know where anything is," Kim said. "D[o] you?"

"Not until the sun rises and I can find a direction, Kim!" Leah cried. "See that black space up there? I[s] that a cave?"

"I don't like caves," Kim said, her jaw tight.

"But maybe we could hide in it, get some sleep, an[d] in the morning we can make our way back to Sweet[-] briar."

"Couldn't we stay here and not hide in that place?"

"John'll see us with our light-colored dresses. W[e] have to hide somewhere. Come on, let's start climb[-] ing."

The climb up the side of the cliff wasn't easy, but the[y] made it in record time and when they slipped inside th[e] little limestone cave, Leah leaned back in relief. Sh[e] hadn't told Kim that her biggest fear had been a bear i[n] the cave, but now she could see it was empty. The cave was about ten feet deep, fifteen feet wide, and eight feet tall.

With a smile she turned to Kim. "We made it."

But her smile was soon wiped off her face, as from outside came John Hammond's voice.

"So my stupid little wife and her stupid friend have trapped themselves," he said with amusement in his voice, his words echoing so they couldn't tell whether he was close or far away. "I gave you a chance, Kimberly, to join me. In fact, I chose you because you seemed to have no useless morals against trying to kill somebody who was in your way."

Kim, flattened against the cave wall, gave a quick look at Leah.

"But my wife," John continued, "disappointed me. Now your lover—oh yes, I know about him—lies dead at our house. What a tragedy everything will seem when the town hears how Justin was killed and two women died all in one night. I'll be the bereaved husband."

"Help me gather rocks," Leah whispered. "Let's make a pile of all we can find. Maybe we can hold him off for a while."

Obediently Kim began to pile rocks near the entrance.

"He can't come in by the side, only from the front. We'll have a clear view of him. If he shoots, fall flat to the floor. Understand?" Leah commanded.

Kim nodded.

With a smile on his face and a pistol in each hand, John stood before the cave entrance, his body outlined in the moonlight.

"Now!" Leah ordered as he took a step forward.

The women began throwing rocks with both hands.

Stunned, John ducked, grunting as stones hit him. When he fired, both women flattened themselves on the ground, bullets whizzing overhead, yet they never stopped throwing their rocks.

Kimberly sent one with force, hitting John on the side of his head, blood running immediately.

Almost staggering, he backed away from the entrance and quickly scrambled out of sight. "So, you bitches think you're smart, do you? Let's see how long you can last in there with no food or water. When you're ready to give up and die a quick death, let me know. I'll be here waiting."

Kim sat up behind what was left of the pile of rock. "We're going to die, aren't we?"

"Of course not!" Leah snapped. "Kim, you have to have courage."

"Courage?" Kim said despondently. "Leah, I have no idea where you've gotten the idea that I want to be anything but a coward. Your bravery gets you in all sorts of trouble while my cowardice keeps me safely at home."

"Safely at home married to a murderer and thief," Leah pointed out. "You let yourself be blackmailed into that marriage, too, because you were afraid of being found out that you'd tried to kill me. And if you weren't so sneaky you'd never have found out about that hidden closet of your husband's and if you'd never found that out we'd not be here now. And furthermore—."

"Leah, I really think you've made your point. Perhaps we both should change. When Justin and I get married, we'll—."

"Justin," Leah said, putting her hand on Kim's arm, "is dead."

"No he's not," Kim said with simple conviction. "I'd know if he were dead. He may have looked as if he were dead but he wasn't."

There was something in her tone that made Leah believe her. "Kim," she said softly, "what John doesn't know is that we left the note for Wesley. And if Justin is still alive that makes a witness. Even if John kills us he won't get away with his murders."

"Let's tell John," Kim said, rising. "He'll have to let us go now."

Leah pulled Kim back down. "I'm sure your honorable husband will smile and let us go and everything will be solved. Maybe he'll even shake hands with us."

"You're right. John has a dreadful temper," Kim said glumly. "He's already killed lots of people, so maybe he'll kill us just to keep in practice. Leah, what in the world are we going to do?"

Leah stood and walked to the far wall of the cave. There was water trickling down. Wesley, she thought. What would Wesley want her to do? She remembered all the times Wesley had said she just ran off and did things rather than asking for help. At least this time she'd thought of asking for help from Bud and Cal, but when they weren't available she'd just gone ahead, dragging Kim behind her, and tried to rescue Justin and capture a murderer all by herself. And now, because of her vanity in thinking she could do everything alone, both she and Kim might die.

"What would Wesley want me to do?" she whispered.

"Wait for him," Kim answered. "He wanted you to wait for him at the farm until he returned from Lexington, but since you wouldn't, I guess waiting in this cave is the next best thing. Could we please just stay here and not do one single brave thing, Leah? Please?"

"But what if—," Leah began but stopped. "We have water but no food and it's going to get awfully cold in here."

"I think graves are probably colder," Kim said. "Leah, someone's bound to find the note I left and when Justin wakes up he can tell them John is a murderer. Someone will come after us."

"But even if Justin is alive it could be weeks before he can speak. He looked badly wounded to me."

It was at that moment that a rock came sailing into the cave.

"Looking for this, ladies?" John said with a laugh.

Leah could see that a piece of paper was tied to the rock. With trembling hands, Leah untied it. "It's the letter you left, isn't it?" she asked, tears in her voice.

"One of them," Kim said without much concern.

"*One* of them?" Leah exclaimed.

"Leah, you just have no idea how mean my husband is. Someday I'll tell you the things he did to me at night. And, too, I knew that if I was going somewhere with you I'd end up in trouble. If you and Wes go out to deliver food, to do a good deed like that, you nearly get killed. I heard how the dogs nearly got you. And it was your fault, Leah. You collect more trouble than a piece of glass collects dust."

"How many notes did you leave, Kim?" Leah whispered.

"Three. One in plain sight, one under the dirty dishes—I knew John would *never* touch a dirty dish— and one under a pillow in the bedroom."

"But I didn't see you," Leah said. "How . . . ?"

Kim stiffened her back. "As you've pointed out, I

can be secretive. Now, Leah, this isn't easy for me to say because I know you can be persuasive, but if you leave this cave, I'm not going with you. I'm staying right here until a real live man, one with muscles and, I hope, a gun, comes to rescue me. If you go, you'll have to go alone."

Leah looked around the ugly, cold little cave. "It could be days before anyone comes."

"I'd rather spend a week in here than arrive dead in Sweetbriar four days early."

"Me too," Leah said, her eyes sparkling.

"You know exactly what I mean. Leah, how long can a person live without food?"

"Maybe we're going to find out," Leah said softly.

Dawn came and with it no sign of help. John Hammond found a perch exactly opposite their cave, across the deep ravine, and at random fired shots into it, making it impossible for the women to rest or even relax.

"Maybe we should try—," Leah began a hundred times, but Kim gave her such quelling looks that she subsided.

When night came they were utterly exhausted. John stepped up his firing and, once, he let go a volley that hit the ledge of the cave.

"Is he trying to shoot it off?" Leah cried out.

"Here!" came a faint voice. "While he's reloadin', help me."

Kim and Leah exchanged quick looks before hurrying to the mouth of the cave.

"Mac!" Leah said, dropping to her stomach to reach out to him. Between the two women they managed to pull him inside.

Mac leaned against the wall of the cave. "It's my leg. It's not too bad, but it's bleedin' a lot so if you ladies have anythin' to wrap it with, I'd sure appreciate it."

Both women tore their petticoats away as they fired questions at him.

"How did you find us?"

"Is Justin hurt badly?"

"Where's Wesley?"

"How are we going to get out of here?"

"Do you have anything to eat?" This was from Kim.

"Hold on a minute," Mac said. "Let me look at my leg. I thought so. Bullet went through. It stunned me so bad I nearly fell off that ledge."

"Does it hurt much?" Leah asked.

"A mite. The worst thing is I don't think I'll be able to walk on it very much. Here." He handed Kim a piece of jerky from a pouch on his belt. "Now, ladies, as for your questions. You were easy to find because you couldn't have left a bigger trail if you'd used a broad ax. I don't know nothin' about Justin. Lynna and me visited the Stanford farm and she found your letter. I sent Lynna back to Sweetbriar to spread the alarm and sent somebody after Wes. I been outside all day but had to wait until dark to get in here to you."

"I don't want to sound ungrateful, but why didn't you go after John?" Leah asked.

"He's holed up in a little cutback in a rock wall across the ravine. To get down there without him knowin' it I'd have to come down from the top with a rope and I ain't got a rope with me, but more'n that I wasn't real sure that maybe he wasn't shootin' at a bear."

"Bears don't live in caves," Kim said, looking around her suspiciously.

Mac only glanced at her. "I didn't figure on gettin'

344

shot while I was climbin' up here. I must be gettin' old."

"I think we ought to—," Leah began.

"Don't listen to anything she says," Kim interrupted. "What do *you* think we should do?"

"We're gonna sit here and wait. Wes and some of the other men will be here soon and I hope they're smart enough to come prepared. I ran off like a—what the hell!"

His exclamation was because Kim had leaned forward and kissed him firmly on the mouth. "I just love men," she said with a sigh. "They're so sensible."

"I'd ask for an explanation for all this," Mac said, "I'd really like to know why two damn fool women ran off after some murderer like the Dancer, but to tell you the truth, I found out a long time ago that women's reasons for things usually make me madder 'n hell, so if you don't mind I'd just as soon talk to John Hammond as you two. I want both you women to lie down on the floor back there, make yourselves as little as you can, and no matter what happens, stay there. You all understand me?"

"*I* do," Kim said pointedly.

"If you're planning something, maybe I can help," Leah said sincerely.

"The last thing I need is—," Mac began, but a gasp of pain from Leah cut him off.

Kim had grabbed Leah's arm and dug her nails in. "Leah's going to do just what you say, Mac. Aren't you, Leah?"

"I was just asking," Leah said defensively.

"Go! Now!" Mac was seething and both women obeyed his orders.

On his stomach Mac crawled near the opening of the

cave. "Come on, Hammond, you not man enough to take on two little women and a wounded man?" Mac shouted across the ravine. "You havin' trouble with us?"

His answer was two shots fired into the cave. Both Leah and Kim covered their heads with their arms as the shots echoed above them.

"That wasn't even a good try, Hammond," Mac yelled.

For hours Mac yelled and John shot into the cave. Leah's ears were ringing and she could tell Mac's voice was giving out. Ignoring Kim's commands to the contrary, Leah crawled forward on her stomach until she was beside Mac.

"Your leg's bothering you, isn't it?" she asked. "Why don't you take a rest?"

"I want all of Hammond's attention on me," Mac said hoarsely. "Look across there."

At first Leah could see nothing, but as she concentrated and strained her eyes, she saw a figure against the lighter rock.

"Hammond, did you kill Revis? I heard how you were there. Is that why the man gave my name?" Mac bellowed.

"Who is that?" Leah whispered.

"From the size of him, I think it's Wes," Mac answered.

"Are you angry, John, because two women discovered who you were?" Leah screamed.

Mac put a hand to her throat. "Don't you *ever* disobey me again. Now get back into that corner."

Meekly, Leah crawled backward to lie beside Kim.

"I saw Wesley," Leah whispered. "He's coming down the cliff on a rope. It'll all be over soon."

"One way or the other," Kim said, burying her face in her arms. "I hope nothing happens to Wesley."

For the next few minutes Leah lay paralyzed with fear. "Please, God," she prayed, "don't let anything happen to Wesley. I'll be obedient from now on and never get into any more trouble and I'll always ask for help with chimneys *and* murderers."

"If we get out of this alive I'm going to make you repeat that every morning," Kim said. "And I'm quite sure Wesley will help me."

Leah had no idea she'd spoken aloud. "If—," she began.

"You two shut up," Mac said. "You're distractin' me."

In the next minute there were several shots fired, then came the awful sound of a man's scream as he fell.

Leah didn't breathe.

"Who was it?" Kim said with a gasp. "Not Wesley?"

"I can't be sure . . ." Mac began.

"Leah!" came what she knew was the sweetest voice she'd ever heard. "Are you all right?"

"Yes," she whispered, then started running, tripping over Mac as he was rising, ignoring Kim's calling her back. She tore down the side of the cliff on the way to the bottom.

Above her came Mac's voice. "Stanford, you better get to the top quick 'cause your wife's comin' after you. And I can tell you she's got no more sense 'n to climb down that rope after you."

"About as much sense as your wife's got, Macalister," Wesley shot back across the ravine. "Linnet's at the top holding the rope."

"Goddamn you, Linnet!" Mac shouted. "I told you to go get help."

347

Leah was halfway up the opposite wall before Wesley came sliding down to her, pulling her to him.

"I don't know whether to beat you or make love to you. Leah, you almost got yourself killed. Why didn't you stay at the farm?"

"I'm glad I didn't because John came sometime and took one of Kimberly's notes and Justin had already run off and Bud and Cal couldn't have helped me because they weren't there and—."

"Shut up, Leah," Wesley said, putting his lips on hers.

"Yes sir," she said obediently.